IRON GATES

MARTINET PRESS

IRON GATES

ISBN-13: 978-0692306581
ISBN-10: 0692306587

MARTINET PRESS
martinet.press@safe-mail.net

© Copyright by Tempel ov Blood (2014)

All rights reserved. No part of this work may be reproduced in any way without the express permission of the publisher.

IRON GATES

IRON GATES

CHAPTER 1

The filthy infant lay screaming upon the moist floor of the forest as her mother, her cries almost as shrill as that of her child, stood several paces away, pinned against a tree by two uniformed, anonymous figures. The field marshal approached the child and gently prodded its clothing with the razor-sharp bayonet point attached to his AK-74 copycat model, specially made for him in the clandestine armaments factory operated directly by members of his unit. Whereas most who were fortunate enough to be equipped with firearms were relegated to utilizing older and carefully maintained weapons from existent stockpiles, certain elite ranking individuals such as himself were supplied with freshly minted firearms such as the one which he now held, for reasons of both practicality and prestige. Hot air infused with his ever-present rage blew from his nostrils, his eyes were wide-open and bloodshot and this along with a heavy black mustache arranged his face in a decidedly intimidating veneer. The cold blue point of the bayonet continued to toy with the flimsy garments of the squiggling child, slowly opening its shirt to reveal a pale white chest holding a fast-beating heart, sped up considerably due to duress, thumping heavily beneath its flesh.

IRON GATES

Seeing this from her location several paces off the mother's cries of distress began to reach horrific proportions. The field marshal raised his left hand in a brief gesture, to which the guards holding her responded by grabbing a handful of her honey-blonde hair and yanking her head downward as another attached a rubber ball-gag to her mouth, stifling her screams so that now only the sound of the infant's cries permeated the wooded landscape. As if on cue, the field marshal suddenly arced his rifle behind his head and drove it down, skewering the child on the tip of the bayonet. The bayonet set deep into the innocent flesh, directly penetrating into the child's heart, causing a stream of arterial flow to shoot several feet into the air. The field marshal raised the rifle back up into the air above his head, the bayonet bloody with the crimson flow from its most recent child sacrifice, a veritable moloch in the form of a machined rifle, the small child's limbs convulsing in its death throes. Deftly and with much skill, as he had assuredly done this before, the field marshal held the rifle at an angle so that the blood flowed downward without soaking the preciously oiled metal of the main part of the gun. Smiling beneath his thick black mustache, the field marshal eyed the mother: his eyes filled with an insane mania, hers filled with a shock beyond all reason. The child's cries were now silent and he placed his mouth in line of the blood flow allowing the rivulets of blood to fill his mouth, staining his face and mustache in hideous ornamentation.

After making his point known and as the blood began to cease its flow, the field marshal lowered the bayonet, still bearing the twitching infant on its point, and unceremoniously pushed the corpse off of the weapon's deadly accoutrement with one heel of his combat boot. The child hit the ground with a dull thump, the last of its blood spreading around in a muddied pool upon the earth, its milky eyes frozen in the pangs of death. The field marshal looked at his guards, their faces revealing nothing but cold, cruel eyes behind the black balaclavas which were the hallmark of the internal security forces. The field marshal raised his left hand in a similar brief gesture as before. 'Do as you want with the woman and with the remains of the child.' With that and a final sardonic smile, this time aimed at his men, he turned from the scene and marched several yards into the forest toward the small tent that functioned as his temporary headquarters for small unit operations in the area. Behind him, the guards paired off with the woman and the corpse of the child respectively, enjoying their peculiar tastes to the hilt.

Inside his tent, the field marshal sat down in a shadowed corner and took a cloth to clean the infant's blood from his face. The child's blood had encrusted in his mustache from his earlier imbibement and his attention to grooming in this respect was left half-undone intentionally, so that his men could visibly view the tell-tale signs of his cannibalistic orgy and so that he himself could enjoy the traces of the harsh iron scent of the child's blood, reminding him of his undertakings, a notch in his myriad successes. Unlike the pathetic excuses for military formations before the nuclear wars had etched their memory of mass murder onto the fields of the earth, the military formations now wore their proclivity for bloodshed on their sleeve. That was as it should be, according to some at least. The field marshal turned to the black screen of his small portable laptop, a scaled-down version more similar to a stand-alone word processor than the more sophisticated equipment that generations before him were once used to and, lighting a cigar and letting the smoke billow around his face, he began to write the minutes of the last several days' operations which were quickly drawing to a close. Soon he would be back at headquarters and then the real work would begin.

Since the last time he had been at HQ the pressure of unfolding events had heightened considerably. The entire organization was undergoing a brutal increase in internal discipline, some referred to it as a purge, commiserate with its continued successes on the field. Usually in charge of a much larger force, the small unit action he had been undertaking during the last several weeks made up for what it lacked in manpower in the level of its sensitivity and the brutality and efficiency with which he had accomplished his orders thus far, assuring him of continued prestige and favor in the eyes of the commander. The commander was the ultimate authority and was the highest deity within the organization, although various death cults worshiping varied demonic entities and past martyred operatives flourished amongst the rank and file, which helped boost their morale in an otherwise hellish situation and also seemed to provide inspiration and increase operational acumen in the fulfillment of their equally hellish missions. As long as the commander remained at the helm as the unquestionable deity, a thousand flowers were allowed to bloom in relation to subversive cult factions. No great wonder, considering that most of them were manufactured directly by the intelligence sector itself and disseminated quietly, giving the impression that they were organic in manifestation.

The headquarters of the organization was housed in a giant and imposing stone structure, the nerve-center which was housed in what was a former high-security federal penitentiary in the old days and which now served as the fortress housing the commander and large numbers of shock troops and internal security forces. The organization had annexed the infrastructure of the surrounding small towns that had once survived economically via employment at the penitentiary, with the security level of the resident operatives living in the area increasing or decreasing according to their proximity to the main compound. In the administrative buildings behind the concertina wire, hundreds of faceless individuals worked in the offices and interrogation rooms of the internal security sector, of which the field marshal's personal security force were members.

The commander stressed the importance of extremely harsh discipline within the organization, with an internal apparatus of repression to match his unmatched megalomania, rising paranoia and fanatic need for cultivating an atmosphere of absolute terror within and without. Punishment of the corporal nature from levels going from conservative to obscene was normative rather than being the exception to the rule. If terror reigned supreme within the organization itself, the commander reasoned, then those so exposed would be perfected as instruments to spread terror outside of territories currently acting as organizational strongholds. The administrative buildings housing the internal security personnel at HQ were split seventy-five twenty-five between offices (some inside former cells) responsible for amassing reports, organizing surveillance material, the drafting of indictments and enhancing internal disciplinary policy and the punitive units, which busied themselves exclusively with interrogation, torture and incarceration.

The former penitentiary had proved an ideal command center and residency for the organization thus far, being virtually impregnable by conventional means from the outside and equally hard to leave from the inside, as appropriate to its former use. On the exercise grounds where convicted murderers and rapists in the old society used to lift weights and walk the track to alleviate the paralysis of a forced sedentary existence in confinement, new murderers and rapists, this time cultivated by the state rather than confined by it, now used the same area as a military drill ground. Black uniformed shock troops, blood lust bred into their very flesh, could be seen training in rotation day and night on the drill grounds, making for a sublimely intimidating sight in the dead of the night as they trained under electric generator powered light, an anomalous sight in the new society where open flame was the standard. The sound of incessant marching, frequent firearms and explosives training, drill masters barking orders from high atop raised platforms overlooking the training areas, frequent alarm sirens piercing the night and the pressurized atmosphere of the prison buildings bathed under gigantic spotlights even in the dead of night were a testament and sign of the commander's undisputed authority and the prowess of the organization which he had built up from nothing.

Once back at HQ the pace of work would take on an intensity that would make the small unit action he had seen here seem like a vacation in comparison. The field marshal relished the stresses of the battlefield and reveled in the gory brutality that was the hallmark of his campaign style yet, like some perverted sexual deviance that was both compelling and revolting simultaneously, nothing could match the stressors of life on the base. It was as if even the presence of the commander behind the walls of the concertina-wire laden fortress, physically unseen the majority of the time but apparent everywhere, was enough to push the entire facility to psychological boiling point at all times. Soon he would be back.

IRON GATES

CHAPTER 2

Instead of being on the drill grounds with the rest of his tactical shock unit at 2:00 A.M. as scheduled, Private Bonn was facing another kind of ordeal altogether. Ten minutes before he should have been marching down the dimly-lit corridors toward the drill grounds with the other men from his barracks a call came over the intercom system. A blistering crackle of distortion erupted from the decrepit wall-mounted speakers followed by an anonymous voice, the standardized organizationally-induced attitude of indiscriminate hatred being the only inflection: 'Private Bonn, report to inquiry center immediately, Private Bonn to inquiry center.'

The fact that this had been broadcast over the intercom system at all, sounded aloud in every last corner of the former penitentiary, was injurious enough in itself. Usually any suspected disciplinary infraction of a degree warranting investigation at the inquiry center would be relayed privately via use of a personal courier acting on behalf of their superiors' orders in internal security. Those who were proven guilty beforehand did not receive a notice, they were simply extracted from their sleeping quarters in the dead of night and never seen again. With the announcement going over the P.A.

at an equally nocturnal juncture, it was obvious that psychological warfare was at play, as even a seemingly simple order to report would mark him with high suspicion amongst all of his peers, a gauntlet which had now been thrown down with no mistaking. With the hard eyes of the other shock troops avoiding his glance as they vacated the barracks for drill, it was glaringly obvious to Bonn that the intercom message itself was already tantamount to an indictment in effect. In an anonymous police state within a police state, as the HQ most certainly was, having his own name publicly associated with the inquiry center in any way whatsoever was much worse than anything that he could have faced at the hands of his unit superiors.

Now Bonn stood alone beneath a vast concrete archway, waiting for the remotely-controlled steel door to the outer portion of the former inmate hospital to open. The entire former hospital building was huge, consisting of three gigantic wings outlaid in steel, concrete and brick and even more secure than the other parts of the high-security installation. Within the former government that held power over the building, one of the stratagems employed for confining those deemed criminally insane was to foster a system of incarceration within incarceration, which meant that not only were such individuals incarcerated but they were also independently committed and confined to certain sections of the institution with its own rules and administration. The organization continued this thread within the arts of penology, but employed it in more diverse fashions than the former administrators of the penitentiary would have ever dreamed. The first wing consisted of administrative offices, main ward and medical operations, the second had been used for the terminally ill and doubled as a medicinal storage repository and the third wing had housed the psychiatric facility. Other than a routine interview held in an adjutant building at the beginning of his enlistment, Bonn had never stepped foot in or near the inquiry center in several years, nor as a sane person did he have any desire to do so.

High above on either side of him and to the right, huge-bodied internal security guards stared down at him from their watchtowers, their faces completely black in balaclavas and tinted goggles, silenced MP5 submachine guns clutched threateningly in their black-gloved hands. A low buzzing sound started as the steel door to the inquiry center's lobby began to slowly open, revealing a brightly-lit foyer, surprisingly antiseptic in feel, with concrete block walls painted cheap white, sparsely decorated with various unit crests from the internal security forces. Bonn entered and was met with surprise when he felt a light tap on his shoulder.

'Private Bonn?'

The voice emanated from a female officer, nearly his own height, dressed in the same black uniform as himself, the only distinguishing feature being the presence of a polished Sam Brown belt and a small inexpensively-minted chrome-colored badge which marked her as part of the building's security detail.

'Private Bonn, officer.'

IRON GATES

The officer nodded at his confirmation and pointed to the far end of the foyer leading towards a heavy metal door with a small wire-mesh window inlaid three-fourths of the way up.

'Follow me.'

They proceeded to the other door and then on through to a long corridor, the officer removing a large set of keys and opening then locking the entrance behind them. The keys were facets of the original infrastructure of the prison, which came ready-made for the commander's purposes. Nearby military installations had been looted of their hardware and then abandoned, manned by heavily armed squadrons of security troops who guarded some of the decaying military hardware still stored there. While built for launching offensive measures in the past, most military installations had focused on waging war abroad, not domestically, whereas the penitentiary served a very local purpose which made it more secure than the former bases.

At the abandoned bases most of the various large land vehicles and aircraft simply sat, pilfered for random parts and materials as needed. The large amounts of refined fuels necessary to run such mechanized behemoths were long gone and the human personnel knowledgeable on how to operate them were generations dead. Easily maintained vehicles that could continue to function well on old, dirty, mixed and experimental fuel, like combat jeeps and certain of the smaller armored trucks represented the extent of the organization's motorization. Use of fuel-driven vehicles amongst the non-military populace in areas run by the organization did not exist and even amongst the organization itself their use was becoming less and less frequent as time went on. Whereas elsewhere in the world there were some backwards-thinking dreamers who sought to squeeze the last drop of hope from remnants of the old civilization, the organization was coldly pragmatic in pursuing new ways of doing things. What the organization lacked in ability to harness still existent technologies of the former era was made up for in their ability to inspire - and inflict - heavily ideologically-based terror. The gadgetry of the decadent consumerist society of the past was now mostly useless, but accounts of former dictatorships and the doctrines and methodologies used to hold them together had a more eternal quality, qualities that had been adeptly mined by the commander in his obsessive rise to power.

Private Bonn and his escort stopped at a closed door to the left, halfway down the corridor, further on which led to a large secure area in which was located the former operating theater. By this point Bonn was sheathed in a cold sweat of mounting paranoia, exacerbated by the presence of his escort, who came across as utterly cold and devoid of any conscience whatsoever. The latter attribute no doubt facilitated her being part of the internal security force, who pleasured like nothing else in feeding on their own. In the shock troop units and squads there was still the necessity of maintaining some sort of mutual consideration in order to be functional on large-scale combat missions, however tinged with sadism that mutual consideration might be. Internal security were under no such restraints and represented a different animal altogether.

In the organization it was an unstated rule that seniority was decided by how cruel and insane one had proven themselves to be, both in nature and application. Considering that, the commander was the supreme in cruelty, supreme in the pathology of applied human control mechanisms, and the internal security units functioned as the direct manifestation of that hideous will.

Bonn's escort rapped on the door twice in rapid succession at which point a buzzer sounded and the door clicked open with a jolt. The uniformed female gestured that Bonn should enter on his own by pushing the door slightly ajar, allowing him to hold it open before turning and marching off back in the direction from which she had come. Not knowing whether he was about to enter an interrogation room or something potentially worse, Bonn entered and the heavy door closed behind him, locking automatically. The room in which he now found himself was several degrees colder than it had been in the corridor. A black internal security unit banner bearing initials and a unit crest involving crossed rifles and a symbol that Bonn did not readily recognize hung behind a large wood frame desk at which sat a severe figure who, like all other personnel on base, was garbed in a black tactical combat uniform. Unlike the uniformed officer who escorted him in the corridor however, this man's uniform was unique in that it bore no distinguishing sign of rank whatsoever: no unit crest, badge or flourish designating status, nothing at all that would betray what section of the organization to which he was attached.

The coldness of the room was offset by the acrid stench of stale cigarettes. Most people smoked the hand-rolled deal these days, which came in do-it-yourself packets produced within the organization for those who choose to so imbibe, however a few of the uppers had access to the old factory-made filtered kind which had been painstakingly preserved through a variety of humidification processes down through the intervening years. Glancing at the brown glass ashtray sitting on the man's desk, the private could see that he had been smoking some of the filtered variety, which marked him as higher on the pecking order than anyone he had ever met with one-on-one in his career thus far. Beside the ashtray sat a large bottle of liquor marked with a factory label. In most cases whatever might be in the bottle would assuredly not be what was on the label due to the growing scarcity of anything before the 'late unpleasantness' (an understatement if there ever was one) however, considering the existent anomalies that he had observed in this man's office thus far, Bonn halfway thought the label and the liquor might match in this particular instance. Directly in front of the man sat a thin black binder.

'Private Bonn, please have a seat.'

The man's voice was rough, perhaps a testament to his obviously high-end tobacco habit, and carried no discernible accent that Bonn could trace. Bonn saluted before taking a seat on the plain metal folding chair at the place it had been positioned, which sat him facing the internal security personnel square on across the desk. The man was completely bald, whether naturally or from shaving could be not ascertained, more than likely he was in his forties and with a face heavily lined from stress. His left hand grasped a pen which he tapped against the desk in rapid staccato fashion, as if gathering his thoughts.

'Let us cut straight to the chase, Private Bonn. You can address me simply as officer, is that sufficient? Right. Take a look at this photograph.'

The officer opened up the black binder, which contained a notepad, several folders and a side pocket containing an envelope and an embossed business card, with no name but bearing the same standard as featured on the crest displayed behind his desk which, in its bizarre and disturbing design, seemed to exude the measure of death in every shape, form and fashion imaginable. The officer removed the business card with one swift motion and replaced it facing face downward, having taken notice of his subordinate's interest. Bonn was impressed, the officer was edging him on, proffering information then concealing it. This was the hallmark of the diplomacy of espionage.

Bonn looked down as the officer placed the envelope in front of him.

'Open it.'

Bonn complied and duly opened the envelope as instructed. Several black and white photographic prints, glossy and thus obviously coming from an organizational surveillance unit operation, featured a youngish girl with black pigtails bearing a penetrating stare and livid countenance. The first photograph showed her sitting on a bench somewhere on the compound, dressed smartly in a tailored black uniform, which intimated implicitly her importance to the chain of command, as such perks as tailored clothing were not often given out and certainly not at random. Most organizational uniforms were of roughly a one-size fits-all variety and it was up to the individual organizational personnel to make any necessary adjustments on their own.

Taken at a distance, the image on the photograph was immediately recognized as one having been taken surreptitiously due to the angle from which the picture was taken, which would have not been ideal had the image been taken in an openly stated and official capacity. She sat cross-legged on the bench, casual in posture, the contours of her black uniform pants revealing a very thin, starved figure. Bonn scrutinized the area in which the photograph was taken, noting some small trees in the background and a building that looked both easily recognizable as being part of the commander's vast compound yet also unrecognizable in terms of its exact location.

'Have you been having sexual intercourse with this individual, Private Bonn?'

Bonn looked at the officer incredulously, his attention snapping from his analysis of the picture to the unnamed officer before him. He had never seen the girl before in his life and was needless to say not at all pleased with the way that the surprise interview at the inquiry center was going thus far, as he now understood that he was inhabiting a dangerous precipice from which it would be very easy to fall very far into hell.

'I have never seen this girl before in my life, officer.'

'I think you've been fucking her.'

Bonn's face began to redden, as the officer's mood began to move into that of a hostile interrogation.

'Admit that you've been fucking her!'

Bonn said nothing.

The officer burst out of his seat, walking around his desk and bending slightly down, putting his face less than two inches from Bonn's ear. His left hand snaked around the back of the folding chair, his palm situated on the private's left arm, thus able to immobilize it immediately should Bonn make the slightest move. Meanwhile, the officer's right hand had raised as to grab a hold of Bonn's collar. The choking was not physically painful to the private, but the message in the forced discomfiture was, as it were, quite resoundingly clear.

'Do you need me to call some people in here to talk to you in a way that you can understand, private? Because you are obviously not understanding me, nor do I believe you are even trying to understand me, isn't that right?'

Bonn could feel the moist breath of the officer on his ear and neck as the officer made his inquiry in an evenly stated tone, while gradually tightening his grip on Bonn's jacket. Any moment the unbridled sadism would break loose, Private Bonn could feel it in his guts.

The officer released his grasp on Bonn and stepped back several paces.

'Put your face against the wall, trooper...'

'I have never seen this...'

'PUT YOUR FACE AGAINST THE FUCKING WALL YOU SON OF A BITCH!!!'

Any move at resistance would only make things considerably worse, so Bonn walked briskly to the nearest wall and put his nose against it as commanded. Once obediently assuming this posture, the officer promptly walked up behind him without warning and slapped his opened palm against the back of the private's head with all the force he could muster, making Bonn lurch forward and bust his nose with a resounding crack against the concrete black wall. Blood begin to pour from Bonn's nostrils in torrents. Bonn grasped at his nose blindly in an attempt to stop the flow of blood before beginning to back away from the surface of the concrete wall.

'DID I TELL YOU TO BACK AWAY FROM THE FUCKING WALL YOU GODDAMN ASSHOLE??? DID I FUCKING TELL YOU TO DO THAT?'

As the screamed admonishment filled the room the officer shot his arm out, grabbing a small fistful of Bonn's hair before driving his face back into the wall, causing Bonn to scream in pain as blood began spurting anew and with great force out from between his fingers, which still held onto his face in a vain attempt to stop the flow coming from his now twice-broken nose.

Whatever test the private was undergoing he now understood that he was losing and losing fast. His vision was blurry from squinting in pain and shock at the sudden brutal facial wound, his head having also absorbed a portion of the impact against the unyielding concrete wall of the small office within the inquiry center. Bonn began staggering backwards as he felt two other sets of hands, not the officers, grab him from either side and lead him toward the officer's desk.

'Put that piece of shit over the table.'

The officer, now visibly more composed and somewhat recovered from his aggressive exertions, walked over to the table and removed the glass ashtray and the bottle of liquor with one hand and the leather folder and photographs with the other, placing them out of harm's way on top of a nearby file cabinet, drab gray in color. Meanwhile, two internal security personnel who apparently had entered while Bonn was in no state for observation, faces completely obscured in black masks and tinted goggles, dragged Bonn over to the desk. Still bleeding heavily, Bonn found himself being bent over the table, his belt being unfastened and his trousers and undergarments being pulled around his ankles.

The officer paused and removed one of the pictures from atop the file cabinet, sliding it into a clear plastic sleeve which he removed from the binder. This he proceeded to slide onto the table directly at eye level with the unfortunate private, now held firmly down on either side by the black-masked and black-attired security guards.

'Dear private, I want to once again ask you to take a very close look at the picture in front of you. Pay very,

very close attention to this face. I am going to ask you several more times if need be, but not for long, certainly not indefinitely, as we are all busy about the organization's work, isn't that right? Well, should I say that is we should be, we should be. Have you seen this individual, private? We know you have. I know you have personally! Have you had sexual intercourse with this individual perhaps, perhaps even engaged in mutual insubordination against the rule of the internal state together, acting in tandem, acting against the wishes of the commander himself even by proxy? Just let us know, private, let us know and you had best let us know right fucking now!' The officer emphasized the last three words by thumping his fist against the table, causing the picture of the girl to fibrillate from the resultant vibrations.

Bonn suddenly felt a cold chill move over him as he recognized the sensation of a gloved finger, greased with some unknown lubricant, being slowly and persistently inserted into his rectum. Bonn stared into the picture, studying the minute counters of the thin-faced girl as the security guard drove his finger deeper into the private's entrails, the gloved knuckles of his other fingers grinding against the exposed flesh of the private's naked backside. The violated walls of his anus, stretched out of capacity with no notice from the cold leather-encased finger, caused indescribably painful protests in his internal nerve-endings. Blood flow from the busted nose had now stopped and the existent blood began congealing nastily, clogging his nostrils and causing the private to breath belabored through his mouth, accenting the mood of the molestation now taking place. Bonn's mind began to race. What was he supposed to do?

'Sir, I have never seen this girl in my life...'

Bonn's voice now sounded like he had been the victim of a three week long cold, as all normal breathing had ceased from his blood-clogged nostrils, causing his mouth to gape open in an attempt to increase oxygen flow into his lungs. The pathetic delivery of his riposte to the officer's accusations was multiplied by the discomforting and revealing position he was now in, bent over the table like some unfortunate wife preparing for the wild thrustings of a drunken husband.

'...but if you want me to say that I have seen her, then I have seen her.'

'DON'T FUCKING PATRONIZE ME YOU PIECE OF FILTH, YOU FUCKING SHIT!'

The officer's mood had now returned to fully hostile in tone and in an ever-increasing degree than before. Bonn attempted to gather himself to provide some split second reasoning that might assist him in the situation. All the while he continued to stare involuntarily into the black and white photograph of the unknown individual placed before him, the edges of which were now splattered with his own blood. Bonn took note of the plastic casing and could feel the turn of the screws within his own mind, the officer was obviously quite thorough and had more than likely gone through this routine before. At this point, Bonn's mental sanity began to crack around the edges. In a brief moment of stress-induced hallucination, he could almost believe that the figure in the picture was smiling slightly at his plight.

Bringing himself back into the present, he garnered his remaining strength and shouted back at the officer the best he could in his uncomfortable position.

'WHAT DO YOU WANT ME TO SAY?'

He could hear low spoken orders exchanged between the officer and the guards and the finger which was jammed into his guts now became two fingers and moved in as deep as possible, while the other guard jammed a nightstick against the small of the private's back, pinning him more securely to the officer's desk and causing him to arch in a posture that was increasingly obscene, as no doubt was appropriate to the situation.

'Private Bonn, I am getting so sick and tired of this endless back and forth. You are now wasting valuable organizational time. You are wasting the shock troopers' time, your comrades' time, soldier, as you should be on the drill grounds right now with the other men, this very second? Isn't that right? This very fucking second?'

Bonn made a groan confirming the officer's inquiry.

'But instead of being out on the drill grounds, under the gaze of the commander, and you know he is watching at all times, instead of being out there training to be a killer, you are here in my office taking it up the ass like a little fucking slut, aren't you, aren't you, you piece of fucking shit!'

As accent to the officer's lecture, the guard inserted a third finger into Bonn's rectum and began thrusting back and forth, causing the private's chin to smear the blood now profusely staining the officer's table. Bonn could feel an uncomfortable rumbling deep within his intestines. Things were going very, very wrong.

'Don't you want to go back to the drill grounds, private?'

Bonn made a guttural sound that somehow managed to communicate his acquiescence to his interrogator.

'Good, now we are getting somewhere, private, you have a goal in mind and goals are important in this life. We have established that you are wasting your unit's time, however something that also bears airing in the open is that you are wasting my valuable time as well, by continuing to prolong this interrogation and yes, you can tell for yourself by this point that it is an interrogation. Self-criticism without self-rectification is nothing, private, nothing whatsoever!'

'When you waste my time and when you waste the time of internal security then you are directly offending the commander himself, the commander's institution, the commander's mission. You like fucking around with internal security or whomever and whoever, no respect for anyone, for any-fucking-body?' The officer picked up a leather blackjack from atop one of the file cabinets and slammed it down on the desk less than an inch from Bonn's face.

'So, private, dear, dear private, if you want to continue to live at all - I repeat - IF YOU ARE NOT INTERESTED IN DYING THIS FUCKING SECOND - then you need simply confess and then we can debrief you, end of story. Do you understand? That is the path to your resolution - I am making it as clear as it possibly can be what your option is.'

'Officer...'

'Yes?'

'I...'

'SPEAK UP, PRIVATE!'

'I confess!'

The words came out strangely due to the stress of his nose injury, which was now certainly beyond all repair, and the continued pressure of the gloved fingers probing him from behind.

'You confess?'

'I confess!'

'You confess? Speak up you piece of shit!'

'I CONFESS! I CONFESS! I CONFESS!'

Bonn felt the nightstick dig deeper into the small of his back.

The officer's face, visible from the corner of his eye, had become a grimace of an even blacker rage which was fast rising to the surface.

'Private Bonn, you do not even DESERVE TO LOOK AT THIS PICTURE!'

The officer snatched the photograph in the plastic casing off the table and out of Bonn's line of vision, replacing it on top of the file cabinet with a resounding thump.

'You confess to seeing this girl? You confess to seeing this girl? Did you just tell me that you 'confess'? Well I say that you have NEVER seen this girl! In fact I am quite sure that you have never seen this girl in your entire miserable life. Are you trying to make me look like an idiot? Well, well now, I think you are the idiot. Soon enough you will be able to discover how much of a goddamned idiot you are for lying to me, lying to internal security, lying to the whole goddamned organization. May as well be lying to the commander himself, right? I say again Private Bonn, and I emphasize this so that it will sink in with no chance of misinterpretation on your part, that based on your response you are a fucking LIAR and furthermore you are more than likely a goddamned TRAITOR AS WELL!'

Bonn began to weep silently, adding the salt of his tears, moistening the still-wet blood stains on the desk.

'Clear him out, he doesn't even deserve that much!'

Bonn felt the gloved fingers withdraw from his anus in one abrupt motion. The nightstick withdrew from the small of his back and with a shove he felt himself being pushed off the table, slumping to the floor involuntarily.

'STRIP THAT TRAITOR!'

The guards, faceless and terrifying, stood him up straight, ripping open his combat jacket and removing every other existent piece of clothing from his body within less than two minutes time. One of the guards removed a large knife from his utility belt and slit all the shoelaces from the private's combat boots before pulling them off and throwing them to the side, thus removing them considerably faster than would have been possible in a more conventional manner.

'DS to control, DS to control, come in control.'

The officer now sat back behind his desk, speaking into a CB-type radio apparatus.

Electronic distortion poured through the attached speaker unit on the small piece of equipment and an anonymous voice spoke on the other end of the line.

'Control.'

'Get two more guards in here and bring some

restraints, we are sending this one into R&D so be ready on your side within the next ten minutes for receipt.'

'Confirm on that DS, guards are on their way.'

Before the officer had even set his microphone down, Bonn could hear the unmistakable sound of combat boots running down the corridor, along with the metallic jangling of chains.

The door buzzed, opening the lock, and two large guards burst in, dressed exactly like their counterparts. They came in shouting and in full raid posture, with firearms drawn, metal chains and leather restraints attached to clips on their belt.

'FACE DOWN ON THE GROUND! ON THE GROUND!'

The first set of guards who had now succeeded in stripping the private naked, Bonn now only wearing the blood stains on his ruined face, pushed Bonn down and spread him out flat onto the ground, face-down, as the other two guards moved in, holstering their weapons and attaching manacles to his ankles. Handcuffs followed, bringing his hands behind his back. Both sets of restraints were then attached to each other, rendering him hog-tied.

'Good-bye, Private Bonn, this could have been considerably easier if you had simply played by the rules.'

Bonn felt himself being painfully gripped at each limb by the four guards and being lifted up from the ground. The coldness of the room was trebled in his state of forced nakedness.

The officer rose from his desk and walked in front of

the guards. Bonn's face stared downward toward the floor and then, as the officer moved closer, he saw the officer's leather boots come into his view.

The officer grabbed Bonn by the hair, raising his head so that he could see his face despite his awkward position. Bonn's eyes, clouded with tears and blood, saw through the painful haze the cruel face of the officer, an angry scowl on his face, sweat dripping from his forehead.

'Next time it won't be so pleasant, I can assure you, hope that you remember that when you get to where they are taking you.'

The door buzzer sounded and the officer walked over, holding the door open for the four guards who proceeded to exit the office with their prisoner.

'Guard.'

The guard holding onto the private's left arm turned his masked face toward the officer.

'If you don't mind, tell them down at control to send someone in here to clean up the mess, I like to keep a tidy desk.' The officer turned back, looking at the reddish stains pooled across the wooden surface of his desk with disapproval.

'Yes, sir.'

The officer retreated into his office, closing his door behind them and leaving the guards to do their duty.

At a breakneck march the guards proceeded down the corridor towards the secure area. A few administrative secretaries were loitering in the corridor outside of one of the investigative offices and cat-called as the guards passed with their bare-assed, hog-tied and weeping captive.

A brunette holding a clipboard turned toward the other secretary who had whistled and lowered her glasses, arching her eyebrows mischievously.

'That little piece of meat is going to be in for the time of his life, sister!'

Both women began laughing. The laughing was not pleasant.

The guards, Bonn in tow, marched past the painted line on the ground designating the beginning of the special secure area leading toward the other wings of the internal security building and, proceeding down another corridor to the right, disappeared into the interior of the facility.

IRON GATES

CHAPTER 3

The field marshal sat at the edge of the forest as a blood red sun began making its descent behind, illuminating the crest of the mountains before him to the east. Weather permitting, it would take a week for his small unit to cross over the mountains on foot and then several more days' march through the foothills before reaching level ground and the base. As he watched the dying rays of the sun casting its crimson light over the wooded mountaintops the field marshal considered what would be happening back at headquarters during this time of day. Most shock troops and other organizational sectors not on duty would be engaged in evening classroom training sessions on a wide variety of topics, including the history of the land's descent into societal breakdown and nuclear war, which had reached its zenith more than seventy-five years before. As such, almost no one living, except perhaps a few isolated individuals (whom he nor anyone he knew had ever met) would remember what the world was like before that time except through books, carefully censored, which had been stored at the institutional library which was accessible, in a controlled degree, to most members of the organization over a certain security ranking.

The field marshal certainly did not remember what the world was like before the apocalypse, as he himself was born right in the midst of the blood and fire of societal anarchy several decades after the collapse. During those days in the territory in which he and his mother lived, in a land north of the organization's present headquarters, there had been considerable more diversity in the armed groups that were in operation. However, operating according to long defunct political and religious ideologies, throw-backs from the old days, coupled with a biological attunement toward obsolete methods of waging guerrilla warfare, their groups were easily absorbed into, forcibly taken over or exterminated by the organization in time.

The field marshal had always admired the organization from the earliest he could remember. His mother worked as an informant against the so-called 'sovereigns' who lived around the area of his birth and who spoke of the organization with fear and loathing, referring to them as communists, criminals and other epitaphs which made no real sense in terms of what such designations meant before the states of the world had cannibalized themselves, with mass loss of human life and permanent loss of advanced infrastructure, in a time that may as well be considered prehistory with the way things were run now.

In exchange for spying against the people in their area, many of them related to her (not that that meant so much these days - and any person with the slightest hint of organization-leaning ideology would understand clearly that familyism as it was practiced traditionally was disgusting, nothing more than a bourgeois aberration), the field marshal's late mother received ration packets, black-market liquor, edged weapons and clandestine ideological training material, all of which she received on a regular basis and all of which was carefully concealed beneath the floorboards in a small abandoned structure in the forest behind their residence.

His mother actively taught him to read at an early age and actively encouraged him to peruse the organizational pamphlets and related materials that she received. This, along with a passion for practicing with the large, serrated-edged weapon that his mother entrusted him with, seared into his consciousness the goal of becoming an enlisted member of the organization as soon as he was of age. At the time the organization recruited at eleven years of age and above, now the age bracket had been lowered considerably and there were many children that were sent on dangerous missions as young as six, having spent their life from the cradle being trained for inflicting death, conducting espionage and executing other sophisticated facets of political and military science according to the needs of the group.

Raising himself from the rock on the outcropping, the field marshal looked one last time toward the east before returning the way from which he had come, back toward the camp. He had finished his report ahead of schedule, allowing him a brief respite and view of the mountains, rising in all the grandeur, in the the east, before sunset.

IRON GATES

At that time his escorts had still been sporting with the woman, her muffled screams of grief and horror being too much for his head to bear after filling out fifteen pages of mandatory documentation and entering more than that in electronic data, all of which was now secured in a padlocked box which he carried with him on all missions outside of the organization's territory. 'Outside of organization territory' was almost a misnomer at this point in relation to his current area, as the few inhabitants they had encountered were little more than savages, existing alone or in small packs, emotional and fragile creatures that marked them as the detritus of the fallen civilization. Detritus is trash and it was amongst the purview and job description of his commission to exterminate such trash, to sweep away the past so that the organization and its brutal, future ethic could take total hold without any traces of pre-apocalypse humanitarian contaminant left to mar their historic work. Like chaff, those who simply lived but did not imbibe the fuel of fanatic desire for geopolitical domination and control could, as simply as that, be blown away suddenly by the incoming, violent wind.

Back near the area where the lone mother and child had been ambushed by the field marshal and his elite guard unit earlier in the day, the level of atrocity had continued apace, managing to maintain itself steadily at an unspeakably horrific pitch, a great success considering the intensity of the inaugural actions taken on the unfortunate victims prior.

After the field marshal had left his two internal security attaches with the woman and the dying child, said attaches who had formerly worked as punishment camp guards for the organization before moving up the ranks into the prestigious position of the field marshal's personal guard, they had availed themselves and taken the blessing of their superior officer quite earnestly when they were instructed to enjoy themselves to the very hilt.

The guards came from a background much like the field marshal himself, albeit being less prodigious in the military sense as normally understood. Both had been exposed to organization ideology early during their childhood, except in their case they had been born in an area that had just recently been taken over by the commander's forces and which contained very little opposition in regards to organizational program.

In areas that were only beginning their new local identities as organizational strongholds, it was considered imperative to make organizational presence dramatically known and to commit at least ten to twelve punitive actions against real or perceived local dissent to organizational control on a regular and consistent basis. In cases where no actual dissent to organizational control existed, the shock troops and associated personnel would perform punitive raids and public criticism rallies and executions aimed against individuals who were earmarked as being potential future problems depending on their background and personal and social history within their respective communities. The investigative work leading to making the choices in this respect were executed by intelligence officers on the ground, information on potential targets being fed to local intelligence handlers by domestic human sources located throughout the area.

Without such repressive political theater as exhibited in the criticism rallies, raids and executions, any potential future dissent would be given the de facto green light to bolster their operations, incipient or active, and loyalists who supported the organization's mission would be demoralized at the lack of mechanistic and applied social brutality. Seventy some-odd years since the last nuclear warhead sent the genocidal rays of its radiation sun shining gleaming death on all known continents, only a considerable amount of bloodshed, butchery and violence would manage to get the attention of the people. The populace had been effectively and realistically ruined for more subtle means of political communication.

The men who were now pulling security for the field marshal both grew up in the same territory. Although they did not interact in their youth, their shared background provided ample basis for strong solidarity in their adulthood and professional lives, especially in the hermetic atmosphere of the field marshal's personal service.

Embedded deep within their psyches lay impregnable imprints from the mandatory propaganda rallies put on by the enlisted organization forces which they had attended as children. In the organization all propaganda activities were formulated and managed exclusively by the intelligence directorate, removing the need for another separate internal branch to handle tasks such as producing literature, forming curricula and holding public events. The purpose of this conglomeration did not intimate, however, an attempt to cut corners, or bespeak any lack of acumen of order on the part of those so concerned, as propaganda was of an unequivocally vital importance to the organization's mission, particularly in the arenas of recruitment and the harvesting of human resources.

With propaganda activities being managed directly by the intelligence branch, the commander could be satisfied that those responsible for the imperative tasks of said propaganda had the full measure of military and intelligence-driven psychological warfare methodologies and advanced police coercion techniques and training at their fingertips at all times. Especially in the context of public rallies, the efficaciousness of such an arrangement could be seen dramatically in stark relief on the parade grounds, as the officials orating and the hand-picked individuals from the local populace recruited by intelligence in the crowd could coordinate seamlessly amongst themselves, in concert, for mass group effect.

Aside from more specific desired results and specialized undertakings, in general, the mass rallies were designed to cultivate an attitude of hubris, total identification with the group and fanaticism for the organization's objectives and leadership in the demographics of moderate to heavy supporters and, in contrast, to inspire blood-curdling terror in those who might possess even the slightest latent seeds of rebellion in their minds. The rallies almost always followed the same formula wherever they were held and invariably began with a shock troop contingent marching through the main strip of town or along the main road if held in a strictly rural environment.

Usually a group of forty shock troops would make up the bulk of the procession, divided into ranks of five abreast. In front of this would be a section of the baby brigades as they were informally referred to in the organization, the youth corps which consisted of boys and girls from five to eleven years in age. The pontifex of the local youth corps, the organization's bizarre equivalent to class president or valedictorian, would head the parade carrying a torch made of a burning human head. The head was always that of a member of the organization itself, not an external enemy as might initially be thought. The pageantry aimed at driving home the commander's policy towards external rebels would come later on, at the end and zenith of the propaganda rally.

The tradition of parading a human head fashioned as a macabre flaming torch had begun early on in the organization, back in the days during which the symptoms of overt radiation poisoning had been seen everywhere as part of the hideous direct aftermath of the worldwide nuclear conflagration. In those days and in days since, the particularly fanatical members of the group would volunteer to commit a grisly act of ritual suicide as a sign of their absolute and total commitment of individual members of the group toward the aims of the collective whole. In those days, closer in proximity to the wars, the volunteers would often be drawn from amongst those who had been adversely affected by radiation, putting the continuation their of long-term service to the organization into question for practical reasons, despite their all-out ideological elan. The esoteric reason behind the ritual suicide was as old as combat itself, being based on the practice amongst certain ancient cultures of offering a severed human head as a sacrifice to the goddess of war, death, night and destruction in exchange for the boon of achieving victory on the field of battle. The practice of turning the head into a burning symbol of martyrdom to be paraded before supporters and potential enemies alike seems to have apparently been the organization's own innovation, although many held that such a practice had been executed within certain formations similar to the organization long beforehand.

In a private ceremony, held directly before the rally and attended only by uniformed members of the group and leadership, the martyr, chosen amongst the volunteers, via secret selection by a special committee composed of ranking members amongst the shock troop and intelligence community, would perform his or her act of martyrdom in a solemn and grim rite.

Amped-up on a specially manufactured liquor laced with stimulants administered by an organization physician, the actual narcotic element based on the original methamphetamine formula as developed and utilized by the Nazis during World War II, the martyr would be led to the stage, flanked on either side by women (or men, in the case that the martyr was female), who acted as the martyr's pleasure concubines and personal attendants in the last few days leading up to the ceremony. A large bonfire and myriad sacrificial pyres contained in large metal urns would be used to light the ghastly scene as the ritual took place.

On a plinth, beneath a large black banner bearing the insignia of the organization, lay a long and large knife of the survival combat variety with a sawing blade on one end and a compartment for holding essential supplies hidden within the handle, a quality piece crafted originally for one of the now defunct governments existing well before the nuclear wars and maintained religiously ever since. Painted black, except for along the edge, which had been sharpened to the keenness of a razor, the bleak and gory instrument lay oiled and gleaming with an evil light, a blasphemous and impersonal idol inside a cult forged within the very nuclear zenith of death.

The insignia of the organization featured a profile image of the commander, dressed in a peculiar black mask embedded with his personal crest, worn only by himself and his own elite guard unit, minutely painted upon the area centering around his third eye. Bandoliers of high gauge bullets crossed his chest, medals covered his width and knives and firearms burst from various military belts attached to his arms, belt and legs, holding sheathes and various holsters custom-made for the armed-to-the-teeth dictator of the organization and supreme authority over all the human inhabitants in areas his forces controlled. His blistering eyes, blank yet enraged simultaneously, stared forth into an even more nightmarish future than anyone could possibly dream. A motif of an enormous bat rose up from behind the leader's profile, prolonged fangs with pouring streams of blood dripping downward, anointing the image of the commander and bringing home the horrific, insane and malicious nature of the organization and its ultimate leader.

Several members of a specially selected youth musical corps, picked from the most succulent and beautiful amongst the children, stood ground-level on either side of the stage, dressed in obscenely revealing uniforms, sounding hideous trumpets and beating strange rhythms on military-style drums. Deranged older men and women, totally destroyed physically and psychologically from that radioactive residue which still permeated its life-destroying poisons from deep within the earth, looked on with milky eyes and pathetic sexual longing upon the lithe limbs and figures of active youth in all their sublime glory.

IRON GATES

CHAPTER 4

'Don't shout or I'll shove it straight up your ass, little bitch!'

A youngish girl with black hair arrayed in a hasty bun upon her smallish skull bucked wildly around, situated on all fours, her pert and youthful buttocks rotating round in a primitive rutting gesture as the lieutenant rammed his cock into her slick genitalia in measured and energetic strokes. At the lieutenant's admonishment, her animalistic grunting tapered into a low, sick hissing sound, not unlike that of an enraged cobra ready to strike.

The lieutenant was attending one of the conferences put on by the elite political figures within the organization, held on a secret base consisting of a vast number of corrugated steel buildings linked together by corridors, containing various meeting halls, residential rooms and offices, the second of which the lieutenant and the daughter of a high-ranking organization military figure now inhabited.

The site of their cohabitation in mutual lust was adorned with all the basic amenities befitting visiting organizational liaison members from abroad. A chest-of-drawers, a bed of variant size depending on what was available and some tables and chairs outfitted a medium-sized room lit by pressurized oil-lamps of the variety that were utilized by the old-order Amish during the era before the wars.

Small, bee-sting tits bobbed chaotically as the lieutenant bore into his night's lover with schizophrenic abandon. His eyes lolled back into his head wildly as spittle dribbled down his handlebar mustache, pooling on the female's upturned buttocks and then streaming in pools upon the dirty desert-tan sheets equipping the dilapidated mattress upon which they now performed their conjugal pastimes.

The lieutenant's flesh was marred with various wounds, inflicted by the enemy and self-inflicted both, bearing testament to the atrocious mental state that the lieutenant, one of the top brass within the organization, wore with an inflated and unapologetic ego. In a group in which insanity was a mark of distinction, the lieutenant was by anyone's account extremely distinguished.

Along with the tell-tale signs of lacerations from razors, combat knives and other edged tools of similar intended purpose, the lieutenant's sadistic-looking frame also carried scars from several gunshot wounds, many years old. Surviving gunshot wounds in the era post the wars was extremely rare, as medicine in general was on the decline and those who were educated in the questionable medical training centers run by the organization had much different priorities than physicians of the former era. Manufacture of stimulants used to increase propensity for violence and battlefield stamina over long periods of time without sleep, truth serums for interrogations and experimental chemical and biological weapons and the methods of their application were the top priority for anyone with medical training or scientific know-how.

Hidden deep within the monolithic complex of steel buildings with no external windows, the residential areas for visiting brass were infamous for being stale and airless. This made the exertions of the lieutenant's intercourse even more pronounced as evidenced by the fact that both he and the girl were drenched in sweat.

The lieutenant massaged the girl's buttocks, moistened with perspiration and his own saliva, which fell from his mouth involuntarily in grotesque rivulets as he took in the beauty of her pale, flawless skin in counter-pose to her night-black hair. Now looking straight forward toward the headboard, the girl's ocean-blue eyes stared from deep rings of black, fashioned with homemade eyeshadow made from soot and the fat of wild swine, obtained from her kitchen at home. Her father, an official in the clandestine armaments business, was an ample sportsman and wild boar still proliferated, having strong constitutions and proving highly adaptable to post-nuclear environs, flourishing as the earth began to naturally reforest itself, providing ample ideal habitats for the tusked beasts.

The girl turned her head, looking backward toward the lieutenant and drawing his attention however briefly away from the upturned curvatures of her delicious derriere, exposed in full swell as he continued to thrust into her moist vagina. She looked at him with a petulant pout, extending her bottom lip and widening her eyes in feigned innocence.

'I don't think you will, lieutenant - all threat!'

'All threat, then? We'll see about that!'

The lieutenant's eyes also widened, not in feigned innocence but in increasing amazement at just how turned on she was making him. She was pushing all the right buttons. They had been fucking since the second night of the conference and now, four days in, this was the next to the last night before the delegates returned to their various assignments elsewhere in the sprawling southern territories now controlled by the organization. The lieutenant slowly inserted one moistened finger into the girl's arse, sliding it back and forth, widening it ever so slightly for the coming sodomy. The girl cooed in delight and her face began to tremble in perverse premeditation of what was to come. Not that this move on behalf of the lieutenant came as any surprise. Manufactured contraceptives no longer existed, all manufacturing being strictly based around military need, not consumer desire. Enlisted personnel and non-military members of the populace were all encouraged to apply more creative ways of preventing unplanned pregnancies. The lieutenant continued to massage and then removed his stiff member from her slit, inserting it between her buttocks. The girl, now fully in the swing of things, let loose with a snarl of excitement as they finished each other off in grecian courtesan fashion.

Afterward they dressed and checked the time, which informed them that it was now late enough in the night that most of the after-session functions for the attending personnel were already well past, unless they wanted to drink rot-gut with varied drill masters and specialized intelligence personnel around burning barrels of refuse in the open-air courtyard at the center of the compound. As they had already enjoyed themselves considerably tonight as it were, they decided that they would pass on seeking out other companionship and instead enjoy their next to last night together alone with one another in the confines of their room. The lieutenant had a bottle of liquor that was much better than the rot-gut the lower ranks would be drinking and some cigars that had been given to him after a military campaign near the coastal regions and he intended to enjoy them with a beautiful girl, not out amidst the rabble. This girl in particular was a treat and a lesson in contrast; he could associate with shock troops and spooks from internal security anytime and usually, due to the rigors of his profession, the association was more frequent than he might desire.

The couple now sat at one of the low tables in the corner of the room, studying each others faces as the lieutenant poured a portion each of the harsh-smelling brown liquid into metal tumblers, passing one to her along with an anise-scented cheroot, part of a stockpile of the same that had been given to him by one of his subordinates during the campaign in the east after his man had found them, naturally humidified in a dank cellar, in the home of one of the many families that he had butchered, exterminating to a person as per organizational edict in relation to persons inhabiting that particular region. The girl, now dressed in her tailored black uniform, lit a punk on one of the gaslights and began taking long draws, causing the burning ember at the end of the cigar to pulsate and sending large billows of white smoke circling round her face.

'Are you going back to headquarters after you finish here, lieutenant?'

Even with their previous activities withstanding, a pronounced degree of formality recommenced once the sex was over. The lieutenant, although technically lower in rank than some of his peers, was indisputably one of the commander's favorites. The lower rank was a technicality, part of the political games that sometimes reared their heads within the organization, making the lieutenant a target from some sectors due to his undisguised psychosis and inability to play well with others as the case may be. Be that as it may, ninety-nine percent of the group brass would give the lieutenant a wide berth under any circumstances. His violence and insanity were mirrors of the commander's own violence and insanity, a similarity that had been well noted by the commander. Within the organization making an offense against one of the commander's favorites was tantamount to making personal offense at the worshipful feet of the commander himself, an act considered by no one except those lusting for a slow and painful death. Those who had been so foolhardy to do the latter often did so unknowingly and after so failing, in a military world dictated by a highly sophisticated but unwritten etiquette, they were quickly dispatched, disappearing into the hells of the internal security department forthwith, often never even understanding for what reason they had been ruined. For the girl, cohabitation with the lieutenant was not only quite pleasurable, it was an honor, and, particularly for a career-minded organizational operative such as herself, it was a potential gateway to better things - or worse - depending on one's perspective. She considered herself innately psychotic and lusted for a partner with whom she could thrive in a bleak world based on ever-dangerous games of one-upmanship amongst competing rabid beasts with the countenances of humans.

'Not this time, Nadezhda.'

Nadezhda thrilled inside, as this was the first time he had called her by her given name. As far as Nadezhda was concerned, she knew better than to ask him his. No one knew the name of the lieutenant and as no one ever asked he was as ever simply known as the lieutenant, a practice of anonymity that was applied amongst the most sensitive of personnel in referring to them only by rank, even within internal organizational documents. There were various rumors within the organization concerning this practice as it was applied to the lieutenant specifically and also as to why he had not been promoted to a higher outward ranking. Some say that when he originally received the rank of lieutenant he went berserk and assassinated several men in his unit, not because of any rationally understood enmity existent between them but rather as a violent and fratricidal celebration of his moving up in rank, his joy - their sorrow. Those who were more in the know concerning the events surrounding the incident believed that the commander himself was directly responsible for the lieutenant's promotion and sent a personal secret message via a headquarters-based courier informing him of the names of several individuals within his unit whose immediate executions were personally commissioned, along with detailed instructions of how and where to perform the deed. The opportunity of committing further, unusual and extraordinary bloodshed was the commander's personal reward to the lieutenant on the occasion of his promotion and the fact that the orders had been personally issued assured an ever spiraling level of elation in the lieutenant in the ferocity and detail with which he went about his orders. With that act, enemies of the commander had been executed as needed, the lieutenant had been forever cemented as a loyalist and, due to the obscurity surrounding the incident, a legend was born concerning the lieutenant's excesses.

Nadezhda nodded her head in assent, pulling a rough slug from her tumbler and taking a deep draw on her cheroot. She knew better than to ask for any details without their being proffered. If he was about to go to the field on a mission it was not her business to know. Secrecy was lifeblood within the organization, without the importance of secrecy remaining heavy in circulation, the organization would collapse. That had been the fate of the less brutal, less malevolent post-nuclear war paramilitary outfits that had risen in spats during and after the nuclear winter. As always it was old ideas, outmoded thinking and a tendency to look back upon a perceived golden age of 'ethics' that spelled the demise of such groups. The laws of survival were not dependent on how well one cultivated an atmosphere of civility amidst chaos and as far as members of the organization were concerned, civility within chaos was an aberration and an impossibility, well worthy of being smashed with extreme prejudice. What the people really lusted for was order and there was no better order than dictatorship, which was exactly what the organization offered.

Nadezhda had grown up firmly in the bosom of the organization and had even been dedicated as a child by the commander himself, although she was too young to remember it, back in the days when the commander would be seen more frequently amidst the higher brass and unlike the present, in which he was wrapped in almost complete obscurity. Nadezhda's father was a particular prize within the organization to this day and especially in the years in which the organization was undergoing its formative stages of consolidating their power and authority. His father, her grandfather, had been a professional gunsmith and amateur lathe operator before the wars, his choice in profession no doubt testament to the fact that he could see the writing on the wall as the geopolitical scene ratcheted up towards the boiling point which caused nuclear death to reign down, obliterating untold numbers of the earth's inhabitants. His skills had been passed down to his son at an early age and Nadezhda's father had proved to be a prodigy in the realm of the manufacture and maintenance of a wide variety of small arms. Coming from an area of the land known in former times as the foundry due to its proliferation of industry, Nadezhda's father had migrated south and away from the large metropolitan areas in the hideous nearly several decade period of nuclear winter, but not before pilfering a significant amount of equipment from government facilities on his trek down through northern Virginia, famous for its military installations and bred-in-the-bone gun culture.

Once in the deep south he linked up with the organization, who readily rolled out the red carpet for someone of his considerable mechanical skill and know-how, not to mention the fact that he had arrived in the southerly clime with both ample supplies of armaments manufacturing equipment as well as a considerable personal arsenal, which he gladly donated to the organization in exchange for assurance of lifelong security and occupation in the furtherance of their mission. Supplied with a decent residential living situation for himself and his daughter, his wife having died of radiation exposure soon after the child's birth on the journey south, the armaments officer settled down near organization headquarters, equipped with a full staff and a facility to work with, and set about the business of manufacturing the sought-after instruments of death that were essential to maintaining current organizational territories and expanding those territories into uncharted areas where life was said to be even more unpredictable and fraught with danger.

Some of Nadezhda's earliest memories were of learning to read in the large glass cubicle formerly utilized as a guard shack in the abandoned cannery that now served as the organization's main armaments factory, located deep in the woods a few miles southwest of headquarters, the location which was guarded heavily both by contingents of shock troops, surveillance teams and via secrecy of the location itself. Once refurbished as a weapons facility, the quaint dimensions of the interior guard shack inside the building itself seemed almost comical in comparison to the machine-gun toting black-masked nightmares who roamed the roof, perimeter and surrounding areas at all hours, thus Nadezhda was bequeathed with this daytime residence so that her father could keep closer supervision on her, easily seen through the plexiglass, while he roamed through the large hangar, troubleshooting and advising the workers in the finer points of firearm craftsmanship.

The lieutenant smoked his cigar, inhaling deeply and exhaling through his nostrils in a great stream of smoke that made him resemble some fire-breathing beast as Nadezhda studied him from across the table. She had been attracted to the lieutenant since an early age, having heard about his various exploits while associating with her schoolmates in the youth corps academy. Various of the girls would stand around the foyers of the administrative offices, featuring large poster renderings of the various military commandants and officials who had received medals and various other honorifics due to the severity of their repression of opposition on the battlefield. While her mates had favored the field marshal almost to a person, she had always favored the lieutenant. Whereas the field marshal appealed to the youths as a sadistic yet somehow grandfatherly figure, the lieutenant was all punishment all the time, unpredictable, privileged within the framework of the commander's favor and always horrific in execution. This fondness for extremes put her in good standing with various of the more brutal elements in the academy, including many of the boys, who she wiled away hours with practicing ambush maneuvers and interrogation techniques long after the mandatory day's training sessions were over.

Now she sat across from him, having mutually enjoyed with him in a conjugal fashion for several nights' time although speaking very little of serious matters until the present. Sitting through hours of tedious programming lectures during the day at the conference, Nadezhda, like the majority of other attendants, was mentally and physically exhausted at the end of the day. Except for those inhabiting the perpetual 'situation room' (field marshals, generals and other war theater decision-makers), whose positions mandated their continued attention long into the night, most of the other attendants sought some sort of diversion in the evening. Getting smashed on the liquor provided for the attendants, discussing events along tables of food (fresh meat hunted with firearms being a welcome delicacy, especially for those from headquarters who subsisted the majority of the time on strange substances laced with pharmaceuticals that kept them going long past the time that they would have passed out under natural circumstances) or, for the loners, holing up in their residential quarters with some propaganda magazines or simply their own dark paranoid minds.

The lieutenant poured himself another snifter of liquor and took a deep drink while keeping his eyes evenly boring into Nadezhda's.

'So I assume you will be back at headquarters yourself soon, correct?'

'That's correct, lieutenant.'

She was pleased with his inquiry, but did not show it, keeping the tone of her voice monotone and without inflection. She had no intention of showing her cards or any vulnerability to his attentions until she could better ascertain the situation. Having heard the tales for many years of the lieutenants split-second moves from amicability to cruelty and also well aware of his tendency for forced rape and murder of past lovers, or dropping an oblique false accusation to internal security that would, due to his rank, almost assure a sudden extraction, she wanted to keep well on his good side.

'What detail do you work in?'

'Code clerk and intelligence analysis, internal security administration.'

The lieutenant took another drag from his cheroot, now burned to the end, and snuffed it out on the ashtray, his mustache twitching slightly under the stress of his exhalation.

'What would you ideally like to be doing for the organization, Nadezhda?'

Now the kicker had come, a surprise for her. Her answer to this question could take several possible courses depending on his mood and his base intentions in asking the question. It could be merely small talk or even a provocation to draw her out concerning her ambitions, or it could be something else altogether. Rather than beat around the bush, Nadezhda decided to answer honestly.

'I would like to work for torture center, incarceration, at HQ internal security.'

The lieutenant was impressed and pleasantly surprised at her proclivity to work in what was considered a dirty assignment even within the sadistic confines of organizational life. Internal security were pariahs in any case, although being the commander's favorite operation, and torture center, housed in a separate secure building adjutant to the inquiry center, was the height of nastiness, the crown jewel of human rights abuse for internal subversives and high-level spies and espionage suspects. Having worked in intelligence analysis of suspect elements within her own organization however, the thought that she might want to move from shoring up investigations and expanding them through interrogation seemed a logical progression from his vantage point.

'Have you put in for a transfer?'

'I have attempted in the past, but internal security said that they rely on me for decoding and associated activities and that there are more qualified individuals lined up for posts at torture center.'

The lieutenant snorted with disgust, no doubt her higher-ups were referring to personnel from the shock troop units and guards from the military concentration camps. He instantly disagreed with their decision - a femme fatale with deeply rooted ties to an armaments background and present employment in intelligence analysis was exactly what torture center needed to add a layer of sophistication to their grisly tasks. He intended to do something about it.

'Ask and you shall receive, Nadezhda. You want the rank of Agent along with it, correct?'

Nadezhda did not pause before answering.

'Special Agent in charge.'

The lieutenant showed no reaction, but Nadezhda seemed to detect that there was the slightest hint of a smile around the corners of his mouth. She reached over the bottle and poured herself another draught, raising the cup to her lips and consuming the majority of it in one swallow. They were well on their way to getting piss-drunk and she was enjoying herself to the hilt, both the intoxication and the interesting turn of events that their post-coitus discussion had taken almost immediately.

'Well officer, I will see what I can do, in fact I will do more than that. I am surprised that you want to stay at headquarters though, most headquarters staff are ready to get out and see the rest of the world outside - see what the organization is doing in the field, perhaps take out a few enemies on the field, do a little hunting...'

The lieutenant's eyes glazed over slightly and he could feel himself begin salivating, considering both the exquisite taste of animal flesh and human flesh alike. Post the nuclear wars, meat was meat and judging on how he had seen the progression over the years, cannibalism was a trend that was going to accelerate. A fresh kill always tasted better than eating some diseased, dehydrated corpse on the compound, which was the extent of natural protein available at headquarters unless a person wanted to go out of their way and risk potential punitive response - that happened sometimes too.

'Have another drink, SAC.'

The lieutenant grinned discernibly this time and reached into the pocket of his black jacket, removing a small wallet and taking out a personal credential card, embossed with a personal insignia and contact information of his headquarters liaison secretary at the base. The personal insignia, not a group insignia of one of the organizational subsections such as intelligence, internal security or the shock troops was a particularly significant distinction, as it marked him as not belonging specifically to any of the known sectors of the organization. Some speculated that the lieutenant was part of a secret outfit reporting directly to direct emissaries of the commander and engaged in secret work. The lieutenant's uniform bore only an organizational crest and no other markings, which could designate him as anything from construction security in armaments to interrogator in intelligence. He removed a small ink pen from the other pocket, a water-proofed variety issued to organizational personnel, and wrote several lines on the back of the card before resheathing the pen and handing the card to Nadezhda.

Nadezhda took the card and turned it around. The words written on the back of the card meant nothing to her, a string of several unrelated words followed by a set of numbers. Her code clerk training began to go into effect but she was not able to readily ascertain the nature of the code.

'Don't bother, Nadezhda.'

The lieutenant looked at her with a bemused

expression.

'You will not be able to crack that code, although feel free to give it a shot when you back to your room later. Don't do too good with it though or they will never let you out of the code office.'

Nadezhda smiled back and put the card into her pocket. She would have to have faith in the good graces of the lieutenant, although she would most certainly attempt to decode the message before she retired for the night and most certainly before she would hand it in to anyone. The ciphers on the back of the card could just as easily be instructing that the person turning the card in should be executed or incarcerated as it could be instructions for assignment.

'Hand that card in to the internal security administration secretary, not your direct boss in internal security. Better yet, put it in the night slot, that way you won't have to deal with anyone directly. Once the person who needs to see the message gets the card you will see that everything will work itself as it should.'

Nadezhda managed a slight smile although the paranoia concerning the potential intentions of the lieutenant bothered her. If she did get promoted to torture center, and at the extraordinarily influential post of SAC no less, without having to work her way up through the ranks in the usual fashion as a clerk, then promotion to Agent, Supervisory Special Agent, etc. then it would be a dream come true. If something else was written on the back of the card, well, she'd rather not think about it at this time. She poured herself another drink and took a long draught to steel her nerves. She was fucking the lieutenant, she was drunk on particularly potent and good quality alcohol and it looked like she may be in charge of her very own chamber of ghastliness in the modern dungeon that was torture center. Life was good. Apparently the lieutenant was pleased with her thus far; she intended to make sure that she had some insurance on her side.

Finishing her drink and standing erect she crossed her arms over her chest, staring down at the lieutenant, his face now ruddy and flushed with intoxication, beginning to overheat in the atmosphere of the enclosed room.

The room was the lieutenant's own - she had been barracked in another several corridors away and other than sleeping it had been barely lived in during her tenure at the conference, as she had been spending most of the time after meetings with the lieutenant in his own quarters, during which time she had gotten to know the lay of the land. She paced over to a chest of drawers and removed from between several uniform shirts a rolled piece of leather.

Taking it and letting it unfurl in her anorexically small right hand, the object was seen to be a utility belt for field missions, more sturdy than what was usually worn at conferences. It was thick, black and highly polished and still smelled of the animal from which it had been made.

'Dear lieutenant, you have put a lot of trust in me in this sudden promotion, I am glad that we are making a strong mutual impression on one another. I think maybe you should give me a forewarning about how life is in torture center. Coming in at your recommendation, I want to make sure that you have full confidence that you are sending in a well-disciplined human resource.'

Nadezhda walked to where the lieutenant still sat and placed the belt on the table in front of him before slinking down onto her knees and beginning to gnaw on the lieutenants arm. The lieutenant shook her off, knocking her to the ground in surprise, before taking the last draught of the liquor from his cup. He stood, inadvertently knocking the chair over as he grabbed the leather belt, coiling the end around one hand and smacking the thick leather onto his other hand.

'Bend over the bed, my little pet, so I can see what exactly you are made of.'

Nadezhda complied immediately.

IRON GATES

CHAPTER 5

As Bonn was carried down the halls into the intestines of the inquiry center he could see very little other than the floor passing by him in feet and yards and the marching boots of the guards which held him. A place of ten-thousand varieties of possible paths, all leading to equally potent vectors of ruination, the inquiry center pulsated with a doom-laden aura so prominent that no one could mistake that this was a place where the most hideous aspects of human nature were allowed, nay, provoked to come to the forefront.

The guards held his arms and legs in a vise-grip, tightening considerably once they had moved past the line on the floor that marked the beginning of the secure area. They had walked through several corridors containing individuals which he could hear but not see because of his awkward position, however the voices were entirely more serious and less flippant than the secretaries that had mocked him on his exodus from the office of the anonymous internal security officer who had conducted his interrogation.

For all he knew the secretaries could have been a staged incident, part of some grand psychological pageant being put on by internal security for the detriment of his mind. The voices that he heard as he moved deeper into the corridors of the inquiry center were hushed, brutal. If a naked man being carried hogtied by a contingent of guards was something that caught the attention of people on the administrative side of the building, it was apparently so unnoticeable here that it did not deserve any pause from whatever black work the personnel were busying themselves with. If his situation was business as usual where he was going then he was in trouble. But, he knew instinctively that he was very much in trouble and he was no innocent after all, he was a shock troop, albeit very low on the totem poll and only having seen action on the field once outside of the confines of headquarters. It seemed like he had been at headquarters for far too long; now he knew that he had obviously been at headquarters far too long indeed.

The guards turned a corner and stopped, letting the private dead-drop the less-than-a-foot between his body and the floor, which had formerly been tile in the administrative section but had given way to a polished concrete as they moved further in. The drop was not enough to cause any serious damage but it was jolting nonetheless and re-opened the bleeding from his broken nose. Since his nostrils were completely clogged with blood however, no blood leaked out onto the floor or, hell forbid, the boots of the guards, but instead simply pooled in his nostrils. He coughed as the iron liquid dripped further into his sinus canals and down his esophagus.

The guards reached around his head and stuffed a black ball-gag into his mouth, fastening the leather straps around the back of his head. With equal rapidity another guard moved in and placed a black hood over his face, another placing a pair of modified guard goggles painted completely black over this and the last placing a pair of large headphones over where his ears were now concealed beneath the thick black fabric. Bonn was now completely enveloped in darkness and all sight and sound stopped. He could feel the guards picking him back up and could tell by the air flow moving over his naked flesh that they had resumed their march, however he now neither saw the direction in which they were going nor could he hear the sounds of the guards' combat boots thumping against the concrete. At some point he felt the air get colder and a breeze flow past him before stopping. When he could feel the guards proceeding again the air was much warmer than it had been in the inquiry center. He had left one building and entered another.

Immediately the scent of strong disinfectant chemicals hit him, exacerbated by the warm air. His mind was in a state of high disorientation already due to the sensory deprivation, and as his body relaxed slightly in its bound state he could tell that the warmness of the air would only serve to increase his susceptibility to the sensory deprivation already driving him toward mental instability. He felt himself being slowly lowered onto a hard metal surface which seemed to be higher than ground floor. Deprived of speech, hearing and movement and atrociously exposed in a state of humiliation, shock and forced immobilization, all he could do was drive further into his own mind, fighting to maintain some semblance of reality and to what might happen to him.

The interior of torture center was all concrete walls lathered in layers of black paint, lit with low-level generator-induced light shining down from their mounting places high in the roof overlooking a vast interior. A monitoring station sat in the center of the room, manned by five guards seated beneath a plexiglass enclosure that was filled with all manner of restraints, chemical sprays, nightsticks and several weapons. Much of the metal was original equipment from when the building had been used as a penitentiary before the nuclear wars. At some point before the nukes went airborne the prisoners went ballistic, not about to sit out Armageddon behind bars, and a massive riot involving over eighty deaths occurred before the strongest of the convicts made their way out into the surrounding countryside. The correctional officers were too easy of an immediate target for the prisoners' rage. There was none of the usual recourse to emergency backup in the case of a prison riot at the institution at the time, as every member of the National Guard and local police were all preparing for a much bigger catastrophe.

The black paint had been the organization's own addition to the internal infrastructure of the main processing area of the high security segregation area, apparently recommended by no less than the commander himself.

Inside the monitoring station all the original computer monitors that had been installed there for the staff had been removed as well as the computers themselves, as well as the electronic monitoring equipment, etc. One organization modified laptop sufficed for the torture center secretary who entered in the essential information onto the local database. For interrogations and tortures, notes would be taken of salient information and quickly hand-encrypted and destroyed. Torture center, in order to apply the highest security possible, always adhered to an even more utilitarian standard than was applied in the organization as a whole.

ECT (External Control Torture) was horrifyingly enough the actual name of the specialized correctional unit controlling the torture center, the full name of which was External Control Torture Administration Center (ECTAC). The broad utilization of this so-called administration had its emphasis on administering punishment. The atmosphere was extremely harsh and this harshness was increased with large doses of pure terror in that the ECT was the staging grounds for the most sadistic minds within the organization. The most brutal of the shock troops, men who had been remanded from their training units for committing particularly harsh hazing practices on other troops, or shock troops who had been operating in the field and had been observed raising the bar in the intensity and creativity of applied atrocity were often selected for service in the ECT. Several small units of hardcore intelligence officers, skilled in interrogation, torture and pioneers of the organization's embryonic punitive mind control program were also stationed in ECTAC.

The intelligence officers in place in ECT were for the most part field operatives, and their brand of applied intelligence (intelligence in the organization equaled terror) bore the stamp of the sort of operations in which the interrogations ended with the termination of the person being interrogated in many cases, and often a butchering of the person's corpse and meal of human flesh to follow, along with the obligatory sharing of bone fragments as souvenirs when it came to particularly high-level targets. The latter practice was more common amongst the elite amongst the shock troops, and the intelligence officers' engagement of similar activity on the field attested to the stark reality of a post-nuclear world and frequent fraternization with the military troops by intelligence. For an intelligence officer, to bed a harsh matron who manned a belt-fed machine gun during large-scale exterminations was more than an exotic experience.

The level of sophistication was primitive despite the high-end working capital of the installation, which boasted mechanical advances in order to operate the steel doors leading to the segregation housing units themselves, which had once been operated frequently throughout the day, opening and closing by electronic impulse. In order to abbreviate the process of guards and ECT personnel moving to and from inmate areas within the institution, several of the cells in the interior of the wings of the segregation units had been appropriated for guard stations. Their steel doors were removed and replaced with heavy black plastic curtains so that personnel could go from guard cell to cell (usually the guards appropriated a row of five cells along the central housing corridor) with minimal difficulty. The door to the segregation housing units leading to the receiving and discharge and outer areas of the prison were built exclusively to work by electronic pulse and were once frequently operated by remote control from the guard stations. This was no longer practical due to restraints on electricity even within the commander's base, which was one of the few places within the organization to have electric lights, the bluish hue of spotlights sending the clear signal to all that the organization was the unequivocal master of the area. Now the door to the segregation cells themselves were only opened a few times per day, with the guards attaching the circuit to the entrance-way to one of the generator hookups which shot one surge of electricity enough to open and close the door.

The private lay on his stomach, the cold metal of the gurney causing goose pimples to rise along his flesh. Although he could not hear, he could feel the jostling of the gurney being rolled for a brief period of time before he felt himself being roughly lifted and placed on a thin mattress. Now he was only left alone with the beginning of debilitating aches from his prolonged state of being manacled in an uncomfortable position along with the building sense of dread and mental incapacitation beginning to set in from the sensory deprivation hood. He had managed to exhale in a snort through one of his nostrils so he was now able to breath slightly. The other nostril would remain totally clogged with blood unless he could get a finger to it, which was impossible in his current state, and the ball-gag, stretching his mouth uncomfortably, provided no air flow. He would remain in this position for quite some time until his formal processing began.

CHAPTER 6

A large podium stretched across the deep interior of a vast corrugated steel building, formerly used for some industrial enterprise but now the site of one of the organization's leadership-level conferences. It was now the afternoon before the final conference meeting to be held in the evening. The installation, technically secret outside leadership and select required personnel, was located in organization territory at a mid-point between the commander's base and the secure areas of the border that marked the most far-flung horizon of the organization's holding operations. Organizational operatives and activities existed beyond this border, however the secure area marked the last geographic line where the land and the populace was entirely in the organization's pocket.

Huge banners representing various sectors of the organization such as intelligence, shock troops and internal security hung high from the rafters above the heads of the participants. The entire hall was lit with large, pressurized gas lamps which cast the entire meeting place in an eerie glow. On the far end of the building a hangar door had been opened, letting in the dull light of the sun, cloaked behind cloud cover and overcast weather that had been steady since the conference began several days prior.

In the post-apocalypse people had gotten used to the absence of the bright electric lights that once lit the vast swathes of the civilized world. If some stray satellite from the old days was still circling the globe, taking automatic photographs of the various portions of the earth, it would see that the globe was now covered in darkness - as appropriate in this, the new Dark Age.

Long work tables with folding metal chairs had been set up across the expanse of the floor and were populated with some three hundred members from a cross section of the organization. Many of them had come to the organization in their own way with different stories to tell and operated in varying sectors of the group, yet their elan and fanaticism toward forwarding the mission of the commander had facilitated their rise within the ranks that put them at the conference today.

Nadezhda, sitting with a contingent from her office in internal security, found it hard to concentrate on the various matters being discussed from the podium, although she duly took notes concerning salient points, particularly when it came to her specialty areas of code decryption and intelligence analysis. The lectures on those two topics from the podium were however quite brief, less than fifteen minutes each, the code and intelligence analysis work being relegated more so to early morning and late afternoon sessions in smaller meeting rooms and attended only by those working in those fields, as well as a few intelligence liaison officers who worked on the ground at shock troop units.

Although part of the purpose of the event was to build cohesiveness and focus amongst the individual sectors of the organization in relation to their work, her mind was on another sector altogether. The last sexual experience of the previous evening had been intense and the lieutenant had been very pleased by the correct strategy of her ministrations, having given her a hard beating with the leather belt that she had offered him followed by taking her over his knee and spanking her like a child, before she led him to orgasm via energetic oral stimulation. Her petite bottom felt quite bruised the second day, but pleasantly so, and it was easy to be reminded of what she had been doing as she attempted to sit for the long hours listening to lectures in the very plain metal chair. Equally on her mind was the lieutenant's card that she had been handed, which sat securely within the wallet on her person - she would not risk any chance of that particular document walking away from her, and she had kept the wallet clutched to her breast the night before when she slept, having finally returned to her own room after spending the entire evening with the lieutenant, too tired to engage in an errant code-breaking of the cipher that the lieutenant had inscribed.

Her father was on the stage now, giving a demonstration of the various guns that armaments were now producing on a regular schedule. Large numbers of firearms had been saved after the nuclear war and carefully maintained, however even tools of metal and oil begin to wear down in time and her father had been key in beginning the production of new pieces as well as replacement parts so that corrective as well as preventative troubleshooting could be easily accomplished.

A MP5 submachine gun was lifted into the air and snarled out with several shots bursting in rapid succession from its mean-looking snout. Nadezhda's father had loaded the various test weapons with blanks carefully produced by himself personally with his own reloading machine that he had built from old plans; he would not entrust this task to a subordinate in case of the rare chance that they might put a live round in the gun and some conference attendee accidentally catch a bullet. He paid close attention to detail, a trait which had assisted him well during the course of his long career.

Nadezhda's father's full name was Felix Zhuvova Yatskaya and he stood imposing behind the speaker's lectern as the last dummy round burst from the MP5 and the majority of the three-hundred strong hall rose in raucous applause. Yatskaya was a total veteran of the organization in every respect and knew exactly how to win over an audience, knowing better than anyone else that machine guns would do the trick in almost every circumstance.

He gave a description of the MP5, how many had been produced in the last five years and what the current production schedule was and then went through similar tests and descriptions over an impressive list of other small arms including the M15, AK-74 and several handguns. Via being the mind behind the post-nuclear rearmament, Yatskaya had found himself in the supremely satisfying position of custom-making the arsenal of the organization's new world according to his particular taste in firearms. The submachine guns and handguns that he selected to become mainstays in the organization's arsenal were picked from a rich history of use by military, guerrilla outfits and street gangs. All prohibitions as to modifications and incremental increases in a firearm's level of inherent lethality had been unceremoniously thrown out the proverbial window after society descended into anarchy, allowing Nadezhda's father's work to come into full flourish in designing and manufacturing a particularly intimidating spectrum of death-dealing instruments. Ammunition clips had begun to be produced in much longer higher-capacity designs on most pieces for accelerated efficiency in direct combat situations without having to change clips. Many of the guns were outfitted with ferocious-looking bayonets sharpened to a razor's edge and some of the weapons had been given semi-official nicknames like 'meat-grinder', 'blood mist' and 'hacker' to intimate to those being so commissioned of the unparalleled capabilities of the weapon and to build the bloodthirsty morale of the ever-growing population of shock troops, elite commandos, internal security executioners and intelligence wing assassins. For the latter, an entire spectrum of weapons had been introduced at lower production levels and designed for their specific purposes in mind, outfitted with hand-crafted silencers and flash suppressors and primitive scopes drawn from old military models.

Assassinations were done in areas that would be harder

to execute a typical land campaign replete with burning buildings, destroying or seizing infrastructure, enslavement of the area youth and raping of the women followed by eventual public executions, enacted after long, well-orchestrated periods of humiliation, of whatever leadership might be present. Some of the small communities, savage in their adherence to long dead modes of living, however backward thinking they might be, still managed to exist far enough afield from organizational strongholds and decently armed with old firepower to dissuade the organization from spending the manpower and resources needed to do a typical land attack. Although the organization would get them eventually, one way or another, there were still limited resources and the commander's forces could not be everywhere at once. In these cases, intelligence officers would be sent in under deep-cover, sometimes cultivating local informants under a false flag and sometimes using commando units who conducted surveillance from a distance for weeks in harsh conditions. Once the leadership and key community members were identified, a sniper would be sent in with the commando unit running back-up to take out the targets. The communities would then be completely shattered, disorganized and, most importantly, terrified. Assassinations were a way that the organization sent a message to recalcitrant communities that clearly stated: even if we aren't in your backyard yet, we can still reach our tendrils into the very heart of your world and destroy it. Do not feel safe, we are breathing down your necks. After a period of time following the assassinations, most of the communities would break down on their own and then conventional organization forces could move in easily. Some areas, after the death of their leaders, upon whom they had become dependent on both for direction and psychologically in general, would voluntarily offer themselves up to the organization, sending an emissary over the line into organization territory and begging the first representative they found to have the organization move in and run things for them. This was always highly morale boosting for the organization and a string of successes had kept intelligence unit assassins continually busy.

Increasingly the commander and his direct plenipotentiaries had been stressing the importance of firearms as being the key necessity in ventures on the field but attempting to limit their use within internal sectors. Internal security guards throughout the main compound and around the perimeter of the conference hall where they met now of course were armed to the teeth but however equipped the guards were with machine guns and other accoutrements, standing orders had them utilize the firearms only when no other option applied. Thus training was increasing across the board on command edict concerning the use of edged weapons as well as psychological training to induce armed organization members to be more enthusiastic to kill with their bare hands. Brandished firearms within the organization were always a good deterrent against internal dissent, however the precious bullets being churned out by the armaments division were best relegated to field use. Although not frequently spoken of, the organization's emphasis on terror and internal discipline and raising up the banner of a new dark age had within its political DNA the seeds for a future in which almost every aspect of the old society would, in time, fade away.

As such, heavy industry was not being developed within the organization territories - nor anywhere else as far as the organization's spies and voices abroad could tell. Seventy-five years after the nuclear war humanity was still in scavenger mode. There were ample empty houses, buildings and infrastructure thus no real need to develop anything but maintenance-level building skills in the generally demoralized and scarcity-driven utilitarianism that was the general rule rather than the exception among the totality of the populace, organization-administrated and otherwise. In the realm of food cultivation the rule of thumb was take what you could find, do what you could do. Other than in the higher ranks and amongst those who could manage to hunt a little themselves, food for organization members consisted of highly processed materials (including rendered products extracted from their former comrades) generously laced with certain chemical extracts to mimic natural health.

As he continued to speak, Yatskaya filled his oratory with rising levels of volume and excitement as each new weapon was shown. At the end of the presentation, along with a set of dignitaries from the commander's liaison coming from headquarters, he revealed a larger piece than had been in use. Well recognized by all members of the organization as a small Palestinian-type guerrilla rocket, the crowd erupted with a diabolic frenzy upon viewing the artillery piece, everyone on their feet, fists raised in the air and screams of bloodlust on every tongue. Nadezhda rose like in a dream and her mouth filled with a hateful screech as her arms raised up straight in the air. Across the hall amongst another sector of attendees, the lieutenant also found himself in the mesmerizing spell of the newly produced upgraded weaponry.

The thirteen foot black cylinder gleamed with a sinister glint, with the initials and make, KVA-1, painted in plain red letters upon the side. The small pulley with the mechanism set atop its tripod mount rolled into the center near Nadezhda's father. Brutal and as imposing as the weapon which he had forged, he too raised his fist in a violent scream as the artillery piece came into the view of the amassed organizational personnel at the conference. This was the day that he had been waiting for, the unveiling of the fruits of a project that he had been working on for many years with complete secrecy within the armaments division. Nadezhda in the audience was floored considering that she had seen no visible signs in her father over time that would have compromised that he was working on something very specific and ambitious such as this.

If she had still been younger and studying at the armaments factory as she had when she was a girl she would have noticed, but code-breaking and intelligence analysis in internal security had become all-consuming work and her visits with her father were almost always at his residence; there had been no specific need to visit the armaments factory as of late. Organization life, even in its mundane particulars, did not mimic the softhearted ways of the familyist-minded bourgeoisie which once ruled the land. If Nadezhda, as a commissioned codebreaker and internal security personnel, frequented the armaments factory without due reason, no matter that her father worked there, she would be noted for potential espionage activities if the action continued. Once she moved out of the youth corps and into full service not too long ago, she had been well aware that the dynamics change when a person joins a subsector within the organization. Shock troops were more lenient and accepted in certain circumstances, but internal security were always suspect. They preyed upon the people and then they preyed upon one another, which would be the scenario as already mentioned. It was a cannibalistic bureaucratic beast that devoured human beings without any understandable discrimination - it was to be avoided.

Yatskaya waved his arms in a gesture for the crowd to quiet and the roar lessened to a degree, although all were still on their feet, then all of a sudden a huge banner that had been rolled up and hidden in the rafters behind the stage was unfurled dramatically, featuring a new insignia of the organization, now no longer featuring the bat but instead crossed rockets behind the profile of the commander. In the corner in blood red stood a new image of a bat, flying down from some ghastly sky as if in the midst of a hunt. The symbolism reverberated with everyone throughout the hall, striking deep chords in the very center of their consciousness. Now they had advanced their death machine into an entirely new level and their domination would be unstoppable. 'DEATH!' shouted the armaments official, howling like a madman through a generator-run speaker system. 'DEATH!' screamed the unhinged audience in response. 'DEATH! DEATH! DEATH!' - the chant resounded like the roaring of ten-thousand tigers throughout the metal hangar, sweat pouring down every face in emotional exertion.

'Esteemed members of the organization,' began Yatskaya. 'We are now entering a new and increasingly weaponized era within the organization. With the assistance of our chemistry sector, in conjunction with armaments over the last several years, we have worked without stop on forwarding this project under the express orders and personal leadership guidance of the commander himself.'

The audience response was now caged chaos.

'Only with the leadership of the commander could we have reached the level that the organization, his dream, now has at its hands. We are going to usher in an era in which death will reign from above onto our enemies and they will recognize without fail that they must submit under the lash of this group, this organization, this spearhead of the new Dark Age! Let the exploded bodies of their kith and kin be the punishing testament for any who would seek to conspire against the might of god-in a-flesh-body, the commander. Let him hear your screams!'

The audience erupted into banshee shrieking, exploding the limits of sanity.

'By being present here today, you are the first outside of the production team and the highest levels to be informed about the existence of this weapon. Propaganda sheets are being printed both in white and black propaganda style, two different versions for the benefit of our group and our enemies respectively, acting as the prophet in the wilderness bringing to light the horrific new level of our organization's might. Within two months' time there will be a mass rally near headquarters in which this lethal arm of the commander, this lethal vessel of death stamped with the mark of our our organization, will be formally unveiled to the organization as a whole. At that time there will also be mass initiations and the conferring of medals and armbands forwarding our new emblem. For those who want to sign up for special initiations please see the processing liaison officer who has a table set up at the back of the room tonight. Attendees will be given priority for choice initiations and will be attended and devised with much circumstance. The commander will be attending this rally personally and your dedication and elan with which you take on the responsibility of setting an example as members of leadership cadre will quadruple the discipline of your subordinates and give untold pleasure to the commander. Avail yourselves of this opportunity!'

Various religious cults, thinly veiled fronts of certain experimental intelligence operations utilizing the population of the organization as its experimental lab rats, would be at the coming event. In the organization the lines between the swelling mystical current within the post-nuclear populace and methods of maintaining organizational cohesiveness on a psychological, sociological and physical level were always blurred. If the tendency existed, it would be co-opted by the organization. Many tendencies of course were crushed, however in the latter doomsday scenario in which they found themselves operating, the leadership of the organization had learned that it behooved them to play certain chords. The majority of the tendencies most in vogue were fabricated by intelligence itself. In the old days, a shadow state like the organization would have been termed religious extremists or most loathsome in their methodology of governance, however, the thrust and sheer scope of the cult programs within the organization were unlike anything the world had ever seen except perhaps as vague intimations of the future during the darkest days of yore.

Lines of masked and goggled internal security guards lined the open door of the hangar; the presentation of the rocket had induced the highest level of security possible for this rally. The project had, in reality, been kept an absolute secret without any chinks in the armor of silence, as none of the attendees outside of the project had seen this coming. The additional

IRON GATES

security personnel had been personally requested by armaments or at least someone going under armaments cover. For a long time the organization had boasted various particularly nasty weapons - chemical, biological and radiological warfare was considered the name of the game, the crest jewel to the organization's usual shootings, dismemberments and more primitively executed atrocities on the field. Now all of this hideous weaponry would have a psychotic means of dispersal. From the times when elite units would make moves against small settlements with poisoning the wells or contaminating the food supply, the organization could now load those same agents into warheads and send them spiraling over the spires of the forests and into unaware and unprepared centers of humanity, inaugurating their actions with explosions, shrapnel and rising casualties and ending them with culling cultured from varied pages of the the organization's encyclopedia of death.

'Esteemed members of the organization.' Yatskaya's voice sounded like hosts of phantoms flying over the three-hundred strong crowd of organizational personnel. A team of guards moved in around the stage surrounding the speaker and the weapon and some activity could be seen commencing at the mouth of the hangar. 'Please head into the courtyard where refreshments have been prepared and enjoy yourselves for the rest of the afternoon. Evening session will begin at the usual time; we have a special session this evening and it will be brief, as all of you are preparing to leave in the morning. In the courtyard you will have the opportunity to receive reports on the scope of the new project and various public strategic outlines that I am sure will be of interest to you. I am looking forward to speaking with you soon and more in-depth. Long live the commander!'

A cheer rose up from the crowd as the people began making their way toward the hangar door. Still guarding the stage, several technicians came and wheeled the rocket in an opposite direction, out a side door and beyond the view of the attendees. The cheer broke down into a minor cacophony of animated conversations as they moved toward the courtyard.

Outside the hangar was a bustle of activity as the delegates began pouring into the area located securely between several of the steel buildings making up the conference location. On huge spits wild boars were rotating in roast, sending a sweet scent of broiling flesh wafting across the grounds. Large open-faced military tents were manned by various low-level clerks from intelligence who were passing out pamphlets and newspapers glorifying the appearance of the rocket in the organization's arsenal. Industrial-sized plastic barrels outfitted with primitive tap mechanisms had been set up at various junctures, dispensing a crude organization-made low-alcohol small beer similar to the potato recipes once utilized by Russian peasants, the difference between it and its historic counterpart being that the organization version was also, as usual, amply fortified with laboratory-produced stimulants.

IRON GATES

The conference had been more exciting than most of the attendees had premeditated. It was within the purview of executive strategy to engineer events such as these during significant successes and this was most certainly a stellar success by all accounts. A several hour period of celebration was soon to begin which would culminate in a final debriefing which was more perfunctory than essential, as by the time the evening session started there would be atrocious levels of intoxication throughout the attendees - the informational meat had been set to the organizational vultures in the afternoon session, as by prior design and culminating with the armaments announcement.

A snowless winter was upon the landscape but due to the southern climes the weather was relatively warm considering, however to both cut the chill in the air and provide atmosphere there were lines of steel drums half-buried in the ground burning a variety of refuse for warmth and additional light in the courtyard, these much similar to how partisans in the old days used to arrange a landing strip for descending support aircraft. Nadezhda looked around the area for her father but he was nowhere to be seen, more than likely he would be locked in serious closed-door sessions well into the evening whilst the rest of the company celebrated the victory which was due highly in part to his design.

Cold chills broke over her neck when she considered what had been said earlier in her father's speech, concerning the commander taking personal leadership of the project from the onset, which meant that the commander had been working with her father face-to-face and – by implication – for some time. The development of the rocket under the joint work of the commander and her father would catapult her into entirely new levels of respect and prestige within the organization and she wondered what this, along with the coded message that the lieutenant had given her, would mean for her future. Driving her wandering thoughts to the side, she approached a small lean-to proffering drinks of a stronger variety than what was in the plastic drums dispensing the potato-based liquor.

Several ebony-skinned men with huge frames stood nearby, smoking large cigars which contained a brutal narcotic favored by some of the members of the organization with a particularly strong constitution. They were hand-rolled with wild-growing tobacco, called rabbit tobacco, but interspersed with ample amounts of a mild hallucinogenic substance called 'cerebranam' and finally dipped into another chemical (often thought to be an equivalent to the embalming fluid of pre-apocalyptic times) which acted as a sedative. The combination of mild hallucinogen, nicotine stimulant and sedative produced a state in which the various substances combated one another, producing a somewhat calming but also violent state in those so using. The black men in the organization received much favor from the commander, who considered them superior to many of the other racial strains and, because their ancestors had lived in the area for hundreds of years before the nuclear wars and had not always been on good terms with the state, they were considered natural resistance fighters who were able to roll with the punches to a higher degree than some of the genetic strains who had socially been raised on the soft tit of luxury, making the latter sub-species all the more neurotic and destroyed when the world came down around their heads in a sea of nuclear fire.

The men did not notice Nadezhda as she walked beneath the awning of the stall, where a small boy around ten years of age manned a primitive non-electric refrigeration unit made of some put-together pieces of insulated material, surrounded by a few cartons and various plastic cups. Nadezhda smiled at the boy, who promptly grinned in return. His beady eyes ran over every inch of her body within a few seconds, greedily imagining the specifics of the slight curvatures that existed under the black uniform.

'Hello, brother,' Nadezhda said smoothly, aware of the young man's interest and fully intending to take advantage of the situation and give the youth a thrill in the process.

'Hello, sister...' said the youth, his voice trailing off inadvertently amidst his rapture.

Obliquely, Nadezhda raised one hand and cupped her breast through the fabric, pursing her lips slightly while nodding toward the tankard. 'Please set me up with one of those, brother, and perhaps I will set you up with one of these later.'

She tapped her small breast, the curvature of which was barely noticeable beneath the fabric.

The youth went to preparing the requested liquid extra quick.

Nadezhda would be enjoying a mixture of

promethazine, codeine syrup and a mild alcohol made from the rotting persimmons that fell down from the boughs of the trees in the fall, combined with ice. The purpose of the drink, which Nadezhda favored, was to produce a state of extreme somnolence, lowering of respiration capacity and producing a dissociative state. As the young boy prepared the concoction she eyed him appraisingly; she would have to show him a thing or two before the night was over.

IRON GATES

CHAPTER 7

As the field marshal returned to his encampment he could smell the unmistakeable aroma of roasting flesh over an open fire. Beneath his thick mustache he smiled and mentally commended the acumen of his guards for their practicality. After he had left them alone with their two victims, they had paired up, one guard holding the baby and the other guard holding the still ball-gagged mother tightly against a tree. By this time the baby was dead, however blood was still trickling from the bayonet wound which had spiked directly through its heart, causing massive internal bleeding in its infantile frame. The guard held the baby, manipulating its dead body parts like a sick marionette and, once close to the mother's face, took great delight in squeezing the baby as hard as he could, causing blood to belch out of the dead mouth. The mother's face widened in a total rictus of horror.

'If we take this gag off of you, are you going to scream?'

The guards looked to the mother's eyes for any sense of comprehension but saw nothing. The fact that the field marshal had told them to have a good time essentially meant that they could do whatever they wanted with her and that more than likely any intelligence she might field them would be of minimal value or else the field marshal simply did not care in this instance. Their motivation in considering taking off the gag was part sense of responsibility that she should be interrogated at least a little bit and partly interest in her mouth in general.

'Listen, bitch, we have listened to your screaming enough for one day. If you scream when we take off this gag do you know what we are going to make you do?'

The woman shook her head in negation.

'We are going to make you eat your baby, isn't that right?' The mother's masked guard nodded in affirmation to his anonymous partner. Fresh tears began streaming down the woman's face.

'We are not going to let you eat all of it, though, because we are most definitely going to be eating most of it ourselves, isn't that right?' The guard nodded at the other guard who nodded in turn.

One guard held the baby in his arms in a mock sense of parenting, gently rocking the corpse and looking at the small bleeding infant through his black goggles.

The other guard had the woman pinned to the tree with one hand and with his other hand he pointed in her face, making sure to psychologically send the message home. He was very interested in interrogating her, or at least pretending to.

'If you make us eat the baby then we are going to have to take our masks off and if we take our masks off that means that you are going to have to die because you can't know our identities, now can you? Can you, you fucking bitch, you stupid fucking whore?' The guard emphasized his misogynistic diatribe by thumping her head against the rough bark of the pine tree, further adding a debilitating measure to the situation.

The guard motioned for the other guard holding the baby to set her down and assist him. He took a hold of the woman's hair and dragged her into the clearing, forcing her to her knees on the forest floor, covered with fallen pine needles. As the guard removed the ball gag from her mouth, the other guard held a huge survival-style combat knife, hefting its weight threateningly in his hands to remind the woman to keep her sound pressure level down.

'There is no one here except for you, me, my friend here,' the guard nodded toward his partner, 'and little what's-his-name over there,' the guard gestured toward the dead baby lying at the foot of the tree. The guard gestured toward the other guard to come closer. 'Let's take a look at what she's got.' The woman said nothing but breathed heavily in sharp, labored inhalations, the removal of the ball-gag being a small respite in an otherwise horrendous situation.

The second guard moved forward and began slowly moving the tip of the large knife down the front of the woman's blouse, snipping her buttons off one-by-one, a testament to the insanely razor-sharp edge of the lethal weapon. The woman did not react. She had just seen her infant child bayoneted and then mutilated in front of her face; whatever the guards intended to do to her would not make an impression after the previous ordeal - or so she thought.

IRON GATES

The guard ripped open the woman's blouse, revealing her breasts, pale white and topped with large, succulent and prominent areolae. The guard reached out and slapped them with his gloved hand, bringing out a gasp from the woman's mouth. Her eyes widened in hatred, but she didn't say anything at the sudden perfunctory humiliation and shock of the sudden blow. The guard moved toward her and began massaging her breasts with one hand and feeling her underneath through her thin cotton pants with the other hand, having resheathed his knife.

The other guard was near the edge of the forest and looking around the trees. Both guards were still completely blacked-out and obscured due to dark-tinted goggles and balaclavas. The forest was becoming dark in the twilight of the hour with shadows forming around the second guard as he reached into a tree and broke off a stout, whippy branch, breaking the cut with a small machete that had been attached to his belt. Smelly sap oozed out the green hardwood branch.

'Get the gag back on her!' yelled the guard massaging the girl. The second guard approached, carrying his freshly cut punishment rod in one hand and removing the ball gag from a small pouch at his belt with the other. 'Got it right here,' he said.

The sense of menacing was made strange and alien by the mens' anonymous and bleak disguises. There was no personalism to relate to and within the horrified mind of the victim. Nothingness oozed forth from the bleak, horrific black-masked faces staring from seas of blackness, the slight microscopic image of herself peering back from their mirrored effect, showing her tortured face and the copses of pine and rough hardwood in the forests surrounding them.

'Put the muzzle on the bitch,' barked the guard. The second guard tossed down his switch and ran up on the woman, jamming the ball-gag in her mouth and fastening the straps around the back of her head, bunching her thin, wheat-blonde hair. He accelerated the attack by ripping her shirt the rest of the way open, revealing a gaunt, starved figure, pale and shivering. He too reached around and smacked the red-tipped breasts with his gloved hand. 'Steady now,' said the other guard.

IRON GATES

CHAPTER 8

Blood spurted nauseously from the shock troop's nose as the lieutenant bashed him in the face with a leather encased blackjack, filled with heavy lead. The trooper crumpled to the ground with a muffled howl as the lieutenant moved in and drove a booted foot into the man's midsection.

'Get up, you filth!' the lieutenant screamed, gobs of spittle flying from his mouth in unrestrained rage.

The lieutenant's body pulsated, the hormones of a blood beast riddled with organization-designed stimulants and seared together in one fleshly package with years of brutal organizational training and brainwashing.

The lieutenant had been called out by a member of internal security ten minutes before the afternoon session had released and led into a foyer leading to a small hall of a few rooms with all the doors tightly shut. The shock troop was within one of the rooms, remanded there due to a breach of security protocol in unloading the rocket from the lorry before the presentation.

The trooper had been smoking while waiting for the internal security retinue to arrive to take the test model into the hangar when the team from internal security arrived. Beneath their masks he could not ascertain their expressions of blearing, black hatred.

'What the fuck are you doing, trooper?' the head guard asked.

The shock troop did not respond immediately and instead blew a ring of smoke out from his lungs, oblivious to the situation and oblivious to the fact that he was adding irredeemable insult to injury by his actions.

'Take a few steps this way, trooper.' The guard pointed to a concrete wall a safe distance away from the live rocket. The shock troop complied. Once reaching the wall the trooper took another drag from his cheap, stinking cigarette at which point the guard summarily smacked it out of his hand.

'You are a fucking idiot, trooper!'

This time the guard smacked him in the face. A red handprint spread across the trooper's face as his cigarette slowly burned out a few feet away.

'You fucking motherfucking stupid fucking idiot!' screamed the guard. 'That rocket is live, brother! You should have felt damn lucky to be responsible for having any part in the transporting of that weapon or being close to it at all!' The shock troop began to backtrack.

'Listen, I had no idea what that thing was, I...'

The shock troop was cut short with one black leather-gloved finger held menacingly in front of his face.

'Shut up! Shut the fuck up! If you do not know now then you are about to learn. Take this filth out of here!' The guard raised his hand in a swift gesture and two other guards marched over and took hold of the errant shock trooper.

'Take that one to out-processing satellite!' The guards took off at a horrid trot, practically dragging the unfortunate trooper along toward a side door leading toward the hangar from the backside.

At the processing satellite guard station ('out-processing' being not a place but a thing) the head guard on duty, making an absurdly incongruous sight sitting behind a desk fully masked, goggled and suited for combat, with a silenced MP5 sitting on the wooden desk, listened with growing ire to the report from his detail.

'He was doing what?' the head guard asked the men incredulously.

The apprehending guards proceeded to brief the resident security chief on the situation in full. The shock troop was summarily ushered into a small enclosed courtyard with high concrete walls rising on either side of him and a pale sun shining above.

'Guard.'

Back at the desk the security chief motioned one of the internal security personnel over to him.

'Do you have a few minutes?'
'Whatever you need.'
'Good.'

The security chief began scribbling a coded note on a small piece of paper bearing an internal security crest on its header.

'Get into the conference and find the lieutenant and give him this, escort him back when he comes in case he doesn't know his way.'

IRON GATES

The lieutenant was in the throes of armaments-induced insanity and martial fanaticism when the guard approached him with the note. Once having finished reading the coded message, which took less than a minute, the lieutenant crumpled the note in his hand and began laughing loudly, his eyes lolling around in his skull in a decidedly maniacal fashion.

'Let's go, guard, let's do it!'

The guard, duly impressed with the lieutenant's zestful demeanor and pleased that he had been given this particular detail, a highlight to an otherwise bad situation, motioned for the lieutenant to follow him toward a plain door located near the back of the conference room.

It did not take much briefing from the security chief after entering the small satellite station to make him understand why they had called him in to perform an act that any of them could have done. It was both an honorific calling him in, a morale booster to the guards having some official interaction with the dreaded and infamous lieutenant and also, at base, throwing blood to the beast - much like tossing a fresh rabbit corpse to a ravening wolf or a slab of raw steak to a rabid dog. At the desk, the security chief smiled to himself as he heard the lieutenant being led into the enclosed courtyard annex and the door slam behind him.

Not far away as the conference of attendees were beginning to get into their own revelry, a few imagined that they could hear the martial barking of a harsh male voice and a few blood-curdling screams wafting across

IRON GATES

the air. It was no surprise however, such sounds were expected and often forthcoming for those living inside the organization; what other events might be happening at the secret base in addition to the conference was anyone's guess.

'Get the fuck up, get the fuck up, get the fuck up!'

The lieutenant chanted his internal mantra aloud as he pounced like an animal upon the shock troop who lay prostrate on the ground, clutching his abused stomach as blood gurgled out of his nose and mouth.

'GET UP GET UP GET UP!'

The lieutenant's hands snarled out at the prone shock troop like enraged asps, grabbing the trooper forcefully around the neck and wrenching him to his feet.

'Don't ask, don't tell!'

The lieutenant was now beyond any semblance of sanity as commonly understood. A few of the guards inside the satellite pressed their ears against the steel door, vainly straining to hear some sounds of the action.

A purplish tongue protruded from beneath the lieutenant's mustache and to the surprise of the shock troop the lieutenant began lapping the blood from his face, swallowing it with strange gurgling noises and feinted 'oohs' and 'ahhs' of an amorous encounter.

The lieutenant, his mouth now amply stained with blood, removed his hands from the trooper's neck and forcibly pushed him with both hands, sending him sprawling on the ground once again, barely missing smashing his head against the concrete floor.

'I thought I told you to get up, you slimy shit, get up! Get up! Get up!'

The groggy soldier began making the motions to attempt to rise, rolling over on his side and supporting himself with one of his hands. The lieutenant promptly walked over and brought his boot down on top of the trooper's hand with a resounding crunch, crushing numerous small bones and bursting blood-vessels and nerve-endings. The trooper screamed pitifully, his bloodied face now a total wreck, contorting at the sudden searing pain of his smashed hand.

The lieutenant walked over to him and whopped his blackjack at a vicious angle onto on the back of the trooper's head, causing his face to rebound on the floor.

'The security guards in there told me everything!'

The lieutenant bent down, hands on his knees, to get his face as close as possible to the trooper.

'They told me everything, trooper!'

The lieutenant emphasized this by widening his eyes and thumping the blackjack against his leg as he rose and began pacing back and forth in front of the trooper's face, now resting on its side upon the ground.

'They told me that you, trooper, have been passing SECRET DOCUMENTS to the ENEMIES of the organization, that you have made PERSONAL ACCUSATIONS against the commander, that you have been CONSPIRING with elements of dissent amongst your unit, and much more as well!'

The trooper went into shock. Dear life itself, what on earth had internal security told him?

'No...'

The shock trooper managed to let loose a pathetic croak from his belabored lungs.

'NO WHAT? NO WHAT? NOW WHAT HAVE YOU BEEN UP TO, YOU MOTHERFUCKING TRAITOR PIG!'

The lieutenant would have gone for the shock trooper's hair, however the shock trooper was bald so the lieutenant improvised by grabbing the back collar of the shock trooper's uniform jacket and began dragging him around the floor of the courtyard annex vigorously.

'TRAITOR! TRAITOR! TRAITOR!'

Spit flew from the lieutenant's mouth as he capered, wetting his already blood-encrusted mustache, as he continued pulling his unwilling victim behind him. Every so often the lieutenant emphasized his message by smacking the shock trooper on the top of the head with his blackjack.

'BLEEEEAAAARRGGGGGG!'

The lieutenant's litanies of crimes and false accusations, all contrived within his own mind as part of his interrogation ruse, began degenerating into animalistic sounds of unchained brutality and fury and sheer violent physical effort.

The lieutenant continued to scream, each time he screamed he beat the lead-weighted blackjack against the shock troop's head a little harder and the shock troop screamed along with him, albeit with a more defeated tone.

The forced dragging had left a neat trail of blood

spiraling around in concentric circles upon the floor of the courtyard annex. The lieutenant stood up, slowly catching his breath, drool dripping down his face causing further streams of filth-encrusted clarity in his otherwise blood-encrusted face, sweat glistening on his forehead in beads.

The shock troop, now punished into total exhaustion, lay like a slug.

The lieutenant walked over to the door back to the satellite and began banging on the door, screaming. The shock troops, their ears still pressed to the door, almost fell over with surprise.

'Lieutenant calling chief!' yelled the guards.

'Well for fuck's sake open it up and see what he wants!'

The guards complied, opening the door to reveal the staring, deranged face of the lieutenant. A hushed conversation ensued and the guards returned to the chief's desk to relay the request. They led the lieutenant into a makeshift lavatory where he slurped up tepid water from an open basin.

The guards returned, one carrying a jug of blue chemical antiseptic, a length of chain and leather restraints, the other guard carrying a black shining martinet, greased to perfection.

'Be so kind as to join me, why don't you?' said the lieutenant, smiling, as he stepped into a small section of light beneath the overcast sky of the courtyard. The guards didn't even consider the implications of the request. Personal service to the lieutenant would catapult them in status far above anything that they could hope to accomplish in the backwater of being stationed at the conference center attached to a small security detail reserved for special duty at intermittent events at the secret base.

The guards brought their items into the courtyard annex, transformed into an arena of sublime punishment through the machinations of the lieutenant, as the shock troop lay on the ground, breath slow in trained survival-reflex relaxation to the severe trauma he had undergone thus far. Such semblance to relaxation would not last long.

'Strip him,' ordered the lieutenant. 'And bind him,' he added, as an afterthought.

The guard carrying the restraints and the antiseptic set the clear container upon the ground and then knelt, removing various chain and leather restraints from his utility belt and arranging them neatly according to their use.

The guard approached the shock troop and began moving the mostly limp body onto its back, beginning to unbutton the uniform shirt. If it wasn't going to be of any use to him anymore then others in the organization could certainly use it. The shock troop began to struggle slightly and the guard got up close on his face.

'Listen to me, trooper, we are going to strip you. If you want me to push my fist straight through your face then let me know. If you don't struggle, who knows? You might have a fighting chance at staying alive.'

The shock troop stopped his feeble struggling and the guard thought to himself in satisfaction how easy it had been to play the false psychological ruse on the prisoner. Being knocked unconscious would definitely be a progressive move in counterpose to waking consciousness prior to what was coming. All was predicated upon the measured heightening of the levels of abusive tactics being applied both psychologically and physically.

The guard finished removing the combat jacket and then took off the shock trooper's shirt, revealing a well-exercised chest and torso and a few grisly tattoos of atomic mushroom clouds, armored skeletons and naked women in various states of undress. The guard noted them internally with favor.

'Put him in the corner and in the second stress position.'

'Get up, trooper' the guard commanded the shock trooper. The shock trooper complied, rising unsteadily to his feet, gore from his face streaking down his neck.

'Take off your boots and trousers.'

The trooper bent over to begin fumbling with his bootlaces and promptly fell over.

'Goddamnit!' screamed the lieutenant and walked over to the shock trooper, kicking him brutally in the midsection, however carefully holding back, the gesture being more for psychological effect than physical, sufficing however to cause the victim a considerable amount of pain without a strong amount of damage, additional damage which could easily move into terminal levels in light of the trooper's present state.

The lieutenant promptly grabbed the shock trooper by the arm and began dragging him over to a corner of the enclosed building, propping his frame face-forward in the corner of harsh and rough concrete blocks. The lieutenant reached around the front of the man's waist and unbuckled his pants in one fell motion, then dragging the man's pants and underwear down his legs, revealing his naked flesh. He left them pooling around the man's ankles.

'Well, I'm sure as hell not taking off those fucking boots myself!' the lieutenant yelled, his head careening toward the general direction of his contracted assistants. The guard whose activity with the prisoner had been taken over by the lieutenant promptly pounced down on the ground and began wrestling the boots off the shock trooper with surprising rapidity.

The guard threw his pants and remaining garments off to the side along with the boots and walked over to where the restraints were laid out on the ground and started expertly and rapidly picking them up and placing them upon the prisoner in a well thought-out and predetermined manner.

The first was handcuffs which were attached behind his back. Following this were several restraints which bound a thick leather strap around the inside of the man's knee pits and around the upper part of his back, immobilizing him and allowing all parts of his body to be easily accessed for whatever the guards and lieutenant were about to do to him.

'Look at that little pussy, that stupid fucking little pussy! What's wrong with him, why is he acting like an idiot?'

The lieutenant taunted the trooper from several paces

away.

The lieutenant walked up to the other guard who had for the extent of the scene thus far simply been standing a few yards away in the courtyard, holding his vicious and expertly oiled martinet, various straps coiling around each other with the ends tied like a knout, ready to pound in the finer points of discipline even into the most recalcitrant of errant personnel.

'Bring that little slut to heel, gentlemen!' the lieutenant roared.

The guard with the whip looked toward the lieutenant at the statement of his orders, as the lieutenant had approached him briskly before speaking, getting directly into his masked face and laughing with an atrocious glee. The lieutenant then, in an unprecedented move, suddenly pulled up the man's ski mask until right below the eye level, where the balaclava was held fast with the elastic strap attaching the dark goggles in the uniform prevalent trend of appearance within the guards of internal security.

The lieutenant stood in front of the guard blocking the vision of the other guard who was in the corner, busying himself with arranging the shock troop in the correct stress position. The shock troop sat on his knees, completely immobile, his head resting on its side, the side of his face resting on the cold stone floor and his crown pressed up against the corner, grating against the edges of the concrete blocking. His buttocks and backs of his legs were exposed fully to the guard who finished attaching the last rings into the apparatus.

The lieutenant darted his tongue into the mouth of the

surprised guard, the latter whose one hand was resting at his side and the other hand grasping the martinet, leaving the lieutenant at leisure to perform whatever molestation was now occurring.

The lieutenant finished with his oral stimulation and ran a finger across the red lips of the guard, before patting his face and pulling the balaclava back down and restoring the guard's usual sense of concealment. The lieutenant finished his gesture by reaching down and gently massaging the guard's member through his pants, checking for signs of sexual stimulation, before sliding his hand around and clutching the guard's right cheek with a firm grasp as he moved his mouth close to the area of the guard's ear and whispered: 'I hope I see something interesting out there, or else you are going to get it!' The lieutenant released the guard and stood aside, as if to gesture the guard forward toward his awaiting captive. The guard moved swiftly out from the area of the lieutenant, duly noting the gravity of his words and reached the corner where the shock troop awaited, pathetic in defeat. Without ceremony, the guard began his work.

The whip flew through the air, its ends splaying and then connecting again firmly on impact as they drove into the prostrate soldier. The bulk of the martinet's sting settled over the curvature of the man's obscenely stationed posterior, the ends of the whip snaking around, hitting his lower back and the small parts of the side of his chest which were able to be exposed in addendum due to his extremely confining level of restraint. The shock troop let out a bleat of pain.

IRON GATES

The guard continued along the same course, striking with full force and as hard as possible, the long snaking tentacles of the whip predictably splaying forth and then reconnecting as they impacted the naked skin of the shock trooper's totally exposed and vulnerable flesh. The shock troop screamed with each impact until, after twenty strokes, the screams began to taper off into a gurgling sound of pure exhaustion, mental collapse and stress-induced psycho-physical breakdown.

'Rape him, why don't you, friend!' the lieutenant laughed.

The guard did not see the humor in the situation, but duly went forward, placing the martinet on the floor and kneeling as he began undoing his pants. Surprisingly, he found that his member was already erect when he pulled his underwear down to his knees. The lieutenant noticed the man's endowment and began a mocking clapping in the background.

'Very good, guard, quite good! Now give us a little show, why don't you?'

The shock troop began grunting in protest as the guard moved his erect member into the shock trooper's entrails, already well lubricated with the sheath of sweat that had formed over his entire body from the already serious martinet whipping and the thorough physical beating that had gone on before. Although trebly humiliating, the current action was well-timed by the lieutenant to keep the prisoner alive for some bit longer, as continued flogging at the intensity that the guard had been delivering thus far would have sent him into shock, comatosis and then death only within a span of ten to fifteen minutes more, and perhaps considerably less. Torture, however sophisticated it might be, was not an exact science and casualties were apt to occur, especially in rough-and-ready conditions such as these.

The guard, suffuse in the blearing and fanatic ecstasy of the exertion of administering torture, held firmly onto the shock trooper's sides as he plunged his erect phallus again and again into the trooper's rectum. The shock trooper could have seen this coming theoretically, but it was always something else participating in something like this than hearing about such goings-on from gossip within the men in his unit. Against all thought and seemingly a physical impossibility due to his generally depleted state, the shock trooper himself felt his own member beginning to harden, the sudden stimulation acting almost in counteraction to the martinet lashing, despite the multiple bleeding lacerations on his buttocks which the guard was now duly agitating as his own body rubbed up against the wounds in the context of his constant thrusting.

From the distance the lieutenant clapped, laughing at the scene unfolding before him. All of this was of course not really necessary, but excess was the pleasure palace of such situations (and duly inhabited in this particular case). The lieutenant clapped harder when he heard the unmistakeable low grunt of the guard achieving orgasm and then waved his hands as a signal for the guards to allow him to make his way to the prisoner. The guards complied.

The lieutenant reached out his hand and received the

proffered martinet from the guard and began laying on the stripes heavy and hard without mercy. The shock trooper, still stunned from the rape, began howling in pain as the lieutenant drove the whip mercilessly into the man's back, thighs, legs and whatever else exposed part the tendrils of the whip decided to impact upon. The lieutenant was going at it as hard and reckless as could be imagined, with little concern at this point for the amount of injury he was causing. The guards looked at each others' masked faces and both knew that the lieutenant was now going in for the terminal gesture.

The shock trooper continued to yell as the lieutenant laid the whip on.

'Hope that you enjoyed the ministrations of the guard there, trooper, for that is the last pleasure that you will ever experience in this lifetime!' The lieutenant punctuated his statement with peals of obscene laughter which echoed throughout the courtyard.

The shock trooper's screams began to fade and although the martinet continued beating without cease into his exposed flesh the cries of pain no longer came. The shock trooper had passed out and gone into mild shock from the heightening levels of pain.

'Bring me the antiseptic!' shouted the lieutenant, drawing the martinet away from the soldier's flesh and massaging its now bloody filaments with his hand. The guard carried the large container of bluish chemical liquid over to the lieutenant and exchanged the container with the whip. 'Clean that up, we don't want a good implement like that being ruined from the blood of that little piece of shit!' The lieutenant gestured to the shock trooper, although it was clear who he was talking about nevertheless.

The lieutenant removed the cap from the container, sending an acrid smell of alcohol-based industrial-strength cleaning liquid wafting into the cold afternoon air. Without any ado, the lieutenant took the base of the container in one hand and the handle near the spout in the other and tossed a large portion of the liquid onto the wounds of the shook trooper. The shock trooper was now awake, screaming in horrid tribulation as the alcohol burned into his exposed wounds. The lieutenant responded by sloshing some more of the liquid upon the man's flesh and kicking him out of the corner so that he know lay bound in some sort of disturbing version of the fetal position.

One of the guards walked over to the shock trooper, kicking him and nudging him with his boot so that he was facing upward toward the lieutenant. The lieutenant pinned him in this posture by standing and straddling the shock trooper's bent knees, holding him in an upright position with his own legs. The lieutenant looked deep into the horrified eyes of the shock trooper and then began pouring the antiseptic chemical straight into the shock trooper's face, the first quantities of which promptly went into the shock trooper's mouth which hung agape, the chemical blue liquid causing him to spurt and begin puking, which only fell back down upon his face and dribbled along the side of his neck. The chemical burn began doing its horrid work upon the shock trooper's eyeballs and flesh. The lieutenant ceased straddling him letting him fall back once again into the perverse version of the fetal position and then continued to douse him with the liquid until the entire fifteen-gallon canister had been completely emptied on the man's naked body.

'If you still want your restraints now is the time to get them off, guards.' A guard scrambled with keys in compliance, removing the handcuffs and other restraints and watching as the man's body collapsed out from the forced stress position, covered in slimy blue liquid and his own blood and filth.

'You could have easily avoided this entire incident, shock trooper, had you not taken it upon yourself to put the commander's mission in jeopardy by your idiotic actions. Had you committed a blunder at another time, perhaps there would have been more leniency for you. Unfortunately for you, you decided to act the fool not only concerning what is arguably the highest priority development for the organization in many years, but doing so at a time when all of us are busy celebrating this newly unveiled device which you, in your stupidity, nearly destroyed by accident! Thankfully there were some knowledgeable persons who were able to identify your mishandling of the situation and correct you before your actions spiraled into real damage. What you have done today is real damage however, because you have dishonored your entire unit and whoever knew you will have to look back in shame at the fact that there was association between you. Isn't that a shame? Your bitch of a mother and bastard of a father, should you have any and should they still be alive, will be subjected to shame upon shame until their last pathetic days are spent, does that please you? Furthermore and most direly, you have put out these fine men,' the lieutenant gestured toward the guards, 'who should have been better spending their time in celebration and revelry at the glorious new armaments development. Thus we have to say goodbye to you now and put this chapter to a close.'

The lieutenant took a few steps away and removed a packet of cigarettes from his jacket pocket and then removed a lighter from the other. The shock trooper's eyes were bare slits, their film covering slowly burning away from the chemicals in the antiseptic and the man was as such unaware of what was transpiring, having barely heard the lieutenant's monologue through the sirens of his own excruciating pain. The guards looked on at the lieutenant in awe. With a brief motion, the lieutenant lit the cigarette and took a heavy draw, creating a burning red ember on the tip and sending up a filament of bluish smoke. As soon as the ember reached its peak of heat the lieutenant threw the cigarette down onto the shock trooper's body which instantly spread with low-intensity flame across the areas that had been soaked by the antiseptic.

'We're done here, men, I am going to request that you two specifically accompany me for the rest of the afternoon and evening's festivities, if you have no objections?'

'None whatsoever, sir.'

The shock trooper's body slowly burned, his semblance

of screaming garbled and low. The incendiary in the liquid would quickly burn down but only after taking a serious amount of flesh off of the unfortunate shock trooper who had deigned to smoke in the presence of the commander's rocket.

'Get a few of your undercorpsmen to come in here and keep watch on him should anything happen. He will probably need some more antiseptic and a good hard scrubbing inside a closed punitive unit to heal those burn wounds.' The black humor of the statement was not lost on the guards. One of the guards gathered up the restraints and empty canister along with the martinet, while the other guard unlocked the door and led the lieutenant out from the courtyard annex and back inside the hallway of the satellite security unit. The three men disappeared into the corridor and the door closed with an audible click. On the ground, slowly burning, lay the half-dead body of the shock trooper, staring listlessly up into the gray and unforgiving sky, beaming down its dead light upon the horrid landscapes of the post-nuclear world.

CHAPTER 9

Meanwhile, back at the much larger courtyard housing the celebration, the revelry was getting into full swing amidst deep and penetrating political conversations amongst the various elite attendees. Nadezhda for herself was working her way deep into a heavy state of intoxication from the mixture that she had purchased from the young man at the stall, who sat between serving other organizational brass, eagerly awaiting the possibility of Nadezhda taking a continuing interest in her promised ministrations of earlier.

Large groups of men and women dressed all alike in the standard organizational uniform, distinguished only slightly by small modifications to their uniform that denoted them as being part of this or that specific organizational sector, stood around the burning barrels of refuse, inhaling the stinking smoke of charred trash and sipping on a variety of putrid liquids designed either to speed one up, slow one down or cause untold combinations beyond the scope of either.

Within the world of the organization in the many decades since the downfall of the world as it once was, the bent of intoxication had taken on new and dangerous properties due to both the desperate state of the populace in general and the unrestricted flow of certain previously restricted chemicals and substances that had once been carefully kept away from the populace in days past in order to not cause an inadvertent breakdown in the social fabric. Such breakdown in the social fabric was no longer a concern, since society as it once had been had simply ceased to exist and, unlike previous times, the rule of dictatorship was strict and more obscene than anyone could have ever imagined in the past - such a small inducement as temporary change in one individual's psycho-physical makeup was not enough to bring down the iron fist of the commander that made its way into the life of every person under the rule of the chain of command of organizational hierarchy.

It would be an understatement to say that the constitution of the average person had become much harsher after the nuclear wars, and those who lived within the confines of organizational facilities and areas controlled by the group were subject to persistent psychic driving techniques without end that custom-made them to face death, commit death and any and all things in between. Although how widespread nuclear war would affect the surviving populace had been the subject matter of various speculative studies in the hallowed halls of academe of old, as well as in the offices and research facilities of large militaries and governmental organizations, nothing could have prepared those individuals (they themselves long since dead from the blasts themselves or having whiled out their last days, their eyeballs melted, bodies sick from radiation poisoning and inhabiting a blind and suffering existence on the outskirts of the once-great metropolises) for the way that humanity had actually been affected. For many of them, observing the way that life went on in the present, it would have not seemed to be deigned with the title of humanity or life as it was once known at all, even in contrast to the premeditated moral degradation present prior to the nuclear conflagration.

With a celebration of this much weight, the situation on the ground at the conference was sure to go in interesting directions before the night was finished and at present it was still only mid-afternoon, with the final conference session (which would be perfunctory and ritual more than a working meeting like the last several days) still several hours away. Already the roasting pork was sending a delicious aroma throughout the air, masking whatever fallback odor there might have been wafting through the wind from the annex courtyard where a certain unfortunate shock trooper had just been lit aflame by the lieutenant.

Nadezhda moved over to an empty space of wall where one of the many corrugated steel buildings was arranged to frame the space of the courtyard and sat down cross-legged, leaning her back against the wall and slowly drinking her beverage. The sedative effect of the drink increased her state of deep thought as she considered the trajectory of the last several days. The conference had been much more than she had bargained for, first with her beginning amorous encounters with the dreaded and infamous lieutenant, followed by his promise to establish her in torture center as a SAC and then finally with the announcement from her father in front of hundreds of people earlier that he had just finished a high-end armaments project under the direction of the commander himself. Although familyism and any sort of patronage based on birth was officially discouraged within the organization, family ties still meant something on a visceral level and despite the organization's level of brainwashing and ideological remolding it was hard to fully eradicate the feelings that came with biological relationship. This was apparent as various members of the organization, passing by her location, would stop briefly and nod or wave as they went about their way. She had positioned herself far enough from the crowd that it would be obvious if someone was approaching her for face-to-face conversation, which might have brought the attention of roaming security guards or surveillance teams in plain uniforms who might be watching for anything off-color following the announcement. The development of the new weaponry was politically the equivalent of throwing a piranha in a tank of fish and everyone was both suffuse with excitement but also on edge and on guard as to what this would mean for life in general within the organization. The commander had been increasing the level of discipline and severity within the organization in a highly graduated fashion over the last several years and the manifestation of their new armed capability had something to do with the preparation that had been ongoing, although they had not known quite what they were preparing for and still didn't fully, only relying on the word of the commander and faith that he would be leading them in the correct direction as he had for decades since soon after the last atomic bomb wreaked its hideous work upon the earth. Within the organization there was really no competition for leadership with the commander. There were more apparent and visible leaders who people interacted with on a more frequent basis yet the commander was untouchable, far beyond the scope of normal consideration and, as such, he was bullet-proof reputation-wise. His practical acumen was without question as could be seen in their collective gradual ascent in power and influence in the post-apocalyptic world under his practical leadership.

Nadezhda had only worked her way a quarter of the way down her drink before she began feeling very disoriented. She was glad that she had stationed her back against the wall because the support now seemed necessary rather than only a welcome respite to standing. She would wind out her time here and look in the crowd, seeing if the lieutenant would make an appearance. She hadn't seen him since before the afternoon conference session began and was surprised, as he was not usually one to break from such revelry. Indeed, in such a momentous occasion as this, his presence would not only be palatable but expected by the other attendees. Her co-workers in internal security code-breaking and surveillance analysis, who had some idea of the relationship between she and the lieutenant during the conference thus far, she had spotted a few yards off, their eyes locked lustily onto the greasy, cooking flesh of one of the gargantuan swine and their large plastic mugs filled to the brim with the potato-based liquor that was flowing like water from the tapped tanks stationed throughout the courtyard.

'Bring them on in, corporal!' a black-masked internal security guard barked to a pock-marked shock trooper wheeling a small camper-like device on wheels. From inside the camper one could hear the faint whimpering of children. All around the courtyard the eyes of the various organizational brass lit up with unconcealed delight. The shock trooper had brought in a cage full of captured children from one of the recently conquered territories. The adults had remained stationed back at the place where the combat took place and set to slave labor at various hard physical tasks in support for the organizational armed forces that were now stationed there, and the children had been taken away as a punitive measure. A secret underlying reason the children had been removed was to provide them as entertainment for the organizational brass on just this occasion. Bald lust showed on the faces of the people present, some more than others, in gratitude at the commander's thoughtfulness in this regard. The corporal brought the trailer to a stop and the end, which would have once hooked to a automobile but was now being pulled by man-power, dropped onto the ground, putting the trailer at a tilt and causing the captives inside to slide around, which elicited some more sounds of discomfort from inside, much to the pleasure of the mass of organizational personnel who were now watching closely. Two masked guards with the usual silenced MP5 submachine guns stationed themselves at either side of the trailer door as the corporal saluted and went off toward the liquor dispensers, intent on getting heavily drunk before all was said and done. The make of the trailer was such that no one could see inside, only the faintest sounds escaped, increasing the speculation and lust of the conference attendees in treble fashion.

A crowd began gathering around the area where the trailer was now parked, various men and women in organizational garb and black-masked security straining to hear the soft sounds of children crying, which filled their loins with delight and feelings of profound satisfaction in their evil hearts. The theft of children amongst the areas that were taken captive by the organization were at once one of the greatest terrors for the inhabitants so targeted and also one of the most piquant delights for those within the organization, who reveled in child abuse, the destruction of the flower of youth in various fashions, also delighting them as well because they, holding themselves to a higher standard than the moth-eaten moralities of the past, which put childhood on a pedestal, found it highly amusing to understand that through the satiating of their own base pleasures that such simple activities would so highly agitate those who were less developed and who had not been conditioned under the merciless discipline of the commander and his organizational apparatus.

A blank-faced woman in her late thirties, stringy yellow hair hastily tied up with strands falling down upon the collar of her black uniform jacket, looked with milky anticipation at the filthy trailer and the two submachine gun-armed security who watched over it.

She had never given birth, always shoving some tense wire into her vaginal canal whenever the telltale signs of pregnancy had hit her years ago when she cavorted with other members of the shock troops and security attaches to the mechanics' brigade on campaigns. Her love life had fallen since then and the thought of young children brought out motherly feelings within her, distorted with sexual perversion and an innate desire to see young blood spilled. Especially blood, rebellious blood, from lands beyond the commander's control. She imagined that the seeds of defiance in those white and red blood corpuscles might act as some magical elixir that would cause her own physical vigor to return to her, what little of it she ever had, being of several generations of those highly affected by residual radiation. She imagined her ideal child victims as one hand snaked down to her crotch, shamelessly masturbating through the black fabric of her uniform pants as her other hand held a cup of harsh liquor which she consumed greedily, the slick rotten-egg color dribbling down her chin. She felt herself being shoved to the side as younger and more healthy attendants moved their way forward to hear the sounds of the child victims. She giggled to herself sickly, before moving toward the side of the crowd to finish herself off in a ruinous act of self-satisfaction, the images of young flesh dancing lecherously in the clouded confines of her mind.

A portal opened up in the side of one of the metal hangar walls and a jeep slowly rolled out, powered by a cacophonous engine spurting pollution from its tailpipe.

IRON GATES

A drab olive gray, the well-maintained monster was driven by two masked guards and standing on the bed stood a monstrous woman, nearly six feet tall. The crowd erupted in screams of frenzy as the machine rolled slowly out, flanked by eight submachine gun carrying members of internal security, armed to the teeth and highly intimidating. The commandant standing on the bed was of super-high rank, wearing a pointed black helmet of fine mesh and one bleak bar of horizontal goggle lens and erstwhile garbed in a shining black outfit of skintight design and unknown fabric origin. Her large breasts shone like bleak and deadly moons encased in the shining black fabric, one of her waspish and skeletal hands carefully holding a vial containing a green poison liquid, her other clasped triumphantly on the bar separating the bed from the cab of the military automotive.

Her waist bore a thick nylon utility belt with a harsh nursery strap hanging to one side along with implements such as night sticks, restraints and then, in the other, a bleak, long-nosed pistol in a stellar black holster. She was of the elite of the elite, a god in the flesh, the touted female known as the commandant - never seen but worshiped throughout organization-run territories as a black mistress of death, destruction and imploding schizophrenic blood lust - creeping like a mustard gas mist across the destroyed and devastated plains of a post-nuclear hell. Her pictures had sprouted up ten years ago, traded and dispensed as icons by a strange cult that had cropped up within the organization. Like many of these intelligence-born viruses, the cult's operational influence over the populace came about overnight, sprouting suddenly like some poisonous mushroom, as livid-sounding characters in the garb of internal security operating off-hours began spreading the rumor about a great black terror, garbed in the most horrific bleeding nightmares of the post-nuclear world, holding the power of total destruction in her hands. Soon pictures of her uniformly disguised face began cropping up on corners of settlements and on bulletin boards, and then they began appearing on the desks of various organizational personnel. One more hideous cult microbe had been released into the superstructure of the organization by the iron will and nightmarish genius of the commander.

From black reinforcement steel poles attached to the back of the jeep flew black flags, emblazoned in the center with a large circular bluish globe depicting a mild sky, with a giant red, orange, yellow and black atomic mushroom cloud filling the firmament, sending black and red rivers of death flying outwards upon all living things. This was her flag, the flag of total death. The crowd of three-hundred or so were divided, some surging toward her, although steering clear of the marching heavily-armed security beside her, and some standing off but watching ever so intently. This was the division between her devotees and her non-devotees. The fanatics of the sect were at once drawn forth into the highlight of the spectacle, well-conditioned and expectant of her eventual arrival, which was now nigh. This reflex was no matter overall, however, considering the fact that many more of these cult gods would begin to manifest 'during the night' according to the sublime psychological plan of the commander and the highest echelons of internal security, devised by the glistening elite amongst intelligence.

Certain members of the audience began bleating like disturbed goats, throwing themselves forwards toward the area where the slowly moving tires of the jeep were proceeding. They were summarily kicked in the face and shoved out of the way by internal security for temporary quarantine - the deaths in her ritual would be carefully controlled for the audience. She was compared to the mother of death, who would nurse her own children then destroy them without any mercy whatsoever, keen on the perverse obliteration of their mortal lives and feeding upon the astral lifeforce of the pain spreading around their dying and pained forms, like a toxic sponge drawing upon the rivulets of surrounding sour blood. The zenith of killing would come soon enough.

The woman on the back of the jeep, known as the deity called the commandant and revered hitherto as some mystic potency residing within the physical body of the commander, had now manifest. From her glistening black hip she removed a large thick-gauge needle nearly the length of a railroad spike and held it aloft as the audience screamed in devotion. Another line of uniformed security emerged from another doorway into the corrugated metal building, forming a flank in front of the jeep as the vehicle came to a halt, idling and then shutting off as deep electronic rumbling erupted from some hidden apparatus beneath the platform on which the commandant stood. The low tone of the harsh sound caused the ground beneath the feet of her adherents to shake disturbingly. Several shock troops fell to the ground weeping, completely in the thrall of a hideous, black devotion.

The shining needle was held at a playful angle by the commandant as the bellowing resonance of the gigantic subwoofers within the floorboard of the military vehicle emitted a deep, hellish roar that mixed with the screaming and howled prayers from the mass of people. A contingent of guards formed a human corridor leading from the area around the jeep to the trailer full of children, two of the guards began removing the huge padlocks and slowly pulling the gate open as the burr from the jeep's sound system grew louder and louder. Now audibly heard within the screams of the crowd and the sound believed to be the voice of the commandant herself was mixed the faint yet unmistakeable whimpering of the children inside the prison wagon who were being slowly and reluctantly led out. They were all naked but surprisingly freshly clean, from toddlers to at least two youth that looked to be in the latter stages of thirteen. The guards were all armed with MP5 submachine guns and those who were not leading the children out all had the snouts of their firesticks pointed threateningly at the members of the crowd, who wisely stayed a respectable distance away. The guards would not hesitate to fire should the need arise. Additionally, interfering with this activity, unprecedented as it was in the history of the organization, was intuitively understood as being an unforgivable offense against the commandant herself, who would no doubt cause a doom more horrific than anything imaginable upon those so infringing. The audience had a clear memory of the would-be martyrs that had been brutally beaten away from the area of the jeep and ushered into punitive quarantine just a few minutes ago. To make their point clear, two huge and vicious-looking guards, loaded with even more heavy weight belt-fed machine guns than the other guards, had started routinely snapping off a few rounds here and there if the crowd deigned to get closer, their random victims sinking to their knees in strangled death. It continued to stay a respectable distance.

As the children were led out into the frightening scene before them, their whimpers turned to screams, which pleased the personnel participating in this bleak sequence of staged horror to no end. A thin specter-like security guard, of long limbs and lank constitution, stood at stark attention to one side of the jeep surveying the reaction of the crowd. During the last few moments the commandant had discreetly handed the vial of poisonous chemicals to the guard in question who took them, cautiously, now cradling them between two gloved hands. The commandant now began lovingly stroking the tip of the giant needle, bringing even more attention to the malign disposition of the instrument which was aligned toward only the most hideous of tortures. As the children were forcibly led from the trailer, screaming in horror, their eyes riveted by the inhuman sound and the sleek, almost robotic-looking female encased in black and a deadly shining sight visor, toward whom their procession was steadily heading. The naked flesh of the children became livid as the cold, late afternoon air seeped into them. Within minutes, as if moving in a nightmare, the children found themselves bunched within a circle of security guards who forced them into a collective huddle of young innocent flesh before their lethal goddess. More than one guard held an infant in his arms, merciless fingers grasped around fragile necks in the very beginning of their development.

The commandant held the needle with one hand and pointed a willowy black-gloved finger toward the group of children as loud thundering sounds began emanating from the speakers. Many personnel had raised their hands in awe and naked worship, their eyes frozen open. Some slumped to the ground or lay flat altogether in total obeisance before the living goddess of death who stood before them, an inverse valkyrie coming from the very black soot fires of the nuclear holocaust itself. A few shock troopers in the audience had made ample open slices into their arms with whatever edged weapons they possessed on their persons, letting the blood drip down upon the ground. Others raised their wounded limbs, mutilated from previous misadventures either internally or externally induced, as if to hope to draw the attention of the commandant, who appeared regal and completely evil in countenance.

At the commandant's gesture, one of the men holding a baby began walking in slow procession toward the metal rail circling round the bed of the jeep. The commandant now leaned against the rail, her black-encased buttocks shining in the pale afternoon light in psychosis-inducing lustiness, her pointed finger now motioning in a come-hither gesture to the child carried by the masked and anonymous guard.

Deep within the bowels of the converted penitentiary many miles away, the commander himself sat deep in concentration amongst his own activities, with a filament of his awareness in meditation upon the events which were happening erstwhile at the conference center.

Meanwhile, the sudden appearance of the commandant had roused Nadezhda from the lethargy of her excesses of intoxication and she too stood riveted, mouth agape in a strange devotion mixed with awe that made it hard for her to look away. Without any conscious purpose that she herself was aware of, she had forced her way through the crowd and now stood only several persons back from the line of internal security as the procession continued and the baby, its small arms pinwheeling in its youthful idiocy, with trunk held firmly by the guard, made its approach toward the waiting arms of the commandant.

Across from the scene, on the other side of the jeep, the lieutenant stood within the crowd, the tell-tale signs of having taken part earlier in the execution of an interrogation and torture still lined into his face, flanked by two black-masked internal security members that he had taken with him in reciprocation for their having acted as willing and dutiful accomplices in said activities. For all the guards knew, their post with the lieutenant might be a permanent assignment from this point on, to which potential fate they would be very conducive indeed. They had arrived in the courtyard a few minutes before the commandant had appeared, which was enough time for one of the guards to supply the lieutenant with the drink of his choice, which he had hastily consumed before sending the guard off for another. By the time the second arrived all hell had begun to unfold in the arena. Through the crowd, the piercing psychotic eyes of the lieutenant had indeed spied Nadezhda in devotional thrall, but due to distance and positioning as well as ample intoxication on her part, she was not aware of his distant stare.

The guard reached the bed of the jeep and raised the infant before the commandant, its face red and smeared with tears, and screaming continuously. The commandant reached out with one gloved hand, still holding the needle deftly in the other, and took the infant in her grasp, moving back to the center of the bed of the jeep, facing the crowd and raising the infant aloft into the air. The bass sounds amplifying from the inbuilt speaker began to fade and now all that could be heard was the roar of the crowd as the mistress of death stood with her sacrifice. The baby continued to scream horribly, its peals of distress echoing within the metal-enclosed courtyard, mixing with the massed adulation of the crowd. With a nodding motion toward one of the senior guards, the guards in the front responded in turn by raising their hands and lowering them to induce the crowd to silence. The assembled personnel duly obeyed. Now the only sound within the courtyard was the shrill crying of the infant, which sounded rather small and insignificant in comparison to the roars that had just been silenced by dint of their obedience in devotion.

The commandant brought the baby closer to her breast, resting it upon the slick black fabric with one hand. The child sputtered and then went completely silent, the deceit of motherly affection completely bought lock, stock and barrel by the traumatized youngster, too young to understand rational intent but animalistic enough to perceive implied physical comfort. The faces of the crowd looked on in absolute awe at the persuasive and highly duplicitous nature of the commandant. The child rested upon her bosom for only a few minutes as the silence continued sinking into the arena. Only a few minutes and then, as quickly as she had brought it to her breast, she grabbed the infant by the head, palming the skull like a ball and, with her other hand, thrusting the long shining needle directly into the child's heart, causing bubbling blood to shoot from the wound and begin pouring down from the child's mouth and nostrils as the burst principal artery sought a passage out from its persistent internal bleeding. Beyond several gasps of delight the crowd continued to maintain its deadly silence.

The silence was over however once the commandant wrapped her hand around the child's throat and with one fell gesture slung the corpse out from her grasp, over the heads of the guards and into the crowd. A strange animal sound of primal bloodlust curled through the courtyard as everyone from shock troops to administrative clerks and all in between scrambled wildly toward the corpse as it began its descent to the ground. It never reached the ground however, for as soon as it came within the grasp of the mob it was ripped limb from limb, those obtaining portions of the child's anatomy greedily sucking the blood from the soft skin and chewing the flesh whole. Those who were not so lucky to obtain a piece of the child tumbled onto the ground on their hands and knees, attempting to suck up any of the red elixir that had fallen to the earthen floor.

The commandant slipped the needle back into the pouch on her utility belt and raised both hands upright, fists clenched in victory and unmitigated authority as her devotees and many who had become devotees just at that moment went berserk around her. The bass sounds from beneath the jeep bed recommenced at this time in full bombast, interspersed with guttural, squealing sounds that reminded one of some massive electrical disaster. The commandant punctuated these particular sounds by shaking her right fist in unison.

Those who were in the know and part of her cult before the event knew that this was the veritable voice of the commandant which could not be understood by mortal comprehension but the message of which would seep into the very depths of the hearts of the devotees themselves, implanting the message, mission and nature of the commandant within them to draw upon until they too met her in some blood-strewn battlefield or fiery death of a new nuclear holocaust.

Nadezhda stared unblinking upon the shining sultry body of the commandant, her nature a black mystery, hidden beneath her strange helm. At that moment Nadezhda decided that she was flesh for the commandant, she would serve the commandant and she would seek to become like the commandant, a lesser replica roaming the earth in horror and blasphemy. If the lieutenant's promise to send her to torture center was in earnest, which she believed it was and which would certainly be possible now in any case due to the situation with her father's breakthrough in armaments, she would make it her life's work to imbue torture center with the cruelty and capriciousness of the commandant, her god.

She opened her mouth wide, guzzling the last drops of the chemical beverage she had still been grasping throughout the proceedings, and dropped the empty cup to the ground. She screamed in devotion, in mania, in insanity. From several yards off, the lieutenant stood more sedately along with his new internal security entourage. Seeing her reaction and the undeniable look of conversion in her eyes, he smiled with knowing satisfaction.

IRON GATES

CHAPTER 10

'Time to see what this little one has under the hood.'

A severe uniformed female wearing spectacles and heavy elbow-length industrial rubber gloves slowly lifted up the thin shirt of the twelve-year-old girl who stood before her, sobbing softly to herself. The nurse lifted the shirt up over the girl's head and tossed it aside, revealing pert small nipples attached to slightly budding yet undeveloped breasts.

'Very good, the commandant will be pleased with this one, I believe.'

The girl had short, auburn-colored hair and a pale complexion, decorated with a few freckles on her face. As the nurse spoke she directed her comments to the two balaclava-clad internal security guards who stood behind her near the entrance to the examining room who would process the object further should she past muster.

The nurse's gloved hands moved down to the waistband of the girls shorts and removed these as well, grasping the hem of the girl's underwear at the same time and removing them both, allowing them to fall around the child's ankles.

'Step out from that.'

The girl did as requested.

The girl was petite but had long limbs. Her pubic area was covered with soft, downy hair and her skin was perfectly smooth. As she stood in front of the nurse one of the guards deftly moved in, removing the bottom garments from the floor and tucking them away with the other articles of clothing which had been tossed off by the nurse, placing them in a refuse bin sitting in the corner.

The nurse turned the girl around, inspecting the curvature of her back. She pressed the girls' small, tight buttocks, nodding to herself admirably at their springy and firm consistency. Turning the girl back around facing her she brushed away a slight shock of hair that had fallen over the girl's face.

'Stand up straight, eyes toward me.'

The frightened child looked toward the woman. She could see a slight reflection of her tear-stained face in the insect-like spectacles worn by the examiner.

The nurse wiped the tell-tale signs of tears from the girls face and then placed her thumbs in the girls mouth, forcing it open as she peered inside. The interior was deep red, with some discoloring denoting malnutrition.

'If we take this one out I want you to bring some of the dried meat and powdered protein to feed her during the trip.'

The guard obeyed without responding in affirmation, moving to a cabinet and removing several metallic packets which he placed in a multi-compartmented rucksack that hung on his back.

'She looks healthy enough, let's move her down the hall for sleep test.'

The nurse stood up and removed her gloves, placing them on a metal table to her right. Firmly grasping the girl by the hand, she marched toward the open door held open by the guard. The second guard departed after the nurse and the first guard shut the door behind them, locking it with a key attached to a large keyring held around his belt. The girl's hand held firmly, the nurse pulled her along at a decent trot, the few areas of tight buoyant curvatures present in her physicality bouncing ever so slightly as they proceeded down the hall, the two guards marching behind them to either side.

They approached a block in the corridor and a large black metal grate which was attached to an even larger steel door. These, like the walls, were covered in thick black paint. The nurse pushed a button on the wall which caused a buzzer to sound deep from within the closed sector. The little brunette at her side grimaced in pain at the nurse's tight grip, her little button nose crinkling in frustration.

With a sudden slight scent of electrical discharge the door slowly and jerkily opened and the group passed through, and they were several paces down the hallway when they heard the door begin closing again. The lighting inside this hallway was dim red from large tubular lights running along the side of the walls. With a curvature to the ceiling and a slight descent the little girl could now assess that she was being led into a tunnel within an underground complex. Her mind held much fascination for this facility and a healthy dose of wonder was mixed in with her fear, as not only the procedures she had been facing but also the building itself and the people within it were entirely alien to her past experiences. Her mother and father had died far back in her faded memory and she had been living here-and-there for several years now, unprotected with only brief socialization amongst other children who roamed about in certain of the outer areas. One day a few black-robed females calling themselves nuns of someone called the commandant had approached her while she was alone in the wilderness.

They gave her rich food and promised that if she came with them that she would be taken care of. Her hesitance was washed away by the food, which was not only exciting in that it nourished her but that she also began feeling strange feelings of euphoria in her body, which caused her reasoning to associate the words 'commandant' and 'sisterhood' with pleasure. The food had been drugged by the cult recruiters beforehand. Although the girl would have probably gone with them willingly, the recruiters did not blanch at using a little extra persuasion and they also had a vested interest in availing themselves of any opportunity to perfect their techniques.

The descent into the tunnel was gradual but consistent and the girl could feel her chest constricting as the pressure increased. The dull red lights shone sickly on her naked flesh and the uniform of the nurse pulling her along. The tunnel leveled out and led shortly to a split in the corridor. They took the left fork and went into the first of a long line of doors which stretched onward into the half-darkness. They proceeded nine doors down to the end of the hall, each of the doors bearing a small card slipcase either bearing a name, number or blank. They entered a door bearing a blank name; the door nearest to it read 'Bonn.'

A room set up like a small bedroom met the girl's gaze upon entering, a surprising sight both because of the incongruity with the rest of the surroundings as well as the fact that she had never seen a room so furnished in her life. The coziness factor mimicked something that would have been familiar in another time, and it struck a chord as some genetic legend living in the mind, a throwback to the pre-nuclear period when things were more comfortable. The cinder block walls had been covered with some sort of synthetic siding and had been painted a dark gray with white borders. A single bed with a rough gray blanket folded down revealing hints of fresh white sheets and a pillow with pillowcase occupied one corner of the room, with a small end table nearby.

A small light bar shone above a highly-polished metal mirror set over a sink. There was no running water but the sink was stoppered and filled with clean water, with more stored in a bucket beneath the sink. A few towels and washrags were set on the edge of another empty bucket similarly situated nearby.

'Please lay down on the bed.'

The nurse led her to the edge of the bed and pushed the girl's shoulder down with a slight but firm authority, causing the youngster to involuntarily sit as instructed. The slightly rough texture of the blanket caused her flesh to further goose-pimple, more from reflex than atmospheric condition, as the air had grown somewhat warmer once entering the room.

'Wait outside.'

The two guards left the room and as the door shut the last glow of the red lights from the corridor disappeared. The electric lights inside the room were of a soft white light which brought out the accents of the small surroundings and seemed very soothing. The girl considered within her mind the events as they had unfolded thus far. She had originally volunteered to go with the cult members, in what seemed like a very far away but also brutally close past. One part of her mind told her that she wanted out, wanted desperately to be back with the stars over her head and only various other semi-wild scavengers as her sometime and often infrequent companions. The other part of her realized that, despite some discomfort and shock in the beginning, whatever she had done with the cult thus far was probably far more engaging than the monotony of day after day without a mission, a goal, a purpose. Sometimes the devil you didn't know was a welcome respite from the devil you did.

The forced stripping and consequent nakedness had been strange for her, not that she hadn't been naked plenty of times before, but not in this clinical and unnerving context. She had had her share of occasional confused ruttings with some of the boys who roamed the countryside but she had stayed safely away from the better known adult predators - her life had been simple and obscure, and she had instinctively avoided the obvious social pitfalls which presented themselves.

Some of the younger children who had closer memories of some semblance of family or community had a superstitious idea about needing protection. A greasy, bearded hoarder with a few baubles and a sweet word would send these children practically falling over themselves, tears in their eyes and emotions aflame, to go with a strange older face. In turn they would in due time find that their protectors had become their de facto captors who would do whatever they wanted with them and usually enlist them in a lifetime of drudgery, assisting in more large scale scavenging than to what she herself was accustomed to and categorizing ancient junk from the pre-nuclear days. Such a life had no appeal for her - let the weak sink! As a counterpose to that possible future, which she saw as even less of a future than being isolated and shiftless for all practical reasons as she had been, the cult recruiters had presented an entirely different animal altogether, something completely outside of any experience or known memory. That was exactly how the cult had designed the nature of their encounter.

The security teams who went out into the wilderness under the guise of clergy were not on any internal security personnel list, although they had received the most extensive training that organizational intelligence had to offer and in the most secretive of facilities. The far areas of the wilderness into which the commandant's devotees inserted themselves, ostensibly on behalf of organizational intelligence, were not on any organizational maps and were long distances from even the farthest organizational battle lines and frontiers of territorial organizational cultivation. She had been recruited by the secret of the secret, non-commissioned contracted special operatives; now she was in their world.

'Lay down now!'

The girl snapped out of her brief mental fugue, the atmosphere of the room was both inviting and unsettling at once, whereas recent memories of the nurse's machine-like process of disrobing her earlier had been disturbing only.

She did not intend to provoke the order of the nurse and she laid down as directed. The feeling of her head hitting the soft pillows, something which was unfamiliar to her, hit her senses like heaven's own hand.

The nurse stared discerningly through her glasses at the girl, her paleness punctuated in contrast to the dark fabric of the blankets, clearly visible ribs moving slowly up her chest cavity and punctuated by hard nipples of brownish hue, the color of ground meat that had been allowed to sit.

'Before I leave for the evening please be advised that you will be staying here for approximately two nights, which I trust will be interesting for you. This will be your room for the remainder of your stay at this location.' The nurse managed to crinkle the side of her mouth slightly which apparently serviced as a smile.

'There is a wash basin there which you may use, also a towel that you can drape around for clothing until we issue you something more substantial. Someone will come in and check on you intermittently.'

The girl had no idea what the last word meant but managed a slight nod in the affirmative nonetheless.

'We will bring you your first meal tomorrow. For now we want you to stay in bed and go to sleep, someone will wake you in due course.'

There was a plain straight-backed chair near the table and the nurse scooted it over, positioning it in reaching distance of both the bed and the table.

From a drawer under the table the woman removed a pair of large headphones with an electrical device attached to the side, which blinked in a dull blue light every few seconds.

'You need to wear these through the night. Have you ever seen anything like this before?'

The girl shook her head in the negative.

The nurse was not surprised.

'There will be sounds that will come into your ears via this device.' The nurse pointed to her own ear to emphasize the point.

'You will wear them like this.'

The nurse put the device on her head to demonstrate, then removed it with an equally efficient motion.

'You will hear some sounds through this device. Keep this on throughout the remainder of the night!'

The naked girl laid upon the bed, her head slightly bent to the right on the pillow, eyes continuously and cautiously watching the nurse.

'Do not remove this device until one of our staff instruct you to do so, this will occur after you wake up in the morning. Do you understand?'

The girl nodded in the affirmative.

Despite herself, as a result of the long schedule she had undergone thus far, she felt herself becoming drowsy. The day had begun early, and she had been in transit on foot for several days prior with the cult members before being transferred to a closed, windowless black van driven by black-masked internal security intelligence attaches in a deep evergreen forest. There were several more of the threatening, silent figures inside the van and being inserted in the back portion of the windowless cargo area she was unable to ascertain anything about her position or whereabouts as she rode, huddled in a corner of the vehicle on the several-hour long ride.

She had napped frequently along the way, somewhat disturbed that the recruiters had passed her off without coming along for the last leg of the journey. The recruiters had assured her that everything would proceed nicely and to be confident in her decision, however their smiles were a bit too wild and concentrated and the disparity between them and the anonymous figures who were quite obviously some sort of military personnel was a bit too abrupt a change. There was no solace to be had in their gesture.

Within several minutes of the nurse's finishing her instructions to the young girl, she was left alone in the room and found herself lying on the deep, downy pillow. Still naked, she was now beneath the covers of the bed and on her head the strange headphone device was attached. There was a dull crackle that sounded like it was coming from deep within a corridor that played faintly in the background. She was amazed. She had never seen an apparatus like this in the duration of her life, much less used one. She wondered where the sounds were coming from. This was unheard-of technology in consideration to her background and the age in general and as she lay there in these strange new environs she felt the overwhelming sense of impending sleep taking her over, yet certain filaments of apprehensiveness remained like lurkers on the cusp of the eventide.

The lights above the polished metal mirror dimmed, and the dull gray walls of the room now turned smoky, seeming to swim in the darkness. She felt herself drifting, drifting, drifting. From the headphones the faint crackling began to be replaced by a tinkling, unearthly-sounding music. She began to move into the early stages of sleep, her eyes closing and a faint smile playing upon her mouth as the music continued, interspersed with various atmospheric sounds, some which she could place and some which she could not. Waves upon a seashore, the sound of wind whistling through trees in a high forest; the latter she knew well, the former she did not. Now some strange flutes began piping and some bells began ringing ominously, as if tolling some future event directly on the horizon.

The girl was well asleep before the voices began, informing her of the destiny that lay rolled out before her, of the commandant who was to be her leader and of what she could do for the commandant, what was expected of her and what she needed to know to succeed. The importance of having a total sacrifice attitude amongst other more weighty instructions were given in an even, reassuring yet unmistakeably authoritative meter. The girl herself heard none of these knowingly, as by the time the voice instructions began she was well into the deeper stages of sleep, the messages penetrating straight into her subconscious mind without being vetted through the decision-making rigors of waking consciousness. With the sound of the voice playing in her ears, her head burrowed into the pillow and, the smile still upon her lips, she slept.

When the morning came she was already awake. The lights had resumed their normal daytime-level glow and she lay obediently on the bed under the covers, the headphones still on her head. As before, there was a faint crackling within them that sounded like it was coming from far, far away. She had been told not to remove the headphones under any circumstances, however, erring on the side of caution, she had decided to lay in the bed as well, maintaining the position in which she had been left the night before until someone came for her. A sharp knock came on the door and the nurse entered, attired exactly as the night before yet seeming somewhat more relaxed than she had been the previous day.

'I trust that you had a good sleep?' she asked politely.

The girl nodded in affirmation.

With measured steps, her boots clicking against the

floor, the nurse approached her and removed the headphones, placing them back in the drawer by the bedside table.

'Freshen up and we will bring you breakfast in one-half hour.'

The nurse carried a small courier satchel over one arm and she removed it, placing it on the edge of the end table and taking out a small pile of clothing.

'Try these on, these should fit you. If not, let us know and we can adjust the size before your morning occupations, understood?' The nurse smiled, surprisingly enough, and the girl could not help but smile back in response in natural mimicry and reaction.

'This is your new uniform, hope that you will like it!'

With one final grin, this time in earnest, the nurse lay the pile of clothing on the chair and turned, retrieving her satchel and leaving the room, locking it behind her with a resounding click.

The girl moved to the sink and looked at herself in the mirror. She was surprised at how surprisingly clean she looked in the reflection of the mirror, but no real wonder as the cult recruiters had told her that cleanliness was important if she was to be a member of the commandant's family and, as an assist to program, they had helped clean her up from her rather filthy state which they had found her in when they first came upon her in the wilderness. This was the first time since being transported to the facility in which she had the opportunity to endeavor to make good on continuing this specific directive given to her by her recruiters, so as she cleaned she proceeded with a sense of mission and importance.

One-half hour until breakfast was more than ample time to clean up. She removed the towels and washcloths from the empty bucket and set them on the floor to the side. She was glad that she was not going to be relegated to wearing a bathing cloth as means of dress to hide her nakedness. Pulling the bucket out from under the sink she squatted, sending a small stream of urine into the bottom of the container. She straightened herself, daubing her genitalia with one of the washrags before pushing the bucket back under the sink.

She looked at her reflection once more in the mirror. Her hair gave her a mischievous, sprite-like look of which she was proud. One of her young friends back in the wilderness had through some strange fashion had an attraction to messing with peoples' hair and she had been a frequent subject of her friend's ministrations. She liked to keep her hair short. With lots of strange bugs around the forests it was simply better and more all-around practical to do so, plus she admired the look that it gave her and she believed that her associates did as well, infrequent as such associations were, however.

She smiled broadly in the mirror and then frowned, watching her reflection intently. She was interested in being aware of the breadth and scope of her potential facial expressions as she might employ in any given situation. Remaining in her slight frown, she turned her attention to the water in the sink and cupped her hands together and brought them up to her mouth, taking several long draughts. Next she took one of the washcloths and moistened it until it was soaking wet but not so wet as to drip water onto the floor. She moistened her short hair and then shook it out like a wild dog to dry it. Next she moved the washcloth over her firm young body, scrubbing first her breasts, chest and stomach, reaching around and doing the same to her back, then her legs, armpits and feet. The water was cool and made her flesh tingle pleasantly. Her decision to accept exodus from the wilderness was seeming more and more to be a wise one, but it was early days yet, she reminded herself. She took one of the larger towels and vigorously dried herself off, walking over to the chair near the bed and hanging the towel over the side to dry while reaching for the small pile of clothes that had been left for her there by the nurse.

The clothes were entirely nicer than anything she had ever seen before in her life, certainly nicer than she had (or more correctly, formerly had) herself and nicer than she had seen on others, excepting the guards and nurse who had been processing her. The cult members that had picked her up in the wilderness wore long black flowing robes that seemed both rich but austere as well, the impression of the garments, strange as they were, made the wearers a bit maniacal looking, which was not incongruous for their character as they had in fact acted a bit like maniacs in all earnestness. Too nice at certain times, too stern at certain times but also certainly nothing to be trifled with - they were different and also serious in such a way that she instantly recognized that they could be very, very dangerous. More dangerous than the most dangerous of the predators that roamed in the wilderness which had been her home. Being dangerous however did not seem like a bad thing in her mind - she would much more prefer to be dangerous than to be pathetic as she herself saw many of the inhabitants of the wilderness had become in their long, shiftless days. Most of the inhabitants of the area that she had been in seemed like they were simply waiting for something to happen, waiting for something to come and move them into some similitude of purposeful activity, said activity which continued to prove elusive. She had also been of such a waiting disposition, but once she saw the black-robed figures coming over the hillside, their sable garments flowing behind them in the breeze and strange songs upon their mouth, she knew that her time had come.

The clothes before her were carefully folded but she felt a lump between them. Curious, she reached and found two shiny black shoes within which were stuffed a pair of small black socks. The shoes were of fine quality, and she slipped them on and found that they fit perfectly. Slipping them off again, she continued her inventory of the items before her. There was a short black jumper upon the breast of which was a pocket embroidered with a small insignia representing the cult and which designated the wearer as belonging to the cause of the commandant. Two small straps on the sides of the garment allowed cinching according to size and also had a few hooks upon which could be attached various items at which time there were none. Along with this was a pair of white, full-coverage panties, a thin black shirt and a length of ribbon. The ribbon particularly pleased her. Still standing naked before the bed, she took the slick black fabric and arranged a small bunch in the back of her hair, tying a small funny little ponytail, the best she could muster with the length of her hair. She sat on the edge of the bed and put on the black socks which were short, reaching only above her ankles. Next she put on the pair of white panties, followed by the shirt and then the jumper which she cinched around her thin waist, causing it to flare out slightly around her hips. Her attire complete, she slipped into the shiny black shoes and made a few circumlocutions of the room. She was pleased to hear that they produced a slight click upon the flooring in mimicry of the nurse to her senior and her sadistic leather boots.

After donning her uniform, she set upon examining various parts of the room, beginning by opening the drawer on the end table by the bed. The headphones sat where the nurse had placed them just thirty minutes earlier, but there was nothing else in the drawer to be seen. She paced back and forth, waiting for the nurse or whomever would arrive with her food; she assumed it would be the nurse, although she could not be sure. At this point she was well-famished, as it had been quite some time since she had eaten. She went before the mirror again and stared at her reflection, smiling slightly at the look of her hair tied back with the ribbon. The hair on her sides was pulled back with the ponytail but leaving two prominent shocks hanging on either side, framing her face.

IRON GATES

CHAPTER 11

A barrage of heavy machine gun fire blasted through the copse of trees heavily interspersed with bush. The time was the wee morning hours and the darkness of a moonless night was even more dense beneath the heavy foliage. All that could be seen was the fire bursting from the unseen muzzles of the guns some distance away, sending showers of metallic death upon the small group of dissidents who had been camping in the area. Pieces of bark flew in raining shrapnel as small trees were burst asunder from the heavy firepower. The caliber of the guns was obviously from some belt-fed mechanism as dissidents saw the bodies of their compatriots blown almost to obliteration, trunkless legs falling down with their upper bodies ground into piles of bloody meat.

The firestorm stopped and then the sound of a deep resounding horn could be heard several times in the distance before the machine guns started again. The dissidents, armed with only a few stolen handguns from their tenure in the organization, were not even able to draw their weapons before they faced death. The machine guns were still firing, and all five of the individuals now lay dead on the ground. The guns silenced and a torch was lit amongst one of the members of the death squad, sending an eerie reddish glow within the sky as they slowly approached. The death squad consisted of eight elite shock troopers and two internal security attaches. As the shock troopers went through and attempted to identify the bodies, cutting off the heads of those who were not completely blown to bits, the internal security attaches set up a small radio apparatus attempting to establish a signal with their main force which was stationed some miles away. Only static was heard as they attempted to beep in several coded messages which may or may not have been received. The thickness of the brush and the atmospheric pressure of the area were not conducive to their attempts at communication.

'We aren't getting any sort of signal out from here, have you identified them all?' one of the internal security attaches asked.

One of the head shock troopers smiled, his hands covered with blood.

'We have them all in hand.'

He emphasized his point by holding up several severed heads, holding them by their bloodied hair and dropping them into a rucksack outfitted with a rubber interior lining designed for just such a grisly purpose. The heads would be brought on to the commanding officer in the field as proof their work and evidence of successful termination.

'Good then, let's get back to the others.'

Leaving a scene of hideous carnage behind them, they proceeded toward the edge of the forest and then began marching along the dark plains leading toward the position of the other members of their force.

IRON GATES

CHAPTER 12

It was only a few minutes after finishing dressing and effecting her vain exploration of the room that little Lynx, as she had been called in the wilderness, heard the sound of the lock being turned back. The nurse entered the room, still seemingly in a particularly good mood compared to how she had seemed the day before. Along with her was a guard who carried a large plate of food containing a pile of unidentified mashed substance, some dried meats, some cheeses and a large glass of reddish liquid. Lynx's eyes opened wide in amazement; this was a veritable feast, comparable at very least to the best of the fare that she had been treated to by the robed women recruiters during their initial meet. Noticing the girl's reaction, the nurse smiled broadly.

'You will be well taken care of here, do not forget that, Lynx. Some of the treatments and training you will undergo within the next several weeks will be arduous and sometimes you will certainly feel some tension directed to you, but remember that this is part of the cleansing process. We must build ourselves into the proper and most disciplined state so that we can better be of service to the commandant, understood?'

Lynx nodded in agreement, her eyes not leaving the food tray which the guard had now placed on the end table before proceeding to the back of the room where he stood at the door, the nurse following suit. From the open door eerie reddish light from the corridor spilled into the entryway to her quarters. Other than the fact that the lights had automatically come on in her room at a certain time titularly denoting the arrival of morning, it was impossible to ascertain whether it was day or night in the subterranean center in which she was now domiciled.

'Eat up and be ready to go along with us for some training within the hour. It will be intense so be prepared.' The look on the nurse's face hardened in a stern expression. Lynx nodded submissively in acquiescence and, without further ado, the nurse and the guard left the room, locking the door behind them and shutting out the reddish glow of the tunnel.

Within seconds of the door having clicked shut Lynx was well into the food. She was absolutely starved and this yield was unlike anything she had ever seen before, especially with the dried meat and the cheese, which she had never had before. Several thick slices of the waxed yellowish substance lay on the plate and she picked one up and, tasting it, her eyes nearly rolled back into her head in ecstasy. The mashed substance was surprisingly flavorful if strange in appearance, and she quickly finished it off, leaving the meat for last, which she gnawed contently while drinking the reddish liquid which had a vague fruit-like taste with a slight bitterness. She hoped that the level of nutrition would continue in this manner - for meals like this she was willing to suffer much. Her decision to go with the cult recruiters was not based on any sort of advanced theoretical understanding of what they were about but primarily on necessities of survival and her own determination to move beyond what she had experienced thus far in her life. She knew that her options were slim and that if she wanted to live beyond age twenty then it was best that she make her decision as to where she wanted to be heading. The cult recruiters had shown her a few pictures of their leader and stated god-in-the-flesh who they referred to only as the commandant, and now she, once obscure, was in service to the same.

As Lynx sipped at the remaining dregs of her beverage she felt a strange sensation running through her body, a great abiding sense of pleasure but also a strange aggression, as if the nourishment had awoken some hidden force within her that made her more similar to the animal which she had been nicknamed after those many years ago in the wilderness by one of her friends who had read the name in some old, old book that came from before the nuclear wars. She drank down the final remaining sips of the reddish drink and let out a large belch. She proceeded to the sink and washed the telltale signs of food from the corners of her mouth and splashed some of the cold liquid on her face, drying it off with one of the towels. She looked at herself squarely in the mirror. She had no idea what might come but she intended to face it with all readiness. She was amazed as she felt a sharp burning sense of confidence thrumming through her body as if it was living right beneath the surface of the skin. The hour drew down quickly and soon enough the door reopened. This time the nurse was not present and only two internal security guards met her, black-masked, goggled and anonymous. She stood waiting for them to motion her out and was not entirely surprised when one of them approached her and took a firm grasp on the side of her arm and led her out himself, the other guard waiting until they had exited the room and without Lynx seeing, examining the plate of food to make sure it had all been eaten. Locking the door behind them he followed them out and continued to follow several paces behind as they marched forward down into the red-lit corridor.

Before she knew it she had entered into another room. The guard released her and either purposefully or by dint of his comparable strength shoved her forward slightly, causing her to trip and fall to her knees, scraping them slightly on the rough concrete floor. She raised herself up and looked with an unmistakeable sign of scorn at the person who had so offended her, but no expression was forthcoming or could indeed be ascertained at all from the masked figure. The guards closed the door and stationed themselves on either side of it and Lynx turned back around, facing into the rest of the room. The area was arranged like an office, with a large desk at the center and a huge poster of the commandant behind the desk, her lusty and lethal figure interposed over a gigantic spreading nuclear mushroom cloud. Two flags on stationary flagpoles were on either side of the desk bearing the nuclear ensign of the cult. A few bookshelves contained what looked to be newly bound volumes encased in greasy leather. Bright electric light tubes over her head illuminated the area. She looked down at her knees and noticed that they were only slightly scratched. Thankfully they hadn't done anything to ruin her uniform. She wished that she could take one of their weapons and blow them to bits. She was surprised at the thought and somewhat taken aback by the anomalously violent feelings which were surfacing within her, which seemed to get more prominent as each second went by. Within a few minutes a firm rap came from the outside of the door and a young woman appearing to be about sixteen, four years Lynx's senior, entered. She was at least a head taller than Lynx and dressed in the exact same attire as Lynx herself, her short jumper revealing muscled but pleasantly plump legs. The girl's hair was tawny and long and tied into two braided pigtails which looped around her ears.

'So you are the new recruit?'

Lynx nodded in the affirmative.

The girl walked around to the desk and opened a drawer, brows furrowed as her eyes beamed down at whatever it was she was contemplating before closing the drawer with a loud bang.

'I heard that you are very spirited, is that true?'

Lynx didn't exactly follow the other girl's linguistic line of reasoning but could tell from the tone that she was being challenged.

'I am here to serve the commandant!' Lynx answered with a tone of unabashed finality and authority. She could feel her heart rate gradually quickening and rising in her chest.

The girl with the braids rocked her head back and let out a long, bellowing laugh, her features looking maniacal if somewhat contrived, yet the scene was given an extra air of grotesqueness by the huge poster of the commandant which loomed down from behind her, the sixteen-year-old obviously being to one degree or another her proxy at this particular juncture as far as Lynx was concerned.

The older girl walked back around the desk and approached Lynx with smartly clicking heels and, reaching out, took both of Lynx's shoulders in either of her hands, looking deep into the younger girl's eyes.

'I am sure that you have some desire to serve the commandant, otherwise you wouldn't be here today. Although I wonder that perhaps you were just wanting to escape from a situation that was pressing on you, gotten in trouble perhaps, stolen something from someone perhaps?'

'I haven't stolen anything from anyone in my entire life!' Lynx snarled, fully riled now.

Once again the older girl let out a long, pealing burst of laughter but cut it off suddenly, her face turning red with rage as she began to shake Lynx by the shoulders.

'You don't shout at me, little girl! I shout at you and only if you are lucky, as that's the least of what I can do!'

The older girl released Lynx and stepped back toward the desk, pulling out a chair and sitting down, drumming her fingers on the hard wooden surface.

'I think that you are going to have to be taught some things about discipline, and I do believe that I myself am going to have to administer some punishment to you, is that clear?'

Internally Lynx wanted to jump across the desk and strangle the girl, but her self-control caught better of her. She was experiencing some weird interaction from whatever she had eaten; she knew that her level of aggression was unnatural. However within the last few seconds the feelings of aggression had begun to be equally coupled with indescribable pleasurable feelings - she was confused, but she knew that she had to keep her bearings about her if she was going to survive whatever ordeal she was being put through. She wanted to spend tonight back in her room with another meal the next day, and she wasn't interested in being dumped in some backwater naked to be left scrounging in the bushes for berries or whatever else might be available. That in mind, she lowered her head and nodded obediently to the older girl's stated intention.

'Very good, very good, I think you are beginning to understand things already, however you are still not in the clear, and it's obvious to me that you need a little attitude adjustment, young lady.'

Lynx could feel aggression and pleasure running through her body in equal measures at the condescension and implication, not sure whether or not the aggression was making her feel pleased or whether the influx of caloric intake itself was fueling aggression. At the mention of attitude adjustment she could feel the blood rushing to her face and began deeply blushing, something not unnoticed by the older teenager seated at the table.

'I think it's time for you and I to come to a little understanding about how things are run around here and what will be expected of you. First of all, respect is tantamount, and we can begin this by way of introduction. My name is Miss Hall, but you can refer to me as 'ma'am', do you understand?'

'Yes,' Lynx replied, her increasingly reddening face turned downward still.

'Yes WHAT?'

Having spent most of her life scavenging in the wilderness, Lynx was totally unconscious of what Miss Hall was aiming at.

'Yes WHAT?'

The older girl's eyes became hard and beady as she stared at Lynx from behind the desk. The younger girl's reasoning skills seemed slightly impaired, but then the connection made sense.

'Yes, MA'AM...' she replied, the last word emphasized in its strangeness, as she had no clue what such a title meant, although it was obviously some sign of respect, an honorific, that the older girl seemed to demand.

'Good! You are beginning to learn, little one.' The older girl eyed her haughtily, leaning back in her chair and splaying her arms on the desk in a suitably executive fashion.

'What is your name?'

'My name is Lynx.'

'WHAT?'

'My name is LYNX!'

The last word was emphasized almost with a shout and Lynx felt her head automatically raising itself and staring assuredly across the room at the other girl seated behind the desk, her face now red from both embarrassment and anger.

'NO, FILTH! LYNX IS AN ANIMAL THAT WALKS AROUND ON ALL FOURS IN THE FUCKING FOREST! YOUR NAME IS RECRUIT! DO YOU UNDERSTAND THAT? RECRUIT! RECRUIT! RECRUIT!' The girl emphasized each repetition by slamming the flat of her hand on the desk.

'WHAT IS YOUR NAME?'
'RECRUIT!'
'RECRUIT WHAT?'
'RECRUIT, MA'AM!'

Knowing that the time for discussion was over and action was at hand, the youth officer rose from her chair, picking it up by its handle and moving it around the table so that it sat to the side of the room, its seat faced outward, near one of the large shelves of books. The female smoothed out the bottom of her skirt and then gestured for Lynx to come forward.

'I am going to teach you how disrespect is commonly dealt with in this level of our organization, do you understand me? In higher levels the punishments are much worse, but as you are still young yet we need to get this out of the way first.'

The sixteen-year-old sat back down in the chair and gestured for Lynx to come and stand beside her, before grasping the young girl's arm and pulling her over her lap. Lynx had never experienced anything like this before and she let out a gasp.

'Oh you'll be making more sounds than that before

its all over with, my dear.'

Lynx's arms inadvertently reached toward the ground, putting her in a perfect position for the older girl's disciplinary ministrations. The masked internal security guards stood unmoving at the sides of the doors as witnesses, silently observing the events as they unfolded.

The older girl firmly pinned Lynx to her lap with one hand and with the other hand brought down a resounding slap on Lynx's bottom, raising her hand again and bringing it down firmly and repeatedly in a brisk tattoo of spanks. Lynx was in shock from the position she found herself in but not necessarily in pain; it was more surprise than anything at this point.

'Are you understanding this, little girl?' the older female intoned.

Lynx did not respond.

Six hard slaps followed in rapid succession.

Lynx let out a small whimper.

'There we go, let's see if we can increase the volume a little.'

Lynx felt the points of her toes enclosed in her polished black shoes involuntarily rise off the floor as the older girl repositioned her so that her bottom was directly beneath her line of vision. With a fell motion the older cult member lifted Lynx's skirt, revealing her young, pert buttocks, perfectly encased in the white panties. In this position, the beating continued.

The older girl alternated her hits, driving her open palm down upon one cheek then the other, then moving toward the plump area where buttocks meet thigh and hitting with a resounding smack where the flesh was exposed.

Lynx felts waves of humiliation come over her but also rising aggression in equal amounts, and she began wriggling beneath the older girl's grasp in attempt to free herself. Not that she knew what exactly she would do should she manage to free herself; her thinking had become automatic and passionate in the context of the situation as it was unfolding.

Within several minutes' time little Lynx found herself with her panties pulled around her ankles and the sharp cracking hand of the sixteen-year old driving her to hot tears of shame and contrition. Her petite buttocks gave little cushioning to the incessant spanking being administered by the older girl, who interspersed the punishment with regular elements of stern lecturing, mostly informing her about the seriousness of the cult that she had joined.

From her shameful vantage point, Lynx could see the two black-masked internal security guards standing at the doorway and wondered what they were thinking of her predicament. Did the scene of a young girl facing such a dressing-down, forced nudity and decidedly domestic-style violence excite them in a sexual fashion? Or had they seen so many similar scenes within their lifetime that they were effectively immune?

The spanking suddenly stopped and Lynx felt herself being grabbed by the back of the neck and stood back upright. Her jumper did not fall into place but stuck on the tightening clasps, leaving her awkward with the fabric pulled up over her small hind and her panties bunched around her ankles. The older girl looked at her appraisingly, lingering perhaps too long around the area of her pudenda.

'Let's take a look at this, shan't we?'

The older girl took her by the arm and slowly turned Lynx around, examining the reddish contours of her well-spanked buttocks. She placed her hand on the younger girl's upper thigh, snaking the tips of her fingers around and digging into the reddened flesh of her buttocks, causing Lynx to gasp slightly. Turning her back around, the older girl stood and removed a handkerchief from the pocket of her jumper, softly rubbing away the tears from the younger girl's face.

'Pull yourself together, you can put your panties back on, straighten yourself up.'

As Lynx complied, the older girl took the chair and moved it back behind the desk. It was all over almost as soon as it had begun. The strange psycho-physical feelings Lynx had been having before being taken into the room and enduring the humiliating punishment had tapered off. Her aggression was now in check, although she felt more potential, more poised if you will, to commit an act of violence should she be called on to do so or should the opportunity avail itself. The pleasurable sensations were also now less prominent, although she could feel a lingering sensation within her flesh that left her feeling more pleasurable than usual. This was surprising considering what she had just undergone. But after all, she did not expect that everything would be roses within a cult that worshiped a form of personified nuclear war. She straightened out the seat of her jumper and turned, standing submissively with her hands at her sides and her eyes downward in front of the desk, where the older girl had once again placed herself.

'My name is Patty, Patty Hall, as you know – though perhaps now you know me better? Now that we have that out of the way...' a vicious little smile curled around the corners of the girl's mouth, 'we can proceed on to more important matters. I am going to be giving you several important documents which it is absolutely essential that you keep with you at all times.' Patty began removing several thick, staple-bound books and clipped-together reams of paper from numerous desk drawers. 'There will also be a satchel for you to carry them in... where is it, now?'

The sixteen-year old conversed with herself as she rummaged through various drawers, then moved to the file cabinets. Squatting down with her back turned toward Lynx she found pay dirt in the bottom drawer. 'Here we go.'

Patty removed a black courier bag with the emblem of the cult emblazoned on its side and then stuffed the documents along with several ink pens into the bag, closing the fastener and extending it over the desk toward Lynx, who still stood with her eyes turned downward.

'Here, here, take it!' Patty said with an overemphasized sense of hastiness. 'I already have one!'

IRON GATES

CHAPTER 13

'It's only going to be a matter of time before they come back down the path and see us!'

The filthy twenty-year-old man with a long scraggly beard, makeshift knife cradled to his chest, sat behind some shrubs contained within a copse of trees some quarter of a mile left of the position of the organizational troops. He and two other men, equally bedraggled in appearance, had been posted as lookouts for the more substantial number of their force that had been stationed up the hill. The problem arose in the fact that rather than coming from the direction which they had suspected, the organizational troops had circled the hillside and come in from the back, leaving the current team still waiting and not clued-in to the lethality of the situation until they heard the massive outpouring of machine gun fire which had left every member of their main force dead. Their stratagem defeated and severed from any potential assistance, they now sat in wait, hoping that they would not be noticed as the members of the organizational team made their way down the hillside directly past their position. It seemed like it would be a miracle if they were not spotted; whatever resistance they would be able to offer against the massive firepower that they had watched from a distance would certainly mean instant death for them. Their only chance now lay in the possibility that they would not be discovered. They had to think quickly and formulate a plan or else they would be as dead as their recently departed compatriots.

'We need to move away from the area.'

The organizational troops had abandoned their sense of stealth now that the force had been eliminated, and they were not considering that there could have been others positioned elsewhere on the same hillside, their muted conversations becoming more and more audible as they moved closer to the position of the stranded resistance. The bearded fellow looked down toward the south side of the hill, spotting another but more substantial copse of trees a distance away. If they could only make it down without being spotted there could be a chance that they could escape without capture. The bearded man was more than disheartened. They had thought that they themselves were about to pull an ambush this night, but instead they had faced a massacre which made their small force almost halved in size. The ancient, decaying barn in the field several miles to the southwest held a few more of their ragtag group of operatives. The resistance option was proving to be suicidal. He wondered now deep within himself whether or not the strategy to resist had been a wise one after all.

If they were to move there was no time like the present and the leader of the miniscule band motioned to his compatriots with a silent motion of his hands to make for the copse of trees down the hill. One of the men being instructed grabbed for his rucksack containing various cooking utensils and in his haste several metallic pots spilled out of the bag, making a noticeable clamor. Hopefully, with the wind the sound would be lost on the organizational troops that were quickly making their way toward the resister's present position. The man hurriedly put the items back in the pack, making even more noise in the process, and then scrambled down the hillside toward the cover. As if watching an unfolding nightmare, the group leader heard a burst of automatic machine gun fire and almost immediately the forward scout's upper body disappeared into a mist of blood, the remainders of his twitching corpse falling with a thump onto the ground. Another round of machine gun fire burst out from another angle to their left. They were surrounded, but only the trees had any hope of sheltering them, if any.

'Everybody make their own way - survivors make recontact at the barn!'

The team leader sprinted on brawny legs toward the copse of trees and once entering kept on going, making his way quickly down a ravine and downward toward a more substantial area of forest where he could slowly wind his way around the perimeter of the fields to get near their headquarters under cover. In the background he could hear another peal of machine gun fire and the sound of his other companions facing death. He was now the only one left surviving.

With belabored breath he scrambled down the slimy root-riddled washout, various thorns and brambles scraping against his flesh, offering his blood to whatever foul spirits inhabited the wood which was now becoming the sight of the doom of his group. He still grasped his knife, which was lowered to his side; intermittently he could hear more gunfire in the background although no sound of human voices. Gradually the gunfire began to sound more distant. He was now in the deeper part of the forest and was making considerable ground. Eventually the sound of the gunfire stopped as the organizational shock troops recognized that they had routed the surprise pocket of resistance.

Meanwhile, the shock troopers had reached the former position and scanned the hillside leading downward to the southeast and southwest, scanning for any movement. One shock trooper carried a pair of primitive binoculars but even those had little utilization in the near pitch black nighttime environment. While they scanned the ground for further resistance, another of the shock troopers worked his way at sawing off a head from one of the bearded corpses that had received a hit in the chest. The scout who had been first to be hit with the machine gun fire effectively had no head - that and the entire upper portion of his body having been decimated into blood spray and finely ground pieces of gore that littered the area here and there. The shock trooper felt some remorse that he would not be able to collect a trophy from that particular casualty, but he did manage to find a nice piece of flesh which he took to gnaw on during the march back to the rest of their formation.

They had an extra gunner stationed on the west side of the hill who opened fire on the position of the resisters soon after they had heard the commotion with the bag of pots and pans. The items of the bag now lay scattered around the area and several shock troopers carefully picked up the materials, secreting them into their own satchels which they would bring back with them. The material would be of potential use, waste not want not, there was also the potential that the items might provide some clues as to the nature and affiliation, if any, of the people that they had encountered. Meanwhile, off to the side, an internal security guard stared blankly into the nocturnal forest, his goggles removed and his pale eyes shining dimly in the cool night atmosphere. He removed a small notebook from his side jacket pocket and wrote down a few notations, scanning the landscape from side to side and making notes of the positioning and area. For the shock troopers on the mission right now, their work would soon be done, however once back with the rest of the troops the internal security personnel would be having a private conference with the field commander on site and soon there would be several elite commandos let loose onto the landscape by way of follow-up. One resistance member had been allowed to escape on purpose; tracking him would lead the organization back to whatever pathetic base they were operating out of and from there their network would be examined. The commander wanted to have an opportunity to test some new weapons, but first they needed at least a sizable amount of victims to act as guinea pigs. He hoped that they found something substantial; this would certainly put his career on the fast track should their forward actions of this evening lead to a massacre.

After his notes were finished, the internal security member put the notebook back in his pocket and shouted to the other internal security members present. 'We need to get this team moving out, let the shock troopers know that we are ready to go.' Under the cover of night, the team departed toward the site of the organizational encampment.

CHAPTER 14

'Bring me the head of that one over there!'

One of the shock troops capered behind the military wagon and grabbed a female's head off the pile of bleeding severed heads collected by the organizational contingent over the last several weeks. Some of the heads were, as it might be expected, in worse condition than others, however some were still fresh. The head of a young blonde woman executed in one of the villages earlier in the day had the eye of the shock trooper on this particular evening.

The pile of heads gleamed sickly in the light of the torches surrounding the encampment. The wagon was an older military truck that had been edited and converted over the years. It was relatively slow-moving and ran on old, dirty gas; the shock troopers could march about as fast as the wagon could drive. The automobile was utilized exclusively for transport of heavy weaponry, everyone else marched except for the those in few seats in the cab. Those seats were reserved for the driver and a few internal security personnel who were as ever armed to the teeth, entrusted with the mission of maintaining communications and other records and also entrusted with the duty to explode the vehicle in suicide-mission fashion rather than have it captured. This of course was simply a contingency, as any professional staged resistance against the organization was ancient history – much less the probability of the capture of a carrier. Overkill was applied in all situations, to prove a point and keep the discipline of the sectors within the organization at razor's edge at all times.

'Bring me that head, trooper!'

Healvan stood resplendent in his black uniform jacket, the sleeves rolled up revealing heavily muscled arms covered with tattoos of butchered children, various black magic symbols from assorted post-doomsday cults operating within the organization and more than a few naked valkyries of death marking him as a headhunter for the commandant. The rest of his contingency recognized his religious proclivities and indulged them by collecting heads along their way. The extra brutality was not a problem so much as the extra work, however all within the unit were obligated to indulge him as the superior officer and more than a few of them also held a degree of devotion for the commandant, although their levels of knowledge concerning the same differed.

Braunfel, his direct assistant, moved his hands along the gory pile of severed heads, the more rotten and gangrenous which lay upon the bottom, but as they had only been out for a few weeks they still bore distinct resemblance to what they would have looked like during the time that whatever spirit had still inhabited the same. Near the top were the fresh kills from earlier in the day, the blood still stinking with the beautiful burnt iron-like

IRON GATES

odor of fresh atrocity.

He settled on his officer's choice, the head of a sharply-featured woman with tanned skin and long blonde hair. The length of the hair made the severed head easy to handle and the shock trooper reached down and plucked the bloodied piece from the pile, walking with an air of procession about him as he approached the officer.

Healvan whisked the grip of hair from Braunfel's hand and held it above his head, allowing the head itself to settle directly within eye view.

'What a pretty one indeed!'

Healvan belched loudly before protruding his tongue and licking some of the blood from around the dead woman's lips where the blood had hemorrhaged outward when the shock troopers had sawed the head from its trunk using one of their razor-sharp serrated edge knives. This was very pleasing, perhaps he would have to take this head for more and further intimate ministrations, later on, inside his tent.

'Out of here, Braunfel, out of here you beast, find your own!'

Peals of laughter enveloped the two as Healvan let out numerous cackles of perverse and insane delight at his find. Other, more conventional persons might wonder that treating the heads in such a fashion might be looked at askance by the religious cult who desired them to be collected, but those in the know knew that Healvan was amped-up enough that such considerations did not matter. Healvan was brutal and ultra-violent in all things, yet lacked the finesse and understanding to go but so far. For now he was subtly manipulated by the present members of internal security attached to his unit and thus guided in correct pursuits of his peculiar abilities by the targeted brainwashing of the commandant's cult. Those that were dealers of death and dealers of death only, first and foremost, whatever their level of sophistication, were to be encouraged and kept in the fray at maximum efficiency. The dual lines of manipulation from internal security and intelligence with added aid of maintaining a subservient unit all assisted in the trajectory of his brief yet bloody career in the organizational shock troops thus far.

Braunfel walked back over to the pile of heads, nonplussed, as Healvan took the blonde and proceeded toward his tent. There he would no doubt be undergoing a night of heavy drinking and manipulation of the head followed by lots of autoerotic practices, with certain practices involving the head's orifices, while not necessarily solitary in nature, still falling under the general autoeroticism header, albeit with a strong lacing of necrophilia.

Braunfel waited until the officer was well ensconced in his tent, then moved around the wagon towards the lit fires where the rest of the men were drinking and enjoying the aftermath of the day's killing. Braunfel eagerly eyed a plastic bucket containing a noxious-looking liquid - this was the rot-gut that had been formulated especially within his unit with a variety of additives, both provided and stolen and which provided a hardcore ending to a hardcore day of killing, maiming, raping and sundry other activities associated with military life within the organization. A few of the men eyed him as he walked up, then returned to their conversations.

'You should have seen this little bitch that I murdered earlier today, I can tell you it was an event to be sure...' A plump, beautifully-uniformed man of Indian descent bounced slightly on the log upon which he sat as he took a draught of the hideous beverage before launching into his monologue for the benefit of the other attendees. Rajiv was known to go far above and beyond the call of duty on a regular basis and as it just so happened he had gone above and beyond only a few hours ago in the little civilian village that marked the edge of organizational territory in the area.

'So me and Peter had just rounded the corner of this filthy little shack - what isn't these days?' A few of the men snickered at the comment, both a telling commentary on the situation in the village and also a telling commentary on the situation in general.

'Standing by the side of the porch is this girl, must have been six or seven years old, black as the ace of spades. Well, first of all we cleared the area and shot her mamma in the face, blew the goddamn bitch's head straight off. She was an ugly piece of shit and you know me, shooting her in the face, what the fuck is Healvan going to think about that?' Rajiv looked at Braunfel and let out a pressurized tittle of laughter, his eyebrows arching and retracting in absolute self-enjoyment. Braunfel ignored the comment and drew himself a large mug of the rot-gut from the bucket.

'So we shoot her mamma, right, then I go up to the little girl and pinch her on the nipple like this?' Rajiv coaxed the tip of his rough-hewn cigar. 'She is crying and all, snot running down her face and tears and all that, oh my it was wonderful. Anyway so I say to her, 'You know your mamma is dead now, don't you?' and she goes, 'I thought you was shooting a chicken.'' Several of the shock troopers burst out laughing and Rajiv looked around the fire circle, arching his eyebrows for further emphasis and letting out a sick little giggle himself. 'So I say to her, 'I think you are the chicken, maybe I can pluck you?'' Chortles progressed to guffaws.

'So I grab her other nipple and squeeze as hard as I can and she goes 'eeeek!' like that, like she seen a ghost or something, right, and I go, 'No no, no 'eeeeek', must go 'squawk, squawk!'' All the shock troopers now were laughing heartily and taking huge slugs of the rot-gut. ''So maybe I stick a feather in your pussy and you go 'squawk, squawk'?' I ask her and she goes, 'Don't mess with my kitten, sir.''

Rajiv's conversation pealed off into more of the same, culminating in his stripping the girl, performing an anal rape on the steps of the porch all the while encouraging the youngster to squawk like a chicken. At the end of the rape, Rajiv instructed the girl to open her mouth and bite a brick before he brought down his boot onto the back of her head, busting out all of her teeth and anointing the rock with the gore of busted lip flesh and shattered facial flesh.

Within several seconds of Rajiv finishing his story,

the situation at the camp was suddenly disrupted as small arms fire burst from the covering of trees several yards' distance away. The gun was light, probably a twenty-two caliber and only a few volleys were fired, however that was more than enough to send the shock troopers into a frenzy of activity. Rajiv and another one of the men quickly threw their mugs of rot-gut onto the fire, effectively extinguishing the blaze and sending up dirty clouds of smoke, further adding to the confusion of the situation.

Immediately and in a highly disciplined and efficient fashion the shock troopers retreated from the smoldering embers of the fire and made their way behind the wagon to the area of the officer's tent. Healvan had already burst out from his own tent, slinging the semen and blood-splattered severed head back toward the direction of the pile. His chest stood rippling with harsh muscles, his combat jacket opened up and wearing no undershirt. His eyes bulged in rage and insanity and his left hand gripped a huge belt-fed machine gun which was his weapon of choice. Breaking the sudden silence arranged by the other shock troopers, the officer let out a howl of rage that reverberated across the area of the camp, sending blood-curdling fear into whatever resistance was presenting itself in the area.

'Arm yourselves and get ready to spread out!' the officer hissed. He strapped the machine gun across his back and removed a large serrated combat knife from his belt, slicing a filthy and jagged wound across his arm, slicing through the designs of several of the cult-oriented tattoos. He grimaced and spat at the thought of resistance from those that he and his comrades had already undertaken a harsh raid against earlier in the day. Did they really want everyone to die? They had left a number of civilians at the small village, as the raid had been a breaking-down tactic designed to soften up the area before organizational forces annexed it into their ever-growing territory. That some resistance and furthermore armed resistance had sprung up suddenly was completely intolerable. It was an infraction which would be prosecuted with extreme prejudice.

As the officer and his troops strapped up with arms and began spreading out over the area to find the culprits, the two internal security personnel crouched inside their own tent some ways away. They had heard the small arms fire but were more concerned with reaching the elite commando unit on their private radio to find out whether or not the escapee from their earlier volley had reached their quarry and where he had been heading. A sudden crackle and a burst of radio interference rang out followed by a low coded voice which relayed information confirming what they had suspected. There was a small resistance faction held up inside the old barn which they had mapped out previously, and soon after the survivor from the organization ambush had arrived, an inconspicuous older lady had departed the area of the barn, going toward the small village to warn her contacts there of imminent organization attack. It had taken the elderly lady until mid-morning to reach the area, however, and by then she was too late, and she arrived in the midst of the organization's punitive raid and had personally witnessed Rajiv's brutalization of the little girl and murder of her mother in the house on the edge of the village. She had arrived under the cover of having gone out scavenging for forest roots and other foods, playing the story that she lived in the village, which she in fact did not. The organizational troops had bashed her across the face, breaking her cheek bone which would leave her maimed for the rest of her life, yet not subjecting her to torture or cursory extermination, which could have been warranted under the suspicious circumstances of her sudden arrival. Considering the meter of the situation, she had laid low in the village until the organizational troops departed, then doubled back to her position at the barn, informing the resisters of the situation and that the civilians that they had been attempting to guard had been the object of an organizational punitive raid.

Emotions ran hot in the barn upon her arrival. She had managed to get back just after nightfall, and the men had been anxiously awaiting news of the situation when she informed them, rather sentimentally, about the death of the young girl and the other telltale signs of the organizational punitive raid as it had been occurring, such as the burning of certain key buildings and other acts, meant to hammer home the fact that any autonomy for the region was over and that the commander had come to call his own unto himself. Several of the men had decided to take action and use one of their few guns to perform a night raid on the organizational encampment. They did not have the firepower nor the manpower to do anything substantial, however they knew if the organizational shock troopers and others present heard the sounds of guns that they would at least know that they were dealing with armed resistance, however minutely so, and that they were not going to roll over and let their territories be taken lock, stock and barrel without some modicum of airing their position of dissatisfaction.

A number of the men had crept out under the cover of night, blackening their faces with soot from the fires of the ancient cast iron stove inside the barn and armed with one gun and an assortment of smaller edged weapons. They did not intend to engage the enemy, simply harass them, as any engagement would mean their sure and certain death. Only some harassment followed by a quick escape without getting trackers on them would suffice. They had already decided not to return directly to the barn but instead hole up in an area of forest on the side of the village, near the edge of where organizational territory began in earnest. It would be a harrowing experience, but they believed if they did not act out against the atrocities now that they might as well pack their bags and head west. All of the people, themselves included, had spent considerable time, pain and effort in building up their area and they were not about to let it all go to the organization, its commander and his sadistic minions without a fight.

As the internal security guards got their confirmation of the whereabouts of the resistance base in the old barn, they signaled for the commandos to proceed with home invasion and extermination of the inhabitants, said action having already been pre-approved by the commander upon the contingency that they found out where the resisters were located. After confirming their marching orders, the internal security got on the radio and summoned several other elite units as well as some conventional forces from organizational headquarters, informing them that they requested they muster directly on the organization side of the border and await the internal security personnel from the small unit to personally appear and debrief them before moving in. They requested demolitions and explosives teams and also several shock trooper units trained in chemical warfare and armed with the substances of their choice. They were going to make an impression and no mistaking.

The internal security got off the radio just as the shock troopers were in formation and about to spread out and enter the woods from which the volley had come. No further gunfire had been heard and the resisters were already doing their best to sneak away in the cover of silence and dark. One of the internal security managed to approach the officer who, although tacitly leading the force, understood to a degree that his position as a shock trooper was subordinate to the machinations of internal security and intelligence. Duly informed that the internal security attaches were proceeding out for approximately one to two days to garner reinforcements, the internal security guard left the officer with a small walkie-talkie which would be the method by which he would be contacted upon their successful liaison with the organizational personnel from headquarters which were already preparing for their imminent departure. The officer grunted in confirmation and took the walkie-talkie, securely clipping it to his utility belt. He had since put himself in a more appropriate manner of dress for a field assignment - his jacket was buttoned and several bandoliers of ammunition criss-crossed his broad chest. The bloodied wound on his arm was congealing but still gave the clear signal of his intent to totally annihilate any of the hostiles he might come across.

'If you find them don't worry about taking any hostages, officer, we already have some more information. Kill them, come back here and get your men ready for a real punishment raid. We will be in touch via the radio soon.'

It was no austerity for the officer to be ordered to simply kill; he approved of this measure, and with one last nod at the internal security guard they went their separate ways.

The shock troopers spread out in a long V-formation as they silently marched into the forest, all heavily armed with the best munitions and armaments that the organization had to offer. The officer Healvan's mind was filled with schizophrenic visions of his deity, the commandant, considering the stark curvatures of her black form, her anonymous and horrid mask and the poisons, weapons and atrocities that dripped from her very aura like the fallout of her own spiraling and unquestionable evil. Her black banner bearing the ensign of the atomic mushroom cloud enlarged and retracted within his mind as he unwillingly let out a hiss of black rage from his lips. Whomever and whatever was attacking them would be feeling a wrath beyond simply an organization, they would be feeling the wrath of the children and servitors of death and hell itself, he would magnify their suffering so as to make a proper gift and sacrifice to his mistress.

The shock trooper on the left corner of the V-formation motioned that he had spotted some movement and waved his hand downward. All of the shock troopers dropped to the ground and began to crawl slowly toward the position of their quarry as the shock trooper who had been doing lookout slowly crept further into the bush. He raised his arm and gave the symbol of 'three' denoting that he had spotted three individuals in the brush. This in fact was the entire amount of the resistance force that had been sent out on their suicidal mission. The person who had escaped from the ambush on the hillside was not among their number, having stayed back at the barn at the encouragement of all the others present. They did not believe that he was fit for another foray, despite the seeming heroism of his escape. Seeing all of one's compatriots killed by massively disproportionate levels of military firepower was enough to put someone off balance, thus they had decided to rotate their human stock in order to maximize the few resisters that they had on hand. They had attempted to recruit more heavily in the village, however this had been met with a mix of varied disinterest but more prominently fear. Despite that, those in the village who knew what they were up to still psychologically attached themselves to the hopes that some would-be heroes such as these might turn back the tide of organizational dominance and let them live outside the boundaries of organizational control. Such was not to be.

Having heard of the disaster of splitting up in the retreat from those involved in the ambush, the resisters who had hit the shock trooper camp with harassing fire had decided to stay together in their withdrawal from their movements on that night. As such, they were all together and would be easy to exterminate by the organizational troops. The organizational troops were still unfamiliar as to just how many of them were present however, so they decided to not blow them all to bits right away and proper. The right side of the V-formation slowly started circling around the back of the location of the resisters so that when the people on the left side of the formation fired the resisters would run right into their hands. Several of the men warranted with the task of interception slowly stalked outward, some with pistols drawn, some holding assault-style machine guns and others with one hands on their holsters and the other hands gripping lethal tanto-bladed combat knives, their metallic shafts painted clandestine black to hide any glint during the course of a night attack. Suddenly one of the men on the left side of the formation shot their folly and, as quick as they could manage, the resisters began scurrying out of their hiding place in the bush, headed directly for the awaiting organizational intercept team.

IRON GATES

Their soot-colored faces were no means of effective camouflage as the crashing of their feet through the brush and the heavy panting of their belabored breath indicated to the awaiting shock troopers where the recalcitrant persons were located just as well as if they had been coming toward them in broad daylight in a treeless field. As the first resister bounded into the intercept area, he felt a sickening pressure in his stomach just as he began to bound downward after jumping over a fallen log. The pressure was the combat knife held at the ready by one of the organizational forces, the pressure increased as the weapon was drawn upward, slicing through the flesh of the man's lungs and ending right beneath the heart area, where it was promptly twisted violently and removed, allowing the man to fall, drowning in a puddle of his own sickening gore. Shots fired into the air and from behind caused the remaining two resisters to freeze in their tracks and they were quickly brought down with a shower of fists and boots.

'Who else is with you?' shouted the officer, his combat boot placed on the neck of one of the resisters now laying on the ground.

'I don't know what... urrggaaaa.' The answer tapered off into a sickening squelching sound as the officer's boot pushed further into the man's throat, then released it suddenly. The man tried to think fast. If they thought there were more around they might let them live in order to provide counterintelligence, if they confirmed that they were the only ones then they would be killed instantly. The attacked resister decided to aim toward a happy medium between the two with an element of the

Benedict Arnold thrown in for extra measure. If he was saved then that was what counted. He had no experience in this sort of activity before joining up with the crew from the barn. Moving west or rolling with the punches when the organization took control would be easier than soaking up this sort of treatment on a regular basis. 'We are the only ones.. but I can take you to our leaders...' The other resister on the ground in a similar predicament shouted with protest as he heard the audible sounds of his compatriot's treason, but was instantly shut off as one of the shock troopers brought a combat boot driving into the side of his ear, fracturing a portion of his skull and busting his eardrum in one fell motion. The man now lay dazed, stunned and silent, his face contorted in a look of shock as he rocked back and forth, holding his hands to his ear from which slowly dripped a gradually increasing quantity of blood.

The officer laughed out loud, staring down at the frightened man who had just answered him. 'I'm pleased to hear that there aren't more of you and even more pleased that you are willing to take us to your leader, however I already know where your leader is so that leaves your life at forfeit, correct?' The man's eyes widened and he choked with a response, however nothing understandable came out except a gurgle of horror. They were surely in the spider's trap now. 'Don't waste your bullets on this filth, men, why not take them apart limb from limb with your combat knives - I have a feeling we will have better things to use our guns on soon enough. See you all back at the encampment, I still have a little business to take care of.'

As the officer withdrew, Rajiv moved forward, staring at the fallen men with slitted and hateful eyes. All he could think about was the full cup of rot-gut that he had thrown onto the fire because of the pathetic attempt at armed harassment of the two men on the ground. The interruption of his retelling of his amorous encounter with a certain ebony-skinned child beauty added further insult to injury. The single firearm possessed by the resisters had already been confiscated, thus nothing stopped the shock troopers present from proceeding along with the officer's order with marked efficiency. With a fell and fluid motion like a panther in slow motion before killing his quarry, Rajiv leaped down upon the ground and began sawing off one of the resister's heads with his combat knife, his high-pitched shrieks of insanity and predatory bliss mixing and intermingling with the resister's own screams of pain.

The last victim fell to a similar fate. Three shock troopers moved in for the kill, all drawing knives as they stalked toward their victim. The first brought down his combat boot with a deep stomp, driving directly into the prone man's midsection, knocking the air out of him and cracking some of his lower ribs. As this occurred the other two moved on either side and began wrestling the man's clothes off. Soon he was stripped naked, shivering in pain and horror beneath the cold night sky as the remaining shock troopers who were not assisting Rajiv in his occupation of slaying the other man moved in and began showering the unfortunate victim with a shower of kicks to all parts of the body.

IRON GATES

'Everyone take a part and start cutting!' laughed the shock trooper, his eyes glinting in the darkness. Each began sawing a different body part and the screams of horror echoed through the night air. When finished, each of the shock troopers making up the formation returned with a grisly souvenir of their night's work: a finger here, an ear there. The heads were duly collected for the officer's collection for the cult of the commandant.

As the men marched back to their encampment, the embers of the fire still glowing and popping under the condensation of the spilled rot-gut used to dampen the flame during the brief attack, each shock trooper's face was chiseled with absolute concentration. There would be no more revelry tonight; now was the time to begin preparing for what was to come. The fire was reignited and a few of the men on watch edged their ragged blankets and makeshift sleeping compartments as near to the fire as possible, huddling beside the subdued blaze and cradling their machine guns in their arms. The other men went to their tents and, before going down for a few hours of sleep, laid out the weapons that they would soon be using on the remaining of the villagers who had supported the rabble that had attacked them. Resistance was not only futile, it was a bad move altogether. Now the punishment of the organization would reign down upon their heads like death angels from the heavens falling onto the earth.

CHAPTER 15

Back at the commandant's training facility, located clandestinely deep in the bowels of torture center within the commander's compound, within only a few weeks the young girl from the outlying areas named Lynx, since re-christened Bluebird by her initial punitive handler, Patty Hall, had begun to come into her own in the programming that the cult provided. As she was traumatized she was also built up in the process and the trauma was like building muscle, the muscle had to be torn in order to grow larger and more formidable. Compared to a life in the wilderness, the environs of the small area of the cult complex that she inhabited was progressive, despite the rigors she had undergone thus far. After undergoing several more nights in the gray bedchamber with the psychic driving mechanism which she was subjected to during the evenings, she had been moved to a dormitory-type setting which was populated by other girls and boys of her age and younger. That she was in fact one of the senior individuals present at the tender age of twelve heightened her sense of authority, along with the accoutrements she had gained from Patty after the corporal punishment episode during her first full day of training at the facility. The accoutrements had found a place in the various tool slots of her organizational jumper, some of them were used by others on her, some she used herself on others. The punishments had continued from other individuals her senior outside of the demographics of the dormitory, many brutal to the point that it made her initial interaction with Miss Hall seem like an amusement in comparison. During one situation she had been led into a large cell painted all black and with a high vaulted ceiling. In the center of the room was an athletic vaulting horse with thick chains and leather manacles attached. In the room with her were six internal security guards lined up on either side of the room and a huge man wearing no shirt but attired in the combat-style pants and balaclavas that the others wore. She had been given a large dose of stimulants beforehand which made her fight-or-flight psychology go into overdrive, accented with a dose of mild hallucinogens and her already natural overwhelming sense of paranoia.

Within seconds of entering the room she had been apprehended by one of the sentry-like guards and placed over the vaulting horse, her ankles manacled to the bottom and her hands equally immobilized on the other side. Her skirt had been lifted and her panties pulled down to her upper thighs, fully exposing her youthful posterior which was then summarily beaten with a huge leather strap attached to a wooden handle, wielded expertly by the shirtless and anonymous man. Her crying interspersed with shouts of pain became screams and then shrieks as her flesh reddened and welted and as the red marks became black and purple bruises, the sounds of her pain echoing eerily and singularly heard within the strangely built chamber, as her torturers made no sound whatsoever behind their anonymous masks. When she thought she could not possibly take anymore of the beating, the person doing the whipping exchanged the thick leather strap for a long metal cane that looked to be made from some sort of antenna. The consistency was thin and extremely whippy and as he began driving it into the ruined flesh of her backside with an ultra-fast 'swish, swish' her bruised skin began to break and tiny red rivulets of blood began dripping down the back of her pale white legs.

'There is only one person who can give you relief!' shouted a stern voice broadcast from some speaker high above her. 'There is only one person who can make the punishment stop!' The swish swish of the cane continued, her legs now covered with spiderwebs of dripping blood. Bluebird cried and began whispering to herself like a mantra, barely audible under her breath, 'Commandant, commandant, commandant.' Swish, swish, swish. Scream, scream, scream.

'Only one person can make this stop, only one person, but if it is her will then you should allow it to continue, will you allow it to continue?' The metal cane continued to rip into her backside and her screams began anew. 'Answer us, will you allow it to continue?' Beneath the strange luminous light from above one could see small specks of blood flying into the air from the ferocity of the lashing as the metal instrument unmercifully punished her exposed flesh. 'Answer us, answer us!'

IRON GATES

Through the confusion and the horror Bluebird managed to let out a screamed answer, driven by pain and whatever strange drugs she had been dosed with earlier. 'Let it continue, commandant, let it continue! Punish me, commandant, punish me!' The disembodied voice high in the ceiling changed from that of a male to the hearty laughter of a woman, echoing strangely. This must be the voice of the commandant herself thought Bluebird, her eyes lolling wildly, her tongue involuntarily protruding from her mouth in some heathen symbol of prostration. Oblivious to the metal cane which continued to beat her, she began crying in devotional ecstasy at having heard the voice, and then she too, like the voice from the speakers, began to laugh.

After her performance in that training ordeal and similar performances elsewhere it became clear to her handlers that she was one that was naturally gifted with a sense of obligation to fulfill the commandant's mission. Deep within the cavernous building, psychological experts from organizational intelligence attached to the commandant's experimental cult pored over the reports of her reactions and progress and gave her very high markings, recommending her career path to be accelerated by orientation toward the fact that she was also part of a political organization and recommending her toward the post of pontifex in the baby brigades in charge of persons of her own age range and beneath. Her reassignment toward the dormitory was laying the groundwork for just this purpose.

CHAPTER 16

The two internal security guards had marched through the night toward the position where they would wait for the arrival of the troopers from headquarters. As they reached the relatively exposed open portion of land they made their camp beneath a large copse of trees anomalously present in the middle of the field. They were not too concerned security-wise at this point, as they were now well within the borders of the organization's territory. Their purpose would be to lead the military contingent to the proper areas for engagement once they had arrived and to liaison with the contingent of shock troopers back across the invisible border. Within several minutes of setting up their temporary arrangements, purposefully small as they did not premeditate too long of a wait until the force from headquarters arrived, they heard a crackle and beginning transmission over the radio. It was the commandos who had been tracking the planned escapee from the operation on the hillside the day prior.

The commandos gave a full report to the internal security personnel in coded language in the remote case that anyone might be listening in. They had scouted out the entire area around the barn where the resisters were encamped and also looked out for any other outlying pockets of resistance linked to their syndicate. Other than a few particular houses in the village which had already been identified there was no other base areas except a few half-rotten sheds deep in the forest about three miles' hike into the woods southwest of the barn. The commandos gave their opinion that this would be the location that the resisters would retreat to should they be able to escape from an armed engagement or should they be allowed the opportunity to escape. The internal security personnel on the radio made note of all the salient points of the report on a small notepad while the other internal security member scanned the horizon looking for the sign of arriving troops. They would more than likely radio in when they were getting close to position however the exactitude of the liaison location had not been worked out completely and the security men wanted to be well ready to receive them and ready to hit the road once they arrived.

CHAPTER 17

Within approximately one week of Bluebird being housed in the dormitory residence hall it was clear that she was emerging and being groomed as a leader. She had not yet heard of the term 'pontifex' nor knew exactly what the organization consisted of other than the fact that it was presented to her as an arm of the commandant's cult which she was to take part in. As this was a reversal of the actual situation was interesting from a theoretical standpoint, however in terms of operability it made no difference. The intelligence plan creating the personality of the commandant and the cult surrounding her had been born from the intimate desires of the commander himself and for years had restricted itself to recruiting within the organization only in order to harden and magnify the already existent ultra-violence amongst its ranks. The situation of recruiting people from outside organizational territories, cold calls as they were termed, was a relatively new development. Children were specifically targeted for their potential to be built into something useful and worthwhile for organizational aims. Most of those who had reached adulthood living in the wilderness had become aberrant to the point that they were basically wrecks of human beings, unfamiliar with order, occupation and many of them without the basic ability to relate to anyone socially in any capacity whatsoever, having spent the majority of their lives communing with diseased nature amongst the post-nuclear wastelands.

Bluebird was something special and that could be well seen in the fact that her leadership abilities and ability to interact with her direct age peers and the younger children inside the dormitory was nearly automatic. That she had survived unscathed for so many years in the wilderness and had socialization amongst what almost amounted to a mobile children's colony did her credit. She had spent much time alone but her intelligence level created a situation in which the solitary time spent in a survivalist mode coupled with interactions with others in the wastelands that necessitated that she be canny served to her credit within her beginning interactions in dormitory life. Most of the children who were in the dormitory had been donated by their parents, most of whom were all either shock troopers or internal security members, the former being the highest amongst parentage demographics. A relationship between the sexes culminating in sexual intercourse and leading to conception and birth of a child could happen within a few days of similar military posting for the shock troops. As easily as they had come together they could just as easily be drawn apart, sent out for differing assignments in the field, to headquarters or smaller bases within the cosmos of the organization's territory or with the relationship purposefully being broken up by the officers in direct control of them in the interest of fluidity of military function or for other ulterior purpose.

For those, and especially for those who had already been inculcated with the mythos of the commandant, donating children in their infancy to the commandant's special schools was the best bargain. They would not only be freed from their domestic burden but they would also be unilaterally respected for their decision even by those who did not subscribe totally to the commandant's cult per se. Any unsubscription in this matter of course was a matter of preference, however that did not mean that those who did not actively participate harbored any innately subversive feelings or negative thoughts about the existence of the commandant's cult within their ranks. Rather, the commandant's image, the cult surrounding her and the vibration of her propaganda struck too close to home for some. While the organization obviously was not a moralist's organization and thrived in the doom-laden atmosphere of the post-nuclear world with veracity, the commandant's cult took certain filaments of that worship of destruction and honed them to a fine point. For some who worked in particularly violent fields within the organization, just hearing the name of the commandant uttered would cause their skin to crawl. While overarchingly psychotic in every way, shape and fashion, the commander was still at the end of the day a military figure, a people's leader who had achieved what he had gained through sheer will to power, unconquerable bloodlust and the spiraling mind of a military genius come from the womb. What the commandant was, how she came to be what she was and exactly what she was doing was entirely unclear to most, and this contributed to the many reasons why certain personages within the organization found her 'too much' at the end of the day and found their own solace in certain of the lesser cults also flourishing within organizational territory, most of them being controlled and formulated by organizational intelligence. Singular amongst the pantheons, only the commandant held the unique position of being considered nuclear death personified.

For those expecting the birth of a child that were not intimately familiar with the commandant's cult, frequently posted fliers on the numerous bulletin boards within the main headquarters complex, posted throughout the towns and villages under the control of the organization and circulated within propaganda sheets for shock troopers and internal security personnel on the field would inform them of the commandant and her willingness to take children on. The mortality rate of children within the organization was very high even for a social grouping existing in the post-nuclear landscape, as formerly many persons who had unwanted children would get rid of them early or, for the more sadistic and desperate, some couples would wait until they were born and torture them for some time for their own grisly amusement before harvesting them for meat. The political and military councils surrounding the commander began to get wind of the latter trend and while not necessarily bemoaning the level of brutality inherent in those who engaged in cannibalization of the children for want of meat for sake of practicality, this level of violent action coming about spontaneously was a sure sign that the killer programming of the organization was taking root in the blood. Their main concern however was that the councils did indeed take issue with the fact that the lives were destroyed on a private level where such a privilege should be the domain of the organization as a collective. While the straight-out organizational youth brigades accepted members for full training at as young of age as four, the parents were still at least somewhat responsible for maintaining the children up to that age. The organization was still not at the point where they could undertake totally communal raising of children on a large scale. The intelligence community running the commandant's outfit on the other hand was able to effect full-responsibility communal child-rearing on a minute scale with certain fail-safes in place, which was the most conducive environment in applying programming of proffered and extracted children in a much more severe and experimental fashion than what existed in the regular organizational youth brigades.

Unlike the regular youth brigades, donating a child to the program of the commandant - her special human garden if you will - was just that, a donation. At the point of signing over the child to the commandant's cult, the parents relinquished all rights to the child from that point on. Whereas the cult preferred that children within the organization come on only as infants (this assisted the breakage from the family unit further also due to the fact that within a few years the parents would certainly not even recognize their child, having relinquished it to the commandant's cult in its infancy), in certain cases the commandant would in fact accept older children, even up to the age of thirteen or fourteen years of age. Children within the organization at large would tell each other frequent rumor-driven horror stories about the sinister machinations that would occur when one's parents decided to give them up to the commandant and were warned amongst themselves to keep careful watch if they saw their parents discussing among themselves too in-depth or casting strange glances at them, as this was a potential sign that passing them over to the commandant was imminent. They would come at night to make the transaction and, before several hours would pass, said the children, they would be embroiled in a hell so complete that it made the most rigorous activity within the organization look like 'the old days' (not that anybody, even their parents, had any sort of clue what the 'old days' genuinely consisted of, yet the phrase was still bandied about among the less devout). The taking of older children was done with a special strategy in mind. It was more of a challenge in breaking them down in one respect, whereas the infants simply came up within the cult with no knowledge whatsoever of the existence of any other environment. Even within families that gave an older child to the cult who were avid followers of the commandant themselves, there was a large difference for a child between their observing rites, such as giving a piece of flesh or powdered stimulant before a picture of the formerly remote cult figure that was the commandant on their home altar in conjunction with their parents activities, versus being sent into a seemingly mythical nowhere where anything was apt to occur.

Bluebird had taken to the first several weeks of cult programming like a charm, even those who had been pushing the agenda of getting children from the wastelands to participate in this way were surprised at the applied acumen by which she had taken to the directions of the commandant heart and soul. The psychic driving techniques utilizing the headphones and various administering of narcotics had been in effect for several years now, however she had been one of the first taken from the wilderness on whom the technique had been tested in full force. The naturally rigorous life she had led up to that point and the sudden imposition of a structure where there had previously been none at all other than what she had imposed upon herself seemed to be part of the reason why she had proven herself so appropriate to programming. As well, certain of the harsher techniques, such as the bloody caning that she had undergone before being transferred to the dormitories, served to exhibit a successful test of the very limits of what the commandant's cult had achieved thus far in provoking a full-blown conversion experience on persons formerly unfamiliar with the commandant and her mission.

Part of the duties that Bluebird was proffered inside the dormitory included keeping discipline in check and being responsible for the general hardening up of the youth outside of their normal routines of testing and experimentation, performing the role of strict den mother rather than drill master. The nurses and the upperclassmen amongst the mid-to-late teenage set were responsible for the day-to-day training of the children in formal environs, however once in the dormitories there was the ability for the youngster to revert to previous ways of thinking and behaving. Bluebird was commissioned with the task of bringing the discipline and order experienced in the course of a day's (or night's, depending on circumstances) training and keep that discipline instilled during their time in the dormitory, extending into basic maintenance activities like ensuring that after-hours study continued to take place, bodily maintenance occurred regularly (bathing, personal hygiene), interpersonal relationships and activities were regulated and all-round enforcement of discipline.

To hammer that message home, Bluebird had been entrusted with a stout wooden paddle painted thick black and bearing a yellow imprint of a stylized vulture descending for the kill, which was the crest of their particular commandant youth unit in a formulation based upon the type of traditional insignia style used by internal sectors within armed forces units extending further than memory. Entering and leaving the building, each child would see the paddle and the potential punishment that they would experience at the capable hands of Bluebird should their behavior not prove up to par.

The dormitory was, as was the rest of the commandant's area, located within the deepest recesses of the most secret parts of the old penitentiary, in this case within a hidden clandestine annex to torture center.

It was not entirely underground as there were certain courtyards and open areas consisting of towers of three stories or more that existed in the internal parts of the building's infrastructure so that they could not be surveilled except via air. As the post-nuclear situation did not include airborne craft, this type of security concern did not come into consideration and thus created an atmosphere of total and secure isolation.

As the twilight fell in the dormitories the areas would be lit sparsely, relying as much as possible on the light coming in from the barred slits of the windows, by whose same light vicious murderers and other criminal elements of the old society had once been contained in the most secure conditions for the safety of the larger society. Now such areas were being used in a world where there was no outer society, the only society was the one that forged with brutal will its manifestation onto a hideous and unforgiving earth. It was on such twilights that those who impugned on the strictly ordered existence of the commandant's regime within the dormitories would face humiliating beatings with the punishment paddle of which all of them were starkly aware. Sometimes the punishments took place in front of the others and at other times Bluebird and her victim would repine to an adjoining room where the punishment would be laid on in unbridled ferocity with every ounce of perversity and controlled violence that Bluebird could muster. Sometimes the disappearance and extraction of a child amongst their ranks and the child's haunted, traumatized return sometime later would prove to be an even higher level of terror-instilling strictness than the public beatings. The concrete effect on the children could certainly be seen, as the depths of their internal world were psychotically shifted with the brutal instrument representative of the commandant's unquestionable authority.

The young girls in the unit were dressed practically identically to Bluebird herself (sans the courier pouch and various small disciplinary tools clipped to the slots of her jumper) whereas the boys wore short pants, black shirts and knee socks. Some of them who performed hazardous work during the course of their training had the benefit of wearing small, ankle-high boots. Both boy and girl alike were under equal dictate to the unmitigated will of Bluebird while within the dormitories, who stood as their cult mother, disciplinarian and ever-constant watcher. She actively encouraged her wards to inform on one another in order for her to possess the highest level of intelligence as to what occurred among her charges.

During the days when the students were operating within other occupations dictated by the cult and of which Bluebird was well aware and sometimes participated in herself, she would most often be drilled in organizational and cult indoctrination by various personnel throughout the commandant's center. The nurse who worked with her early on had not seen by her since, neither had she seen the sixteen-year old girl, Miss Hall, whom gave Bluebird the first taste of cult punishment and had provided her with her courier satchel, organizational handbooks and later a few disciplinary items for her to have on her person in premeditation of her dormitory position. Outside of Bluebird's knowledge, the nurse had been moved on to the position of a personal attache working with the commandant herself and had traveled to the area of the organizational conference to take place in the commandant's unprecedented and spectacular appearance after the unveiling of the organization surface-to-air rocket. Miss Hall had been whisked away on special assignment involving an advanced photo manipulation plot centered around extracting a certain shock trooper into punitive confinement via the auspices of the inquiry center.

Although her figure was slight, Bluebird's thin frame possessed a wiry strength which the other children feared in its oftentimes cruel application. She was an all-round mother to the children, instilling them with the ethos of the commandant and as such she was both the disciplinarian and also the principal caregiver. Whereas virtually all of the other children came from organizational territories, the fact that Bluebird was from the wilderness gave her a marked physical advantage as to her physical strength and constitution as she was used to covering much more territory and used to the open air which in general gave her a better degree of health than those cloistered within the various compounds and territorial schools, despite their having participated in organized physical training.

She herself had adjusted to the relative confinement of living within the cult compound well considering, and the lack of fresher airs had only served to birth a strange, hostile nature within her. As might be expected, due to her being on the cusp of puberty, she enjoyed punishing the boys particularly and often she would take advantage of her position and authority to conduct semi-public punishments within the confines of the dormitory to show her prowess in exhibiting the draconian side of her feminine nature. A small boy in particular of the age of six who had a certain aversion to her authority was often the target of her beatings. She would bark for all of the children's attention, at which point they would duly assemble in an orderly formation at the front of the dormitory, which, being formerly part of the prison, was arranged much like a barracks in a military basic training facility. Her two personal attendants would bring her a metal chair and she would begin by sitting and launching into an emphatic lecture concerning what was expected of them as full-time adherents of the commandant, reciting with her own special flourishes the information that she had been indoctrinated with through listening to the tapes that were provided to her by her handlers and her intensive study of organizational texts. After making her general introduction she would call out the person who was to be punished. Usually, rather than conducting several punishments at one point, she would scatter them throughout the day, schedule allowing, in order to assure that her ferocity was at its height. Often in the late afternoon session, as the dull glow of the afternoon sun illuminated the communal living quarters, she would choose that time for her most pronounced punishments, which often as not fell on the young boy. Calling him to the front and having him escorted prisoner-style with her assistants holding his arms on either side, he would be brought before Bluebird who would give him a stern dressing-down and then request that he remove the punishment paddle from the wall by the door.

Dead silence would ensue as the boy made the procession to remove the instrument, having to stretch to lift it over the hook upon which it hung. Once returning to Bluebird he was expected to present it to her with both hands, at which time she would take it and sling it by the strand attached to its handle over one corner of the back of the chair and then pull the boy toward her, informing him to remove his shoes and afterward his shorts and underwear which left him completely exposed from the waist down, wearing only his black shirt emblazoned with the commandant's principal organizational insignia. Thus disrobed, the boy would be pulled over her knee and the paddle retrieved, at which point she would pound into his backside until his buttocks were a dark deep red, his legs kicking in protest and tears streaming down his face. Bluebird always made sure that she punished until the child was visibly repentant, which translated in her reasoning as visibly humiliated and in pain. As much as the boy would kick, he could not dislodge himself from off her knee, being pinned down by her wiry yet iron-like grip. Once she had engaged him enough in this manner she would gingerly lift him off her lap and then stand, forcing him to kneel with his arms resting on the seat of the chair, his knees on the ground and his reddened buttocks facing the other students. She would then give him a paddling much more painfully executed than what was possible over her knee, arcing the paddle over her head before bringing it driving down onto his naked flesh, causing him to scream in protest again and again. When she was feeling particularly sadistic she would call up some of the boys of her own age who were beginning to experience the beginning of their sexual awakening. She had schooled these particular boys on her own time in private and, thus aware of what their members in an erect state were capable of, they would, at her request, go to the front and take turns sodomizing the younger boy, grinding their erections deep into his entrails and sometimes smacking the sides of his legs and his upturned rear as if they were taking a ride on some pathetic beast. Bluebird would watch these scenes with great relish, standing several paces behind the chair, her arms crossed in a mood of unabashed hubris, the paddle danging from her hand. She would array herself where she was assured a good look at the sobbing face of the little boy, making sure that he was experiencing just that much more pain and horror than the last time that she had administered similar discipline. Her stratagem was not in itself simply born from the burgeoning psychotic cruelty that had been cultivated and fanned to a fiery blaze by her cult indoctrination. She intended to take some of the younger ones like this, who had some streak of defiance against her authority in them, and cultivate lasting marks that would echo throughout the rest of their lives, causing the existence of a consistent subconscious flashpoint that could be activated so that such human resources could be used for particularly brutal assignments within the cult. Even at the seemingly tender age of twelve, Bluebird was instinctively laying the groundwork for her ascent in the career ladder of the commandant's grim mission.

IRON GATES

CHAPTER 18

Little nine-year-old Britta laid upon the filthy covers inside the soldier's hut, her firm stomach grating against the half-cured boarskin covering of the rough wooden rack. Across the room, his visage dimly lit by the burning embers of the fire, sat the field marshal; twirling his jet-black mustache which was amply seasoned by grease and the fat of a boar of not too dissimilar breed as the sort utilized for the resting place of his current night's pleasure. From the small slit in the canvas of the tent one could hear the frenzied flapping of bat wings and the ever-incessant alarm signal of the military encampment.

The field marshal and his personal security retinue had been recalled to headquarters from the field for several weeks now, however only recently he had received contrary orders; whether these orders were to his relief or to his chagrin he himself could not readily ascertain.

A few days' march from the organization's furthest border the field marshal had been told via radio transmission to hold off his march to headquarters proper and to reroute to a recent organizational encampment that had sprouted up on the territorial border to their south. The encampment consisted of a wide cross-section of organizational field operatives including internal security, death squads, commandos and shock troops from headquarters as well as regiments coming in from the field who had been involved in resistance skirmishes in the border territory.

His night's mistress, whom he had already enjoyed thoroughly, he had met spontaneously on the road during the first day's march toward the encampment courtesy of her adult handlers. Britta had been (and still was, her visit to his tent a temporary diversion) in the company of female members of the commandant's recruiters; strange, black-robed women known for their mystic airs and eerie chants and songs in praise of nuclear war personified in the person-deity known as the commandant. They had intersected with the field marshal some days before during the course of their march (he had spotted them long before they spotted him), the recruiters on their way back from the far territories with only the single female child in tow.

Apparently an internal security transport team who had been tasked to meet them and bring the recruiters and their new recruit to headquarters had not appeared and, based only on secret information of the landscape not committed to maps, they had themselves been traveling on foot for several days back to the borders of the organizational territory to fulfill their mission in an elsewise more arduous fashion. Upon meeting them the field marshal had volunteered to take them on to the makeshift encampment at the border to which he was now headed, from there they would be better able to make recontact with the appropriate sectors of internal security in order to bring their charge back to the commander's headquarters. In reciprocation for this favor, the leader among the commandant's recruitment party had offered up the flesh of young Britta to slake the field marshal's nocturnal lusts while along the march route. From his own perceptiveness and tell-tale signs during the night he understood that several of the commandant's lady recruiters had themselves in similar fashion provided their own more willing services to his personal guard detail. He remained appreciative of having been given license with the choicest among their number.

Arrival at the encampment had been a sight to behold. The field marshal knew little of what was transpiring along the section of the border to which he had been directed, having been well engaged himself in his own mission to date prior to his ordered diversion in course. It was deep during the night as he, his guards and the commandant's recruiters, engaged in hushed but animated conversations with their charge, had rounded a hill and found themselves observing nearly one hundred small campfires lit in the shallow valley below, around which crouched, like flies, small black tents filled with organizational shock troopers, internal security and support staff representing a broad cross-section of organizational expertise and tasking. A primitive guard tower hewn from logs and supported with black-painted corrugated metal sheeting stood threateningly among the scene, torches lit around its highest point and the commander's crest emblazoned on a black banner sheathing its side facing the border.

A few short radio transmissions later, the field marshal and his companions found themselves safely escorted inside the camp and provided with quarters, making preparation of their own tents unnecessary, a fact for which they were particularly thankful after the long march. The field marshal's personal guards, with his leave, took tents nearer to where some of the shock troopers were lodged but not too far from the field marshal's small wooden hut, so as to facilitate them some welcome comradeship amongst their peers after many weeks in the field with only their superior officer and occasional victim as company (the commandant's recruiters being the one exception) while still keeping them within shouting distance should he need them. The field marshal himself, the commandant's recruiters and the girl were directed to a spot not too far off but far enough away to be generally outside the brunt of the activity, that being a smattering of tents and primitive quickly-constructed huts inhabited mainly by higher members of internal security near a small copse of dark trees.

An internal security delegation attached to the situation planning committee behind the reason for the encampment's erection quickly made liaison with the field marshal upon his arrival in the camp, informing him that a full debriefing would follow in the morning and deferring further explanation until then as a courtesy. The commandant's recruiters, after arrival at their quarters, were obviously anxious to make haste in contacting their own appropriate internal security liaisons to facilitate the transport of themselves and their charge back to headquarters as soon as possible, which they premeditated to be effected the next day if they acted in haste. As a parting gesture to the camaraderie they had built with the field marshal during their tenure as travel companions, they left him Britta for one last night before her return to headquarters, her fate there which the field marshal himself could not guess.

IRON GATES

IRON GATES

CHAPTER 19

The weeks since Nadezhda's return to headquarters had gone by in a whirlwind of activity. She and the lieutenant had managed one more frenzied rutting after the commandant's appearance, the memory of which lay enshrouded within the strange haze of narcotics and cult-induced frenzy of the commandant's physical manifestation which brought all the attendees of the conference, herself included, to the fever pitch of organizational rapture. The lieutenant had been called away to parts unknown on secret work after the conference and she had no direct idea when she would be seeing him again, although she was almost certain that he would be making an appearance at the next scheduled event involving her father's weaponized breakthrough which he had been working on in close liaison with the commander's direct orders and instruction.

Since the conference Nadezhda had avidly taken up the cult of the commandant like many other leadership who attended but were not yet affiliated or committed at that time. Now a small shrine inhabited a corner of the tiny cell that she shared with another female code clerk, the bleak goggled eyes of the commandant watching over her from a small plastic-encased photograph which she worshiped by cult-prescribed methods daily, involving burning certain substances and chanting specific incantations in a certain way while focusing on the photograph and petitioning her blessings. As to codes, she had yet to break the coded message that had been inscribed on the back of the card the lieutenant gave her, and, after admitting defeat for her lack of ability to decipher it, she had taken it on a leap of faith that the lieutenant's intentions were as he said and she had inserted it, on the way back from an evening feeding at the communal dining hall, in the administrative secretary's drop-box after hours.

Within two days she had been called to the signal officer's desk at the code clerk office, the twenty-something-year-old man eying her with a look of incredulity as he held a small black dossier which he tapped lightly against the table.

'Well, Nadezhda, it looks like we will no longer have the pleasure of your services here at internal security administration, it's a shame, you are one of our best.' The man sighed with resignation and a slightly forlorn look passed over his face before straightening up, standing and handing Nadezhda the dossier.

'Here are your tentative marching orders. This contains your severance paperwork from intelligence analysis and a personal recommendation from my person on your good work over the past years, not that my recommendation is really necessary, all considering.' Nadezhda felt sure that this was a thinly veiled reference to her father's even more lustrous reputation as of late among organizational leadership during the last several weeks, as the signal officer too had been present during the conference, vetted as a speaker during one of the closed intelligence training sessions held on location.

'There is also a notice for you to report to the inquiry center at three o'clock this afternoon for further instructions - that's for your new job I assume, not for a hostile interrogation.' The signal officer managed a weak smile.

Nadezhda had been relieved of her code clerk duties immediately after she had been given notice by the signal officer, her junior co-workers taking possession of her code cards and charts and some of them vying for who was going to be able to take over her slot, which was enviable within intelligence analysis, although few possessed the professional acumen comparable to their predecessor. It only took a few minutes for Nadezhda to clear out the few personal possessions on her desk, dropping these and the dossier into a small satchel she kept with her at all times while on duty.

Her co-workers, a smattering of pale-faced and sallow individuals, waved with little enthusiasm as she left internal security administration for the last time, quickly returning to their tedious work of codebreaking and analysis of intercepted radio transmissions and organizational security memorandums. As she walked down the corridors toward the door to the walkways of the headquarters compound and out of the building she could feel herself smiling involuntarily. Soon her destiny would be leading her in an altogether more action-oriented direction, she could feel sure of it.

She stopped off at her quarters in order to unload a few of the items from her desk before proceeding to the communal dining hall for midday meal, carrying her satchel and dossier for further investigation while eating in order to kill two birds with one stone and save time. From the corner of her cell, the inconceivable visage of the commandant gazed stationary from her shrine. Nadezhda had been tempted to immediately access the contents of the dossier as soon as she had reached the semi-privacy of her own quarters, however the hours of the day were passing quickly and sooner than she expected she would be reporting to the inquiry center, not a good prospect on an empty stomach.

As she walked to the dining hall the sounds of drill masters shouting over loudspeakers permeated the atmosphere, with so many booted marching feet on the parade ground that she could feel the earth rumbling through the foundation of the concrete walkways which criss-crossed the compound leading to and from the numerous buildings. There had been an excess of activity on the compound lately, even according to the normal pace of headquarters life which was intense even during its calmest point. She knew that the formal unveiling of the commander's rocket built by her father, the prequel event which had been held at the conference, was now less than six weeks away. That being the case, no public notice regarding the event had been announced, the information at present only known to those who had attended the private meeting some weeks before and those who were privy to such information, herself included, were strictly prohibited from preempting disclosure regarding the same.

The type and pace of the activity at headquarters at present however, in contradistinction to the upcoming unveiling, seemed to spell more than a building up of internal security-driven protective measures for the commander's appearance and subsequent potential shock troop martial exhibitions. Rather, it bore the unmistakable feel of a major military buildup for a definitive offensive action the likes of which had not been seen in some time. The intelligence reports that had come over her desk during the last several weeks since the conference had belied nothing to this effect, however there was a definite feeling in the air that could not be ignored and, in light of the tone she ascertained among her contemporaries, she was not the only one who could detect the unmistakable scent of future bloodshed being prepared in earnest.

The sounds emanating from the parade grounds became muted as she entered through steel doors and into the corridor for the feeding queue. The cavernous mess hall was relatively subdued at this time of the day, being toward the tail end of the midday dining period. Several scattered tables were filled with teams of fifteen to twenty shock troops who were all invariably boasting loudly about their grisly adventures in the field, many of them laughing and gesticulating wildly with their spoons in between mouthfuls of thin speed-laced gruel.

Decidedly more subdued conversations were taking place elsewhere in the hall in groups of threes and fours, these personages being unmasked members of internal security and organizational intelligence, engaging in hushed conspiratorial discussions no less spirited and intense despite their difference in inflection. A dim roar of pots and trays being vigorously scoured could be heard from the other side of a small portal near the doorway of the mess hall where dishes were handed in at the end of the meal, while off to one side of the hall, which was mostly deserted, stood several strange women in black robes who stood by a table of propaganda and paraphernalia relating to the cult of the commandant, singing odes to nuclear death in arrhythmic, lilting voices.

Nadezhda moved through the queue and obtained her own bowl of thin gruel, a cup of thick, whitish beverage and a small dense block made from rendered fats and other flesh-based substances. The sounds of the singing women filled her head with reminiscences of her first vision of the commandant in the flesh at the conference and she felt her body tightening reactively, her hands assuming a white-knuckled grasp on her tray while a strange pointed feeling rose up within her, visceral to the very core of her being and bespeaking of violence beyond any known violence. As she sat down and began her meal she glanced toward the women and, from far across the mess hall, she could see the center among their number returning her glance - as the mouth of the cult member moved in her song of devotion her eyes gazed across at Nadezhda, twinkling in such a fashion that Nadezhda felt that the commandant's recruiters themselves could ascertain her own devotion even from sight. She had never seen these particular women before, however their dusty robes and thin countenances belied the fact that they had recently returned from somewhere in the field, and she had never encountered them at the small chapel where she had visited regularly in the weeks since the conference. The strange gray eyes of the middle songstress twinkled once more, filled with seemingly contradictory menace and delight all at once, and it almost seemed as if a smile crossed her face as she sang before breaking Nadezhda's gaze and nodding in cursory greeting to a small band of internal security personnel on their way out from the hall.

As Nadezhda began working her way into her meal she removed the dossier from her bag - small, black and not bearing any organizational seal on the outside. The signal officer's report recommendation was thorough and couched in the usual technical language found in organizational performance appraisals: 'Nadezhda Yatskaya continues to develop the skills needed to maintain the highest standards of professional excellence', 'Nadezhda Yatskaya writes reports that achieve maximum impact in their clarity and consistency in regard to applied intelligence', 'As a member of internal security administration, Nadezhda Yatskaya avails herself of all available resources and anticipates the needs of internal security and intelligence forces in the field.' The words 'Internal security and intelligence forces in the field' brought her mind around to the lieutenant. What was his present mission? What part of the organization's territory, or indeed beyond, did he now inhabit? A part of her very much wanted him to return to headquarters when she did, after the conference, however she had found his insistence on his preference for the field to be enlivening, what to speak of leading to a validation of her own professional ambitions by someone who amounted to a childhood hero.

Nadezhda's eyes lingered on the final note in the last part of the signal officer's recommendation: 'applied intelligence.' This brought her a supreme sense of satisfaction, for in torture center she herself would now have an opportunity to administer and practice this aptly named 'applied intelligence' in a much more hands-on fashion than she had been used to in internal security administration under the auspices of codes and intelligence analysis, which she herself considered, at best, to amount to glorified secretarial duty. The lieutenant had stressed his preference for the 'field' during his private conversations with her in his quarters at the conference base; Nadezhda believed, with every fiber of her grim intent, that torture center would be her own equivalent, the place that she could flourish in the mission of the organization, in the mission of the commander, and under the ever watchful gaze of the commandant.

CHAPTER 20

Little Wendy bent over the wooden barrel, exposing her pert backside to all present, albeit encased within the fabric of her plain, neutral-colored cloth dress. Still, the contours revealed were enough for any discerning party to take notice of, even though she herself was not yet seven years of age. As the wind blew audibly outside amidst the cold mountains, carrying the sounds of screeching birds of prey, accompanied by the grating of various metals and primitive machinery being utilized in the adjoining workshop, still, psychologically, it seemed quiet enough to hear a pin drop as the small entourage of the lieutenant's personal detail viewed the scene unfolding before their eyes on this particular afternoon.

The lieutenant approached the girl, lifting the dress to expose long, thin, white legs and miniscule white panties. As the latter were well worn and sufficiently dry-rotted as a result, it only took a firm grasp from the lieutenant at their hem and one brief motion to rip them off and asunder, said garment which the lieutenant then subsequently dropped without fanfare upon the filthy floor of the engineering center. With a booted foot the lieutenant kicked the girls legs apart one by one, forcing them to spread and causing her to clumsily attempt to find firmer grip on the barrel to balance her tiny frame.

With a deft motion the lieutenant unfastened the front of his trousers, withdrawing his solid member and plunging it into the girl. Noticing that the hymen had already been broken, he laughed to himself, considering which and indeed how many of the workers at the engineering center had enjoyed her singularly youthful pleasures to date.

The engineering center itself was located far to the north and slightly to the west of the commander's headquarters, inhabiting a region at the very limits of the borders of the northwestern territories of the organization. It was the beginning of the mountains that stretched into the western horizon, the looming ranges of what was once known as the Smoky Mountains and which still bore the curious phenomena of being seemingly drifted in a continuous dread fog as per its namesake.

The eastern ridges while marking the beginning of the mountains were already formidable in scope, with myriad and profuse great rocky outcroppings and huge forests, steep-graded and dangerous in proportion, as well as great drops into valley abysses along the primitive paths, an atmosphere requiring constant vigilance for the wayward traveler and seasoned inhabitant alike.

The mountain region had taken particularly well in comparison to some areas to the untold devastation caused by the nuclear wars by dint of its natural hardiness. A sudden and complete lack of commercial development had allowed violent and profuse reforestation and subsequently, like the rise of the wild boar population elsewhere in the organization's territory, certain rough and tumble species seemed not only to not have been too adversely effected by the devastation of nuclear war but rather to have flourished in the absence of an excess of human predators.

Great and mighty screech owls, black bears and grizzly bears were all in great profusion, the cries of the birds of prey upon the wind heard constantly and the tell-tale signs of the bears' presence (such as great jagged and craggy scratch marks on the trees and footprints along the path) made the traveler aware of their persistent presence. The black bears and grizzlies were able to eat the fish that swam in the streams with no ill-effect, enlarging their already considerable width, whereas the same which would often spell death for a human so consuming depending on the levels of residual radioactive content that might be present in the water.

The lieutenant continued to thrust into the young girl with relish and lusty enthusiasm, the silence remaining within the room and interspersed with only the girl's own soft sobs of resignation. With an animalistic grunt the lieutenant finished himself in the young flesh and pushed the girl off from him, causing both the girl and the barrel itself to go toppling onto the ground, eliciting a great ring of mirthful laughter from the members of the lieutenant's personal detail present who sat around the room on rough-hewn tables sipping a black, tarry-colored drink from tarnished brass tankards, the local moonshine made from dubious substances which was flavored with various roots and mountain herbs known to the locals.

A large internal security personnel member with a great black beard stood up from his table and moved over to the scene of the lieutenant's recent ministrations, uprighting the barrel to its proper position and grasping young Wendy lightly by her arm, lifting her up into standing position, said motion which caused her thin dress to automatically fall into place. Her face wet with tears, Wendy squirmed out of his grasp and knelt down onto the filth-encrusted floor, clutching her ruined undergarments which were now nothing more than rags, her weeping beginning anew and in earnest at the loss of her only other garment. The internal security member grasped her arm once again, more firmly this time but with some small, inaudible words of consolation before he began leading her toward the door.

As Wendy and her escort moved toward the exit the lieutenant brushed some spittle off his mustache and then refastened his pants. Noting the motions of the bearded organization member and Wendy out of the corner of his eye the lieutenant hissed for the party to cease their movement. Walking over to them with measured strides, he lifted the girl's hand which were grasping the pair of panties, lightly running his fingers over the worn fabric. Wendy's tears tapered off at the touch of the lieutenant's fingers upon her wrist and looked up at him, delicate eyes moistly glistening in the early afternoon light streaming in from the open doorway. The lieutenant let go of her hand and lifted his own hand to her face, gently daubing the tears beneath her eyes and smiling down at her before addressing his assistant.

'Go take this one down to the quartermaster and see if you can't get her a decent uniform, baby brigade fitting, full-weather operable, my personal crest attached. Get someone to clean her up, get her fed and keep her billeted in my quarters until this evening. I like this one, she is going to be a member of my personal entourage from now on, I do believe.' The lieutenant patted Wendy on the shoulder and then gestured with his hand briefly, at which point the internal security man and the girl departed, out the door and down a craggy mountain path, toward the lieutenant's encampment at the base of the hill at the crest of which sat the engineering center.

From the adjoining workshop the sound of a machine lathe winding down could be heard, ending in a rumble and an audible screech. Footsteps could be heard making their way down the wooden catwalk that served as the hallway between the workshop and the all-purpose meeting room and a few seconds later a figure appeared, stout, bald, bespectacled and wearing a leather apron, methodically wiping off accumulated soot from his hands with a red-colored rag.

'Lieutenant, it is good to see you again, comrade! It is always a pleasure to have you here at engineering, not only are you the most welcome and skilled headquarters liaison, in addition it's also exceedingly nice to be around someone from headquarters with a particular appreciation for the area!' The bald man grinned broadly, extending his hand in greeting.

'Engineer, it is good to see you at long last - I have been waiting with great anticipation for this meeting.'

The lieutenant gripped the bald man's extended hand, pumping it enthusiastically as he spoke.

'Let's go into the workshop, shall we?' The engineer gestured toward the entrance and the catwalk beyond it before turning to face the five men sitting at the varied tables sipping their grog and addressing them. 'You fellows continue to enjoy yourselves and help yourself to refills at your leisure, we'll be back in due course.' The lieutenant's entourage gestured with their mugs upraised in unison appreciation, at which point the lieutenant and the engineer disappeared behind the old rusty door leading to the workshop.

The lieutenant and the engineer proceeded to the workshop, chatting amicably along the way, both full of a certain gleeful mood due to their shared secret and complementary parts in a project that would prove to be one of the commander's most terrifying to date in his many long years. As they walked slowly upward along the rise of the covered catwalk the lieutenant could see through the slits in the wall planks the hints of the great mountainous forests that laid all around them, sequestering the engineering center in secrecy and arraying it, fortress-like, due to its sitting high upon the ridge as a natural fortification.

Everyone in the area surrounding the engineering center, sparse as the population might be, were all counted amongst the more qualified loyalists of the organization. The area itself was generally not visited by those within the organization, except for supply couriers and internal security members on organizational business and acting in the capacity of official review delegations. For those at and around headquarters and in the surrounding areas the mountain areas to the west had mostly passed from common memory. Even among those from the organization who had visited the outpost, few were aware of the location of the valley nearby which had been the site of a great massacre by the commander generations before.

Within organizational legend, this single act of mass murder on the part of the commander and the organization in its earliest stages was one of the reasons why there were no known autonomous parties anywhere else in the area, including the other side of the frontier. The details of the event itself lay lost in the history of the myriad excesses enacted by the commander during the formative years of the organization, yet, a lingering testament remained in the wastes of the valley, the form of an expanse of bony remains so profuse that many layers of skulls and skeletal fragments stretched hundreds of yards across.

The engineer and lieutenant reached the end of the catwalk and proceeded through a large iron-wrought doorframe which the engineer closed with a deafening clang behind him. The odors of smelting metal, chemicals and ozone hit the lieutenant full in the face, said smells which were only discerned in fractional amounts in the all-purpose room from which he had just proceeded and in the air around the engineering center itself.

The central workshop was a vast structure, more than likely the remnants of a warehouse which had been converted over decades for clandestine manufacturing purposes within the organization. The vastness of the structure contrasted with the relatively sparse workforce for a building of this size, a tell-tale sign of both global human depopulation as well as bespeaking of the extremely secretive nature of the work that went on inside.

The residents around the engineering center, diehard to the commander's cause one and all, were without exception absolutely stationary in their existence in the mountains. Due to the secretive nature of the work conducted they were inculcated, since birth, by organizational programmers with internal security-driven propaganda ensuring their insularity and continued blanket silence to inquiry. At the pinnacle of this posture of necessary compartmentalization, the inhabitants of the mountain region were also barred, without exception, from any travel outside of their own area. Even the engineer himself had never once been outside the area surrounding his sole place of work, not to headquarters, nor to liaison at the organization's clandestine armaments factory. The work here, on site, was too crucial for any chink in the armor of absolute security.

The engineer led the lieutenant into the center of the warehouse, passing by large stacks of corroded metal barrels and long worktables covered with various primitive instruments as well as several large pieces of electricity-driven machinery which, as ever, were linked up with the obligatory generators run on semi-fuel. In the distance, in one far, lonely corner of the warehouse, the lieutenant could spot an area that was roped off from the rest. In front of this area stood a small squadron of menacing internal security members, masked and goggled in anonymity, with severe black and shining fully automatic machine guns resting threateningly in their hands. Beyond them, behind thick plexiglass walls and a fortified air-sealed door could be seen numerous individuals in white coats, wearing gas-masks and carefully arranging vials of evil, blue-colored liquid with hands protected by rubberized gloves going up to their elbows.

'We are in the process of arming your test device even as we speak,' intoned the engineer, quickening his pace toward what appeared to be an entrance to a makeshift hallway created by heavy metal crates stacked high on either side that led toward a series of shipping containers that had been converted to closed workshop areas.

'The test device should be ready for you by morning. Mind you, it will only give you an idea of the more passive properties of the payload for the commander's warhead - the dispersal potential once fitted to the new unit will raise the devastation levels considerably.' The engineer chuckled to himself and signaled to two internal security guards who stood at the entrance-way to the makeshift hallway who stepped aside smartly, holding their arms to their sides.

IRON GATES

The engineer and the lieutenant then proceeded toward the engineer's personal workspace.

As they marched, the lieutenant noted with appreciation that there were a couple more internal security members stationed crouched atop the crates on either side of them, their presence only noticeable by the dread muzzles of their machine pistols which could be seen peering over the edge, ready to eradicate any unauthorized persons nearing the engineer's secure area at a moment's notice.

The lieutenant followed the engineer and stooped through a low door into the converted shipping container which was dimly lit with low wattage bulbs positioned over several long worktables filled with various devices and tools. At the far end the lieutenant could spy the engineer's personal altar which had a shrine to the commandant at its center as well as smaller shrines to various of the lesser-known and hideous gods who were worshiped in these parts and which were peculiar to this geographic region in particular.

Various flags of diverse organizational regiments and sectors as well as large posters of the commander graced the paneled walls of the workshop, the former representative of the many units who had been equipped with special weaponry by the engineer and whom had provided them with banners of their units, many of which had been carried into action, as a token of their appreciation to the continued unparalleled work done by the engineering center and the engineer himself.

On one side of the table the clutter had been cleared and a small device, shaped like a large, rounded bullet, sat upon small base.

'This is my prototype for the test device - an identical version, properly armed, will be ready for you at the security desk any time tomorrow morning for your field test at your leisure. The commander's warheads will be ready for your pickup as soon as you are done, our workers are doing their final safety inspection right now and crating them up for transport.'

The engineer reached into a low drawer and drew out a small handheld device, equipped with two buttons, two colored lights and a small antenna.

'This will work exactly like yours, except that once the device is triggered you will want to be well out of the way and wearing one of these for good measure.' The engineer used the antenna length as a pointer to tap a gas mask that sat nearby. 'Make sure you get a full seal when you put it on.'

'If you push this button, the device will arm.' The engineer pressed a black button, triggering a pale light beside it, at which point the device on the table emitted a low humming.

'As soon as the signal light is on, you are ready to go.'

After a few minutes, another light on the device

began a slow blinking.

'Press the black button, the light will go solid and dispersion will begin, like so.'

The engineer pressed the black button, the light beside it went solid and the sides of the bullet-shaped object began opening up slowly, spreading outward like the blossoming of a flower. A small hissing sound could be heard which continued until the filaments of the device were fully splayed outward.

'Tomorrow yours will be equipped with an ultra-light payload which you will see can cause considerable damage even in a relatively minute amount. The parcels for the commander will be filled considerably heavier.'

The engineer let out another small chuckle. The lieutenant smiled in response, patting him on the back.

'It's going to be quite a show before it's all said and done, comrade, quite a show indeed.'

The engineer smiled himself and then let out a sigh. 'If only I could be there to watch.'

The two organizational brass finished up their business and said their goodbyes until the next morning, and the lieutenant made his way out from the engineering center to his quarters near the base of the hill, as the sun turned the sickly orange of late afternoon that signaled that twilight would soon be near.

A demented grin flitted across the lieutenant's face beneath the thick, filth-encrusted mustache, and his spirits began to soar in a strange direction as he walked purposefully, nearing the perimeter of his encampment. He had other business to attend to before the night was out.

CHAPTER 21

The morning sun rose orange and strange above the cold encampment at the border area as the field marshal stood outside his hut, smoking solidly on a cigar that he had obtained while on site, his personal supply having long run out during his erstwhile march toward headquarters.

Britta had been whisked away in the deep of night, one of the commandant's recruiters entering his hut with a silent gesture of greeting toward the field marshal and thenceforth removing the child, throwing her old clothes into the still-crackling fire and draping the drowsy girl in a shapeless black garment similar to their own before departing. As they left, the field marshal had caught the girl's eyes one last time; they stared back at him blankly but with a cold harshness beneath that could be readily ascertained by discerning eyes.

Once the girl and her handler had left his hut he had walked outside himself, watching them and the others among the commandant's delegation steal into the darkness and become small dark specks negotiating the slight rise of a treeless knoll on the other side of the encampment. As they neared the summit, lights suddenly shone, two beams of headlights from a black, unmarked organizational van, black silhouettes of internal security members outlined in their light. Within minutes the lights and the people had disappeared, trailing into the distance, toward the east - toward headquarters.

The field marshal took one last long drag from his cigar which was rapidly becoming no more than a stub and threw the remainder onto the ground, snuffing it out with his boot. Shutting the door of his hut, he quickly walked along the perimeter of the encampment, avoiding the activity in the middle. At a certain predesignated point two of his personal security men fell in behind him, neither speaking as the three of them marched with purpose toward a large tent near the back of the encampment that functioned as the command center.

As they neared the tent a line of internal security members moved aside, allowing the field marshal entrance. The two internal security members attached to the field marshal's personal security detail remained outside, talking in low voices to the personnel conducting security for the encampment's command center.

The field marshal entered and was greeted by high-ranking brass from both internal security and one of the most feared shock troop regiments within the organization before being offered a seat at a long table that was covered with various maps and documents. At one far end of the table sat a masked internal security member, acting in a secretarial position, typing reports on a small laptop. As soon as the field marshal was seated, the internal security representative began the briefing.

'We want to first of all express our gratitude that you were able to liaison with us so quickly in this matter, field marshal. Your reputation precedes you within the organization and insistence on your participation in this venture came from the very highest level.'

The field marshal's face remained blank, however he felt satisfaction at the wording utilized, intimating that his diverted route to the encampment was requested by direct representatives of the commander himself. The internal security representative cleared his throat before continuing.

'We are in the process of a significant force buildup that will reach several-hundred more personnel on the ground before fighting season commences. From headquarters we have been informed that action will begin in less than two months' time. There is a hostile populace of semi-organized resisters located several clicks over the southwestern border here...' The internal security representative pointed to a small circled area on the map that the internal security secretary had placed between them.

'There are already several contingents of commandos, shock troopers and signal intelligence on the ground in the direct vicinity that have been working the area for awhile now. The area is an old semi-rural town with medium populace, however there is a small faction of resisters who have been radicalizing them and have engaged in some harassing fire against organization elements patrolling the area. The resisters have some informants among the population who are passing on information about organizational activity in the area as they observe it. There was a punitive raid a few days ago which resulted in an attempted ambush near a small shock trooper encampment, since then signal intelligence and commandos have been tightening the noose. Interaction between the organization and the resident populace in the area in question has been relatively muted - no propaganda teams, no recruitment, only the occasional strike and continued surveillance. The commander is pursuing a policy of building up animosity.'

This piqued the field marshal's attention.

'From what we have been told the commander has this area pegged for a future experimental zone - thus no forward processing as of yet. The people on the ground in camp at present are going to be part of a mopping-up operation after a decisive strike of some magnitude. The contingent that is going to come from headquarters several weeks from now will be part of an intelligence and security deployment that will be engaging in semi-permanent occupation once we have finished the initial cleanup.'

'What sort of decisive strike does the commander have in mind?' inquired the field marshal.

The internal security representative raised his eyebrows before a look of clarity came across his face.

'That's right... you weren't at the conference, were you?'

The field marshal grunted in reactive response before

speaking, 'Unfortunately not, was on assignment elsewhere during that event, although had some foreknowledge of it from headquarters, communications have been sparse since then, however.'

The internal security representative motioned one of the shock troopers toward a large pile of wooden crates that stood in the back part of the tent behind the desks.

'Perhaps this will give you an idea.'

The shock trooper removed a small iron implement from his utility belt and popped open the top crate, removing a gleaming rubber gas mask which was obviously of pre-nuclear war grade make.

The field marshal leaned forward in his chair to get a better view and then sat back, smiling appreciably.

'What's my direct role going to be in the forthcoming mission, then?'

The internal security representative smiled in response.

'Coordination of troops on the ground, first wave in.'

IRON GATES

CHAPTER 22

Nadezhda arrived at the inquiry center well within fifteen minutes prior to her scheduled appointment, checking in with an internal security member, anonymous as ever, who had met her at the end of the walkway leading to the building, obviously having already premeditated her arrival for some time. The reception had both pleased her as well as filled her with an unmistakeable sense of dread, as the sudden presence of the armed, balaclava-clad internal security member could denote a myriad of potential outcomes. At present, however, and in consideration of the pointedly ghastly nature of her desired work assignment, she passed off the method of receipt of her person at the inquiry center as a professional courtesy and followed the security guard, who gestured to her with a wordless nod of his submachine gun toward the door.

The internal security member and Nadezhda proceeded to the doorway under a large archway straddling the roof of the inquiry center, on top of which could be seen several heavily armed guards scanning the area, the snouts of their lethal weapons matching in synchronized sweeps the slow survey of their eyes, obscured beneath their masks and heavy black tactical goggles. The internal security guard accompanying

Nadezhda waved his leather-gloved hand to an unseen operator behind the thick glass of the entrance-way to the former inmate hospital and an audible click was heard from the door which was then opened, the internal security member ushering Nadezhda forward.

The processing area of the center was empty excepting the sole internal security guard and whomever was behind the thick glass of the entrance-way operating the external doors. Grasping Nadezhda's upper arm lightly, the masked internal security member led Nadezhda further into the inquiry center, stopping after some distance at a door, halfway down from which in the corridor could be seen the red slash of line painted on the floor that led to the secure area. Somewhere beyond this threshold, Nadezhda knew, lay torture center and her potential destiny.

The internal security guard gave a sharp rap on the door facing them before a buzzer sounded signaling that the door had been unlocked by central control of the facility at which time she was ushered in, the guard accompanying her into an office-like setting and shutting the door behind him before stationing himself in one corner. Before her sat a middle-aged internal security member behind a large desk, bald and wearing the telltale uniform of internal security yet bearing no insignia or rank which was in contrast to herself who still bore the small patch designating herself as a member of signal intelligence.

Behind the desk, enshrined in a large glass frame, was an ominous black flag, denoting an organizational branch unknown to her, framing the unknown person at the desk. The insignia on the flag, bearing crossed rifles and a strange symbol, unknown and seemingly alien to her own eyes yet infinitely ensconced with the atmosphere and suffuse with the burning unflagging will of the commander and, to Nadezhda's reckoning, likewise the commandant as well. That it was framed was further indicative that the person sitting behind the desk and the detachment to which he was assigned were of a decidedly high-tier status.

The bald officer rapped his fingers in rhythmic fashion on the desk, drawing the last desperate dregs from what appeared to be a rather ancient cigarette before snuffing out the miniscule remainder in a heavy ashtray of equally pre-apocalyptic make and model. Nadezhda stood, confident yet unsure in the uncertain surroundings, several paces from his desk. With a wave of his hand the officer indicated a chair stationed across from the desk and she responded in kind with a nod and quick movement, taking the seat which had been proffered her.

The officer pointed the finger of his right hand toward a leather-covered dossier which lay before him on his desk, smiling coldly at Nadezhda.

'So, we understand that you are to be surged into the position of SAC for torture center? Per the favors of your father or perhaps rather the lieutenant?'

The officer's smile widened into a leer as Nadezhda continued to sit before him, silent.

'Take a look at these photographs.' With a purposeful motion, the officer slid the leather dossier across the desk toward Nadezhda, who in turn shifted her chair forward for better view.

Opening the dossier she saw two photographs of herself from several years prior, encased in a sheet of clear plastic. The plastic was partially stained in places, appearing to be blood or other bodily fluid that had been wiped away carelessly. In the photograph she had been sitting on a bench within the compound and by the specific area and age of the photograph she knew exactly when it had been taken. It was taken three years prior when she had just begun her job as a member of internal security signals intelligence, and she had been waiting for her father to arrive from the commander's clandestine armaments factory to headquarters where he was scheduled for a liaison with ranking brass the next day. The photograph had been taken from a concealed vantage point, without her knowledge. Her mind began to race for how exactly to respond; she chose the direct route.

'Well, that's me, officer.'

The officer's leer turned downward into a grimace.

'I know that's you, what's the context?'

'I don't know the context, officer.'

'The context, Miss Yatskaya, is a damned security breach.' The officer slammed his opened palm onto the surface of the desk for emphasis, causing the photographs in their individual slipcases to move several centimeters askew.

IRON GATES

The officer snaked his hand across the desk and slid the dossier back toward him, flipping further into its covers and removing a small stack of papers with a small identification photograph tacked to the left-hand corner. He sat reviewing the document for several minutes, lighting and smoking another cigarette in the process, not speaking and allowing the tension to build. After he seemed satisfied with his review he held up the front of the papers toward her, making her squint across the desk for a proper view rather than handing it to her. A blank-faced shock trooper stared back at her from the photograph, the legend PVT BONN could be clearly read under the larger header reading ECTAC. This was her first on-hand view of an inmate file.

'Recognize this one, Miss Yatskaya?'

'Never seen him before in my life, officer.'

'Take another look.'

The officer removed the photograph from the stack of papers and slid it across the table to her for a closer view. She picked up the photograph and stared at it intently. The shock trooper in the photograph was unremarkable in every respect. Clean-shaven, cropped hair and the abysmal, blank stare typical to lower-ranking members of the shock trooper regiments stationed at headquarters who were usually in one of various states of being broken down by training and many of whom had yet to taste the carnage of the battlefield which she knew of by proxy through reports in signals intelligence. She placed the photograph back down on the table and slid it across the desk back to the officer.

'I have never seen him before in my life, officer.'

'Well, he says that he has seen you, he says that he has had sexual relations with you, is this true?'

'I've never seen him before, officer, so I would consider his claim to be erroneous in this respect.'

'It's your word against his, Miss.'

Nadezhda frowned at the patronizing tone of the officer and the familiarity of lack of formal address.

'Whose word would you be more inclined to accept, officer?'

The officer didn't respond but instead waved to the internal security guard who had been stationed behind her. He moved forward and placed his gloved hand, lightly but with firmness of intent, on her shoulder.

'Take her down to see the prisoner, guard.'

With that the officer stood and extended his hand toward Nadezhda, who grasped it and shook it out of a sense of ingrained automatic etiquette, this type of familiarity also strange but not in the negative sense as before as it was usually not the custom of superior officers to shake hands with their lessers within the course of organizational protocol.

'It was nice to meet you, Miss Yatskaya,' the officer said with a sense of sincerity, dropping his hand back to his side. 'I don't think that we'll be seeing each other again.'

Nadezhda's eyes raised and with that and one last look toward the bald officer, the strange insignia behind him and his office, Nadezhda was led out by the internal security guard, now grasping her upper arm lightly, leading her down the hall and across the red line on the floor which marked the beginning of the secure area. Her lips whispered a silent prayer. Her fate was now totally in the hand of the commandant's good graces.

IRON GATES

CHAPTER 23

The lieutenant fastened a large survival knife with a razor-sharp, serrated edge blade onto the side of his belt before leaving his tent, bracing himself against the cold winds of the mountains which blew in from the north. Within his line of vision he could see the foothills stretching for miles and miles, entering seamlessly into the main ranges of the mist-shrouded Appalachians. The sun had nearly set behind the hills and the area and the forests in which his encampment had been made was lit by an orange glow of the fading daylight as twilight approached.

It had only been a few hours since the lieutenant left the engineering center and, knowing that he had intended a full schedule during the evening as well as the main experimental action in the morning, he had taken it upon himself to utilize the time for some private rest and contemplation within his tent in the meantime. Now the lieutenant strode toward the small wagon holding the quartermaster's stores. At the sound of his booted footsteps outside of the wagon a small, wiry internal security guard appeared, his mask removed and thin face covered with the sort of scars that were tell-tale signs of frequent engagement in hand-to-hand combat training. The man quickly lit a lamp hanging from pole, providing a pale working light for the area to stave off the encroaching night.

'Quartermaster, how are you enjoying this fine evening?' the lieutenant asked, a smile stretched across his face.

'Excellent, lieutenant, excellent. Also, as you will be pleased to know, your young charge has been properly outfitted and is waiting in the tent near the forest's edge.' The quartermaster pointed toward a small tent stationed near an outcropping of mighty oaks that descended down a ridge toward earnest wilderness. A small fire burned outside it, causing ghostly shadows to dance against its closed entrance flap. The lieutenant could feel a sadistic stirring in his mind and the throb of unmistakable arousal in his loins - he had been well-rested since his encounter with the little girl earlier in the afternoon and was overdue for a second course.

'Splendid to hear, quartermaster, splendid to hear - we as ever appreciate your attentiveness in this regard. In the matter of my young charge, her name is Wendy, as you know...' The lieutenant smiled blankly, his eyes transfixed on the distant tent. The quartermaster bobbed his head happily, rubbing his hands together, warming them against the night air.

'We will be going on an expedition later, not too far off, but it will be in a particularly dark spot.'

The quartermaster's eyes widened at the lieutenant's words, for by this subtle but direct indication, for those in the know, it could be ascertained readily to what destination the lieutenant and his girl would be headed.

'And you will be needing some stout torches I assume?'

'Precisely, quartermaster, precisely. As well, pack a few small provisions, some meat and whatever grog you can find in a bottle - doesn't have to be fancy, rough would be preferred - by way of an offering.'

'Right, sir, right away, lieutenant!' The thin figure of the quartermaster chuckled to himself and began to busy himself about his business, tying off torn rags on the ends of stout staves cut from mountain hardwoods and dipping them to soak in a large vat of black-colored fuel near the far side of his wagon.

'How long to have all this together, quartermaster?'

'Within fifteen minutes, sir, it will be ready for you to go, we'll have it here waiting for you when you're ready to go, should you wish to have a bit of fun in the meantime.'

The quartermaster's eyes met the lieutenant's in a knowing grin, their eyes sparkling coldly as twilight descended in full upon their encampment at the base of the hill, the churning of grim machinery and the sounds of hammering echoing across the valley from the work at the engineering center located at the hill's peak. The lieutenant nodded in silent acquiescence to the quartermaster's implied recommendation and headed toward the little girl's tent as the quartermaster continued about his business in preparation of their nocturnal expedition.

Within a few minutes the lieutenant traversed the area, barren of other party members, that led from the quartermaster's wagon to the auxiliary tent and the forest beyond. Stopping at the small fire that burned outside her tent he listened quietly for any sounds from within, warming himself against the cold by the fire and withdrawing a small metal flask from his jacket which he slurped from greedily, its caustic liquid burning hot as it made its way down his throat and into his stomach. At exactly that moment he noticed a stirring at the entrance to the tent, the drape was pulled back and Wendy stepped through, framing herself at the entrance-way of the tent.

The lieutenant noticed with appreciation the transformation that had been caused by only a few hours under the care of the quartermaster and the attentions of a more centralized organizational unit. Her hair, almost shoulder-length and as black as the coal of her mountainous home, had been oiled and pulled back with a small fastener revealing a recently freshly-scrubbed face, white and ruddy with the night air. Instead of a torn, moth-eaten dress of indeterminable color, her lean and youthful frame was now encased in the sleek and startlingly black uniform of the organization's baby brigades in its full-weather version which included sturdy black combat boots and a small coat with a hood which was currently thrown back, framing the back of her neck.

The lieutenant took another swig of liquor from his shiny metal flask and then stretched it out toward Wendy, inviting her to share the drink and the warmness of the fire. Her gray eyes stared toward him and her lips parted ever so slightly which she wetted with her tongue before moving toward the lieutenant and the proffered drink. Her movements were crisp and purposeful and her body, not yet seven years of age, had been hardened again and again by the everyday rigors of living not only in a landscape ravaged by the nuclear wars but in a secret and disciplined wilderness outpost of the commander's design and purpose. Compared to children of comparable age in the decadent and soft societies that were prevalent before the great conflagration her mind and body was, despite its slight constitution, pure steel, pure predator in nature.

Wendy took the proffered flask from the lieutenant in her small hand and tilted it back, swallowing deeply the fiery liquor which the lieutenant kept in his stocks as he traveled on various organizational assignments. While the grog that was served at the engineering center was equally potent and in some respects more so due to the varied ingredients which could oftentimes be found within it, the liquor that the lieutenant kept with him was of a much more quality distillation, usually only circulated among the higher ranks within the organizational internal security apparatus. The little girl's eyes glazed over with unconcealed pleasure at the drink and turned her gaze toward the lieutenant who with a nod encouraged her to take another, which she did with pleasure. After a second draught she handed the flask back to the lieutenant, wiping her mouth with the back of her hand. The lieutenant took another drink himself before secreting the flask back into his jacket while Wendy looked toward him, musing upon the small beads of the liquor, shining crystalline, that had been caught in the hair of his thick mustache.

The lieutenant knelt and Wendy moved toward him, her arms outstretched, coiling around his neck. He picked her up, one hand cradling the soft contours of her backside and the other grasping her to his chest. She cooed softly as he began kissing the soft contours of her face and neck, her body shuddering under the heightened sensuality effected by his soft caresses and the general physical care that she had experienced during her several hours being attended to by the lieutenant's organizational sector.

The lieutenant's mouth met her own and she reciprocated in kind, both of their breaths smelling of distilled liquor, the extreme softness of her small lips driving the lieutenant toward ever-careening heights of pedophilic lust. His hand gripped her small buttocks even tighter as she hungrily kissed his mouth, biting at his lips. A low growl emitted from beneath the lieutenant's mustache as he walked with her in his arms, away from the fire, kicking open the entrance to the tent with one booted foot and falling to his knees, releasing Wendy in prone position onto the ground-level military bedding. He moved with predatory speed, lifting her ankles and rapidly unlacing and removing her black combat boots and then unbuttoning and pulling off in one quick motion her combat fatigue pants.

As she had fallen lightly onto the bedding within the tent her head had secreted itself inside the hood of her jacket which had been thrown back when she had left the tent earlier to investigate the lieutenant's arrival. This cowled appearance, in conjunction with the flickering light of the fire outside their tent, caused her to assume the appearance of some fell monk, sheathed within a hellish glow. The lieutenant massaged the soft white flesh of Wendy's pale thin legs and the curvature of her buttocks, snaking his hands under the black fabric of her baby brigade issued undergarments before removing them as well and unbuttoning his own trousers, removing his pulsating member, eager to plunge into the waiting flesh of his newest concubine.

As he entered into her, her lithe legs wrapped around him automatically, her mouth panting in response to his amorous attentions which her young frame was unable to fully comprehend or enjoy despite the many times that she had been bedded by the sometimes bleak-eyed and grim and often wildly intoxicated workers in some grimy corridor or remote backroom at the engineering center. Despite this, she sensed something altogether different with the lieutenant. He was, on this night, more attentive than his brutal taking of her earlier on the hill in front of his men, yet this same gentleness belied an inherently deceptive posture. Whereas most of the workers at the engineering center and the men in the surrounding area had always been easy for her to case, there was something both deeply attractive and deeply unsettling about the lieutenant. He was dangerous in a much more pronounced fashion for, whereas it was an open secret among the mountain folk that the engineering center's purpose was to create instruments of death (as it indeed was, though as they were quarantined to the area for life there was little chance of this information leaking elsewhere), it was people like the lieutenant who were the wielders of these instruments in all their gory and hideous strength. The lieutenant was dangerous, yet also infinitely powerful - it was this power that attracted Wendy and perhaps it was this attraction that had caused her to be selected. Quarantine or no quarantine, she now wore the uniform of the baby brigades and she had every intention of leaving the area with the lieutenant on the morrow; whatever means might be necessary, she was willing to take them.

As the lieutenant neared his sexual climax he began hissing and growling, his bloodshot eyes lolling in ecstasy as he held onto the lower hem of Wendy's jacket in each fist, moving her entire body toward him again and again in rapidly accelerating rhythmic fashion, allowing him to penetrate deeper and deeper into her flesh. With a final brutal thrust the lieutenant climaxed, veins popping from his neck and both he and Wendy's foreheads glistening with the perspiration of their endeavors despite the cold.

Both Wendy and lieutenant stood up in unison, Wendy's head still cowled in her black hood as she stepped into her pants and fastened them back into position. She picked up her boots and began to step into them as well however the lieutenant placed a restraining hand on her shoulder.

'Here,' he said, motioning her to sit upon a low crate in the corner of the room. She complied, taking a seat, and the lieutenant replaced her combat boots over her black-socked feet, lacing them up with somewhat less speed than he had unlaced them, still affected by post-coitus languor.

'Lieutenant...' Wendy spoke the word that was both his rank and his only known name, her voice feminine silk to the ears of the hardened organization man.

'Wendy...' said the lieutenant, interrupting her stream of speech and resting one hand upon her thigh, the task of lacing up her boots accomplished. The little girl's eyes gleamed with pleasure at the sound of her name.

'Lieutenant, you said that I am going to be part of your 'personal entourage.' Does that mean that I am going to leave with you, leave the engineering center I mean?'

The lieutenant looked at her squarely, examining her face framed in coal-black hair with lust, lust that was almost close to reawakening instantly despite his recent slaking of the same.

'Wherever I go, you will go.'

A look of confused anticipation crossed Wendy's face as she paused before responding.

'Lieutenant, people from the mountains, our people, from the engineering center, we never leave the mountains, are never allowed to leave the mountains - it's a security mandate.'

The lieutenant looked at her discerningly before raising his hand and curling his fingers into a fist. Wendy winced automatically, premeditating that the gesture was a precursor to a blow, yet she steeled herself from cowering before the authority figure before her - if she was to become part of his entourage, she wanted to show her fortitude early on.

'Do you see this fist, Wendy?'

Wendy nodded.

'This is the fist of the commander's dictatorship, this fist makes the law - what I say is secure, is secure, who I say goes, goes, who I say stays, stays. And I have decided that you and you alone will go, anyone who speaks of it will be dealt with. If I say you are a god, you are a god, do you understand?'

'Yes, lieutenant.' Wendy spoke, yet her mind still processed, the lieutenant was reckless, insane even, yet apparently was set on taking her out of the mountains, which was more than she could have hoped for; he had made the decision himself without her having to resort to any subterfuge of her own.

The lieutenant smiled, opening up the entrance to the outside and gesturing for her to exit with him. She did so, he exiting last, his eyes opened wildly, staring at her uniformed figure in admiration, lust and a yearning for something he could not quite ascertain yet might be revealed during their expedition, the time for their departure for such being well nigh. Yes, she would be principal to him from here on out. Should anyone have a problem with his smuggling the girl from the secure area that would rest on them, he was known for breaking the rules from time to time without great problem, he was the commander's man - his word was law.

The twilight had now given way to the type of darkness that can only be seen in the wilderness and indeed, darkness such as this had never been seen at all prior to the nuclear wars for now no lights from even distant cities penetrated the night skies, for those cities, their people and their infrastructure were long since perished, the satellites which monitored them from space now orbiting in limbo around a harsh post-nuclear landscape that had been plunged into a new Dark Age from which it might never come out.

The lieutenant looked up into the firmament, filled with stars and planets whose names he did not know but which he identified with various extraterrestrial powers of evil, powers of evil which could be accessed through certain vectors known only to the most adept black wizards within the organization, powers of evil which kept the commander, and those under his control, ever at the zenith of power on the terra firma.

Wendy stood stonily, her face staring into the embers of the fire before her tent. The lieutenant approached her and put both hands on her shoulders, looking down into her face which turned upward, her eyes meeting his.

'If I say you are a god, then you are a god....' he mused, almost as if to himself alone. His eyes refocused on the little girl.

'Perhaps you are a god, a new god. We will see, in time, we will see. For now we must go to meet another new god, not quite as new as you - but very vicious.'

A cruel smile broke across the lieutenant's face and, grasping her hand in his own, the pair turned their backs to the fire, walking across the empty expanse toward the quartermaster's wagon and, from there, their nocturnal assignment as yet unfulfilled.

CHAPTER 24

An iron gate clanged shut as the last of Bluebird's dormitory entered into their residential quarters at the commandant's training center, deep within the bowels of the torture center housed within organizational headquarters. As she continued her intensive training she had been informed that the commandant's training center was also known as the 'torture center annex' and that a special participant would soon be arriving with whom Bluebird was to be intimately involved. She had also been formally conferred the status of pontifex, which she understood to be the supreme authority rank among all the dormitories of the commandant's children trainees and would eventually confer her a status as a very close accessory to the commandant herself. Her understanding of her authority position at present did not extend far beyond her firm control of the dormitory - identifying heart and soul with its crest, the training of its residents and the punitive implement which hung upon the wall in dire warning to any who would defy her. Outside of the dormitory and away from her juniors she continued to be drilled harshly in the course of multiple experiments, indoctrination sessions and physical exertions. Even activities that would in normative contexts be considered classroom sessions, such as listening to lectures or perusing stacks of flashcards assisting her in learning the names and nature of various organizational sectors, possessed the unmistakeable elements of torture and abuse.

When she failed to properly identify an obscure organizational standard etched onto a flashcard just a few days prior, as an example, she had been made to march to the front of the cavernous cement room in which her lessons took place, alternately administrated by some harsh female her senior or an anonymous masked internal security guard. Upon reaching the speakers lectern, behind which at this time had stood a masked member of internal security, presumably male, she had been made to present the offending flashcard as well as the small leather punishment strap that hung on her jumper to the teacher, the latter which she herself had used many times on her charges within the dormitory. Placing the flashcard inside a hollowed out cabinet in the speakers lectern, the internal security guard proceeded to grab Bluebird by the hair, forcing her head down into the cabinet facing the flashcard and forcing her hands to stretch out grasping the sides of the lectern. Her skirt was raised, her panties lowered and the lashings of the strap came down forcefully and continually until her backside was marbled black and purple with bruises. All the while the security guard shouted in an inhuman voice one word, over and over again, 'RECALL! RECALL! RECALL!' When the beating had finished the shouting continued, as the internal guard reached around to reattach the strap to her jumper

IRON GATES

before plunging a gloved finger into her rectum, anally raping her until she could repeat the proper rank designation audibly and clearly enough to be overheard above his own shouted commands. At this point Bluebird was released, and marched out of the classroom and to a nurse's station where she would be injected with a large syringe, the contents unknown to her but which always effected in increasing her violent propensities. Soon thereafter she would be unleashed into the dormitory where she would descend like a whirlwind upon her charges, as hateful and merciless as the commandant herself.

It was in her fourth week after a similar session where the punishment had been somewhat more cursory (this time administered by a steely-eyed female who had given her several hard swats bent over her desk, given because she had been dozing while viewing a photographic account of the commander's weapons advancement programs in the years following nuclear fallout) that instead of her usual visit to the nurses station her course had been rerouted to an area which she was unfamiliar with.

Two masked internal security guards led her along the black-painted concrete block corridors up a slightly ascending path, turning along several bends and then entering a stairwell, climbing several flights of stairs, each one covered in hard rubberized coating that was beginning to fracture and chip with age. At last they reached an open corridor painted an anonymous but not unpleasant gray and proceeded to the middle of three doors along its length which was flanked by two chairs on either side.

One security guard raised a large gloved fist and gave three resounding bangs on the steel door, a muffled sound of acquiescence came from within in response and the door was opened and Bluebird was ushered in with the internal security guards closing it behind them, stationing themselves in the chairs flanking the doorway, resting the muzzles of their deadly automatic machine guns on the worn wooden armrests.

The room was large but not so much that it gave an impression of severity like in the dormitory or even the classrooms in which she spent much of her time that was not engaged in disciplining and spying on her charges. The ceiling was lower and covered with various glossy colored posters relating to the commandant's cult, one in the center of the back wall of the room which she now faced being the most prominent, nearly life-size in scale and featuring the commandant in all of her deathly glory, her black helmet of fine mesh and one bleak bar of horizontal goggle lens obscuring any humanity that might lie within, garbed in her shining black suit of skintight design and equipped with various instruments hanging from her thin nylon belt that by sight promised to be implements of excruciating torture, her form superimposed over an image of a reddish-orange mushroom cloud.

Beneath the largest poster of the commandant set a large blue divan which was unoccupied, beside it a smaller one of similar color upon which sat a small girl, from appearance only a few years younger than Bluebird herself, dressed in an identical female jumper that was the standard attire for child recruits of the commandant's training center.

In both corners of the room on either side of the divans and against the side walls sat black-robed females, some chanting eerie songs in praise of the commandant while ringing small, tinkling bells or making time on miniscule drum-like instruments, others staring intently at Bluebird as she entered. She noticed immediately that the cult recruiters who had taken her out of the wilderness only one month ago, which now seemed like years, were among their number - smiling at her in pleasure, but with eyes that seemed cold and strange and belying many hidden secrets.

'Bluebird!' cried the youngest among them, raising herself fluidly from her seated posture and moving across the room, her black robes flapping like bat wings with a sudden gust of wind that arose from outside where a small portal led to an observation stand. The cult recruiter reached Bluebird and reached out to the girl, rubbing her short auburn hair affectionately and silently exclaiming as her hand reached the small black ribbon that managed to tie up some of her locks into an obscure bob of sorts. The cult recruiter pointed a bony finger toward the nursery strap that hung on the rung in Bluebird's jumper, raising an eyebrow appreciably. Bluebird smiled in response, feeling a natural sense of camaraderie with this lady, she and the other cult recruiters being the only link here at the training center between herself and the land from which she had once come. The cult recruiter's bony finger still pointed at the nursery strap hanging on Bluebird's jumper and then, her eyes continuing to widen, moved her hand, still pointing, toward the poster of the commandant before them.

There, on one gleaming hip, hung a nursery strap of identical design, appearing somewhat smaller only due to the gargantuan proportions of the commandant's imposing figure. Bluebird's face crinkled with pleasure - she had made this connection somewhat in her private thoughts however had not dared to breathe it to her trainers, much less the younger children under her control in the dormitory. Now, having confirmation of the similarity from her cult recruiter she was able to ascertain fully that indeed her strap was an identical copy. As she made a mental inventory of the other punitive instruments she had encountered during her time at the training center she could not remember any such exact copy nor even an approximate copy of the instrument that hung upon the commandant's hip – excepting the one in her possession.

The cult recruiter clapped her hands together in pleasure and smiled broadly. 'Yes, very auspicious, is it not?' She winked conspiratorially at Bluebird who felt a spontaneous laugh emanating from her lips at the cult recruiter's word and mood, so different than the formal severity which marked her interaction with others at the commandant's training center. She almost felt transported to those early days sitting on the barren hillsides in the wilderness where the cult members had joked with her while sharing their rich preserved food in the days before the black van manned by the masked internal security members had taken her over paths unknown to her present place of domicile. And yet, now, after four weeks of training at the facility, she felt her joy much increased in their presence, for via the rigors she had undergone and the transformation that had begun to take place in her she knew that she approached them now on a much more equal footing - where they once reached out to her as a potential recruit she now felt an unmistakable sense of sisterhood between them.

'Come, Bluebird, I want you to meet someone.' The cult recruiter grasped Bluebird's hand and led her over to the large blue divan sitting beneath the poster of the commandant, gesturing her to sit.

The younger girl sat kneeling with a look of some trepidation on the accompanying divan as Bluebird situated herself cross-legged on the largest, her hand automatically fingering the ultra-heavy leather of her strap as she gazed across the short distance at the younger girl with a decidedly imperious squint. Only the sound of the cult recruiter's laughter broke her concentration.

'Now, now Bluebird - this is someone special we have brought for you to meet, not one of your dormitory shills!' The cult recruiter laughed again and the singing of the other recruiters around the room stopped as they joined in with a softly mirthful twittering. Bluebird could feel herself involuntarily blushing in self-consciousness at the sound of the cult recruiters' laughter, however she straightened her back and gazed at the younger girl firmly, extending her hand in greeting.

'My name is Bluebird, dormitory pontifex, and you are?'

The younger girl accepted her outstretched hand and gave it a firm shake before releasing it.

'Britta is my name, these are my friends who have brought me here to meet you.' Britta waved her hand in an arcing fashion toward the cult recruiters around the room who smiled in return.

Bluebird could detect an unknown accent in the girl's voice, nothing she could recognize in the other children in the dormitories nor in any of the scavengers she had known in the wilderness, however the underlying husky tones and singular inflection distinguished, along with the unusual name, that Britta was from far afield indeed and had probably not been at the commandant's training center for long.

The cult recruiter who had introduced them sat down before them at the feet of the divans in a posture intimating supplication, which was somewhat surprising to Bluebird but more surprising to Britta. The cult recruiter continued to beam at them and out of the corners of her eyes Bluebird could detect that the others also had their gaze intently set on the two girls beneath the image of the commandant, the room now quiet enough that one could hear oneself breathing.

'Bluebird, Britta has been brought from very far away in order to assist you in some very special work, in fact, she will be assisting you in a very specific work that will be the diadem of both of your destinies.' The cult recruiter glanced between the two of them.

'How long have you been a member of the

commandant's cult, Britta?' queried Bluebird.

'Since meeting these, my friends.' Britta moved her hand in an arc like before, indicating the cult recruiters that sat around the room watching them.

'How long have you been at the commandant's training center?' asked Bluebird in follow-up, her tone somewhat more stern.

'Ah, well, Bluebird, she has only been here a few days as of yet and mostly in care of the sisters - she was brought from the outlying territories only a few days ago and in that context has had some very interesting experiences in the meantime, have you not?'

Britta nodded solemnly in response to the cult recruiter's inquiry.

'She has had quite a long journey and has been chosen specifically to help you.' The cult recruiter paused, allowing the words to linger and sink in.

'Both of you come from areas far afield, far from the direct control of the commander and the organization, yet the commandant sees all. She saw you and chose you both for a very special purpose. Beyond this, you also exhibited the self-determination to leave the lands of your previous habitation and join the cult of the commandant specifically, this is a sign of your self-determination and veracity towards achieving success, such veracity which is the hallmark of a leader. Both of you shall become leaders - in fact, much more than leaders.' The cult recruiter directed her gaze to the image of the commandant which loomed directly in front of her, and Bluebird and Britta turned their heads toward the image as well, following her gaze. A strong breeze whipped through the room as if underlining the cult recruiter's statement.

'As of tomorrow evening the both of you will be enacting training jointly.' The cult recruiter looked toward the two girls who listened attentively, bisecting their gazes between her and the poster of the commandant on the wall, still absorbing the implicit message of her prior statement.

'Whereas your individual training has been just that up till now, Bluebird, individual, from this point on Britta will be undergoing training with you. Furthermore, the pace and intensity of training will increase to a quantum degree. Britta is already one month behind your regimen and as such she needs to be brought up to par - and both of you need to be properly conditioned for what will await you in the not too distant future.'

'Britta, are you aware that the commandant's training center is also referred to as the 'torture center annex'?'

Britta shook her head in the negative.

'Bluebird, are you aware that the commandant's training center is also referred to as the 'torture center annex'?'

Bluebird nodded her head in the affirmative, her hand once more fiddling with the leather edges of her nursery strap as she kept one eye peeled on the identical instrument depicted in the image of the commandant above her.

'Well, Britta, you will soon learn and I do not doubt that Bluebird will give you some indication of what to expect, if not a direct demonstration. As of tomorrow evening both of you as mentioned will be engaging in training together. As to dormitory life and your direct position as pontifex, Bluebird, Britta here will be your direct assistant rather than your charge - that does not mean that she will be outside of your jurisdiction as to applied discipline, quite the contrary, however, within the context of dormitory life, among the other children, you must present a united front, your cohesiveness must be seamless, even if Britta is your junior. Think of her as your plenipotentiary, she will be there to assist you whilst you are present and act as your proxy according to her knowledge or ascertaining of your mood and desires.

'In order to facilitate this transition appropriately, from now on you will have a room which you will share which is located just outside the door of the dormitory allowing you swift entrance at any time, you will be issued a key both to the door and the dormitory, as such, you will be expected to report to training sessions outside the dormitory on your own without accompaniment, with the understanding that all areas should be secured prior to your departure.' The cult recruiter raised her hand and snapped her finger at which time one of her fellow companions came forward and proffered two large keys on a ring to Bluebird and Britta respectively, which they fastened onto the clasps at the waistlines of their jumpers.

'In addition to shared quarters and increased responsibility as to security and in addition to the increased intensity of your broad-based training, you will both be engaging in specialized tactical combat training as well. In normal circumstances this type of training would have been deferred toward much later in the process and some of it may have not been proffered whatsoever except in extraordinary circumstances, however the commander - and the commandant - have shortened the timetable in relation to activities to which you are both to be assigned, so this acceleration is necessary. As to tactical training, upon entering your shared quarters for the first time tomorrow evening you will find that both of you have been issued combat uniforms in addition to your regular uniform - these should be worn when engaging in tactical combat training only, your regular uniforms should be worn by default for all other activities unless specifically mentioned.'

The girls looked at each other with looks of interest but only partial comprehension at the cult recruiter's explanation of their forthcoming additional training activities. Bluebird had only the slightest idea of military combat - the scavengers and wastrels of the wilderness from where she originated had only the most primitive of weapons at their disposal and were more often than not prone to fighting like animals, scratching, biting and pummeling whenever the situation called for it, usually in dispute for some foodstuff or abandoned pre-nuclear objects that were desired by the parties so engaging or considered to be useful in trading or selling to the hoarders who made their business collecting every manner of historical artifact from the time before the wars, whether it was of practical use or no. While she had been vigorously schooled in various battles and martial victories perpetrated by the commander's organization during her tenure thus far at the commandant's training facility, her only real exposure to weapons had been viewing the evil devices carried by the masked internal security guards who accompanied her to and from various training sessions; beyond that her knowledge was strictly theoretical. Britta on the other hand had no knowledge of the tales concerning the commander's various campaigns over the many decades, her only schooling in such had been brief descriptions and photographs in thick leather-bound volumes that the cult recruiters had shown to her before transporting her on the long trek from her former place of residence.

Whereas Bluebird herself had heard some rumors of the organization's nature and activities within her wilderness home, the place from which Britta had been taken was so far afield that no knowledge or information concerning the organization nor the fearsome leaders at its helm had reached her until the cult recruiters had begun their initial indoctrination. In this sense she was in all respects a blank slate upon which the will of the commandant might be imprinted without any programming turbulence from ideas preconceived before her recruitment. That being the case, Britta had by a twist of fate been exposed to many more examples of on-the-ground military life than she would have been otherwise due to the fact that the cult recruiter's internal security guard transport liaison had failed to show up at the proper time which in turn led them to trekking across many leagues in the company of the field marshal and his men and eventually leading to their brief encampment on the far border of the organization's territory.

While her experiences were by no means comprehensive by any stretch of the imagination, the fact that she had lived in the company of the field marshal and his personal guard detachment for many days, what to speak of having been the concubine of the field marshal himself, who was one of the most feared and respected military leaders within the organization's armed apparatus, had made indelible marks upon her consciousness. Despite the fact that her cult recruiters had attempted to shield her from camp life on the night prior to her departure for the commandant's training center, with her night's liaison with the field marshal being the exception, Britta had eagerly watched and listened with acute observation to each and every sight and sound that made its way into her purview. She was in awe of the military apparatus of the organization and their power and violence, which they wore like a badge of distinction, a quality which was something she wished to emulate and possess beyond all other attributes. It was in this martial sense that she most desired to serve the commandant.

IRON GATES

Despite the fact that the commandant's training center laid within the most secure and innermost areas of the commander's headquarters, with many parts of it being actually situated underground or with its only access to the outside being secured internal courtyards, the sounds and atmosphere of unmistakable military buildup could be heard consistently echoing across the concrete expanse of the former federal penitentiary. Bluebird, due to her much more substantial residency at headquarters in comparison to Britta, could especially attest to the increase in these sounds which came often at night, rumbling across the grounds and into the windows of the dormitories where the children lay awake listening to the harsh barked orders of the drill masters, the marching of hundreds of booted feet upon the parade grounds and with increasing regularity the sounds of live-fire exercises being performed. The commander preferred the training of his elite shock troops to take place in the dead of night and in the unholy early hours of morning prior to dawn, suffusing the headquarters in the unnatural glow of huge electrical spotlights which caused a hideous shining light in the erstwhile total darkness that could be seen for many miles in the surrounding area. This grotesque display of resource-driven power combined with the explicitly intimidating sounds of shock troops being drilled for constant vigilance to enact missions of great violence served as a signal and constant warning to all within and without and inevitably the presence of the commander in his calculated schedules of regimentation served the purpose of causing his will and poisoned aura of psychological terror to penetrate deep into the subconscious of those who searched for sleep that was hard to find amidst the ever-constant audible and visual reminders of the commander's unwavering will and hideous presence.

The cult recruiter who had been coordinating the initial liaison between Bluebird and Britta left them alone to become more acquainted with one another and informed them that they would be staying with them until the following evening when their joint training would begin. Until that time they would be housed together in the unknown room in which they had been brought together which, by the numerous flights of stairs required to reach and the fell wind which blew in from the outside, was understood to be an attachment to some form of guard or observation tower.

Bluebird initially protested that her presence was required in the dormitories during late afternoon, her sadistic sensibilities eager to mete out scheduled punishments and a wary consideration of any slip in her authority during an absence, however the cult recruiters soothed her to the fact that all was being taken care of among her charges until the following day and that the nature of her absence and that those who would be tending her fellow dormitory residents in the meantime would only enhance her authority in the long run, not diminish it. The cult recruiters in the corners and the sides of the room resumed their lilting trance-like songs in praise of the commandant, enumerating upon her myriad features with descriptions that underlined that she and she alone was the inherent spiritual power that resided within the nuclear warheads that had destroyed most of the inhabitants of the earth planet and that her wrath and potency lived within each of her disciples, a hideous flame within that burned like the fires of hell itself and which would fortify them as they marched ever-forward into a post-apocalyptic future of their own grisly design, the hell on earth made possible by the commandant's nuclear potency and the commander's insatiable will to domination.

Bluebird was reluctant in her interactions with Britta at first, a natural shyness and wariness at this outsider who had been thrust into her world with an indelible permanency if the intentions of the cult recruiters were correct. Yet at the same time she felt, as Britta did, that their liaison, despite the fact that it had been arranged by forces outside of their control, was one of undeniable mutual benefit. Their being put together came hand-in-hand with their being informed, albeit with less details than they might have liked, that their rise in power would be stratospheric in nature and thus as they looked into each others' faces they realized that they were dual links in the organizational chain of terror and that their bind was now cemented if not yet blossomed. The two girls gradually opened up more and more in their conversation with one another, the cult recruiters keeping a respectable distance and courteously refraining from their intent stares of earlier, instead busying themselves about various tasks and talking among themselves in hushed tones. The conversant abilities of Bluebird and Britta began to improve concurrent to the fact that certain of the cult recruiters began supplying them with beverages regularly carried in on small trays and held within small silver-colored tankards. The drinks were sweet to the taste, belying a freshness and wholesome quality to which neither Bluebird nor Britta were used to, yet they possessed a distinctive soothing and intoxicating quality which became more prominent as the afternoon slowly transitioned into twilight.

As they became more relaxed with each other, in large part due to the expert ministrations of the cult recruiters who had engineered the scenario for just such a purpose, they began to share some information concerning their pasts as well as their expectations for the immediate future as per the orientation that they had been given by the cult recruiters thus far. Britta was intensely interested in what lay in store for her in the daily schedule at the training center including the administration of the dormitories which she was premeditating. Bluebird endeavored to avail herself of the opportunity to give some intimation of what the physical and psychological training consisted of although she well knew that no spoken description would suffice to properly apprehend the stress-induced psycho-physical onslaught that would be in store for Britta. She herself wondered despite her month's experience what exactly the 'enhanced measures' and 'accelerated pacing' would look like. Both of them were of the same mind in that both of them were, despite no firm knowledge concerning what it would consist of, eager to approach the specialized tactical combat training. Britta was able to share with Bluebird some of her own observations from her time accompanying the field marshal and his detachment as well as her brief time at the border camp, which were intensively fascinating for Bluebird to hear about. Her only interaction with armed segments of the organization were internal security and the fact that Britta had acted as the concubine of the field marshal during her journey thrilled her. Bluebird had been schooled on certain upper echelon members of the organization's military apparatus in the concourse of her classroom training and knew the field marshal well, at least in an academic sense. That the intrepid nine-year-old with the obscure accent before her had taken part in numerous amorous couplings with this organizational giant was wondrous to contemplate. Despite their mutual intoxication, Britta was loath to reveal any sordid details yet, via bargaining for information regarding some of the more sexually intrusive practices that were employed during the course of punitive actions in the commandant's training center, Britta did manage to relay some of her pastimes with the field marshal that managed to curl Bluebird's toes and cause no small amount of jealousy. Be that as it may, Bluebird could tell that her fortunes within the commandant's cult were changing rapidly, more rapidly than she could have ever suspected and, as such, she considered that very few things would be beyond her reach in due course of time.

As time progressed and twilight made its way into night

the cult recruiters began supplementing the two girls' beverages with trays of rich food. Rather than the porridges of indistinguishable content laced with speed-producing narcotics and the thick slabs of dark protein source produced from rendered corpse meat the sustenance on the trays which were brought before them now were pure delight beyond even the most elaborate offerings that had been given to them during their initial cult recruitment. A variety of smoked meats accompanied small pieces of dried fruit, far different than the foul berries that were their usual fare in the wildernesses from which they had come. The more of the meat that they consumed the more mischievous their minds became, one meat in particular Bluebird found delectable in comparison to all the others and which she began to consume with abandon, with the cult recruiters resupplying her with more before her final morsel had been consumed.

Britta ate as well but with not quite so much gusto as her older compatriot, in some instances looking toward Bluebird with a sense of curiosity as she picked up a handful of her favored meat at a time before dropping it into her mouth, grinding the rough smoked delicacies down with her molars before swallowing and washing the whole lot down with a swig from her tankard. Bluebird noticed the attentive gaze of Britta and decided to take her to task, beginning to speak even as she chewed, yet Britta herself interjected before Bluebird had a chance to vocalize her concerns.

IRON GATES

'Do you know what these different meats are from?' Britta asked, sounding audibly solemn to Bluebird due to her thick accent yet also with an underlying sense of bemusement present which Bluebird found somewhat antagonizing but which piqued her interest further.

'Canine? Deer? You tell me!' Bluebird exclaimed, belching loudly and involuntarily allowing some of the liquor from the tankard to dribble from her chin. Britta conservatively failed to laugh to herself despite her rising amusement, the stifling of which altogether would have been obvious.

Britta smoothed out the fabric of her jumper and placed her tray upon her lap. With her small index finger she began to move the pieces of meat, of which there were considerably more left in comparison to Bluebird's tray, into three neat rows. The only discernible difference that could be ascertained were slight variations of color and texture as they had all been seasoned heavily with a hot spice that seemed to provide a conducive impetus for the girls to continue their drinking apace. Britta began to point and she intoned the source of their evening victuals. Pork was no surprise to Bluebird, bear somewhat more surprising and with the identification of the last pile of meat as human, which happened to be the meat which Bluebird had most been most relishing, she gave a lazy smile and took another large gulp from her tankard, the thin feminine arm of a cult recruiter attendant snaking around Bluebird's frame and refilling from a carafe likewise silver in color.

'Human meat is very good, and this is fresh.' Britta

punctuated her statement with taking a large handful and stuffing it into her mouth, her chewing audible and following up with a great slug of the liquor, her tankard also being replenished by the cult recruiter attendant who stood nearby. Bluebird gave her a quizzical look and raised a piece of the specified meat to eye level, examining it for any distinguishing signs that might verify Britta's assessment. Britta, ascertaining her analysis, shook her head in the negative before responding.

'You will not be able to tell by looking at it, you will be able to tell by the feeling.'

Bluebird raised a questioning eyebrow at Britta and then popped the meat into her mouth, chewing slowly and thoughtfully. Bluebird's eyes looked toward her as Britta herself descended into her own private reverie, remembering aspects of her own background as it related to the subject matter now at hand. She could remember her earliest memories from childhood when she had lived with her mother and siblings in the cold mountainous region which was once known as the state of West Virginia. Her geographic region in comparison to many others had been less affected by nuclear fallout due to the natural situation of the land and the arctic wind currents coming down from the north. At the same time, the remoteness of the region had become more treacherous in isolation and the people had become cut off and, like the animals, more vicious.

Her mother had no aptitude for hunting or trapping and so Britta's family had subsisted on the use of trickery to provide them with what they needed to survive. While the rest of them hid in the shadows of the trees, Britta's mother, a woman of comely appearance despite her hard and rustic lifestyle, would loiter near the main local travel route in the area which was once a logging road used to transport timber from the deep native forests to the rail yards that shipped it throughout the northeastern parts of the United States. From her vantage point on the rise of a hill she could see far down the old logging road as it dipped before curving and making its way toward the south. If more than one person could be seen along the road she would withdraw into the forest shadows along with her children, however, if a lone traveler approached she would utilize one or more ruses to lure them off the path and into her presence where they would swiftly become her victims.

For men she would use a sexual entreaty, for women, a promise of sharing a meal or deception regarding an alleged injury to her own children, thus playing on their motherly instincts and thus so entrap them. For children she would more often than not dispense with more elaborate methods and simply ambush them by force, a mimic whistle of a local bird coming from her mouth would summon Britta and the other children for assistance and aid should such be needed.

Once off the path by whatever method and whomever was so lured (or forcibly taken), Britta and the other children would move in for the kill, utilizing small and primitive but very sharp and decidedly lethal knives that they had fashioned from scrap metal found in the abandoned rail cars near the northernmost trail head of the logging road. As she entered into her fourth year Britta had moved from the small knives favored by her siblings to a stout club fashioned by nature from the broken-off root of an ancient tree, a bulbous knob at the end serving as the main business part of the primitive weapon.

Once dead, Britta's party would take their quarry deep into an obscure mountain hollow, reached through twisting and dangerous footpaths and situated so deep within the woods and hills that no one could hope to find it except their mother - even the children with their senses well-honed in the outdoors environment would be hard pressed to find the hollow on their own. To this effect, they never traveled alone.

Once secured in their hideout the corpse would be butchered by the mother alone, as the brute strength required to harvest the meat and cut through ligaments and muscles was beyond the physical ability of the children, of whom Britta was the eldest. They would help instead by collecting small bits of kindling to build the evening fire, which was contained within a recess at the base of a ridge, thousands of years of precipitation and erosion having formed a small passageway to the mountaintop and which acted as a flue for smoke that would rise once ignited, further protecting their area from detection and obscuring the location of the fire.

Once prepared, the cooking and eating of the raw meat was done simply, the larger parts being wrapped in wet leaves and placed directly in the fire for a longer and tenderizing cook, the choice morsels being skewered on small limbs and cooked by the children themselves or in some circumstances eaten raw. Whereas the eating of human flesh by Britta's mother had at one time been employed as an emergency survival method, after the death of Britta's father it had become the norm rather than the exception. The more she ate the more she wished to consume and the more her mind was ever-turned towards means and methods by which she might secure victims to provide her with this particular sustenance. The children had naturally assumed this posture by behavioral example yet it seemed more so that the practice of cannibalism itself, in some unknown fashion, provided a self-propelled impetus to continue. As time passed Britta's mother found herself ever isolated with her small brood, a misanthropy that accrued in an incremental fashion respective to each new victim. What is more, both she and her children found that as they became more vicious of mind they also became unnaturally strong in body.

Despite this strength, Britta at a still relatively tender age did not possess the navigational skills of her mother and on one dim afternoon in the hills she had been separated from her mother and siblings as they were carrying a body back to the hollow, having stayed behind along the bend of a trail to examine some small filaments of metallic dust that seemed to shine with an internal light, seemingly glowing despite the gray overcast day. Before she fully realized it she had become separated completely from her party, yet due to the seemingly small time period that had elapsed she felt that she would be able to follow the trail in order to catch up with them.

Her assessment had been wrong.

Before an hour had passed the pale sun had sunk behind the mountains and she found herself alone, lost and inhabiting total darkness. Only by blind luck did she manage to make her way back to the logging road and then walked, in darkness, unaware of her direction. By the time dawn arrived she was many miles away from the place on the logging road where she and her family had enacted so many ambushes and, unbeknownst to her, she had been heading south rather than north toward the railway, further confusing her sense of placement.

Seemingly by chance the first individuals that she had encountered had been a group of strange women, clothed in flowing, black robes, their hands upraised in some unknown worship as they walked along singing songs that Britta had never before heard. They had spotted her before she had a chance to withdraw to the treeline and despite the fact that her better judgment would have advised her to flee, she found herself strangely transfixed at the sight of these unusual pilgrims, almost as if under some enchantment. She thought briefly of the odd glowing substance that she had spied on the trail the prior afternoon, her preoccupation with which had been the lead-in to her present quandary. Being well established in her ninth year, that being in specific nine years of trickery and subsequent nine years of murder, she had a more honed sense of subterfuge than she did of direction and by dint of the same she half wondered if she had been the victim herself of a purposeful swindle, though the logistics of how such could have occurred was beyond her.

Her reminisces regarding her recent past was suddenly broken, like a spell, as one of the cult recruiters approached her and Bluebird as they sat on the divan beneath the poster of the commandant. Looking up, Britta saw that the cult recruiter before her was one of the first that she had seen those many weeks ago in the mountains, and via some implicit intimation Britta was almost sure that she knew upon what topic that she had been remembering, for a certain twinkling of the eyes and a slight curl of a grin seemed to pass her face before she turned her attention to Bluebird who sat attentively, her plate now completely bereft of the meat that had been proffered to her, human and otherwise, and her tankard drained. From the opening at the fire side of the room Bluebird and Britta could hear what sounded like a deep rumbling, however it did not seem to be from any thunder or impending storm as the tone was distinctively different, being much more immediate in its resonance.

'Come with me, Bluebird, Britta, we have something to show you.'

All the cult recruiters now stood together behind the young one which seemed to be their main representative, all staring intensely at the two girls with a sense of great expectancy, their features appearing somewhat maniacal in posture.

Britta raised herself from sitting posture first in one swift motion and then extended a hand down to Bluebird, assisting her up from the thick, soft blue divan. The gesture surprised Bluebird but she quickly took it in stride, as Britta was destined to be her close assistant then her action in this regard was well and proper. The head cult recruiter looked down upon them, smiling. The latter intended dynamics of their relationship were already beginning to come into early fruition after only a few short hours.

Britta and Bluebird glanced at each other briefly and intently before following the cult recruiters toward the door-size opening which was the source of the breezes that had entered the room throughout the afternoon. As they stepped out onto a covered balcony type area, closed except for an area which served as an observation window, slitted with heavy rebar, the distant rumbling became louder and more pronounced and Bluebird at once realized that it was the sound of hundreds of booted feet marching on the commander's parade ground. Bluebird glanced down out of the observation window but no troops could be seen, only a lone balaclava-clad internal security guard patrolling an otherwise empty concrete alleyway several stories below.

'Come, Bluebird,' beckoned one of the cult recruiters, gesturing her toward a stairwell at the far end of the balcony into which Britta and the other cult recruiters had already disappeared.

IRON GATES

After ascending four small flights of stairs Bluebird found herself within a large open-air observation center directly overlooking the commander's parade ground which had formerly served as a secure inmate recreational area in the years before the nuclear wars when the headquarters had served another purpose as a United States penitentiary, housing the most dangerous inmates within the federal prison system. On each of the four corners of the grounds rose high guard towers upon which huge surveillance lights were mounted, patrolled by small squads consisting of three armed internal security personnel per tower, each equipped with a high-powered sniper rifle in addition to the standard silenced MP5 that was the preferred weapon of choice among internal security. Now stationed within the observation center, both Bluebird and Britta felt the cold chill of the night air whipping against their faces and skin with brutal strength due to their raised position above the parade grounds, their organizational jumpers being little protection against the weather on the cloudless winter night. The sound of the marching boots was now nearly deafening, interspersed with the intermittent shrill barks of the drill masters and the aggregate sounds of assault rifles being shouldered and presented within the concourse of their drill.

The group of cult recruiters stood toward the back of the observation chamber beyond the terraced ledge that provided a view of the parade grounds below. Bluebird could not fully ascertain, however she saw, amidst their black robes rippling under the force of the wind currents, that certain of the cult recruiters looked to be shedding tears of some unknown elation or rapture, though it could have been caused by the exposure to weather, although her instincts argued against such a natural causation. What exactly the case may be Bluebird could still not ascertain yet she felt a distinctive chill as two of the cult recruiters separated themselves from the group and stationed themselves on either side of her and Britta, one grasping her arm and one grasping Britta's own and leading them, gently but firmly, slowly but persistently, toward the edge of the terrace within full sight of the as yet unseen marching organizational forces below.

Gradually and surely along with whispered words of encouragement coming from the cult recruiters which neither Bluebird nor Britta could decipher over the increasing roar from below, the two girls were brought forward until they stood at the very edge of the observation deck many stories above the field beneath them, a harsh and nearly blinding light beaming down from a directional surveillance apparatus installed above them within the fortress-like infrastructure of the former prison. Beneath them upon the parade grounds stood well over one hundred organizational personnel, all of whom were armed to the teeth, rows upon rows of shock troopers with bayoneted assault rifles flanked by squads of balaclava-clad internal security personnel. Upon raised platforms stationed intermittently along the periphery of the yard stood fiery-eyed drill masters, their bodies pulsating with poised violence and suffuse with unbridled fanaticism for the most pointed type of work within the commander's organization. At seemingly random spots throughout the yard away from the main contingent of personnel were small mobile signals intelligence units crouched near the ground as they commandeered their low-frequency radio equipment, wearing large backpacks carrying additional equipment out from which stout antennas projected and, protected by a signals intelligence unit, gunners stationed behind small piles of sandbags, manning large and lethal belt-fed machine-guns within the training mock-ups meant to mirror field conditions.

As the two girls and the two cult recruiters which accompanied them entered the lit area at the edge of the observation deck and became visible to the troops in the parade grounds below, a particularly violent drill master, helmeted and wearing dark glasses, heavily muscled and thickly mustached, raised a thick wooden baton and shouted an indiscernible order from his position at the top of a raised platform stationed along the left flank of the contingent of armed organizational personnel. The marching soldiers began to turn in a complicated formation while the small teams of signals intelligence stationed throughout the stadium area withdrew from their machinations in relation to their equipment and stood at rigid attention, facing the direction of the observation deck upon which the girls and the cult recruiters stood in full view of the troops below.

The armed organizational personnel continued their complicated marching maneuvers, the long black lines of brute human strength stretching out across the field in twisted and bleak patterns beneath the cold star-filled sky above them, shouldering and presenting their rifles frequently in strict unison. The main drill master raised his baton high above him once again before rapping it forcefully upon the railing of his platform and then proceeding to press a button upon a small electrical apparatus beside him, at which point shrill alarm sirens began to emit from all corners of the parade ground, further adding to the unnerving din of the marching bodies. On the far side of the parade ground two separated ports ground opened with a scream of metal raking upon metal, revealing dark tunnels leading to subterranean areas of the commander's headquarters. These areas had once been utilized as storage facilities but had now been sequestered for the training of specialized closed units in preparation for an event centered around the formal unveiling of a new weapon within the organization's arsenal to be held at headquarters, an event which had only recently been announced within the organization in general but for which preparations had been ongoing for quite some time. Even still, despite that the date for an organization-wide event held at headquarters had been announced, no one except for those participating in the most confidential preparations for the same knew the details of what the purpose of the event was - and even among those sectors information was highly compartmentalized.

Bluebird squinted her eyes against the glaring of the spotlights, straining to detect any signs of movement from within the darkened corridors which had just been opened on the far side of the parade grounds. The armed organizational personnel's marching pattern began to change as the many diverse circles and columns began to form into two central columns which marched with their faces toward the observation chamber looming above them, widening the gap between them and forming a corridor leading from the base of the observation structure to the two black openings at the far end of the field. With a resounding snap, the marching armed organizational personnel halted in position, solidifying into two long black lines forming a living breathing roadway between the base of the observation chamber and the far end of the parade grounds. As the shock troop regiments and internal security guard units halted, the drill masters also ceased their barking of commands, turning an about face toward the observation chamber, their gazes turned upward onto the spotlighted terrace where Bluebird, Britta and the cult recruiters watched them and their troops reciprocally.

The entire parade ground was now suddenly enveloped in a tense silence, all armed organizational personnel members on the field standing in rigid military stance facing toward the observation chamber. As Bluebird continued to squint in the direction of the far end of the parade ground she could feel warm flesh against her right hand and she glanced down to see that Britta had by some automatic gesture grasped her hand in her own. Bluebird pumped her hand once to verify her acknowledgment and Britta looked up at her, the younger girl's eyes wide in a reactive response somewhat akin to terror in the circumstance which she found herself in now, which no picture books showed to her on a rutted roadside in former West Virginia by cult recruiters could have ever prepared her for. Yet, in the same instance, Bluebird saw that a careening psychotic strain lay beneath that look of terror, as well as a cold pragmatism that made Bluebird cognizant that Britta was, as she was herself, aware that all that lay before them now might be utilized as vehicles of their own violence under the auspices of the commandant's mission.

In the silence there could be discerned the unmistakable sound of marching feet approaching, coming up from the bowels of the former prison along the dual tunnel routes. The sound was distinctively different from the former ministrations of the armed organizational personnel who now stood stationary and silent. Rather than the unbridled and brutal din of martial repression made by the hundred-some armed organizational personnel earlier during their drill maneuvers, the sounds coming closer and ever closer from within the tunnels was of a more subdued note, yet no less intimidating nature.

The muffled footsteps from within the tunnels became more prominent as the first contingent of persons, two-abreast, emerged from the entrance-ways of both of the tunnels into the light of the parade grounds. The individuals emerging from the right tunnel were of absolute alien appearance, dressed from head to foot in large white hazardous material suits obscuring from view any idea of their identity, sex or natural physical form. After ever third or fourth line of two abreast could be seen others equally attired manually pulling low trolleys upon which sat large metal barrels painted blue and marked BIOHAZARD, along with other written and symbolic insignia such as the dreaded skull and crossbones denoting the extreme danger of their contents.

'HAZARDOUS AND INFECTIOUS MATERIALS', *'CORROSIVE'* and *'POISONOUS'* were stamped on the side of some, the beginning telltale signs of the corrosive material eating through the metal lids themselves apparent on several barrels while others of a sickly yellowish color were stamped 'Radiation Hazard.' This hitherto alien force, attired in the practical anonymity of their bulbous hazmat suits and pulling behind them the building blocks of a myriad and potentially vast number of area denial weapons trod forward through the black-clad ranks of the armed organizational personnel beneath flags colored a light bluish color in hue, upon which was imprinted an insignia in black consisting of an outline of a human figure from the middle-chest level up with a bluish starburst extending outward from an area between the heart and the throat. Its design by sight intimated the horrors of acute and fatal toxicity, mutagenicity, target organ toxicity and reproductive toxicity.

A separate contingent had marched out of the tunnel to the left, consisting of persons equally clothed in white hazmat suits yet of a more close-fitting and lower-grade variety in terms of protection, bereft of the heavy air-circulation apparatus and large hermetically sealed square-shaped and impermeable aluminized shell SCBA face-shields of their compatriots and instead equipped with standard black gas masks covering their heads, the white on black contrast giving them an aura of some ghastly humanoid, insect-like beings infused with an anger and will to repress beyond all known human and ethical limits. Dual bandoliers bearing rows of small, can-shaped gas grenades crossed their chests and on either side of their hips rode two machine pistols along with an open bolt blowback-operated submachine gun attached on riggings of nylon belts that hung on the sides of their chests. On their backs were strapped sharpened entrenching tools.

Britta and Bluebird watched with rapt attention as the two units marched forward between the other armed organizational personnel, their white hazmat suits forming two white lines amongst a sea of black. Finally they too reached the base foundation of the observation chamber and their lines stopped, the chemical handlers lined directly in front of Bluebird and the more conventionally armed contingent in gas masks lined directly in front of Britta. The cult recruiter beside Bluebird leaned toward the girls, addressing them both.

'One day soon, Bluebird, you will command these forces,' nodding her head toward the amassed armed organizational personnel on the parade ground which, now with the addition of the recently formed chemical, radiological, biological and nuclear units, numbered well over two hundred persons.

IRON GATES

'These here,' the cult recruiter pointed toward the column of hazmat-suited personnel beneath their pale blue flags, addressing Bluebird, 'are your personal unit.'
'Those,' the cult recruiter addressed Britta, pointing toward the second column, equipped for contaminant dangerous environments yet also heavily armed in the conventional sense, 'will be under your command, Britta, armed chemical squadrons, which you will lead as Bluebird's iron right hand.'

A particularly strong wind whipped through the observation chamber and the black ribbon that held Bluebird's hair, the tie of which had gradually become loosened during the course of her evening in the company of Britta and the cult recruiters, came undone, careening wildly in the wind-currents before descending, like a black feather, toward the parade grounds below. It floated gently downward for several seconds before falling to rest upon the concrete-covered earth, several paces from a balaclava-clad internal security personnel member. Without any hesitation the internal security personnel member strode forward and retrieved the ribbon, grasping it in his leather-gloved hand and touching it to his forehead in respect before marching toward the hazmat-suited personnel member closest to him who carried the standard of Bluebird's unit. With a careful motion the hazmat-uniformed personnel member lowered the banner and the internal security guard took the ribbon and tied it upon the peak of the flag pole. As the standard-bearer raised the flag, once again the winds blew harder still, the blue flag rippling in the brutal, cold air currents.

Upon the terrace of the observation center Bluebird herself stood wild-eyed, her short hair, now unbound, blowing wildly and giving her an electric, maniacal appearance. Behind and on either side of her and Britta the cult recruiters, with their black robes billowing around them, seemed to the armed organizational security personnel below to appear like some species of evil flittermice keeping watch over their leaders. With an automatic sense of command Bluebird raised both of her hands into the air in salutation, her right hand, still grasping Britta's, causing it too to rise into the air in salutation to the armed chemical squadrons which would become her personal force and to all the assembled armed organizational personnel on the parade grounds. The amassed organization members responded with a deafening roar that echoed through the yard in a visceral sign of allegiance.

CHAPTER 25

It had been several hours since Wendy and the lieutenant had picked up the supplies from the quartermaster's wagon and headed into the woods. Although Wendy had lived in the mountains all of her life she was not aware of the path that was being taken by the lieutenant, which seemed to meander along the base of a ridge, sometimes running beside a small stream that gurgled and splashed along, its water a cold transparent black within the night's darkness. In time however their meandering path led them to a rocky gulley at the base of a foaming waterfall and at this landmark Wendy became situated as to her present whereabouts. The waterfall was a place well beloved by the local people, with the continual fresh water from the melting of the snow being free of large amounts of trace radiation, the locals being well acclimatized at present to whatever small traces it might contain. Beautiful patches of mountain laurel grew throughout the rocky ridges and sandy beach at the bottom of the falls and Wendy herself remembered with fondness the last time that she had visited this place, although it had been too long, for as she had grown older her days and nights had become much more supervised and structured. Rather than exploring at her ease as she once did she found herself increasingly confined to the area directly around the engineering center, trading the freedom and green and open spaces of her mountain haunts for the grime, filth and secrecy of the converted warehouse.

Whereas the waterfalls gave all who came into their presence a sense of wonder and joy, although certainly possessing an atmosphere of mystery, the tunnel into the rocks that lay nearby, down a wide, gently sloping road, had a fell reputation and was avoided by all of the children in the area. This tunnel, called the stumphouse tunnel in years gone by, had been an aborted project during the nineteenth century. Immigrants from across the Atlantic ocean had begun the tunneling into the rock with the intention of the spot being the beginning of a railroad that, once out of the mountains, would traverse many states. This intention was never realized however as the tunneling was halted at the beginning of civil strife and military conflict that divided the country and lasted for many years. By the time the war had ended the immigrants who had begun the task of the tunnel were long gone, dead in the fighting or having decamped to areas far beyond the location of the tunnel, which was in those days a hotbed of political unrest.

What was left was never utilized for its intended purpose, an abandoned monstrosity consisting of a great black opening into the mountain that led into an unlit tunnel extending several thousand feet into the rock. Around fifty yards into the tunnel was an air shaft drilled into the roof, extending sixty feet up to the mountain slope causing a constant breeze that flowed out of the tunnel, strong enough that it could be felt many paces from the entrance. In the years prior to the onset of the nuclear wars a locked iron gate was built near the air shaft to keep explorers out of the innermost section of the tunnel, which had a reputation for being a place of danger, with falling rocks frequently injuring and sometimes killing those who had ventured within. As well, although it was less known, the innermost area beyond having a reputation for natural danger had also become a fixation for unsavory elements who utilized the area for an out-of-the-way and hard-to-reach spot for engaging in various illegal activities. At various times during the several hundred years since it was built, the nefarious activities that had occurred there indicated the breadth and scope of some men for possessing an indomitable desire to act in ways transgressive to the rule of law and society, being a site where acts as innocent as illicit intoxication among groups of youth to more capital offenses such as murder and aggravated child molestation enacted by lone schizophrenics and career criminals had taken place.

In the years that led up to the nuclear wars and during the most horrible days after the last barrage of missiles had landed, plunging the world into the darkness of a radioactive, nuclear winter, the area had served as the base for the most survivalist-minded among the mountain folk who utilized the fortification as a spot to hide themselves away as chaos descended around them. The newer people in the mountains - those who had begun to inhabit the area for decades because of its scenic beauty and rural charm yet possessing no real ties to the land - had died early on from starvation or sickness, purposefully attempting to travel to more populated areas and in the process going outside of the natural safety zone from nuclear fallout that the particular region of the mountains afforded.

Those who had stayed behind quickly became victims of the more native among the mountain folk for whom the interlopers who had moved in from the cities were easy prey indeed. While the patriarchs of their luxury homes were summarily executed, some choice targets among the bourgeois households such as young daughters or infants who might be raised for labor were abducted in the course of their raids. Some of these were taken deep into the stumphouse tunnel and dispatched, oftentimes after lengthy months of systematic torture and sexual and psychological abuse, their death being offerings to a strange and hideous god whom the mountain folk had begun to worship in light of the nuclear wars, when the old faiths of their forefathers began to fade along with their former hopes and dreams for the future.

The hideous and new god that they worshiped now, called Gaubni, represented new hopes and dreams - aspirations that fit in with the ultra-violent post-apocalyptic state of affairs in the deep wilderness. In time, as the pointed chaos directly before and after the nuclear wars began to transition into a more stable and grueling state of anarchy, the stumphouse tunnel was once more abandoned as the mountain survivalists who had inhabited it moved out, free now of any threat of fallout and years enough past that the necessity for their thieves' den having expired. Many of them decamped to their old home sites if they still existed or moved on. The most hardcore of them stayed in the area and became, decades into the future, the core population of the mountain region under the strict control of the commander and his organization, in whom the mountain folk found a solid allegiance which had continued to endure.

The cult of their strange god, named Gaubni, went underground during the changes that took place when the population first came under the commander's authority, not for any sense that there was a great contradiction to be found in the ethos (if it could be called that) between the visions of the two but more out of a sense of instinctive concealment and preservation. The stumphouse tunnel was now the main visitation place for the secretive cult, only which a filament of devotion had continued since the old days around the time of the nuclear holocaust. Many within the mountain region were not even aware of the cult's existence, however the tunnel itself and the area surrounding it, anything beyond the waterfalls, had an evil reputation via stories that had been passed down from generation to generation as to its hideous qualities and the monstrous entities which lived inside, always looking to entrap erstwhile people. Wendy herself had grown up on these horror stories and, despite the fact that many believed the cult to be separate from the commander's organization, it had in fact been absorbed into the control of organizational intelligence and psychological operations units in the early days of the occupation and carefully tended to since that time.

Within several minutes of arrival at the waterfalls, the lieutenant could ascertain a noticed change in atmosphere and an enhanced dynamic between himself and the young girl who accompanied him. A charged apprehensiveness suffused the area, black with darkness and lit only by the celestial stars within the firmament, as the lieutenant had kept his kerosene-soaked torches in reserve for their expedition into the tunnel which lay further ahead, the domicile of Gaubni, his patron deity.

The lieutenant observed with appreciation how Wendy was able to keep pace with him during their hike through the woods almost without effort, quite a feat considering her considerably slighter frame. Nevertheless, the lieutenant considered that she had no doubt traveled these or similar paths many times in her life. He had for many years now lusted after the girls of the mountain region, a particular forbidden fruit not in the sense that they could not be enjoyed but that they could not be brought out - and by dint of the commander's demands on his time the lieutenant was never domiciled near the area of the engineering center for more than a week at a time. Sometimes in the past when a particular girl had taken his fancy and he could not bear the thought of leaving her for some other lesser organizational member to handle and possess after he had gone, he would take them to the altar of Gaubni at the end of the same tunnel which he now approached and sacrifice them - never to be seen or heard from again in the mountain regions around the engineering center. In these cases he would take himself a souvenir from his sacrificial victim as an amulet, usually in the form of a severed finger which he would wrap carefully in thick leather and carry with him during the course of his performing various more military-style atrocities elsewhere within the organization's territories. He himself had been far from the first to perform human sacrifice at the altar and as long as organizational intelligence and psychological operations units continued to pour time and resources into making sure that the cult continued to thrive, albeit covertly, he would be far from the last.

Wendy would be the first child that he had taken into the stumphouse tunnel in over two years' time and as the case might be she would be the first child that he had ever intended to take out again, congruent to his purpose of smuggling her outside of the organization's mountain territory. Though he had longed for procuring one of the mountain girls as his own personal concubine for some time, he had never acted on his burning desire for whatever reason. What made this circumstance and this girl in particular the one exception he could not readily ascertain, however he had been feeling more and more of a sinister elation ever since the conference where the new weapon was unveiled and the commandant showed herself in the flesh within the organization for the first time, creating in him a sense of license hitherto unexperienced prior. He could feel with no mistake or misunderstanding whatsoever that a new era was dawning among the organization with the public appearance of cult figures that had only been worshiped remotely before and with the promise of a great outpouring of violence at whatever point the new weapon would be tested. That he would be in charge of transporting the warheads from the engineering center to headquarters was a great honor and one that further cemented his position as the commander's favorite; he felt that no time was ripe like the present to avail himself of the young flesh of a mountain girl whom had succeeded in capturing his imagination like none other to date. On this night she would be exposed to a particularly more brutal side of his affections than she had experienced earlier in her tent at the encampment. With these thoughts on his mind he reached down and gently stroked the back of her jacket, causing her to turn and peer up at him with her twinkling child eyes from within the hood of her jacket. Yes, it was going to be an interesting night indeed.

Before long they reached the wide, graveled road that led down a gentle slope toward the mouth of the tunnel. Having been carefully inculcated with the myths surrounding this area and the alleged monstrosities that lay within and the belief that it should be avoided at all costs, Wendy felt a chill run up her spine. What did this situation intimate? Was the lieutenant fooling her, leading her along with promises of taking her out of the mountain territory, vowing to execute an act without precedent, only to soften her up so that he could lead her into the bowels of the rock and kill her without struggle?

IRON GATES

She had heard the stories, as had all the children, and she knew as well as anyone else in the mountain territory that children who went out into these areas at night were seldom seen again. She could remember from a very young age a rumor about some other young girls disappearing, young girls that were around the same age as herself at present.

As they neared the mouth of the tunnel she could feel the ever-present wind gusting from within, a phantom breeze that presented itself to her as both a sign and a warning, for this was the first time that she had ever been directly in the presence of the tunnel's opening. Though the stories about the evil winds that emanated from within without any known explanation were well known to her, tonight was her first experience of the same. She let out a slight whimper which caused the lieutenant to turn to her, wearing a leering grin upon his combat-hardened face. They stood some twenty feet away from the tunnel's entrance now and the lieutenant stopped, removing a torch from his supplies and with a knock of flint while grasping its stem between his legs and lighting it, causing an instant flame to catch from the fuel-soaked rags which the quartermaster had prepared during the late afternoon before their departure. Great billows of smoke rose up into the air from the filthy reconstituted fuel, bathing him and Wendy in a hellish and smoky glow. The torch's flame visibly blew back at an angle, resistant to the cold breeze that emanated ultimately from the air shaft within, though the lieutenant did nothing to dispel Wendy's native superstition. Whatever discrepancy there might be between what she had been told about this place and the reality, she would herself experience her fair degree of trauma on this night, which was to be her initiation into the cult of the Great Demon, even though she herself did not yet know it. Let her decide how what she had been told and what she would experience were congruent or no.

The lieutenant raised his torch into the air and with his other hand grasped Wendy's own firmly, pulling her along while marching in a steady gait toward the entrance of the tunnel. The little girl let out another, more pronounced whimper in protest and began to pull back from his grasp, to which the lieutenant responded by releasing her hand, whirling to face her and grabbing an area near her shoulder.

Even through the ample padding of her baby brigade field jacket, the lieutenant's iron grasp easily managed to pinch the pressure point to which he had instinctively aimed.

The little girl's whimper caught in her throat at the searing pain and she felt herself being forced down to her knees. The lieutenant knelt down in front of her, his hand still grasping her shoulder within his excruciating grip as Wendy's ruddy face began to turn white under the strain. It did not require a lengthy diatribe on the lieutenant's part to make her understand that she was going to go into the tunnel one way or the other as his steely eyes bored into her own. The lieutenant raised one eyebrow and Wendy nodded in acquiescence to the unspoken demand which his gesture intimated. Respond

IRON GATES

properly, obey, proceed.

With that he released her shoulder, grasped her hand once again in his own and the pair of them proceeded through the arched entrance-way and into darkness.

Within only a few minutes of entering the tunnel, both the lieutenant and his young charge were ensconced in an inky blackness all around them, the light from the torch serving to illuminate the area directly around them yet obscuring what lay ahead. Wendy turned briefly to look behind her, with the consideration that this might be her last chance to look upon anything except the eldritch passageway into which her fell guardian was now inexorably leading her. She could see clearly in the distance that the faint circular outline of the tunnel's entrance had grown to a small pinpoint, their procession into the rock of the mountain being firm and steady. The lieutenant walked with purpose and with no hesitancy despite the treacherous path, for he had gone this way many times before, the walk now surging his mind with memories of the many times he had gone to this place, sometimes with a sacrificial victim and sometimes with lesser offerings befitting the mode of darkness, during which he would engage in solitary meditation upon his deity. As Wendy walked along she every so often gazed up at the lieutenant, attempting to determine his mood and thoughts, however there was no succor in her vision as the lieutenant's expression was unreadable, though his face, stone-hard and gleaming in the open flame of the torch-light and the smoke from its fuel-soaked flames gave him a distinctively demonic visage.

The tunnel was relatively quiet beyond the soft tread of their booted feet as they made their way forward. The soft drip of water running down the stone sides of the tunnel could be heard softly and Wendy noticed that small streams of this black cold liquid flowed by them on either side of their path. Wendy thought that on occasion she could hear the distant flapping of bat wings, however she was unsure if the sound was real, a trick of the strange environment or something more sinister in nature altogether. Eventually they reached the point, several hundred yards in, where the air shaft had been drilled down from the mountain above into the tunnel. A few feet beyond it lay the iron gate to the innermost area of the tunnel, still closed but its locks having been broken long, long ago.

Wendy stared up into the ceiling of the tunnel, her face turned toward the air shaft. Cold mountain air blew down upon her face. The lieutenant released his grasp on her hand and strode forward, opening the iron gate before them and beckoning her on, which she did without question or hesitancy this time around. She was now far into the tunnel and should she desire to attempt to escape at this point her efforts would have come to naught, for the faint light of the night sky visible from the opening before was now long gone, their progression not only being too far to view such a sight but also obscured via their almost imperceptible yet steady descent. Her chances stumbling around in the darkness attempting to escape from her predatory minder did not seem stacked in her favor. As she had made it this far in, she considered that she may as well meet whatever fate awaited her with a degree of dignity, what little solace that was.

She entered first and the lieutenant pressed her forward with a hand on her back before reaching back and closing the gate behind him. She could feel his hand intently and though his grip upon her prior to entering the tunnel had been one of violent warning she could tell without any mistake that his mind now fixated upon more lustful pursuits, even if they be laced generously with the additive of cruelty.

Wendy and the lieutenant walked forward into the tunnel, his hand still upon her back, until she could see at the far end the beginning of the end of the tunnel through the flickering light of the torch. Grasping another unlit torch from his pack the lieutenant lit it upon the one already burning and, walking forward, stationed one on either side of the tunnel's end, illuminating the rocky surface of the tunnel's wall.

The first thing that Wendy noticed was that there was a line of human skulls on the rocky surface of the tunnel's floor, many of them obviously the skulls of full-grown adults yet some decidedly intimating the heads of adolescents and others, even smaller, denoting that the sacrifice of infants had taken place in this area. Other bones of various degree were piled willy-nilly around the area of the altar, some of them, as well as some of the skulls, still possessing old flesh, sapped of the majority of its moisture, stretching nauseatingly across their skeletal frames. At the center of the shrine was a great black idol that was featureless in appearance but undeniably horrific in demeanor. A strange and blasphemous glow seemed to emanate from the black stone from which it had been wrought, polished by the dripping water from the fissures in the rock above and charged relentlessly by blood sacrifices performed by its secretive cult. At the base of the idol stood a great slab of rock standing several feet off from the ground. On its side and along its base thick leather manacles fortified by polished steel had been attached with deep spikes hammered in and securing it to the stone base. Telltale signs of blood could be seen clearly on its rough gray surface.

Having secured the torches on either side of the altar the lieutenant turned toward Wendy, his face suddenly pale in concentration and veneration toward his patron deity, a cold sweat dripping down his brow. Though Wendy had long been inculcated into the horrors that lay within the stumphouse tunnel, tales that ultimately rested with the combined mythos created by mountain inhabitants long ago and engineered further by organizational intelligence and psychological operations units, she somehow found the stationary nature of the altar which stood before her to be more terrifying on a concrete level. Though the sort of beasts and atrocities which had been spread about the tunnel and what lay within it had been known to her for many years, the presence of skulls and bones around the altar, indicating a very concrete cult of death, caused her skin to crawl. Though the situation of the tunnel was decidedly cold and well-aired, even more so due to the presence of a second air shaft that lay just above the idol of the Great Demon itself, she felt a feeling of suffocation coming on her, the air thick and heavy and with a blasphemous stench that seemed to grow as each slow tedious minute passed before the lit area of the central altar.

With a brief verbal command the lieutenant instructed Wendy to shed her overcoat and seat herself cross-legged before the altar of Gaubni. The little girl reciprocated to his request immediately, her eyes stationed unblinking upon the idol before her. With small, tender hands, Wendy unzipped and removed her outer jacket, folding it carefully and placing it on the ground to the side of the stone altar, its black insulated fabric resting gently against the line of skeletal remains that served as the border between the stone altar and the area beyond in which resided the idol, an impenetrable barrier upon which no human would or should cross lest he or she be in the trance of the Great Demon himself.

As Wendy sat staring into the inconceivable face of the idol before her she could feel her consciousness twisting and churning in a fashion that she had never experienced until this point. She felt herself, just being in the presence of the deity for only a few minutes, to have stepped across a irrevocable threshold - the confrontation between herself and this alien power in itself an act of initiation into something altogether different than she had ever known. It was within this state of consciousness that she felt her left arm being lifted gently from its station in her lap and positioned upon the cold stone of the altar, the clasping sleeve of her tactical battle-ready jacket being unbuttoned and her sleeve being gently raised, revealing a thin but wiry arm, its skin a milky white due to her almost constant habitation as of late within the manufactured confines of the commander's engineering center.

With a swift motion the lieutenant withdrew the large survival knife from his belt, the frighteningly oversized proportions of which were accentuated in intimidation by its bleak, black-painted blade which was effected for covert purposes, the only testament of its tempered steel constitution being the gleam along the blade which shone in the light of the flaming torches, its razor-sharp edge horrible in nature and appearance. He held it in front of Wendy's face, forcing her to divert her gaze from the deity of the Great Demon onto the fleshly demon before her as he presented the instrument of her own potential premature demise.

The lieutenant pinned Wendy's arm to the sacrificial stone and without warning brought down the large survival knife in an expert arc, cutting a jagged line across her small wrist and palm. The slash was executed carefully so as to not be fatal, yet still the razor-like properties of the knife could be seen as the cut first appeared pale before the flesh blossomed open and a steady stream of blood began to flow. At the pain and sudden shock Wendy thought that she had screamed, however, although her mouth had opened, no sound had come from her throat as she sat, transfixed at the blood oozing steadily from her hand. The lieutenant released her arm and with a similar motion cut a slash across his own wrist and palm, his own blood coming forth with great large drops like the rain from a storm cloud.

The lieutenant sat down beside her, wrapping his legs around her middle and massaging her non-existent breasts with one hand while forcing his bleeding wrist up to her mouth. She began to choke and spit as the hot liquid ran inexorably down her throat, hot tears of panic and confusion running down her face, intermingling with the recent juices of her now blood-stained mouth. The lieutenant removed himself, standing and rummaging among a pile of mixed bones and rubble nearby. Wendy had raised herself up into kneeling position, cradling her injured arm with her good one. Although the blood loss had been significant, the flow had already begun to congeal with now only small rivulets dripping from her arm onto the stone altar and the base around it.

The lieutenant had found what he had been looking for and sprung back into her line of vision, his eyes wild and crazed, a great leering grin stretched across his face. He grabbed Wendy's injured arm and pressed her wound against his own, clumsily tying their wrists together with a small leather thong that he had retrieved from the pile of debris only a few minutes ago.

'See this, Wendy, see it!' Wendy watched as her blood and the lieutenant's began to commingle with one another.

'This marks you not only as my concubine but indeed as my very wife! And I your husband! Say it, Wendy, confirm before the Great Demon! Confirm our union!'

'I am your wife!' The little girls' voice sounded small and pathetic in comparison to the booming commands of the lieutenant who crouched before her in a state of pure and unbridled psychosis.

'And I am your husband!' The lieutenant shouted the words, their echo reverberating throughout the stumphouse tunnel, the echoed responses pealing off the rock as if his own voice was but one of many.

The lieutenant unwrapped the thong from their hands and cut it in twain with his knife, taking one half and tying it around Wendy's wrist and the other around his own. 'Before long, my little wife, I will get us both a charm to attach to these, the symbols of our troth. However, for now, it is now time to consummate before the Great Demon.'

Wendy was aware enough that she understood his meaning, the pain from the wound having begun to subside and her mind now focused on what had just taken place. The commingling of blood, especially before an altar or a high official within the organization was the standard form of marriage in the organizational territories - its bonds were irrevocable. Not only had she been promised to be the travel companion of the lieutenant and be taken out of the area of the engineering center, but now she found herself bound together by marriage, oath and blood to this violent and powerful man. She could not help but feel herself swoon in ecstasy over her good fortune and suddenly the confines of the tunnel did not seem as horrible as they did before, because she knew that now that they had been joined together that he would not kill her after all. Yet, at the foreknowledge that their conjugal conjoining under the bounds of marriage would now take place, she gulped and steadied herself for whatever type and style of ministrations might come.

As Wendy considered her immediate future, the lieutenant busily rummaged through the sack which he had carried with him and which the quartermaster had prepared for them prior to their departure. He removed another two stout torches and lit them off the one already burning to the left corner, placing them in holders stationed on either side of the stone altar. Now the area around the deity of the Great Demon was brightly lit, the idol's black surface gleaming greasy and unnerving in the illumination of the torch light.

Next, the lieutenant removed a small leather package, placing it on the altar before Gaubni, then a small package of dried meat, next a bladder of strong mountain liquor. As he set each item before the deity, with his left hand he rung a small bell which signified that the item was being offered. After he had finished he would remove the item once more, placing it on the ground next to the altar. Having finished offering the liquor, the lieutenant removed the cap from the wine-bladder and took a long pull of the fiery beverage before proffering it to Wendy who, particularly in mind that the already eventful evening might be even more long and vigorous than she had expected in relation to her recent nuptials, took into herself a pull of the alcohol at least as deep as had the lieutenant, causing her to sputter and gasp as she removed the flagon from her soft, blood-stained lips.

Their preliminary libations having been established, the lieutenant moved in on his tender bride with the speed and efficiency of a wilderness beast cornering its prey. It took only a moment to shift her from her kneeling position to have her bent over, knees on the ground, her stomach and chest flat upon the stone surface of the altar which had only recently been the site of their marriage ritual. Now the more visceral aspect of their binding would take place.

The lieutenant spread her arms out in front of her and to her sides, fastening them securely with the leather manacles that had been driven into the stone of the altar with large steel spikes. This having been effected he followed suit by unfastening and pulling down her baby brigade tactical uniform pants and her panties beneath, allowing them to pool near the pits of her knees before spreading her thighs and manacling both to the backside of the stone altar. The lieutenant's manhood roused fierce at the sight of her shamefully exposed buttocks, with the hint of her sex peaking out from between them due to her forced spread position. Wendy, now his bride, allowed herself to be bound without any struggle and, once manacled in, struggle was in fact impossible, as she lightly tested her bonds and found that even the slightest movement was beyond her ability thus restrained. She rested her head on its side, her cheek upon the cold stone of the altar. From this vantage point she was able to glance back to see the lieutenant as he finished strapping her in, testing the bonds. All around her lay the pathetic skeletal remains of the sacrificial victims that had been offered to Gaubni. How many of them were children of her own age? How many of them had been offered by the lieutenant himself, her husband?

The lieutenant proceeded toward the far corner of the tunnel where upon a large metal hook drilled into the rock hung a long and vicious leather strap, its proportions frighteningly thick and its edges and surface well-oiled as to avoid any damage via the moisture of the area. This object had been in the cult of Gaubni before even the organization had ingratiated itself into and eventually took over control of the same. It had always resided in the stumphouse tunnel and was never removed despite the fact that no one guarded it, nor the hideous deity to which its usage it was consecrated. No one in the mountains, even those with skeptical minds, would have considered for a moment removing an item that was considered to be a possession of the deity. Like others who had wielded it before him, the lieutenant only made use of it at the Great Demon's allowance, it was never his possession or the possession of any other than the Great Demon himself.

Wendy gulped as she viewed the lieutenant stalking around the tunnel from the corner of her eyes, hefting the great leather strap to test its weight. Though she had been the object of many beatings in her few years she had never seen, much less been the recipient of, an item of such calculated menace as the one held by the lieutenant now, nor had she received such punitive ministrations by an individual such as the lieutenant who was well-known even in the relative obscurity of the organization's mountain territory for his ultra-violence and sadistic excesses.

She turned her head slightly, peering up at him with pleading eyes as he stationed himself behind her, the strap in his hands. From beneath his thick mustache Wendy believed that she could ascertain that he was mouthing some words which were unknown to her, only the barest whisper reaching her ears. His eyes were intent upon the deity as he spoke his unknown incantation and then they fell onto her, his eyes roving hungrily over her exposed flesh and then locking onto her own, their gaze frozen together for a split second before he raised his hand holding the strap and then bringing it down upon her naked and exposed flesh with a resounding pop that echoed throughout the tunnel.

The sound of the leather strap meeting bare flesh was followed immediately by a piercing scream from Wendy. Though she had found it impossible to audibly express herself earlier when the lieutenant's survival knife had slashed across her upraised wrist and palm, she found that her lungs had reasserted themselves as the cruel and evil leather strap of the Great Demon, Gaubni, slashed itself in a similar fashion across the innocent flesh of her upturned backside and the exposed parts of her upper legs. The lashes came again and again, all expertly aimed, however the length of the strap was such that it caused the end to not only strike its target but curl around her flesh as well, causing the most painful strikes against the sides of her legs and the lowest parts of her back. The lieutenant's pacing was relentless with no more than five seconds elapsing between one lash and the next, her screams following apace which seemed to electrify the environment - the sounds of pain and molestation via discipline being sucked up by the idol of the Great Demon in a frenzied state of vampiric feeding.

Though Wendy had begun the punishment with her head turned back toward the lieutenant, eying him as he moved in to strike, she found this position now too painful, a crick in her neck adding to the more arduous injury that she was receiving on the opposite end. To that effect and due to the fact that she no longer wished to see and predict when each strike would fall, she had jutted her face forward, straining with all her might against the bonds so that her face stared toward the base of the idol before her. To her disgust and surprise she saw that the otherwise formless idol possessed one noticeably attribute, namely a large protruding male sexual member also of the same polished black rock form which the rest of the Great Demon's effigy had been forged.

The merciless beating continued for what seemed like hours, all sense of time and proportion passing as Wendy's head begin to droop, her screams of protest becoming hoarse and then degenerating into soft whimpers and cries, the tears from her eyes flowing copiously and further commingling with the blood which had been smeared upon her mouth from the lieutenant's wound, giving her the ghastly appearance of some young ghoul recently returned from a nocturnal assignation. Her buttocks had become swollen red orbs before marbling into the black and blue of heavy bruising with faint lines of red where the edges of the heavy strap had broken the skin. Despite the seemingly endless duration of the punishment it had been in fact less than half an hour's time since the lieutenant had begun, the efficiency of her flesh's ruination being enhanced by his prodigiously consistent pacing. As the blows of the strap continued to fall, her entire body was forced forward against the stone of the altar, the torque of the lieutenant's blows and the heaviness of the leather strap driving her small frame forward painfully against the unyielding surface of the altar.

All of a sudden the beating ceased, with Wendy so barely aware that she could only slightly register the fact that she could no longer hear the sound of the leather pummeling her naked flesh. Exhausted and spent of all energy, her posterior throbbing in pain, she turned her head from the idol before her and once again rested her cheek upon the cold stone of the altar. At that very moment and suddenly from far above her and the lieutenant came a hideous ghostly wail, seeming to emanate from the second air shaft located directly behind the idol of the Great Demon itself. This sound was immediately joined by the sound of the lieutenant bursting forth in a great peal of maniacal laughter, the sound of which careened and bounced off the walls of the tunnel, his eyes rolled back into his head, spittle dribbling from his mouth as his face turned upward toward the roof of the cavern.

According to the tradition of the cult of the Great Demon in the organization's mountain territory, an omen, often auditory, would accompany Gaubni's acceptance of an offering or sacrifice. In this case the hideous wail that had echoed throughout the tunnel indicated that the offering of pain which had been culled from the little girl whom the lieutenant had brought for joining before the idol had been accepted, wrested from her by the leather punishment strap which had been utilized in his service for generations upon generations. Now Wendy was not only the lieutenant's bride but, as well, a fellow traveler in the cult of the the Great Demon, accepted by a sign from the Great Demon himself.

The lieutenant proceeded to the far corner of the tunnel, replacing the thick leather strap upon the hook from which he had retrieved it earlier. Wendy breathed a silent sigh of relief at this small fact; at least she would not be facing the strap again on this night. The howling that had come from the air shaft seemed to have entered into her like a cold filament sending a feeling of steel through her spine. What exactly it was she could not say, though she felt somewhat changed; what sort of change it would be was yet to be seen.

Her eyes followed the lieutenant as he returned from replacing the leather strap upon the hook on the wall of the tunnel, his laughter having subsided with the fading of the ghostly wailing into small, strange animalistic sounds, as though he was conversing with himself and only tentatively aware of her presence. Yet, as soon as he reached within touching distance, he crouched down and patted the little girl with an uncharacteristic tenderness on the head, smoothing our her coal-black hair and looking into her still tear-filled eyes with a look that seemed to intimate that he was once again himself, though certainly bearing the residual signs of his earlier craze.

From the small pile of materials that had been offered before the idol prior to the lieutenant's having administered Wendy's lengthy discipline he took the flagon of mountain liquor once more, removing the cap and bringing it to Wendy's lips and holding it there for several seconds, allowing the liquor to trickle down her throat as the little girl's hands and arms were still bound and as such she was unable to grasp the flagon herself, forcing her to suckle. After recapping and replacing the flagon upon the ground, having taken a slug for himself after Wendy had her fill, the lieutenant removed the first of two small leather packets that she had noticed him offering earlier. As he opened it up she could see that it was a small packet of bear grease, harvested no doubt from the wild black bears that had been hunted and killed during the recently past autumn here in the mountains. That the lieutenant's quartermaster had a supply of the same was interesting as it would intimate that either he had obtained it only recently or the off chance that he kept a steady supply. In any case, the meaning was clear for what it would be utilized for tonight.

The lieutenant moved behind Wendy who, still bound, could only turn her head slightly backward to observe whatever ministrations he would be proceeding with presently. Her backside was in a state of ruination from the strapping which she had just endured, with even the slightest touch causing immense pain. The lieutenant, grinning widely as he handled the packet of bear grease, slathered the index finger of his right hand with the same and then began to rub it copiously into the area between her buttocks, slowly working it into her anal cavity with a single finger. Wendy felt herself whimper softly despite herself as the soreness of the beating, moving effortlessly into the pain and pleasure mixture she felt from the lieutenant's penetration as he moved his finger in and out of her tight sphincter. Wendy let out a second whimper, this time more audible and less voluntary, as the lieutenant inserted another finger into her anus, his rough knuckles rubbing against the brutalized skin of her buttocks. His pace quickened and she felt herself wanting to reciprocate and move further down onto his stretched fingers, however the immobility of her bonds only allowed for the ever so slight rotation and protrusion of her exposed rear, a move which, although slight, was not lost on the lieutenant.

The lieutenant removed his greased fingers and with a deft motion unfastened the front of his trousers, pulling them down and settling himself on his knees directly behind her. With his grease-covered hand he guided the tip of his sexual member into the upraised and exposed sphincter of the little girl wriggling on the stone altar before him before grasping each side of the altar himself with muscled arms and entering into her fully with a deep thrust, eliciting a high-pitched cry from Wendy's small, blood-stained lips. Again and again he thrust into her, his motions gliding the full length of himself again and again into the little girl's entrails, her cries and sobs mingled into a state of combined discomfiture and perverse ecstasy. His hands left the altar and began fondling her swollen and bruised buttocks, admiring the feel of the raised stripes from the leather strap beating that were the still enduring testaments to his earlier handiwork.

The lieutenant withdrew from Wendy, stopping to unstrap her from the stone altar, her body crumpling to the floor from exhaustion and the stress of the beating and the lieutenant's subsequent sodomy. The lieutenant drew her toward him, cradling her against his chest and quickly pulled her pants the rest of the way down before pulling her combat jacket and shirt up and over her head, revealing creamy white skin and only the slightest hint of budding breasts. Kneeling with his pants now around his ankles, the lieutenant lifted her onto him, her back toward him and her face toward the altar of the Great Demon, re-entering her anally and pulling her weight down upon his erect member with ferocious intensity, his arms held across her chest and his teeth biting into the exposed flesh of her neck and shoulders. Both the lieutenant and Wendy now panted together in their shared exertion, the feel of her feather-soft thighs straddled against him and the nub of her pert underaged nipples between his fingers driving him ever and ever closer to a hideous climax.

CHAPTER 26

Several days had passed now since Nadezhda's initial interview and orientation for torture center in the large building at the commander's headquarters which had formerly served as the inmate hospital before the nuclear wars during the time that the headquarters compound had itself served as a U.S. Penitentiary, a federal prison for the most dangerous criminals in the United States, a country which, like much of the former societal and national structures, did not endure the sickening gleam of the hydrogen-powered mushroom clouds which had sprouted throughout the world leaving only untold death and devastation in its wake.

She had been taken by her balaclava-masked internal security handlers across the red line on the floor of the inquiry center, marking the beginning of the 'secure area' as it was politely called which, in more plain language, denoted that the area beyond it was reserved for the more hands-on aspects of ECTAC, thus the designation of this area as the 'torture center' specifically.

IRON GATES

She had been led to the cell of Private Bonn, her alleged paramour, where the internal security personnel had given a rap of his ever-present nightstick upon the cell door which caused a feeble fluttering of Private Bonn's eyes and nothing more. As their alleged sexual liaison at anytime was patently fraudulent, Nadezhda wondered whether or not her minders really expected some sort of enthusiastic response from the prisoner inside the cell or if the action was a further part of their intelligence-driven theater, contrived or otherwise.

Beyond any potential reality to the claims, the physical state of Private Bonn was enough to negate any noticeable response. His body lay naked upon a thin cot which rested upon the bottom rack of a steel bunk-bed, with no apparent resident on the top bunk. A thin sheet which had been provided as his only guard against the wintry weather which now reigned down on the commander's headquarters, all the more apparent because of the exclusively concrete block and steel composition of the installation, lay beside him bunched up and unused, or alternately thrown off him in the course of some sort of nightmarish state during sleep. No chains or bonds beyond the cell door itself now restrained the shock trooper, who had become a fragile shell of himself after only a mere few days under the conscientious attentions of the torture center's expert staff.

The bonds which now afflicted the shock trooper in question were in the form of a chemical straight-jacket rather than a literal one, for he had come under the care of the experimental units within torture center who availed themselves of testing the old psychotropic drugs, many of them more than one hundred years past their stated 'use by' designations, of which a near warehouse full had been found on the now site of the commander's headquarters many decades before. Rather than applying such medications conventionally, the experimental units out of a sense of practicality due to the highly degenerated states of the various pills and serums at their disposal had long established the practice of creating their own combinations and concoctions with the drugs, sometimes added to with substances of their own creation as well as with donated substances from abroad elsewhere in the organization's territory (and sometimes beyond) which were supplied to them by internal security personnel who acted as attaches to various intelligence-run cult recruiters who scoured the parched landscape of the post-nuclear world, conducting missions of analysis, reconnaissance and recruitment.

Nadezhda was only stationed in front of Private Bonn's cell for a minute or so, enough for her to ascertain the state of his present situation which was formerly unbeknownst to her, and also exacerbating on the psychological level the demarcation between the scene she now saw with the former courtesy of the man who had interviewed her previously and his anonymous assistants who now accompanied her further into the bowels of the torture center.

After some time of traversing the bleak and seemingly endless corridors lined on either side with cells, some of them containing persons in custody and some of them relegated for the most secretive of torture center administration duties by way of offices - the less secure administrative offices for ECTAC being located on the other side of the red line - she had finally reached the destination for which the internal security personnel had been accompanying her which was a large, open-air room dominated on the far side by an observation station, behind which at a desk sat an imposing matronly woman of prodigious girth. Her stout figure was well complimented however by her equally prodigious height, as by the time Nadezhda had been brought forward to the plexiglass wall separating herself from the observation office, it could be readily observed that even seated the woman behind the glass was equal to Nadezhda's own height standing.

As Nadezhda stood before the plexiglass pane separating her from the woman on the other side, herself flanked by two masked internal security guards who had not uttered a word since their departure from the interviewing officer, she wondered as to whether or not her previous request to the lieutenant to be made SAC of torture center had been the correct choice, or whether or not there was an implicit ruse in his willing acquiescence to her desire for the same. Although she now found herself within the domicile of the specific internal security sector of her desired assignment, she felt that she was being handled more like an inmate than an incoming officer, the disdainful and dismissive glance of the woman behind the pane before her bearing further testament to her doubts in this regard.

At long last the torture center personnel behind the glass acknowledged her directly, setting aside a large stack of files to her right and leaning toward the area of drilled holes arrayed in the pattern of a circle that served as the means of auditory communications between herself and those on the other side of the pane, the rest of the plexiglass being otherwise impenetrable to sound in general.

'Name please,' stated the stout woman, her bulky form having to crouch forward in her chair slightly for her mouth to be level with the drilled sound portals which were obviously made for more conventionally-sized personnel during their construction prior to the nuclear wars.

Nadezhda stood at rest position, her hands clasped behind her back and began speaking.

'My name is Nadezhda Yatskaya, I have been transferred from signals intelligence to torture center to...'

Her monologue was met with a shrill screech of protest from the woman behind the pane of plexiglass, a great ham-sized fist beating the desk in front of her, causing the formidable twelve-inch stacks of files to the side to jump off the surface in physical reaction. From her left side, Nadezhda felt the painful touch of one of the internal security guards pinching her side, leaning his masked anonymous face towards ear and whispering in a harsh monotone audible only to her and the other internal security personnel, 'Name only, nothing more.'

Nadezhda repositioned herself, bringing her arms to her sides in a full attention posture before responding again.

'Yatskaya, Nadezhda!'

IRON GATES

The emphasis on Nadezhda's surname caused the woman behind the pane to grimace considerably before she brought herself together towards the purpose of further discourse, her face already having become beet-red and sweating the cold sweat of rage despite the ever-deepening coldness of the former prison infrastructure in which she toiled.

The woman glowered before Nadezhda, not looking at her directly but her gaze turned down toward the thick file dealing with Nadezhda that had been compiled for her within the last week since Nadezhda had surreptitiously placed the card from the lieutenant in the night-drop, thus putting into motion the chain of events under which Nadezhda now felt herself irrevocably bound, the most direct feature being that she was now at the mercy of the monstrous creature directly before her whose large hands held her life in the balance in the form of a stapled mass of paperwork, the contents of which Nadezhda herself was woefully unaware. The file contained detailed reports of Nadezhda stemming from since her childhood, the surveillance of her person having been effected with extra rigorousness due to the advanced position of her father in the commander's hierarchy. The commander, ever a pragmatist at heart, had always endeavored to keep his friends as close as his enemies in an edited form of the traditional phrase, knowing full well that those who had intimate access to the power praxes of the organization were those who needed the closest watch, well-closer than the most irascible rebels at the farthest borders of the organization's territory.

IRON GATES

Time moved slowly for Nadezhda as she stood awaiting the initial analysis of her file by the female torture center personnel member behind the plexiglass pane. From the internal security guard personnel before her, Nadezhda heard no further verbal communication excepting the brief command which she had been issued earlier. As she waited, Nadezhda took the opportunity to observe the area around her. The large room once upon a distant time had served as a visitation area between civilians and the most physically debilitated of the federal inmate hospital, the risk of potential health infection being born brunt upon the visitors while the employees of the prison itself were protected in the area beyond the plexiglass where Nadezhda's female interrogator now sat. In some fashion Nadezhda felt that the term interrogator was too harsh to project upon her, yet in another, more immediate sense Nadezhda was well aware that her prospects could be worse than she expected, as the undeniable scent of threat hung heavily in the air.

Suddenly the torture center personnel member behind the desk raised her head and, avoiding Nadezhda's eyes in an almost compassionate sense, so very different than the demeanor which she had hitherto exhibited, nodded briefly to the internal security members flanking Nadezhda. A buzzer sounded, indicating that the door into the areas behind the plexiglass and guard shack had been unlocked and, within a few steps Nadezhda and her handlers had entered the innermost hell of torture center. With a resounding click, Nadezhda heard the door lock behind her as she was led down the corridor.

CHAPTER 27

Several days had passed since Nadezhda entered the bowels of torture center and thus far things had become worse as she herself had premeditated. The internal security members had taken her far down a black-painted corridor which seemed to slowly descend on a downward grade which indicated to her that they were in fact going into areas that were subterranean to the rest of the torture center itself.

The first part of her journey with her attendants had been in the area directly behind the guard shack and the accompanying wall of plexiglass and seemed somewhat intimidating yet in the usual clinical sense of the term, with utilitarian-proportioned well-scrubbed areas and expanses of light-colored flooring interspersed with doorways on either sides, the residents of which were hidden from sight due to obscuring mesh that had been inserted over the windows to the cells. After several minutes however they had reached an area bearing yet another locked door which had to be opened by external control, though the door itself and its obscure area of placement could have very well been a service entrance or a closet from outward appearance, bearing neither distinguishing markings nor overt or covert indicators as to its ultimate destination.

Apparently the deception was intentional, as once opened, the door led into seemingly endless labyrinthine corridors which bore the unmistakeable secret police imprint of the sadistically-wielded blackjack under harsh lights and other beatings administered in any number of curious fashions, indicative in every sense of applied intelligence in its most brutal and on-the-ground fashion. This was, as it were, the atmosphere of torture center which Nadezhda herself had speculated about in all of her career-driven daydreams in the years working the desks of intelligence analysis and, as she passed through the hushed corridors, eerily bereft of personnel and so quiet otherwise that to outside ears it could almost be considered uninhabited, she knew then that she had entered the arena of her destiny - for weal or for woe.

The internal security members turned toward a corridor snaking off to the left away from the main hallway and they proceeded in concert for some minutes before being met by a black-robed female, her face obscured by a large cowl and wearing a thick, black utility belt about her waist upon which was attached a bundle of large keys upon one side and a penitentiary strop upon the other. The female, who was easily recognizable as being a member of the commandant's cult, thus signaling the collusion between torture center and the religion which Nadezhda had suspected for sometime, removed one key and opened up the cell directly in front of Nadezhda as her handlers from internal security promptly and without fanfare shoved Nadezhda roughly into the dark area, causing her to fall upon the cement floor and summarily slamming the door shut behind her. The footsteps of the internal security members could be heard audibly proceeding in one direction and the robed member of the commandant's cult proceeding in another, leaving Nadezhda alone in the black cell, effectively without light, the exception being the dim glow from the aerial corridor lights which were situated some cells away. With a sense of dread yet also indisputable anticipation, Nadezhda crouched against the nearest wall, her knees brought up to her chest, awaiting whatever fate would deign to bring her.

IRON GATES

CHAPTER 28

It was several days since the last encounter with the rebels, yet the field marshal could still smell the blood of the hunt upon his nostrils, as could his coterie of shock troopers and varied elite personnel who had accompanied him into the field, drawn from a diverse arrangement of organizational intelligence and non-disclosed sectors, the latter of whom allegedly had direct contact with the commander's liaison at headquarters.

The fact that certain elements were present, only under his direct authority within a titular sense and effectively circumventing the chain of command as such did not bother the field marshal in the least bit but rather enlivened his sense of mission and made him consider the chance for unknown variables in the campaign which lay ahead.

Effectively he was in the dark as to specifics, though he realized without a doubt that there was an unequivocal territorial push being made due to the fact that the organizational forces were proceeding further into the hinterlands than they ever had prior. He had been made aware, only by courier transmission, of the fact that there had been an unveiling of a new projectile-style weapon hitherto unemployed in the history of the organization in its post-apocalyptic context, however the course and trajectory of such an employment were still - details-wise - a matter of speculation.

What mattered, to him, in the moment, and for the foreseeable moments to come, was that he was on the brink of something incalculably horrific in scope - something wrought within the bloody mind of the megalomaniac vanguard that was the organization itself - encapsulated in its most horrific visage in the entity of the commander and in the qualitative parts and parcels of which he, the field marshal himself, was counted and furthermore inhabited in a position of some prominence.

He would do his part, his subordinates would do their parts and together, with the influx of all manner of organizational forces converging on the border region, they would coalesce into a whirlwind of indescribable nightmare and make history. Not the stale history of days gone by, but that new history, that history without moral qualm or reservation, that new and devastating history wrought on the radiation-soaked graveyard of the old civilization with every constraint and consideration which had held it back from the nightmarish crescendos of which the organization availed itself as the ultimate composer in current and future climes effectively obliterated.

Since Britta and the cult recruiters had left for headquarters, his schedule had been a frenzy of activity as more and more organizational personnel poured into the border encampment. Much of his time had been taken up inside the administrative tent along with other higher ranking combat coordinators working out potential strategies and points of entry for when the hostilities began in earnest, though the fact that they were still operating with far less than complete information about the exact nature of the prime method to be employed in the assault did not make the planning any easier. Even still however, what information they did have was acted upon with no small degree of meticulousness and the word coming down from the rumor mill of recently arrived organizational personnel from headquarters seemed to indicate that certain unveilings as to the new weaponry would be made sooner than later in order to expedite the campaign. The field marshal had been fully briefed concerning the rocket mechanism that had been disclosed at the private armaments convention sometime back and that, along with the prodigious stock of gas masks he had been shown during his first meeting at field administration, did not make it difficult to put two and two together.

As the effective commander for coordination of forces on the ground the field marshal had availed himself of the expert personnel at his disposal and the increasing new numbers of specialists who were entering into camp at often up to between ten to twenty new organizational members per day, said numbers which had swollen the encampment to several hundred more people than had originally been inhabiting the area upon his initial arrival. With more personnel and in light of his executive position, he had delegated much of the administrative work, certain of which was becoming redundant due to the fact that they were still effectively on hold for more ambitious undertakings - per word of the commander himself - for anything except the briefest of engagements in self-defense in the context of outward scouting - until the weapon system had been delivered.

With this delegation of duties by the field marshal he had taken his own small entourage out into the field beyond the encampment and some several miles deep into the territory outside the auspices of organizational control. There had been some brief encounters which had by the actions of him and his staff gone more than somewhat beyond the allowable limits as had been specified by orders, however with no reporting of the incidents up the chain of command since and no survivors in the isolated skirmishes, he and his men were effectively concealed in their actions, or at least hoped to be. Should word somehow trickle out among the rebels of certain of their more isolated compatriots having been 'disappeared' there was in all likelihood the unerring possibility that they themselves would also be facing death in the not too distant future in the concourse of the main campaign, thus mitigating any immediate threat - though functioning at such a level within the commander's organization was threat enough in and of itself for all participants, whether such threats were internally or externally driven.

On the third day of their outward patrol they had come upon a small contingent of scouts from the so-called rebel territories who were, as the case may be, on a similar mission not unlike their own - that being taking a

IRON GATES

cursory examination of the area and testing the present outward capabilities of their respective foe. In this case, given their opposite trajectory, attempting to see if the organization had placed any outward scouting posts beyond the large encampment directly on the border which, given its scope and its position in a valley amidst the surrounding hills, could be seen for many miles past the border area properly.

As the field marshal's retinue were of a much more highly disciplined and trained demographic than the rebels, the field marshal's forward guard had spotted the small patrol some hours before the confrontation proper and had watched them from the periphery of the deeply forested hillside in the vicinity of a narrow and barely perceptible path through the mountain passes. The opposition's patrol was grossly outnumbered to the field marshal's twenty men, consisting only of five nearly starved persons with only a few operable weapons between them, one of which was an antique yet very well maintained double-barrel shotgun which bore no match against the berth of organizational-produced weaponry routinely toted by members of the organization.

After several hours of watching and watching only, with the understanding now that the five members of the opposition patrol were many miles from any of their associates and continually unaware of the field marshal's contingent, the action was swift and executed with precision as two squads of shock troopers swept down from the hillsides on either side of the rebel patrol, taking out with silenced drill-like report two of the patrol members bearing arms and quickly routing the others into a quick and unequivocal surrender.

The surviving three members of the patrol were forcibly laid face-down on the cool dirt of the mountain path and immediately surrounded by masked members of internal security who had come up the main route from the southern trailhead as the shock troopers removed themselves to begin stripping the dead of any possible valuables and then stripping them proper before dragging the corpses back down the path to be butchered and rendered for food at the small encampment which the field marshal had set up the night prior.

The interrogations were conducted quickly and with minimal fanfare, with three internal security personnel taking a captive per team and leading them off into the woods beyond comprehensible hearing distance of the others, with one intelligence officer making rounds between them and noting any actionable intelligence procured by the interrogators. On every third go around or so the intelligence personnel would make the quick hike down the southern path and up the ridge to where the field marshal himself was stationed at the encampment and pass on any intelligence highlights of note and receive any appropriate instructions to pass on to the interrogators before proceeding back down the ridge and up the path to the staging area.

Of the three persons being interrogated it could be quickly ascertained that of the three one of the patrol knew nothing of significance whereas the remainder carried some actionable intelligence of varying degrees. What the two arms-bearing persons who had been dispatched upon the inauguration of the ambush knew no one could tell. That being said, the field marshal in general did not see this as a priority action, though he made sure that the personnel under his direct leadership saw him approach the situation with all gravity so that they would do likewise, as this small action as perhaps insignificant as it was in the long term would provide valuable training for the shock troopers, internal security personnel and organizational intelligence officers, the skills which were being honed which could be applied all the more sharply once the campaign had commenced in earnest.

The third patrol member amongst the opposition who was obviously kept in the dark regarding the activities of the rebels due to either titular rank designation or general ineptitude was, by strategy and design, the person that the organizational internal security personnel began grilling the hardest about potential enemy activities. The other interrogation teams and their quarry which had hitherto been stationed out of earshot were gradually moved about within the forest operating theater so that they could audibly hear the level of intensity being increased in a continual and graduated fashion on the one unlucky member of their patrol team who was now bearing the brunt of the collective interrogation team's wrath, with the most aggressive interrogators among the field marshal's team being cycled to that particular target specifically.

In time the interrogation teams had coalesced not

only to within earshot of the others but within plain viewing of the associated captives as the organizational men slowly moved their quarry into a small clearing within the forest arranged within a circle of tall standing pines, with a cool yet circumstantially unsettling breeze whistling within.

While the two potentially lucrative intelligence targets and the three-man teams of internal security personnel conducting the interrogations on their respective targets were positioned to the northeastern and northwestern quadrants of the clearing respectively, the three-man internal security team with the harshest interrogators and the target example stationed themselves in the center of the clearing to provide full view of the associated captives and facilitating more fluid communication capabilities betwixt the organizational personnel themselves.

In time, the unlucky member of the opposition's patrol, still answering in the negative to the inquiries of the internal security members, was stripped and bound to a stout wooden stake which was quickly brought in and installed by a team consisting of several heavily-muscled shock troopers, their bulging arms visible capped off by their rolled-up BDU jackets and all to a man covered in grisly tattoos consisting of numerous crude depictions of child rape, torture and a myriad of bizarre symbols bearing testament to their membership in one or the other of the various cults that flourished like poisonous mushrooms within the organization.

The prisoner's clothes were thrown to the side and disregarded - too ragged and dry-rotted to serve any purpose except perhaps acting as ancillary incendiary fuel for the evening meal back at the encampment later, though in any case they would be disposed of (more than likely by burning, whatever the context) as to erase any sign of the field marshal's men having been in the area.

Though the field marshal was as the case may be extending significantly the acceptable line of action for this juncture prior to the campaign proper, he was going to make sure that even the most insignificant tell-tale signs of his presence here or his actions in the surrounding area were concealed, concealed from members of the opposition who may come across such evidences firstly though most pressingly from other organizational forces who may come through the area once the campaign had started in earnest.

In situations that involved great territorial pushes and other ambitious martial objectives invariably that was the time that internal politics began to rear their head and he knew that there were more than a few members within the organization who would be interested in exploiting any opportunity of advantage to inveigle themselves into his station within the organization's military force whether by hook or crook. As he considered these things, having been briefed about the acceleration of the interrogation and the ruse that was currently being employed by the intelligence officer who was now walking back down the ridge, he felt a cold feeling arise within himself as he began to speculate on the number of spies that were involved in the ongoing operation at present, those men not loyal to him but only to the commander or perhaps in fact to some strange and unknown non-disclosed organizational sector of whose administration and objectives he could only guess.

The intelligence officer trotted down the ridge and onto the path leading toward the staging area of the interrogation with an extra spring in his step, having been informed by the field marshal that terminal maneuvers could be employed in the case of the recalcitrant know-nothing that the shock troopers had recently secured to the stake in the center of the clearing. If anything, this would loosen the lips of the other and soon to be last surviving members of the patrol so that they might be induced to provide some details in furtherance of organizational intelligence before they too met a fate similar to the one among their remnant who would be the first to face organizational bullets since the initial ambush casualties. The intelligence officer smiled to himself as he made the last bend of the ridge and began walking on the path proper, a small sheaf of rolled paper within his hand containing his notes on the interrogation thus far but also, in code, personal observations on the psychological state of the field marshal during the present field activities, to be delivered via hand-courier to certain of his superiors in one of the secret detachments of internal security once they had arrived back at the main border encampment. Wheels within wheels of intrigue were churning within the organization at present and the intelligence officer felt great pleasure that his own deceptive activities to which he had been assigned would assist in calibrating these great and terrible wheels, which turned incessantly under the maniacal gaze of the commander within the bleak landscapes of the post-nuclear earth.

At long last the intelligence officer arrived at the forest clearing where the principal prisoner now was situated bound fully nude and in an upright standing position against the large wooden stake facing the other prisoners and the interrogation teams which surrounded them, the latter now no longer conducting the usual business but holding their charges firmly by the arms and forcing them to face their compatriot who was soon to be made an example of in no uncertain terms.

The intelligence officer approached the senior internal security personnel on duty, whispering into his ear the instructions he had received from the field marshal and receiving a cold nod from within the featureless black mask and goggles as the internal security member turned and began tightening the fastenings of the silencer to his MP5, inserting a fresh clip and filling several more for easy access which he inserted into appropriate slots on his tactical vest.

As the senior internal security personnel prepared his weapon, the intelligence officer proceeded to several of the nearby shock troopers and issued instructions in a low voice which elicited sadistic gleams in every eye and expressions of mirth punctuated with bloodlust upon every visage so concerned. The forest clearing became a scene of low murmurings and strange suppressed sounds as the two interrogation teams threatened their charges in low voices while the shock troopers made their own preparations for the principal captive.

A piece of the rotten clothing which had been stripped from the prisoner was plucked from the ground and torn into a stout rag, which one of the shock troopers then doused with an unknown liquid drawn from one of the ancillary canteens strapped to his utility belt before shoving it into the prisoner's mouth and wrapping another strip of rag around his head, securing it tightly.

Two of the shock troopers occupied themselves with building and stoking a small fire into which were set two makeshift torches made from small tree limbs, wrapped at the ends with the remainder of the prisoner's rotted clothing and similarly doused with the liquid from the canteen of the shock trooper who had busied himself with the binding of the principal captive directly prior.

With a hiss the largest among the shock troopers withdrew a large and sadistically gleaming combat survival knife from a sheath hanging upon his hip, holding it out in front of him and slowly approaching the bound captive with the paced and assured gait of the born predator. The bound captive's eyes widened and his mouth grimaced into a rictus of horror as the shock trooper smiled and extended the knife, rubbing the side of the cold steel blade slowly against the face of the prisoner and watching as equally cold sweat began to drip down the face of his quarry in expectation of what horrors the organization man might have in store for him.

The preamble over, the shock trooper went directly into business mode, plunging his blade with the

IRON GATES

expertise of an experienced butcher into the crevice between the prisoner's shoulder and arm and sawing furiously, his muscles straining and veins pulsating with vascularity under the strain of the work. The prisoner's body began shaking uncontrollably as the shock trooper moved his blade deeper and deeper into the flesh, the muffled screams coming from the chemical-drenched rag inserted into his mouth sounding for all effective purposes like an animal trapped in the unforgiving metal teeth of a lethal snare.

The two other captured patrol members began wailing at the sight of their compatriot's fate, a reaction for which the respective interrogation teams were prepared as they quickly grasped black-gloved hands over the men's mouths, stifling their screams, the weak struggling of their feeble and starved bodies easily overwhelmed by the cannibalistic and speed-induced strength of the organizational men.

With a horrific and final push the shock trooper finished cutting through the arm, with the entire limb falling with a sickening thud onto the ground beside the wooden stake and arterial blood shooting through the air. The shock trooper reared back his head and let loose an involuntary and hideous laugh, his eyes rolling back into his head, as the shock troopers who had been tending the fire rushed forward and thrust their burning torches into the prisoner's bloody wound, effecting a crude cauterization and filling the air with the nauseating smell of burning blood and human meat.

Systematically the scene was repeated upon the other arm - the intimidation followed by the methodical butchery - the gloating of the largest and most sadistic among the shock troopers as the others cauterized the wound. By the time the second limb had been removed the principal captive was barely conscious except for the properties of whatever chemical had been sublingually administered to him through the vector of the gag cloth, the purpose of which seemed to be keeping him conscious at least to a titular degree while experiencing a level of torture that would have easily caused him to black out in shock under normal circumstances. The other captives held by the additional interrogation teams were still being kept muzzled by the unyielding leather-gloved hands of their captors with not an audible sound escaping, their confessions and coerced intelligence reports being waylaid until after the demonstration with the more recalcitrant of their number having been duly effected and completed.

The shock trooper moved onto the legs, a more arduous task in general but effected with an effort more than grim, with the limbs held on tenaciously with the last remaining strings of flesh being ripped off with a brutal pulling before being slung to the side where they were collected along with the rest before being wrapped by one of the other shock troopers and carried down the trailhead and up the ridge toward the main encampment to be prepared with the rest of the flesh for the organization's nocturnal mastication.

As the shock trooper cauterized the last two wounds, only the slightest hint of consciousness could be seen upon the captive's face, a dim flickering deep within the eyes testament to a consciousness driven to the brink and then beyond the pale of induced insanity and held aware only by artificial means and compartmentalization of the mind in some hidden internal place of comprehension to shield from the incomprehensible situation in which he had found himself for falling in with the rebels, for failing to submit to the iron fist of the commander due to the proclivities of his geographic region. Had he been a smarter man, had he been ambitious, he would have been proactive in his treason, sneaking across the border into the large organizational encampment whose flickering lights in the valley distance bore the promise of a life beyond the marginal existence to which he and his compatriots so stubbornly held.

But now that hope was gone, his only solace being that his spirit - if there was such a thing - might be drawn into some strange blood abyss by dint of his having become, albeit involuntarily, a sacrifice to the organization whose gods were strange and some of which were gods-in-flesh-bodies, such as the commander. Night fell upon his consciousness as the shock troopers moved away, the area beneath the wooden stake and the patrolman himself gratuitously soaked in sopping blood.

The senior internal security personnel moved forward, black and anonymous goggled eyes staring strange and alien out toward his victim as he raised the black and lethal snub of his silenced MP5 toward the patrolman from a distance of only a few feet and then began shooting - the sound of the suppressed fire resonating like some strange ground wasp beneath the surface - the body of the opposition member being machine-gunned beyond all recognition as the senior internal security personnel unloaded clip after clip into the head-bearing trunk, churning and grinding the flesh into quivering meat. A fell wind blew and a mist of blood caught upon the wind, wafting into the darkening twilight.

CHAPTER 29

The light had not yet risen on the area surrounding the engineering center in the organization's clandestine mountain fastness when the lieutenant rose to begin preparations for the day's expedition for the testing of the chemical warhead which the engineer had prepared. He bent down and rubbed Wendy's soot-black hair away from her head, kissing her gently upon the cheek which elicited a slight parting of her eyes and a look of sleepy recognition.

'Soon,' whispered the lieutenant. 'Be prepared upon my return.' With that he drew out a fresh cigar from his rucksack which lay upon the small wooden table near the corner of the canvas walls of the tent, lighting it in several strong healthy draws before exiting on his way for the retrieval of the test weapon, the tent's entrance flap opened only for a moment, showing a clear blackish-blue pale of emerging dawn and letting in a cold breeze which made Wendy shiver.

She had passed out asleep while still within the tunnel during their previous night's assignations, partly from exhaustion and partly from the atmosphere which had come down upon her consciousness near the end which seemed almost too much for her waking state of mind to bear. Now that she was awake, after several hours of sleep only, the night before seemed almost like some strange nightmare. Having apparently fallen unconscious while still in the tunnel itself and still engaged in ministrations with the lieutenant she did not remember the exit journey and assumed that the lieutenant had to have carried her out himself.

She drew the rough blanket away from her, naked only for a worn uniform shirt of the lieutenant's which he had apparently dressed her in himself, its bottom edges hanging almost to her knees and testament to their stark difference in both age and physicality. In the corner lay her baby brigade uniform which had been issued to her only the day before, crumpled in a careless pile yet situated with intent so that she would be able to find it upon awakening.

She sniffled with rising emotion at seeing the uniform, in part that she herself had not been awake and aware to properly care for it, the sight of the finest garments she had ever known thrown aside like some rags causing her no small guilt and discontent at her own perceived ineptness. This seemingly trifle emotion was compounded also with an overwhelming sense of now being possessed by the lieutenant and in turn possessing him and with premeditation of all that such might entail for the future as she began her first day as his bride.

Still dressed in the makeshift nightshirt, she crept out of the tent and around to the back where a small bucket of mountain stream water sat upon a small crate for washing. She splashed some of the cold water on her face, her eyes instantly focusing more intently as the shock of the cold liquid compounded with the frosty air of the early morning mountains in the darker season of the year. A few yards' walk into the small copse of trees at the base of the ridge and she proceeded to relieve herself before returning to the wash bucket, pulling the large uniform shirt up and over her head, folding it carefully and laying it aside the crate before cupping her hands in the cold water and allowing it to sluice down over her naked body, goose-pimpled from the cold and shining pale and luminescent in the fragile light of predawn.

Already the sounds of the lieutenant's men beginning their activities could be heard around her in the area, though she was shielded from their vision by dint of the wooded nature of the area and the various grades and slopes which kept the lieutenant's personal tent relatively shielded from the rest of his entourage. Should any of them have seen her in her nakedness she would have had little care, for she was not so demure, having grown up in the harsh rigors of the engineering center, harsh in every sense both physically, psychologically and sexually. She was furthermore emboldened knowing now her special position as it related to the specific loyalties of the men who surrounded her, whose rough voices and various physical tasks being performed could be heard as she continued her morning washing in the growing early morning light. Did they know that she was his wife?

At the thought she laughed to herself. How could they? As they had only wed the night before, in reality only a few hours before, in fact. She rubbed her hands gently against the vicious red bite wounds that liberally covered her neck, back and shoulders and even more tenderly the bruised and blood-encrusted weals that covered her posterior from the cruel ministrations of Gaubni's whip. Those latter marks of her husband's devotion would stay with her for some time to come.

She felt the cold water on her naked flesh begin to cool her skin and realized that she had failed to procure any sort of towel to dry herself with and looking around saw that there was nothing available in the direct area excepting the lieutenant's shirt which she had only recently removed. She drew the cloth to her body and began spot-drying lightly as to not unnecessarily drench the garment, the black cloth which was undoubtedly rough once upon a time now soft from years of wear, the black now being somewhat faded and marked with telltale signs of old blood darkening the fabric here and there, smelling of the lieutenant's sweat and tobacco with the faintest hint of the mountain liquor he had consumed the day before.

A murder of crows flew from the sky, now beginning to show the harsh light of morning in more fullness as the sun arose over the mist-shrouded eastern ridge, their shrill voices piercing the relative quiet as the sounds of activity among the organization began to become more pronounced with the pace of work increasing.

The black shirt held over the front of her slight, naked frame, her black hair still dripping moisture, she walked with intent back into the tent, changing into her baby brigade uniform and sitting upon the small wooden stool near the back amidst the flickering light of the dim and smoky oil lamp which burned within, awaiting the return of the lieutenant and the commencement of her day's assignations in full.

As she sat in the cool, dark interior of the lieutenant's tent, surrounded by the atmosphere of his recent presence and reminded of him by his sparse belongings which were set about the room, Wendy began to feel herself dozing, the coolness and the dark interior combined with her lack of sleep and remaining fatigue from her wedding night. As her eyes closed she began to see images in her mind arising from the darkness - a line of black-masked figures armed to the teeth marching over a verdant grassy expanse, a large flag, similarly black, whipping amidst a strong wind. Another figure on his own, within the uttermost heights of concrete towers that seemed to spiral into the sky, crossed bandoliers of bullets across his chest, his fist clenched and pressed upon a small table, rivulets of blood slowly seeping from between his fingers.

The dream visions morphed into one another, alternately gaining and losing solidity as she moved with the patterns of fitful sleep, her slight frame slumping forward ever so gently. Almost as soon as she felt like she had descended into a proper sleep she awoke with a start - a strong wind from the outside blowing the flaps of the tent and letting in the light of morning proper. Wendy slipped into her baby brigade overcoat, pulling the ample hood over her head and exiting the tent just in time to see the lieutenant and one of his retinue ascending slowly toward her position on a sloping ridge some several hundred yards' distance. Upon the back of the personnel member walking beside him was a large backpack, covered with numerous heavy nylon straps securing the contents within with extra prodigiousness.

Within only a few minutes they met near the slope upon which the lieutenant's tent was situated, he himself drawing near her and wrapping an arm around her shoulder in a public display of tenderness and affection that could not be mistaken by the member of his entourage who waited politely some few feet away, his gray eyes and blank stare belying no discernible emotion or reaction other than perhaps the faintest hint of an internal jealousy deep within, though that could have well been Wendy's own vanity at play in her own mind, the consciousness of a new and chosen bride.

Arm still wrapped around her and with a small but lethal tactical automatic assault rifle slung casually over his other shoulder they walked the short distance to the quartermaster's tent, receiving gratefully some small tin cups of mountain grog proffered by the smiling man as he prepared a small rucksack with various foodstuffs and flagons for their day's hike. Wendy felt equal surprise and pleasure as the lieutenant, having once received the pack from the quartermaster, pulled the straps over her own small but sturdy shoulders. He himself was given a decidedly larger pack, with an antenna emerging from the uppermost portion and various devices of a nature unknown to Wendy excepting that they were of an electronic variety and utilized in some clandestine communications context.

Properly equipped, the three began their march at a

leisurely yet intentional pace and it was not long before a small sheen of cold sweat began to moisten the pale skin of Wendy's cheeks, becoming increasingly rosy as the mountain wind whipped about them, its sound through the coniferous pines rustling like a strange portent-giving entity alive within the wood and limbs themselves.

She looked up and saw that the sky had in the short hours between dawn and the present become completely overcast with iron-gray clouds in an endless stream extending into the horizon. Not the sort of clouds that gave rain, but those that simply darkened the landscape ever so slightly and filtered the light into an ominous glow. The lieutenant noticed her attention and looked up himself, his eyes squinting with a grim recognition of the nature of weather in the post-apocalyptic landscape. How many years had gone by in the earliest days of the organization directly after the nuclear conflagration when there was no natural sunlight to be had? The skies ever-covered with their clouds of ash and those even more impenetrable walls of fell natural clouds turned sinister and hostile under the effects of the multiple-megaton nuclear blasts upon the earth's atmosphere, all rain poisoned, all light hidden from that which might grow under the rays of the sun creating a diseased and poisonous landscape. Scorched by the blazes of the atomic-driven inferno yet not healing, but dying still further.

Those dark days were now many years into the past and many areas such as the mountains around the engineering center - which had in fact been spared comparatively in levels of damage in differentiation to the sort of havoc that was wreaked in the more metropolitan areas and areas without the natural barriers that the mountains provided - had flourished in a new revival of wilderness with the absence of people and the reemergence of many species once near disappearance in the days prior. Yet the unmistakeable poisonous atmosphere remained and one could see it, just as the lieutenant's small child bride could see it now with the ebb and flow of those foreboding iron-gray clouds which were quintessentially alien to the old earth - a new sort of phenomena bred in the foul mutations of the earth and atmosphere surrounding it as a result of the nuclear wars. That which once was profoundly unnatural had in essence become the new natural, the new nature - so profuse, so violent and unchained and with that ever-present underlying poisonous atmosphere evidenced by a myriad of indicators.

The hike continued at the same leisurely yet intentional pace and as they continued to walk Wendy felt her limbs become more limber as they stretched in the motions of walking along the old sodden path which they followed - up and down the hillsides, atop treeless ridges and through pockets of deep forest. The rucksack upon her back which had once been heavy felt lighter and more integrated with her own frame as each hour passed, yet she was glad when the lieutenant had motioned them to stop briefly at one point upon a bald hillside overlooking the vastness of the surrounding mountains and had lightened the rucksack in earnest, sharing some of the contents among the three of them for nourishment before continuing on.

Being out and about in the wilderness in this way made Wendy feel more similar to how she remembered the days of her earliest youth before her lot had been primarily confined to the engineering center itself. There was little discussion between the three of them along the concourse of the journey, though at times the lieutenant would point out some area to Wendy and comment in a low voice which their other travel companion could not discern, said comments sometimes issuing a small laugh and always a smile from the lieutenant's bride. At other times the lieutenant would address the officer who traveled with him, sometimes stopping him in mid-stride and tightening the straps of the man's rucksack to assure that the contents within were properly secured.

Eventually they made their way up a steep, narrow ancillary path that veered off ascending in a twisting concourse through a rock-strewn landscape, interspersed here and there with small twisted trees and desiccated shrubs amidst the treacherous pebble-strewn soil. Even though she had been raised all her life in the organization's mountain territory Wendy had never been in these sectors of the wilderness and the grade of the path made it difficult going for her, yet she managed, scrambling behind the lieutenant and his associate, both of whom seemed to be lost in some private reverie as they negotiated the path before them.

Almost without warning the ridge that they had been

climbing crested and below them stretched a deep valley bearing no foliage whatsoever, surrounded on all sides by hazardous walls of sandy soil, deceptive in their appearance as the actual integrity of their solidity.

The principal feature of the landscape however was the piles upon piles of human bones strewn across the flat of the valley floor, all of them decades old and bleached of all color, the skin and flesh once covering them having long melted into the sands or having been picked by the ever-watchful buzzards which proliferated in the region. This was a site that they all knew, if not by sight then by description, as the story concerning the commander's great historic massacre in the region during days long past was ground in within the narrative fabric of the area, though the details always had been and still were quite vague as to particulars.

The lieutenant had himself however been to the site before on several occasions, once in the company of the commander himself during a visit in which the commander and an elite personal guard had skirted the area near the engineering area - entering the territory in a covert fashion with no announcement of their presence even to the resident brass within the area - in the course of a surveying mission for the establishment of certain secret facilities unrelated to the primary mission of the engineering center proper. It had long been predetermined that this would be the site utilized for the testing of the sort of mechanism which now, at long last, was in the organization's possession, wrought by the ingenuity of the organization itself.

IRON GATES

As soon as they arrived, the lieutenant and the accompanying officer began to go about their initial preparations for the test. The lieutenant removed his large pack and slowly began to remove certain items from the same including a small radio handheld device which he tested for power, turning it on and off again before inserting it into his black BDU jacket.

The officer in turn removed a strange gleaming metallic item from his own sack, the item having a very pointed and distinct appearance - a shining metal cylinder with striations snaking across its side and a small base. By the intensely cautious manner in which the man handled the object Wendy could ascertain that this was the crucial weapon which was to be tested. She herself had no information about the device, other than knowing it was the focal point of a highly clandestine project and one to which her husband had been entrusted with special care and authority.

The plan was for the officer to establish the preliminary set-up of the weapon upon the ground level of the valley and then join the lieutenant and Wendy on the side of the ridge for observation.

Both Wendy and the lieutenant had been issued gas masks by the quartermaster that morning in order to effect close observation of the properties of the weapon - the officer's main task being the initial setup of the device prior then returning back to the ridge line at which time the device would be activated and deployed - done so at a time wherein the officer effecting the setup would be well beyond the line of fallout at the significantly higher altitude of the ridge.

IRON GATES

With cautious steps the three began a slow descent toward the valley's bottom - the lieutenant and Wendy stopping only a short distance down and situating themselves upon a rocky outcropping, the radio equipment which the lieutenant had been carrying with him being left on the uppermost crest of the hill prior to the commencement of their descent. As the lieutenant had observably turned various switches and positioned the antenna in a certain directional area it was presumed that the communications device would be relaying information about the test to the headquarters of the organization via some clandestine channel as the experiment proceeded on-the-ground.

Situated together on the escarpment, Wendy pressed her small body against that of the lieutenant and as she cradled her body against the lieutenant's own she could feel that her touch had elicited his own reciprocal attentions, his rough hands slowly stroking her thighs and hips which were casually straddled against his own as they watched in unison the descent of the organizational man who made up the third and sole other member of their party, the metallic device once again safely secured in the sack upon his back. His figure became smaller and smaller as he slowly reached the bottom of the valley, the ground leveling off near the final descent and then he was there, a black speck moving amidst the charnel ground of skulls, standing alone amidst that grim testament to the particularly lethal aspects of the legacy of the commander and the organization.

As per instruction, the speck-like figure moved forward until the very center point of the valley floor was reached, at that point kneeling and removing the metal sphere from the confines of his pack and proceeding to secure it in an upright position utilizing a small base plate.

As the officer went about the final stages of prepping the device, high on the ledge the lieutenant reached into his satchel and removed the two gas masks which he had procured from the quartermaster, turning Wendy toward him and placing the black rubber mask on her face and checking the seal before donning his own. Beneath the thick plastic covering his face he gave Wendy a knowing look before pointing down emphatically at the floor of the valley.

From his pocket the lieutenant removed a small handheld device equipped with two buttons, two colored lights and a small ballistic antenna which he extended to its maximum length, pointing its extended metal tip in an arc over the valley circumference.

The lieutenant pressed a black button on the device at which point a pale light beside it was triggered. Far on the valley floor the device began to emit a low humming sound. The officer, now understanding the ruse that he was to be the sacrificial lamb in the test, scurried away from the device as soon as the sound began to vibrate from the same, screaming until his voice became hoarse and waving his hands at the two black figures ensconced high on the ledge.

Another light on the lieutenant's remote module for

the weapon began blinking and the lieutenant pressed the black button again, and the light went solid. With sickening glee, the lieutenant stared down toward the floor of the valley as the sides of the bullet-like device began to open slowly, spreading outward like the blossoming of some deadly lotus.

With a hiss, the gleaming device continued its opening and from within a thin stream of yellowish smoke began to flow out into the air from its depths, increasing in volume and intensity of release as the device slowly made its way toward full-open position.

The officer on the ground had long since begun running in a desperate attempt to avoid what he knew at base was unavoidable, tripping now and again on the crests of human bones which were scattered in thick piles across the valley floor.

With a sudden gust the wind from the cliffsides overlooking the valley picked up, sending a strong current downward, at which point the yellow gas began making frenzied and sickening patterns in the air, superimposed upon the backdrop of death.

In moments the poison had taken hold of its host, the officer's eyes becoming large and sickeningly pronounced, both hands rose to clutch his throat desperately, clawing in an attempt to open the breathing passages which had now become blocked with the yellowish fumes which wafted around him. The lieutenant watched gleefully from afar as the man fell to his knees, the officer's eyes now bulging unnaturally, laced with veins and bloodshot as the beginning trickles of blood began to roll slowly down his face like tears.

Alarmingly the officer fell as his muscles involuntarily stiffened, the blood issuing from his eyes now also issuing from his ears as his tongue protruded, black and discolored.

Within the confines of his gas mask the lieutenant uttered a guttural howl in his observation place high atop the ridge, one hand clenching his knee until his knuckles turned white while his other hand stretched out and rested itself between Wendy's legs, massaging her sex in firm strokes over her uniform pants as he became more and more aroused by the violence of the scene beneath him.

At long last they could tell that the man on the bone-strewn expanse below them had expired as all struggling had ceased - the eyeballs enlarged seemingly to the point of bursting, blood covering the ground near his head as blood had continued to flow more and more copiously from his eye sockets, ears and finally nostrils as the poison reached and then began to eat away at the principal cerebral centers.

The lieutenant removed his hand from its current molestation and pointed toward the former member of his retinue, then curled his thumb upward into that universal symbol denoting a successful mission. Within the black-tinted plastic sights of the gas mask Wendy's face crinkled with a smile and an unheard laughter and then too returned the lieutenant's gesture. With that, they grasped each other hand-in-hand and began the ascent to the top of the ridge where the lieutenant would radio news of the test completion to the appropriate sectors, leaving the body, the shell of the test device and the electronic equipment - some of which functioned to monitor residual toxicity in the area - for the follow-up team that would come after him.

Another night at the engineering center and then - his task accomplished - he would be heading back in caravan with barrels of payload in tow back toward the heart of the organization's terror, back to headquarters and back to the commander.

CHAPTER 30

Without knowing it Nadezhda had found herself the subject of an experiment, or more precisely, the experimental subject in the training regimen of two young and exceedingly cruel girls, one a mere youth and one but a child, however both possessed of the acumen for inflicting pain of those many years their senior.

Nadezhda had been left in the solitary and dark cell by the robed cult recruiter who held the keys to her confinement and the accompanying guards with little interruption over a period of several days except for the delivery of trays of food which, by its astringent smell, she could tell was liberally laced with the type of chemical additives only dispersed on interrogation subjects (she was familiar with it in name and usage, if not in person previously, through her work in signals intelligence).

As the case was, those chemical additives immediately took hold of her, causing both increasing fugue states and physical discomfort including intestinal problems which quickly led to her being very cleaned out and also very filthy. Under the effects of the drugs and the continuing darkness time began to have little meaning as day passed into night and night passed into day, further tray deliveries always being brought at uneven and intermittent intervals as to not allow the detainee to develop or be able to ascertain any set schedule on behalf of her captors.

After some days the door of her cell was opened and, thankfully for her eyes, due to her pupils being now quite wide and enlarged from the continual dark and from the chemicals coursing through her veins, the hallway was dim, lit only with the red emergency lights that burned with minimal intensity. Beneath that reddish glow stood the cult recruiter from before, who stood with her arms crossed in a posture of sternness yet with eyes which were blank and belied nothing except an ever-present filament of wildness and fanaticism that seemed to shine deep within her own mind, a sign of a life so touched by the commandant that it could not be hidden even by her own force of will.

In that moment Nadezhda felt within herself the fanaticism of the commandant, the fanaticism, embryonic as it was, that had been instilled in that relatively short time since she herself had subscribed to the cult and performed her devotions with all attention and faith within the small confines of her living quarters after her initial confrontation at the armaments conference.

Had this change in her fortunes, apparently for the worse, come about as a result of the lieutenant's facilitating her wish to be transferred to torture center - a ruse, his ruse - since the beginning, or had the shift come about when she herself joined - albeit within the

IRON GATES

periphery - the religion of the commandant? Her eyes met with that of the cult recruiter standing before her, briefly, before a hood was drawn over her head by an internal security member who had approached her from the side and led her, arms held in painful stress position holds, down the red-lit corridor deeper into the commandant's training center.

With a rough shoving she was brought through a doorway after some fifteen minutes of being walked along the downward grade of the corridor, all the while the internal security member alternately decreasing and increasing the painful bending of her arms and fingers pinioned under his grasp, though she knew better than to cry out and receive more pointed attentions. His boots clicked along with several others that she could hear, indicating that her prisoner's retinue had grown since leaving the cell. That thought, of the apparent honorifics of the situation made her smile, albeit grimly, as was only appropriate to the situation at hand.

A blast of cold air could be felt even through the hood as she fell after the shove, catching her fall with her hands and luckily not causing injury due to her state of blindness. The door from which she had entered closed slowly by its own volition, being controlled by an outside security device and bearing no manual means for entrance or exiting of any sort. The hood which had been placed over her head was not secured with anything other than a small drawstring fastening which she quickly released, now sitting on her knees, the sudden exposure to bright light cascading down above her after loosening the ties causing her to hiss involuntarily and her eyes to redden and swell.

After some time she regained her vision and saw that she had been brought into a large circular white room, a single small but no doubt military-grade in quality speaker situated not so obliquely in one high corner of the ceiling and one portion of wall bearing a large wall-length mirror, ceiling to floor, behind which no doubt certain personnel of the training center situated themselves on the other side, monitoring their quarry.

All at once the door opened and through it stepped a lithe female youth, walking with clipped predatory steps through the passage which immediately closed behind her, leaving only her and Nadezhda within the white chamber. The figure was sheathed in a skin-tight gleaming suit of white latex, zippered from the back and accompanied with cruel shining boots of a similar color. Her hair was dark, reddish and shoulder-length, hanging wet and lank, surrounding a face belying great evil which bore upon its pale visage a small and recently sutured scar, the stitches still visible and above which set eyes that exuded an unbridled insanity.

Elbow-length white gloves covered the lower portion of her thin arms and upon each thin finger were inlaid malicious metallic nails which acted as as collective weapons of evisceration and torment.

Bluebird had undergone an indescribably harsh transformation over the several weeks since she and Britta had been taken onto the terrace to view their assembled legions who would take them into the territories over which they would dominate and possess in time, so doing under the blessings of the commandant and facilitated by the auspices of the martial might of the commander's amassed organizational forces.

She would not simply be entering those lands for so long existing, wasted, outside of the auspices of the organization's control, as some mere administrator, but rather, so inhabiting as a symbol of all that the organization had become and was to be for all those that found themselves under her iron fist. She who would be then more than an authority, more than a mere repository of governance, but rather an embodiment of all those horrific chemicals and sundry mechanisms of delivery that would decimate and mutilate the populace and by doing so fashion a scar that would mar that land eternally to come – she, not a human any longer, but instead - a god.

As such, those several weeks of brutal training since the nature of her destiny had unfolded before her very eyes below on the drill grounds in that fateful moment of realization had necessitated the training befitting a god, the harsh discipline befitting a god and those myriad punishments and incalculable transfigurative acts that changed the girl - already transformed during her time at the commandant's training facility well prior - into an even more fell and predatory being than she had ever considered possible, something conceived of only at the very frontiers and distant limits of human experience, veering into the realms of that which could only be considered as inhuman in nature and scope. Her past now seemed like a far-off memory though through a decidedly darker glass as she had found herself, day by day, having her consciousness mercilessly shattered and re-created again and again in in an obscenely surgical fashion within the rigors of such ordeals – certain recent ordeals which far exceeded those formidable and lengthy days of trial and terror which she had suffered under from the time she arrived from the outer territories up until the time she had found herself as the acting pontifex of the incipient baby brigades.

The white-sheathed figure approached Nadezhda with a sensual yet predatory gait, almost seeming to float across the floor within the purview of Nadezhda's vision, however she could hear the report of the young girl's boots upon the highly-polished concrete floor, though the sound and the girl's movements seemed to be out of synch with one another. Nadezhda struggled to get some firm hold of her own awareness of the person before her and the events presently transpiring, as the drugs she had been administered, coupled with profuse sleep deprivation, caused the clarity of her perception to rise and fall in waves. As such she could not be sure exactly what was occurring in earnest, though she knew that she was in the midst of a confrontation that marked a pivotal juncture both for her person and perhaps for the organization in whose service she had committed herself body and soul.

Bluebird smiled sadistically at Nadezhda and Nadezhda, misreading her purpose, smiled in return and attempted to rise from her kneeling position to issue a more formal greeting.

With an astounding swiftness Bluebird was upon her, the needle-bearing fingers of her white gloves snaking around the exposed flesh beneath Nadezhda's uniform collar, forcing her down and drawing small rivulets of blood from pale skin as the claw-like metal extensions pierced without restraint into Nadezhda's flesh.

Nadezhda's eyes widened in reactive shock at the very sudden and very vulnerable position in which she now found herself, the young girl's slight frame standing menacingly before her and belying a hideous strength quite deceptive to her size. Bluebird's body swayed slightly, accentuating her dominance over her quarry in a mockingly yet insidiously sexual fashion.

With one hand situated on her hip and the other still grasped firmly around Nadezhda's neck, Bluebird slowly shifted Nadezhda's head upward so that their gazes met. A cold sweat dripped steadily down Nadezhda's brow and cheeks, commingling with the small droplets of blood that issued from the wounds where Bluebird's claw-like nails still pierced her flesh.

The young girl smiled again, her eyes squinting conspiratorially as they gazed into Nadezhda's own.

'It has been a long time coming that you have been scheduled for arrival here, dearest Nadezhda. We have been very well briefed from certain unquestionable authorities. Plots within plots have brought you to us.'

Nadezhda stared forward silently, Bluebird's voice seemed to take on an inhuman lilt and inflection as she spoke. Was it the continued effects of the drugs inducing this seeming distortion or was there something decidedly more sinister afoot? In that moment Nadezhda could not be sure as the atmosphere became increasingly more disturbing and surreal.

'You, Nadezhda, are to be our little pet - though we may name you something more fitting in due course. My personal property you are from this point on - though with a very special purpose, perhaps quite more quintessentially important than the profession you intended for yourself. But, my little pet, nonetheless - we will train you, oh yes, we will train you well - and soon!'

From across the room the door opened again, the electronic pulse of its outside control groaning harshly as the metal mechanism grated against the gate operator apparatus.

Through the passageway came a girl several years younger than Bluebird, eight or nine at the oldest. She was naked except for an obscene garment of shining black leather cross-straps upon her upper body that framed small budding breasts and a black leather thong of similar construction upon her lower half. Her hair was barely shoulder length, brunette and of a thick and lustrous hue, framing a small freckled face bearing brown eyes and cruel thin lips which were smeared with the unmistakeable gleam of fresh blood.

One hand extended jauntily upward holding a leash constructed of a similar leather of her very own garments, at the end of which crawled an emaciated male figure on all fours. He was naked and obviously the subject of many unspeakable hideous tortures, the least of which perhaps being the multiple recent and bloody bite marks which stood as proof-positive to the presence of the crimson stains upon his young handler's mouth.

IRON GATES

Britta gazed at the sight of Bluebird, her older sister in service of the commandant's conspiracy, and issued a hoarse hiss in salutation, opening her mouth slightly and causing a bubbling of blood to emanate from her exhalation in the form of an understandable yet grotesque greeting.

Bluebird returned the greeting in kind, transferring her claws to the back of Nadezhda's neck and shoving her face against the shining contours of her own latex-sheathed body, Nadezhda's pathetic and drooling mouth now pressed in a questionably consensual posture against Bluebird's midsection, her victim's chin resting slightly upon the swell of her captors thin hips.

Britta writhed her near-naked flesh in an unmistakably provocative undulating motion, doing so while tightening the reins upon Private Bonn and bringing him closer and closer to heel upon the periphery of her bare feet which sat with a springing posture upon the cold concrete floor of the chamber.

'What a beautiful little pet you have there, my little sister!' Bluebird cooed in a surprisingly sincere and heartfelt sounding of her voice, so doing even as she continued to press Nadezhda's tortured face against her rocking hip.

Britta cooed with delight at Bluebird's comment and nodded emphatically in response, slowly rolling the restraining leash within her hand inward around her wrists and forcing her quarry to come closer and ever closer to her person.

Bonn's face quaked with pain at his movements and

made Britta laugh harshly, her neck nodding from side to side in a corrective but perversely loving gesture at the very point which Bonn collapsed before her under the stress of his earlier punishments.

'Yes! We have had fun with this one, big sister!' Britta laughed and eyed Bluebird coyly, slowly pulling on the leash upon which the naked Private Bonn found himself at the end of, his form only skin set upon bones after months upon months of torture before being further processed in finishing and transferred to Britta's capable command - though those few weeks upon the regimen of his younger and in fact youngest of all handlers had been the harshest of them all.

Britta snapped her fingers while giving a tug on the leash with her other hand and Private Bonn immediately rose to his knees, his breathing ragged and hollow eyes staring forward with a look of expectancy at his young mistress.

Bluebird grabbed Nadezhda by the hair and wrenched her neck in the direction of Britta and the private.

At long last the two individuals, whose fate under the contrivances and machinations of the organization faced each other - both having been accused and tortured, the private more so among the two, for an alleged liaison which was only now taking place.

With a quick shoving motion Bluebird released her grip upon Nadezhda, slinging her with maximum force at the feet of Britta and the kneeling private.

Simultaneously Britta extended her own slender

hand and unclasped the leash from the collar around Private Bonn's neck. The private crawled forward with staggered gait toward Nadezhda's prone body, collapsing into her arms just as she began to rise from the floor. Thus Nadezhda held him in an uncomforting embrace as their joint handlers leered down upon them.

Bluebird moved to Britta's side, her arm wrapping around her younger co-conspirator's shoulders and then snaking down to cup one of the girl's small exposed buttocks, lightly tracing her clawed fingertips over the leather-strap and metal punitive-cane induced weals which still bore appreciable marks and which had been administered by herself personally only a few days before in the context of a hideous bonding ritual among the commandant's cult which they had engaged in hundreds of times in a several week period.

Britta cooed softly at her older sister's embrace and amorous ministrations and wrapped her own arm around Bluebird's waist, her leather leash previously restraining Private Bonn now coiled in snake-like fashion about her arm.

The two looked into the eyes of the other, and, as Bluebird nodded, Britta raised her free arm in a gesture of salute and salutation before the wall-length mirror before them which reflected the scene of the union of Nadezhda and Private Bonn and of themselves in stark and perverse relief. With a groaning and harsh metallic squeal the mirror began to slowly fold itself upward into the ceiling of the white chamber - a cold blast of air issuing forth as the growing portal of the opening grew inch by inch.

IRON GATES

CHAPTER 31

Across the long cavernous corridor framed by huge black cylinder-shaped concrete support beams a small area of light began to grow.

At the opposite end of the corridor sat the commandant, her satanic body tense and sheathed in shining black, accentuating her lean muscled limbs and the overtly sexual yet intensely threatening curvatures punctuating the same.

Lines of black-masked members of internal security armed to the teeth flanked her from behind and down the sides of the walls of the former holding cell. Between the support beams stood large steel cages of naked and screaming children, their cries echoing in futility as other children, robed in the fashion of the commandant's cult recruiters in miniature strode slowly through their midst, carefully minding their quarry.

Across the way within the area of light now fully open, several figures emerged - two girls, comprising the zenith of her high-tier trainees, accompanied by their two prisoners - expertly conditioned - now entering into the initiation toward the hideous destiny that awaited them.

Their grim procession was halted halfway down the concourse as four members of internal security converged upon them, two from either side of the hall, quickly stripping the female prisoner of her signals intelligence uniform and leaving her bare before the sight of the commandant and her assembled acolytes.

At a concurrent moment two of the robed child servants of the commandant emerged from behind black support beams near a cage of captured children, each handing an identical horrific leather device of punishment to the female figure sheathed in white and her younger associate garbed in obscene leather straps, the latter who received the instrument proffered to her with much enthusiasm.

Within her foul helmet the commandant smiled - smiled as the internal security members pushed the prisoners roughly upon the ground - smiled as the emaciated male prisoner mounted the female and began to copulate with her as the dual whip blows of her high-tier trainees began raining down from above.

Thus the well-laid bloodlining for the re-population of the outer areas began. These two united now in perverse union before her feet, chosen carefully through the ministrations of her intelligence network, would be the first to breed. They then, after, would breed with the fruits of their union - father with daughter, mother with son. Soon those latter would seed and they too would breed with their own offspring and then latter sister with brother, brother with sister - igniting a genetic chain of terror, imbued with trauma, forged under the blinding gaze of her new gods that would rule that harsh land soon to be dominated by an iron fist.

The area of light at the end of the corridor began to slowly recede and the commandant extended the antenna of her mind to those lands - those bleak frontiers to come - beyond the iron gates.

IRON GATES

IRON GATES

IRON GATES

MARTINET PRESS

CPSIA information can be obtained
at www.ICGtesting.com
Printed in the USA
BVHW042016181218
535900BV00012B/746/P